The Write Off

The Write Off

Kara McDowell

Berkley Romance
New York

BERKLEY ROMANCE
Published by Berkley
An imprint of Penguin Random House LLC
1745 Broadway, New York, NY 10019
penguinrandomhouse.com

Book design by Alison Cnockaert

ISBN: 9780593955697

An application to register this book for cataloging has been submitted to the Library of Congress.

First Edition: April 2026

Printed in the United States of America
1st Printing

The authorized representative in the EU for product safety and compliance is Penguin Random House Ireland, Morrison Chambers, 32 Nassau Street, Dublin D02 YH68, Ireland, https://eu-contact.penguin.ie.

To my grandma, who filled my childhood with stories.
I hope this one would have made you proud.

The Write Off

1

Present Day

I didn't write West Emerson into my manuscript on purpose. It's just that when I close my eyes and try to picture an apple, I'm one of those people who sees nothing but black. I think that's the reason that writing descriptions of anything—landscapes, people, clothing—feels like death by a thousand cuts. It's slow, it's painful, and worst of all, it's *boring*. The number one rule of my writing has always been *Don't be boring*—even when it gets me into trouble.

West was sitting on his bed playing video games when it happened. It was during our junior year of college, and I was stuck on writing a description of my love interest (*what do people even look like?*) when I glanced up, and there he was. West Emerson had long black eyelashes and a crooked nose, and before I even gave my fingers permission, Fox Caldwell did, too.

I didn't plan to do it again, but then West and I were in the library, both of us claiming we needed to work on our Nineteenth-Century British Lit essays, both of us procrastinating. And Fox needed an eye color. Brown didn't feel right for an immortal. Blue felt like a cliché. Green felt like the color writers pick when they're trying not to pick blue. (I was twenty-one and thought I knew everything, but I still stand by this.)

I slipped my headphones off and kicked West's shin under the table.

He didn't even blink. He was in one of his trances, eyes still on his screen, pen cap hanging from his mouth, blue ink staining his lips.

"West!" I whisper-hissed, annoyed that he wasn't paying attention to me. I had a crisis on my hands. Were gray eyes pretentious or mysterious? I had to know immediately. He looked up from his laptop, his eyes landing directly on mine.

It was pretty much game over after that.

In addition to familiar lashes and a bent nose that indicates that he's been through some shit, Fox Caldwell has multicolored eyes and ink-black hair. He has charcoal stains on his skin, and when he's thinking, he drums his fingers against his thigh. He's also a five-hundred-year-old immortal faerie king.

It was those damn eyes that incriminated me, though. Ocean blue with an amber ring in the center—mentioned an embarrassing fourteen times in *Torched*.

What the fuck was I thinking?

Those multicolored Fox Caldwell eyes are approaching me now, and a zip of anticipation twists up my spine. If I weren't so damn needy, I'd make a hard pivot into the campus bookstore. But curiosity gets the better of me, and I drag my gaze from the T-shirt displaying Fox Caldwell's face to the woman wearing him on her chest. She has pink hair, a full tote bag slung over one shoulder, a lanyard covered in enamel pins.

We make eye contact; I hold my breath. What happens next has the power to ruin my whole life. Her brow furrows in confusion, and then her eyes widen in slow recognition. I'm rooted to the spot, waiting for an adrenaline shot of validation. *Or, more likely, the other thing.* I'm hardly ever recognized in my real life, but this weekend isn't real life, not anymore. This is a book festival, and experience has taught me that the type of readers who attend book festivals in faded Fox Caldwell merch are the same type of people who want me dead.

I paste on a smile and brace myself for whatever's coming. It's the oddest thing, having a rabid fan base that also hates you. I stopped attending book conferences and festivals years ago, turned off the comments on my social media profiles, and hid from the world. The Tucson Festival of Books is my first event in years, and I have no idea what to expect.

The woman grips a campus map tightly in both hands and strides toward me, eyes sparkling. That can only be a good sign—angry people don't *sparkle*. I reach into my own tote bag, and my fingers close around a signing pen. Brand-new. Full of ink that doesn't bleed through the page. With my free hand, I brush my fingers through my hair for when she inevitably asks for a selfie. But then she glides past me like I'm a part of the scenery—a palm tree to study under or a lecture hall constructed in the early 1900s—and throws her arms around a woman behind me.

I stand in the middle of the quad, blinking stupidly, while the excited notes of their conversation float on the early spring breeze. *It's been too long! The flight was rough, the drive was good, one of them saw* THE *Daphne Castle drinking a smoothie (!!!), and the romantasy panel starts in five. They'd better hurry if they want seats.*

My *own* plan to attend the fantasy romance panel evaporates, and all I'm left with is a sour burning in the pit of my stomach. Maybe she didn't recognize me, or she didn't care. And not to be a vain fucking cliché, but I hate the idea of either. I've stumbled upon the only thing worse than my fans wanting me dead: a world in which they don't care at all.

I glance through the bookstore windows toward the retractable eight-foot banner with my name and face on it. *That* Margot Darling is twenty-two years old, and I admit it might be time for new headshots. It's been a decade since my Central Park photo shoot, and unlike some aloof authors, with their black turtlenecks and their curated bookshelves and their I'm-smarter-than-you expressions, in my picture, optimism and enthusiasm radiate from every inch of me.

Back then, I believed that being a published author could save me, and that nothing else in the world could possibly make me as happy as seeing my name on the cover of a book. I study my naive, collagen-filled face on the banner and admit that sometimes I'm still that same starry-eyed girl. So maybe I once went eleven days without washing my hair or changing my pants while I was on deadline, and maybe I've been tagged in reviews telling me that my book sucked so bad I should kill myself, but I can't escape the truth. Despite everything that has happened, I still believe books will save me—I wouldn't be here if I didn't. Nothing has ruined my life like being an author has, but when it's good, there's nothing better.

My phone buzzes with an email from my publicist. I swipe the notification away without reading it and get a glimpse of the scary countdown on my lock screen that reminds me just how little time I've got left until *Shattered* publishes. I feel myself tipping into an anxiety spiral when my eye catches another woman walking toward me. She's six feet tall with wavy red hair and a long floral dress that belongs on a prairie, and every inch of exposed skin below her collarbones is covered in tattoos. She looks like she could bake a killer loaf of sourdough *and* be a guest judge on the newest season of *Ink Master*. I pull out my signing pen and thrust it into her hands.

"Will you sign my book? Or better yet—my bra?" I jokingly tug on the collar of my shirt.

She rolls her eyes, takes the pen cap off with her mouth, and signs her name on the inside of my forearm—just below my tattoo.

"Daphne Castle," I read out loud. "I know at least two people who would be extremely jealous of me right now."

"My parents?"

"Four people, then. I overheard two women fangirling over you."

"You did not," she says reflexively.

"If it'd been anyone else, I would have combusted from jealousy."

I think of the saying "comparison is the thief of joy." It's most often painted in watercolor and used as inspiration porn, just as Teddy Roosevelt intended. It might be a throwaway Pinterest cliché, but when it comes to the life of a writer, it's as true as it is irrelevant. To be a writer is to exist in a perpetual state of jealousy. Writers' conferences and authors' group chats are filled with anxious, overly caffeinated people doing career math in their heads. Advances, marketing budgets, reviews, conference invites, movie deals . . . they're all whispered metrics we use to try to objectively compare one another in a wildly subjective industry, and we all want what someone else has. My only exception is my friends. If anyone else had the year Daphne did, they'd be laid out on a gurney. But because it's Daphne, I've never been happier for anyone.

"No one needs to be jealous of me." She pretends to flip her hair over her shoulder only for it to get stuck in her big hoop earrings.

"Are you kidding? You have infinite aura points," I say. When she stares at me blankly, I add, "Did I say that right?"

"You're the one who writes for teenagers, not me," she says, shaking her head. "I don't need to have my finger on the pulse of Gen Z slang."

"Your finger *is* on the pulse, but only when a character's bleeding out," I concede. Daphne's career started with two historical fiction novels that didn't sell well before she pivoted to bloodier pastures. She wrote a queer thriller in a fevered daydream of a writers' retreat several years back, blew up on social media, and hit the *USA Today* bestseller list when it released last year. She hasn't quite come to terms with it yet, but she is publishing's new superstar, and I get to say I knew her when.

She takes a long drag of coffee before shaking the empty cup in front of me. "Do you want coffee? It's free in the authors' lounge! Oh, and I filled my bag with snacks for later." She opens her READ BANNED BOOKS tote to show me the dozen granola bars and breakfast pastries she's smuggled from the school-library-turned-authors'-lounge. "Shoot. I forgot to grab a bagel."

I shake my head. I'm already three espressos deep and should cut myself off from the caffeine IV drip. "You should set your standards higher than free campus coffee and stale granola. Didn't your publisher give you a per diem?"

"I think so, but if I don't have to spend it—"

"You should," I tell her as my phone buzzes. I need to teach Daphne how to survive these long weekends, and it starts with DoorDashing overly expensive food to her room after a long day. There's something about hotel sheets, HGTV, and a burrito the size of your face that hits the spot after socializing for twelve hours. The buzzing continues. "My publicist is calling."

"Answer it. I'll be inside stealing bagels." Daphne walks back in the direction of the authors' lounge as I answer my phone.

"Hey, Amina."

"Mars! I'm so glad you picked up. Did you see my email?"

My anxiety radar goes off. "No. I just got to the festival."

"I received an email from the director of the conference. You were copied on it, too. Did you see that one?"

My inbox is always out of control, and the closer we get to publication, the less likely I am to wander into its murky depths. "Not yet."

"I didn't think so," she mutters, her tone hesitant in a way I'm not used to hearing. When there's bad news—like the time my third book got eviscerated by *The New York Times Book Review*—she sends an email, and I get to cry in peace. (Which I did. For several days.) The part of me that hates crying in public more than writer's block flares to life. I duck between buildings and walk toward a quiet spot on campus. At least I'll be alone if this ends in disaster.

"What's going on, Amina?" I prompt.

"There's been a change to the general session on Sunday."

My stomach drops, but I'm not surprised. I wonder if they're rolling up the banner with my face on it as we speak. "Have I been cut?"

Daphne thinks my constant worry is unfounded, but after the shit show that's been my career over the past several years, it's hard not to feel like I'm one wrong move from losing my last chance.

"No! No, of course not, not anything like that."

The vise around my throat loosens slightly. "Then why do

you sound like you'd rather give yourself a paper cut than be on this call?"

She laughs—light and airy and fake as hell. "There's been a change to the schedule—it's really not something you should worry about."

"What's the change?"

"Wendell Tyler has the flu and had to drop out this morning." I can practically hear her wince.

Wendell Tyler is one of the best YA sci-fi authors of the past decade, but it's not like authors are in short supply this weekend. "I can hold down the fort on my own, but if they want a replacement, I'm sure Daphne would be happy to step in," I say.

"Mmm." Amina clears her throat. "Well, the thing is, you know how hectic it can be to schedule these things."

I don't, actually. I spend most of my days sitting alone at a computer while made-up characters talk in my head, but it doesn't sound that complicated. "The Sunday general session is the biggest event of the weekend. Finding a conference author who wants more attention should be as easy as finding a newly released James Patterson book."

Amina laughs again, this time high-pitched and panicked. "It sounds like they've already found someone, but without Wendell, it doesn't make sense to keep the theme around YA—"

"That's fine. I can talk about anything." I once spent an entire hour talking about how to write faithful retellings (which I've never done), because someone in charge of something thought my first novel, *Torched*, was a retelling of Dante's *Inferno*. (It's not.) "What's the new topic?"

Amina is silent on the other end of the line as I walk farther from the busy festival, down a tree-lined path winding through brick buildings. I hear a quick *knock knock knock* that matches the pounding of my heart, followed by muffled voices, like she's covered the phone with her hand, and then she says, "Because you're a University of Arizona graduate, they thought it'd be fun to invite another former Wildcat to the panel. You two can talk about your journeys from students to authors."

Awareness prickles the back of my neck. "Who?"

The phone goes silent again until I hear a different voice. Amina has passed the phone to my editor. "Mars! How are you?" Whitney asks.

"Who is it?" I rasp, the words lodged in my throat.

It can't be. They wouldn't.

"West Emerson."

I'm in free fall, my feet tracing steps from pure muscle memory. "They can't."

"I can get you out of it," Whitney says quickly.

"Get *him* out of it," I snap.

"I'll see what I can do. Talk soon." The line goes dead, and it's just as well, because I'm speechless. My brain is a swirling haze of anger, but my feet are still carrying me toward a shaded bench, down a path I walked a thousand times as an undergrad. It's my favorite place on campus, maybe my favorite spot in all of Tucson. Half of *Torched* was written on this bench, and I need to get to it so I can fume in peace. This is my first event in years, and I'll light myself on fire before I bow out in favor of the guy who almost nuked my career. I turn the corner behind the languages building and stop short.

A man is reading in the shade of a large palm tree. He looks up, and for the second time today, I'm staring directly into those multicolored Fox Caldwell eyes. Only this time, they belong to their inspiration and the person I hate most in this world.

West Emerson.

2

13 Years Ago
Freshman Year, First Semester

I didn't pay attention to West Emerson until he forced me to. I was sitting outside the Modern Languages building after Intro to Creative Writing the first time we met. I'd stumbled on this small niche of trees and benches when I got turned around trying to find the exit during the first week of school, and now I slip out the back after every class and kill time until my late geology lab kills me. (There's a special place in hell for the person who invented five p.m. labs.)

I'm usually alone out here. The campus starts to empty in the late afternoon, and this spot is off the beaten path, away from the student union and any of the good food or smoking hangouts. Today, though, a boy in eyeliner stands under drooping palm fronds and motions for me to take off my headphones.

"Mind if I sit?" He points to the bench across from mine.

I slide one side of my headphones off and crane my neck to look up at him. "Go for it." I put my headphones back on and type another sentence, but in my periphery, I see his mouth move again. I pause my music. "Sorry, what?"

"You're in Bachmann's class, right?"

He has straight dark hair that's falling in his eyes, a hoodie, and a spiral notebook I remember him using to take notes in class while the rest of us use laptops. He's interrupting my writing, but I grin at the excuse to talk about my favorite thing. "Yes! Dr. B's a genius."

He makes a *huh* sound like he's never considered it. "The egg thing is weird, though."

"What egg thing?"

"The loose egg he carries in his pocket?"

I have no idea what he's talking about. "I have no idea what you're talking about."

"The egg he eats every day during our writing warm-up."

"Why would he carry a loose egg in his pocket?"

He holds his hands out. "You're the one who said he's a genius."

I wonder if maybe he's high and decide to keep the conversation moving. "I love the writing prompts, don't you? Not the two-sentence horror stories, though." I shudder. I'm *terrible* with scary stories. I've read Stephen King's memoir, *On Writing*, three times, but I dipped out of *Cujo* three pages in.

My classmate laughs. At me, possibly. "You're going to enter his competition, aren't you?"

At the end of his first lesson, Dr. Bachmann announced that every fall he holds a short story competition among his freshman classes. The finalists are picked by him, and the winner is decided by popular vote. The prize is a spot in his creative writing workshop in the spring—a class otherwise off-limits to first-year students. Obviously, I'm entering.

"What gave me away?"

"Other than the"—he bobs his head back and forth as he

hums, searching for the correct word—"*intense* look in your eyes when you had about a million questions for Dr. B?"

The emphasis he places on the word *intense* makes it clear he wants to use a less flattering one.

He motions to my open laptop. "Is that what you're working on?" Even slouched like he is now, with his arms outstretched across the back of the bench and one ankle resting on his knee, he looks tall. Long. His stature is highlighted by his extremely skinny jeans and his black Dr. Martens; he's dressed like he doesn't realize that emo is going out of style.

I should be doing math homework, but he's right. Apparently, my "intense" expression has made me an open book. "Yes. Are you going to enter?"

"Doubt it."

"Why not?"

He shrugs. "It's not really my thing."

"Then why are you in a creative writing class?"

He tips his head back like he's going to find the answer to my *very* difficult question in the palm tree. Finally, his eyes return to mine; I squint but can't figure out what colors they are. Long eyelashes, though. Lucky bastard. He shrugs again. "It seemed more interesting than mapping out sentence trees in Grammar 101."

I think about the way I set my alarm for seven a.m. on the morning registration opened to make sure I got a spot in this class; meanwhile, he shows up with a Top Flight notebook that is probably filled with cartoon penises and swear words and whatever boys doodle instead of the M.A.S.H. game. Angsty song lyrics, maybe. The cool S. *Who knows how the minds of human boys work?* I don't, which is why I rarely write humans.

His notebook should have been my first clue that we are not the same. If this guy isn't committed enough to take proper notes, he probably didn't spend his high school years writing half-finished novels and bad poetry in his bedroom.

"I'm going to be a writer when I graduate, and I still don't want to map out sentence trees," I tell him. Sentence trees are boring. *Stories*, however, are fun. Stories are an escape. Stories are what I want to spend the rest of my life creating. "I'm Mars, by the way."

"Like the planet?"

I roll my eyes. Everyone thinks they're the first one to say that. "It's short for Margot."

"I'm West."

I cock my head to the side. "Like Mae?"

"Who?"

"American actress and sex symbol Mae West."

He laughs in surprise. "Yeah. I guess so. Just like Mae."

I brighten. Slacker or not (and guyliner aside), I like him.

He leans forward and rests his elbows on his knees. "What are you going to write when you graduate?"

"Novels. And I don't know why I said it like that. I'm not waiting for graduation."

"What kind of novels?"

I sit up straighter. "Oh. I don't know. Just . . . whatever."

He sits back. "Uh-huh."

He doesn't believe me.

The next few minutes are uncomfortably silent as I go back to work. My short story—about two traveling con artists who deal in magical potions and eventually fall in love—is on the screen in front of me. It's nearly impossible to write, though, because West just sits there, coloring the fingernails of his right hand with black Sharpie. (I'm impressed with how neat it is until I realize he's probably just left-handed.) It feels rude to put my headphones back on and ignore him, not to mention that I don't have a single friend in Tucson. At least Mae West here is willing to pretend he's interested in my writing.

"Fantasy," I say as the chemical scent of Sharpie stings my nostrils. He's going to read my story eventually—the entire class will—so there's no use pretending it's something it's not. "And romance."

He puts the cap back on his marker with two and a half nails to go (*slacker*) and leans forward again. "Like *Twilight*?"

Yes. And also no. My stories are second-world fantasy, not contemporary paranormal. But the blueprint is there. And look, it's not like I'm embarrassed. I like what I like, and millions of other people like it, too. YA books kick ass. They're *fun*. And while there are some literary classics I'll ride or die for, I still harbor emotional trauma from trying to get through *Heart of Darkness* without dropping dead of sheer boredom.

But—and it's a big *but*—I don't know West. He might be the kind of guy who forces me to defend my taste. "Kind of," I say at last.

"Cool."

That's it? No defense necessary? I narrow my eyes in suspicion. "Have you read it?" Now that the movie franchise has taken over the world, everyone has either read the book or made it a point not to.

"Should I?"

I tilt my head, wondering if I'm about to make my first friend at college. The tall, skinny boy from my writing class. I could do worse. "You can borrow my copy if you want."

He nods his head. "Okay. Maybe I will."

West sits across from me on the bench after our next class. And the one after that. Before long, he sits next to me in class, too, and we walk out the back doors together every Tuesday and Thursday.

Two months after we first meet, West enters Dr. B's competition with a funny but heartbreaking short story about a kid growing up in small-town Arizona. In the story, the boy wants a bike for Christmas and instead gets a maybe-magical Chia Pet that becomes his best (and only) friend. It makes me cry on my dorm bed.

Moments before Dr. B announces the winner, West turns to me with a smirk on his lips, and that's the first time I see the *real* West Emerson.

I feel violently sick.

Dr. B says West's name, but West is still staring at me. "I loved your story. You're not half bad, Mars."

I blink at him in shock. I didn't win?

I didn't win.

"I know," I snap. I don't need his half-assed compliments.

West winces. "I wish you were going to be in his workshop, too. What am I going to do if I hear the word 'heartsick'?"

"You'll figure it out."

"Right." He turns back to the front of the class, but as I look at his profile, all I'm thinking is that I failed, and he beat me, and there are forty-five thousand people in this school, and I might never see him again.

Before him, no one was ever better than me. At writing,

anyway. At sports, math, public speaking, making friends, clapping on beat, juggling, and anything else that can be qualified as a skill, the line of people better than me could reach the moon. But as luck would have it, the only thing I've ever really cared about also happens to be the only thing I'm any good at. So the fact that West Emerson is better than me?

It's a problem.

3

Present Day

West Emerson looks at me, and for a long, breathless moment, I feel trapped, held in place by gravity or inertia or premonition. He pushes his curls back from his eyes, and it triggers a flood of relief.

Thank god for the strength I had not to give Fox Caldwell curls.

It helped that back then West straightened his locks within an inch of their life. If his hair looked back then like it does now, twenty-one-year-old me wouldn't have stood a chance.

West's eyes are wide with horror, matching my own dismay. "Mars?" He takes half a step toward me.

I take half a step back. "West."

"Mars. I . . ." He shakes his head, as lost for words as I am.

Good. This is normal. We'll just keep saying each other's names, as if we didn't use to be . . . whatever we were. As if I haven't seen him standing in this exact same spot hundreds of times. We stare at each other for a beat, and my obnoxious, hyper-fixated brain can't help but compare him to the skinny kid I knew more than a decade ago.

The multicolored eyes and the crooked nose are the same, but nearly everything else is different. West's wild curls now brush his cheekbones and the collar of his button-up, and his face is covered in a dark scruff he could only dream of at nineteen. He's always been tall, but now his height seems impossible, and his shoulders have broadened to a stupid degree. It's almost suspicious. Writers don't look like that; writers have bad posture and eye strain from too many hours at the keyboard. We have sallow skin and mismatched socks and Cheetos dust on our fingers. If West were a character, he'd be a gravedigger. A lumberjack. A professor moonlighting as a hit man.

A five-hundred-year-old fae king.

You know all that cringey, hormones-out-of-whack, so-lovesick-you-can't-see-straight nonsense you did before your prefrontal cortex was fully developed? Stuff like posting vague attention-seeking lyrics on social media. Texting the person you have a crush on and pretending you meant it for someone else. Getting drunk and sobbing his name in front of all his friends. The things that are so borderline unbearable, the memory of them makes you want to walk into the sea. Well, imagine that the most revealing, embarrassing thing you ever did was write a three-hundred-page book (with his unwitting fingerprints all over it) that sat on the *New York Times* Best Seller list for 142 weeks and got made into a movie (plus two more books and their subsequent films).

My cheeks heat with familiar, ancient humiliation.

"How have you been?" West asks. His eyes roam over my face in a way that makes me want to fidget away my discomfort. That kind of searching look was only okay when we didn't hate each other.

I open my mouth and let a lie fall out. "Busy." In truth, I've done very little in the last few months except daydream about how happy I'll be when I've redeemed myself and I'm back on top.

His eyes narrow as he tries to interpret my answer. It thrills me that he can't. He has no idea what I've been up to for the last seven years, and I *love* that for me. I might not be able to take back what I've done, but I can bask in the luxury of having secrets (even boring ones). For once, West doesn't know every-fucking-thing.

Blatant curiosity is printed in his expression. "What are you doing here?" He motions around us, and I don't know if he means Tucson, the festival, or this exact spot.

"I have every right to be here."

He makes eye contact. Holds on. A sickening ache settles in my stomach. When he finally tears his gaze away, I don't know if he found the answer he was searching for. "So, you're good?"

I lift my chin. "Never better." Another lie. Every day that gets closer to my book release has me vibrating with stomach-churning anxiety.

"Right," he says, and I'm delighted to see the color on his cheekbones. I've flustered him. He can write a sentence that wrings the tears from my body, but *I've* flustered *him*. My stomach warms with vindictive pride.

He takes a deep breath. "You might have heard by now that my new book came out a few weeks ago, and—"

"I know." I cut him off, his reminder killing my buzz. He's now a headlining presenter. With me. Crashing my first panel in years. I don't need to hear him say the words.

"You do?" He looks momentarily confused, but when I nod, a familiar smirk plays on the corner of his lips.

I've seen that look before, in a classroom not that far from here. A cold shock douses me, draining the fire from my belly, and I'm nineteen *and* twenty-two *and* twenty-five all over again. Sideswiped by what I should have seen coming from a mile away.

"Did you hear my phone call?" I ask, my voice a calm contrast to the riot happening in my chest. He's smiling like he knows he just ruined my weekend. My year. My whole entire life.

He hesitates, his brows dipping. "No," he says slowly.

I nod, sucking in a deep breath. Good. That's good. The last thing I need is for West Emerson to hear me snapping at my editor. I don't want him to know how much it bothers me that he's here, although I wonder if this forced collaboration is as baffling to him as it is to me. It makes no sense why anyone thinks it's appropriate to put us on a panel together after what he did, but publishers have been known to make interesting choices in the name of selling books (every time a political figure who is deeply rotten inside lands a seven-figure deal for their memoir, for example).

The open secret in the industry is that commercial success can be something of a mystery, even in the hands of booklovers who have all the passion and experience in the world. You can throw all the money and marketing and Times Square billboards at a book, but sometimes it doesn't work. It's alchemy, making a bestseller. It requires the right mixture of timing and luck and a bit of magic that's nearly impossible to capture. So instead of investing in new voices, fairly paid employees, or innovative marketing strategies, more and more lately, we see publishers crossing their fingers and hoping a book goes viral. Putting West and me together might be his underpaid and overworked publicist's way of stirring up controversy to build buzz.

Or maybe this just happened because West is a former student with a book to promote. Maybe it's because through the amalgam of bad timing and worse luck, West has waltzed back into my life when I least want to see him.

He steps closer and lowers his voice. "Are you okay?" he asks, pity in every syllable.

"I have something to take care of."

"I'll walk with you." His long strides quickly catch up to mine.

"No need!" I want to kick him in the crotch and sprint away, but I force myself to stay calm and even. When I speed up, he does, too. Any minute now we'll be competitive racewalkers, vying for a spot in the Olympics' silliest sport. His bare forearm brushes against mine, and I swear to Jane Austen, I feel it in the soles of my feet. I jerk my arm away dramatically, and his eyes slide sideways in a devastating assessment of my sanity.

Fuck. I need to chill out.

"Congratulations on your new book," West says, as if that's a thing he's allowed to say.

I give him a quick look. The book isn't out for another couple of weeks, and I have no sales numbers or bestseller lists or metrics to measure it with. "For what?"

"For finishing it," he says, his gaze sharpening on mine. "You should be proud."

I snort. I can't remember the last time I felt proud of a personal achievement. Only relieved. Either way, he's mocking me. He must know about all the missed deadlines, the pushed release dates, the years when I couldn't string together a coherent paragraph. My expression morphs into an annoyed scowl. "Save the congratulations for after it comes out. Then we'll see if there's anything worth celebrating."

He whistles under his breath, and I can't help but wonder

what he's thinking. I glance up at him and imagine the words *head case* flashing in a thought bubble.

We both stop short as we reach the white tents on the lawn in the center of the U of A campus. The tents are filled with stages, signing tables, and books in every category and genre imaginable. In the grassy space between them, festival attendees weave around performers and food trucks, pausing occasionally to browse handmade merch, including stickers, bookmarks, and tote bags. (Where there are bookish people, there are tote bags.) I inhale a lungful of orange blossoms. If I concentrate on the festival, I can almost forget the years West and I spent walking across this lawn together.

"Some people would say writing and publishing a book is reason enough to celebrate," West muses.

"Those people have never received death threats for writing 'cringey teen romance novels.'"

His face pales. "Did you—" He clears his throat. "Did you really?"

"Don't look so appalled. It's not like it was *your* fault."

I head toward the Old Main building and am aghast when West follows. I glance up in time to see a muscle in his jaw jump. "Did you tell the police?" he asks.

I roll my eyes. "They cared about as much as they care about the dick pics in my inbox." He looks so disturbed by that, I almost feel bad for him. "My editor doesn't think there will be backlash this time."

"I'm sure there won't be," he says, and I bristle at his unwarranted confidence. It's obnoxious the way he thinks he knows my career better than I do.

"You don't know that."

"You could write anything, and people would eat it up."

"You would think that," I reply, monotone. Leave it to him to say the worst possible thing.

"How *are* the early reviews?"

I bite my lip, unsure of what to say. I should have invented a million little lies to tell him about all the reading lists I've made and awards that I've won since we last talked. One book? Child's play. I'll tell him that I've written twelve and sold them all at auction. He'll never bother to double-check.

At the very least, I should have mentally prepared myself to see him again. The first time after a break is always disorienting. It makes me feel like I need to book a physical ASAP, because why should a thirty-two-year-old feel like there's an ice cube in her chest that won't melt? If I'd known he'd be here, I'd have looked at his picture every night before bed to desensitize myself.

"The book's been embargoed. There won't be any early reviews," I hear myself admitting out loud. It was one of the requests (read: demands) I had for my publisher. They would've had to pry that manuscript out of my cold, dead hands if they hadn't agreed to this stipulation. My mental health wouldn't have survived otherwise.

The sun is beating down on my neck as we round Old Main and stop short in front of the large fountain. He exhales a soft huff of air that telegraphs shared memories. His and mine.

"Do you remember—"

"Don't," I say before his words unleash a dam of counterfeit nostalgia.

He stuffs his hands in his pockets and rocks on his feet. "There was a time when you would have killed to be in this position: a published author and festival headliner."

Resentment slices red-hot through my chest. "And there

was a time when you weren't a pretentious asshole, but people change." I sidestep him with purpose.

My name doesn't carry the gravitas it once did, but on this campus, I still have some sway, and I'm going to use every ounce of it to get West Emerson kicked off my panel.

4

13 Years Ago
Freshman Year, Second Semester

I guess I shouldn't have been surprised by the way everything went down, because West was a surprise from the very beginning. I didn't know he had any intention of entering the writing competition, had no idea the Chia Pet story was his until he smirked at me on that last day of class and I realized too late that the train was about to hit.

When second semester starts, I keep an eye out for West on campus, but our schedules don't match up, and eventually I stop thinking about him. Mostly. And every time I sit in Grammar 101 and am forced through the hell that is mapping sentence trees, I definitely don't wonder what's going on in Dr. B's workshop. More or less. And on a Saturday night in February when my roommate, Amber, insists that I go to a basketball game with her and some friends, I agree, because I don't expect her friends to include West.

But like I said, he's always been a surprise.

My breath clouds in front of me in the fading sunlight as Amber and I wait outside the boys' dorm. It's cold for Tucson;

the air has an unfamiliar bite. I breathe into my hands to warm them up.

"It's about time you came out with us. You study too much," Amber says. She likes to grumble that I never hang out, but because she's with her boyfriend ninety percent of the time, I doubt I'm hindering her social life *that* much.

"I'm failing math," I say instead of explaining that most of my time is spent writing fantasy worlds that have nothing to do with school. I *am* failing math, but that has very little to do with anything. Going out is just . . . harder than staying in. Always has been.

"Have you seen a tutor?"

"I'll figure it out." I brush off her question, not in the mood to think about it.

The front door of the Graham-Greenlee dorm swings open, and I can tell from Amber's happy squeal that the frat boy wearing a Pi Beta Phi shirt and shorts that hit mid-thigh is her boyfriend.

"Kyle, this is Mars—"

"Like the planet?" Kyle asks, draping his arm around his girlfriend. "Does anyone ever call you Saturn?" He laughs at his own joke.

"Kyle, like Kyle Cotton?" I ask, my head cocked to the side. Out of the corner of my eye, I see three guys approaching us in the cold, and I do a double take.

"Who?"

I snap my attention back to Amber's boyfriend. "Kyle Cotton? Brown hair. Yea high." I hold my hand at chest level. "He was in my third-grade class. Or wait—fourth grade? No, third grade."

Kyle blinks at me. "How the fuck would I know him?"

I shrug innocently.

"It's a joke!" Amber says. "When we met, she said, 'Like the resin from *Jurassic Park*?' Isn't that hilarious? She does this to *everyone*."

"Not everyone," I say with a smile.

Amber waves and makes introductions. "Mars, these are Kyle's friends Aaron and Nathan, like Aaron, um . . . Wait, this is hard." She bites her lip.

"Aaron Burr and the famous hot dogs?" I supply.

"No. I was thinking of Nick Carter's little brother. Anyway . . ." She points to the third friend, who's towering over the rest of us in a hoodie and jeans. "This is Kyle's roommate—"

"West, like Mae," he says, nodding at me. "We've met."

Amber's eyes light up like this is extraordinary news. "Really? Oh, that's perfect! We're meeting up with a few more people at the game, and I didn't want either of you to feel left out, but you can hang together. It actually makes sense. You're both a little weird."

"Ouch?" I cover my heart with my hand.

She rolls her eyes playfully. "Said with *affection*!"

"How am I weird?"

"C'mon, Mars! You never party with us, you're always in some fantasyland in your head, and you brush your teeth in the shower!"

"Do people not do that?"

"They don't." West shakes his head emphatically as Amber and Kyle lead the way to the McKale Center. "Did I sound like Kyle when we met?" he whispers as he falls into step next to me at the back of the group.

"With my name? No. You didn't try to call me Uranus, for one thing."

"Did he really?"

"He would have gotten there if I'd given him two more minutes."

"Is this a bad time to point out that you're saved as 'Jupiter' in my phone?"

I roll my eyes. "I'm not even in your phone."

West stuffs his hands in his pockets. "So, your roommate is the reason I have to spend all my time at the library?"

"Wait—really? They're . . ." I raise an eyebrow.

"Banging? Oh yeah. *All* the time."

I laugh. "Not in my room, they're not."

"Consider yourself lucky. The things I've heard . . ." He shudders.

We cross the street with a growing horde of students decked out in cardinal red and navy blue. We meet up with three girls I don't recognize, and it becomes clear pretty quickly that West and I are the odd ones out, and without anything else to talk about while we wait in the security line, I find myself asking, "How's Dr. B's class? Any 'heartsick' appearances yet?"

Hands still in his pockets, West looks at me out of the corner of his eye. "Oh, *now* she's in the mood to joke about it."

Last semester we had a classmate who was fixated on the word *heartsick*. Her characters were overwrought with emotion, all of them weeping and fainting and perpetually lovelorn. Every time she used the word, West caught my eye with a meaningful glance and held up his fingers under the table. One for each flagrant abuse of the word. By November, he'd lost count and would clutch my knee while our shoulders shook from silent laughter.

"In my defense, I'm a sore loser." I cross my arms.

"That's your defense?"

"I don't like failing. Is that so bad?"

"Ah yes, the abject failure known as second place." His tone is dry enough to catch fire.

"Second isn't—"

"I voted for you," he says as we come to an abrupt halt in one of the security lines. The rest of our group gets swallowed up by the crowd.

"You *did*?" I don't bother to hide my shock.

"Obviously. Why? Who did you vote for?"

"Myself!"

He shakes his head, the corner of his mouth twitching. "I don't know why I asked."

"Whatever. Second place or last, it's all the same."

"Which story do you think came in last?" He leans in, crowding me, his voice low in my ear. I stare up into his eyes, slightly hypnotized by the strange ring of amber around his pupils.

"Heartsick," we say at the same time.

West finally cracks a smile and ushers me toward the student section. "We can talk about it now? No hard feelings?"

"As long as you don't lie to me."

The crowd presses us closer together, and I'm in front of West now, his hand on my shoulder so we don't get separated. I crane my neck all the way back to look up at him when he scoffs. "When did I ever lie to you?"

"When you said you weren't entering the competition because it wasn't 'your thing.'"

His eyes narrow as he looks down at me, his gaze nearly as heavy as his palm on my shoulder. "People are allowed to change their minds, Mars." His voice curls pleasantly around my name.

"Why did you?" I'm knocked back into him, shoulder blades slamming flush against his chest.

He steadies me, keeping me pressed against him in a way that I definitely don't hate until space opens around us. When I move, he clears his throat and finally answers my question. "Lots of reasons. You, for one."

"*Me?*" I'm incredulous.

"Seeing how much you love writing made me want to love it, too." He looks away. "Whatever. It's mostly because Dr. B encouraged me to enter. Told me I had a good shot."

He points to our group in the student section, and we squeeze our way through the crowd. I stand on my tiptoes and shout so he can hear me over the roar as the Wildcats' starting lineup is announced. "Is that why you didn't tell me? Because Dr. B put you up to it?"

"No," he shouts back, his attention now on the game. He cups his hands around his mouth and cheers for our star player. He nudges me with his elbow, motioning for me to join in, but I have a one-track mind. Obsessive, some people have said. Focused. Determined. A buzzkill.

I put my hand on my hip, annoyed. I thought West and I were friends. He's the one who would kick my foot under the table when the pocket egg made its daily appearance. He'd doodle cartoons for me on the corners of his notebook when he was bored. He read *Twilight* because I told him to. West Emerson knew how much I wanted to win that contest, and he couldn't even give me the heads-up that he was competing against me.

"Then why didn't you tell me?" I whisper. The national anthem is starting, but I'm a dog with a bone, and I can't let it go.

West looks down at me, a puzzled expression on his face. "I

wanted plausible deniability. If my story sucked, I never would have told you it was mine."

"But *why*?"

He shakes his head like I'm missing the point. "I was just trying to impress you, Mars."

5

Present Day

I open the door to Old Main, and a whoosh of icy air-conditioning blasts me in the face. Goose bumps and nostalgia skitter across my skin. I close my eyes with my hand still on the open door, fighting the wave of nausea that swells in my throat. It's the first weekend in March, and half the country is under a freeze warning, but not Tucson. Almost never Tucson. The high is eighty degrees today, and it's during months like this, when New York is still sludgy and gray, that I miss the desert.

"Are you okay?"

I startle out of my homesickness for a place that was never really home and land back in the small administrative lobby, where a young woman is sitting behind a wooden reception desk littered with campus maps and conference schedules. While she stares at me over the top of her phone, with AirPods in both ears and a please-don't-talk-to-me expression on her face, the anger simmering in the pit of my stomach slowly eases. In its place, uncertainty curls around my ribs. Now that I'm here, I'm not sure what to do.

I waver in the doorway, torn between the cool, quiet lobby and the warm, bustling festival. In the end, it's not a choice. I can't turn around and walk back down the Old Main steps, not when West might still be lurking, waiting to tell me how lucky I am because my mindless fans will read whatever drivel I put on paper.

I clear my throat as I approach the table. "Hi! I'm Mars, and I'm hoping to speak with the director of the conference."

She blinks at me. "I don't even know who that is."

Not a surprise, but I've never been one to give up so easily. "Is there anyone you can put me in contact with?"

"I can give you a parking map."

I crane my neck to see down the hall behind her. "Is there anyone in charge here?"

Her eyes travel over my shoulder, and somehow, I just *know*.

"No one told me the Karen Convention is in town." West's deadpan voice scrapes my spine like gravel as his shadow falls over the tile floor.

"I need to report a stalker," I say as blandly as possible.

His answering scoff sounds equal parts amused and annoyed. "She's kidding."

"She's not." I glare at him as he strides smoothly toward me. All my senses perk up at West's sudden nearness, and it sends me into a nearly unbearable state of fight-or-flight. I shuffle back. "Why are you *here*?"

He stops next to me—balanced on the line between close and *too* close—and reaches around me to pick up a conference schedule. Determined not to give him the satisfaction of my attention, I look down at the brown commercial carpeting. Straight ahead at the wood trim around the baseboards and doors. Up toward the recessed lighting in the ceiling. My hand clenches, fingernails leaving crescent moons in my skin.

His fingers drum a rhythm against his thigh as his eyes rove over the schedule, and it's a trait so shockingly familiar that I can't help but look. West's eyebrow ticks up. "Okay, I have to know what Crock-Pot Romance is. Starts in ten minutes. Want to go?" He flashes a smile that gives shades of Fox the fae king. Teasing and irresistible. I hate him for it.

I straighten my spine and turn toward the reception desk. "This is urgent," I tell the helpless undergrad. "I'm a presenting author, and there's an issue with the schedule—"

"It's me. I'm the issue." West extends his hand across the table, and the girl's eyes widen as she shakes it.

"No, he's not."

West angles his body and dips his head so that I have no choice but to make eye contact. "This *isn't* about a pretentious asshole being added to your keynote?" he asks with the mildest interest. He might as well be asking about my car's long-term warranty.

I roll my eyes. "Not everything is about you."

"But some things explicitly are." He nods to the girl behind the table. "Ever heard of Fox Caldwell?"

I haven't heard him say that name in years, and it sets off a red alarm in me that triggers all my nerve endings. It feels like pins and needles, with heat prickling at the back of my neck and pressure building behind my eyes.

"Mars Darling?" A voice booms across the lobby, saving me from certain mortification.

"Dr. B!" I can't help but smile at the man walking down the hall. I hurry to meet him, impatient to shrug off the specter of West. My old professor must be in his seventies now, but from the long gray ponytail that hangs down his back to his cargo shorts to the socks-and-Birks combo on his feet, he looks exactly the same as he did when I was a freshman. "How are you?"

"Better now that my star pupil is here!" he says as he tucks a stack of file folders under his arm.

I know West can hear us from the lobby, and I bite the inside of my cheek to keep from laughing. "Did I ever tell you that you're my favorite professor?"

"Don't say that unless you're here to fulfill the promise you made when you were my student." He must see the confusion on my face, because he raises his hand and says, "'I promise that when I'm a published author, I will come talk to Dr. B's class—'"

"'For *free*,'" we both finish at the same time. I laugh, now remembering vividly how Dr. B would extract that same promise from every student who sat in his upper-division courses.

"I'm leaving early Monday morning," I say with real regret.

"Next time." He waves it off. "Walk with me? I have a few minutes before I have to run." He nods down the hall, and I can't help but turn my eyes to West, who is scowling darkly at the desk of maps and schedules, riffling through them as if his life depends on locating the Second Street garage.

"I'd love to," I tell Dr. B, throwing a smirk over my shoulder at West.

He clears his throat intentionally, drawing the professor's attention. Dr. B does a double take before his eyes light with recognition and a healthy dose of delight. "West Emerson?" He walks down the hall and rounds the desk to clap West on the shoulder. "Apologies, I was blinded by our celebrity here, but I should have known that where Mars is, you wouldn't be far behind! My *two* star pupils!" He motions for West to join us.

He falls into step on the other side of Dr. B and returns my gloating smile with one of his own.

"I owe you an email, Mr. Emerson," Dr. B says. "I found your novel quite moving. In fact—"

"We don't have to talk about it." West pinches the bridge of his nose, giving the distinct impression that he regrets drawing attention to himself.

"Ah. Some things never change," Dr. B says. I snort, and West glares daggers at his feet as Dr. B turns his attention to me. "And *you*, Mars." I straighten my spine instinctively. "You wouldn't believe how proud I am of you," he says with such sincerity that my stomach drops. "I claim credit for your success in all of my classes," he adds with a wink. "Is the world ready for another Mars Darling adventure?"

I cringe under the pressure of his praise. "Not sure *I'm* ready, to be honest."

He hums thoughtfully. "Some things *do* change. Is your new book another sequel?"

"No, thank god." One of my favorite things about *Shattered* is that it takes place in a completely separate universe from my Fox Caldwell series. It's as free from West's inspiration as anything I've written in more than a decade.

Dr. B pulls open the door to an empty office and drops his stack of folders on the corner of the desk. "I have a meeting in a few minutes, but you both know where to find me. And really, Mars. I'm glad you're back. I'll be in the audience on Sunday if you need a friendly face."

It takes everything in me to force a miserable smile.

"I'll be there, too," West tells him.

"In the audience?"

West nods his head at me. "On the stage. With Mars."

"Nothing's finalized yet," I say quickly.

"Interesting." Dr. B's eyes flit between us. "It's with sincere regret that I don't have more time."

Back in the hall, West glances at me as I press my tongue to the roof of my mouth; it's a trick I've learned to stem the tears.

"You keep in touch?" I ask, half as a distraction from the tears building in the corners of my eyes and half in accusation. It would be unfair and, yes, immature to ask Dr. B to choose sides, but it stings that he didn't choose mine.

"A little." West shrugs uneasily.

Please withdraw. The plea sits too close to the edge of my lips, but I quickly swallow it down, hating the implied vulnerability in the request.

West follows as I retrace our steps to the lobby, and I can tell by the way he runs his tongue along the inside of his cheek that he wants to say something. My phone saves me from having to listen. He'll have to inflict his unwelcome presence on someone else.

I close the door in his face as I step outside and answer the call. "Hi, Amina. Sorry I snapped at you earlier," I say as I lean against sun-drenched brick. The warmth seeps into my shoulder blades and slows my heart rate. I pinch the bridge of my nose for half a second before I realize it's a West mannerism and drop my hand.

"No, no, no, not at all. Please don't worry about it," Amina says a little too quickly, and I feel a sense of guilt for once again being a "difficult" author. I've dug in my heels with my publishing team before, and I'm still paying for it. And just like last time, this is all West's fault.

"People won't want to see me with him."

"I'm working on it," she assures me.

"Thank you." I take a deep breath. "I appreciate you trying, especially on a Friday afternoon."

"I'll keep at it," she assures me. "And you absolutely do *not* have to do this event if you don't feel comfortable. Say the word and I can pull you out of any of your scheduled appearances."

The door swings open, and West ducks outside, pushing his curls off his forehead. I wonder what it would feel like to run my hand across the stubble on his jaw, which is an insane thought I should not have. The scent of orange blossoms is screwing with my brain.

He hesitates under the brick archway, and for an agonizing moment, I think he's going to stay. I imagine he'll lean against the bricks and cross his legs at the ankles, arms folded over his broad chest as he pins me with a heavy stare. He catches me watching him, and as we blink at each other in silence, I admit that I've never been able to predict his moves as well as I thought.

"Mars?" Amina's voice carries through the phone. "Do you want to think about canceling and get back to me?"

"No," I tell her quickly, the weight of West's gaze hot on my face. I force myself to hold his eye contact even though it makes me feel like my skin is stretched too tight over my bones, paper-thin and ready to crack. "He's the one who needs to drop out. I don't want *anything* to do with him."

His jaw clenches as his features turn to stone. Nothing about West is soft these days, and the way he looks at me is sharp enough to draw blood. He brushes past me and jogs down the stairs.

"Likewise, Darling." His words carry over his shoulder, bruising me between the ribs.

6

13 Years Ago
Freshman Year, Second Semester

The next time I hear from West, it's a Sunday night and I'm drowning in a sea of math homework that might as well be in a foreign language. I'm not good at math, and I hate that about myself. *A writer who sucks with numbers? How novel.* If I could write books *and* understand how to double the measurements in a recipe, I'd be unstoppable. The world needs more women in STEM, and as much as I wish I could contribute, I'm not going to be one of them. I'm going to be an Enneagram type 3 (wing 4) who likes library-scented candles, moody music, and books with dragons and magic and hot guys.

As if he's been summoned by my thoughts, my phone buzzes with a message from an unknown number.

I'm getting kicked out of my room.

I push my textbook off my lap and tuck my legs under me with a smile. Amber sprayed perfume between her boobs and dry-shaved her legs before she left our room ten minutes ago, which means this could only be one person.

Don't freeze to death.

It's not exactly freeze-to-death cold outside, but the mid-thirties *is* cold for Tucson. My windows are dark and frosty, and the dorm heater is struggling to keep up.

Heading to the library now. Might not make it alive.

Sucks to be you. I'm buried under three layers of fuzzy blankets, in a roommate-less room.

Now you're just being cruel.

Not that I mind, but how'd you get my number?

Amber. It was my condition for leaving tonight. This is Jupiter, right?

It's been a week since the basketball game with West, and I won't lie and say I haven't thought about him since. And every time I think of *him*, I think of his story about a lonely boy, which made me cry, and how I can't help but wonder if that story showed me a part of West he otherwise keeps hidden. I think about how he voted for me to win, despite wanting the prize for himself. I feel the weight of his hand on my shoulder and his multicolored eyes trained on mine when he said, *I was just trying to impress you*. I had no idea he cared so much about my opinion, especially when he can write like *that*. Funny and bittersweet. I was laughing all the way to the end, right up until the moment a tear landed on my keyboard.

Are you saying my roommate sold me out for sex?

She thinks we're friends.

Is she right?

When my phone buzzes again, my reflexive grin is idiotic.

Meet me on the second floor of the main library and we can find out.

I glance again at the frosty windows. Nothing has ever sounded less pleasant than trudging across campus in the cold.

Too cold. You'd have to pry me out of these blankets.

Is that an invitation?

I blink at my screen, phone clutched in my hands, my mouth forming a small O. I quickly scan back through our conversation, trying to decipher anything suggestive in it. I brought up sex, but in a funny way. I mentioned my bed (more than once!). I *dared* him to pry me out of it.

But he's not—he wouldn't—I didn't summon him here for a Sunday-night hookup.

Right?

Room 314.

I send the text with shaky fingers, and then I press my face into my pillow.

Eight minutes later, he knocks.

"Hey." West stands with his shoes toeing the threshold of my room, his cheeks pink from the cold and his chest heaving like he ran here. His hands are on my doorframe, his fingernails a scratched-up Sharpie-purple that I would hate on literally anyone but him.

"Hi." A beat passes in which neither of us moves, but then I stand back so he can shut the door behind him, shrinking the room by a factor of five thousand. He shifts his weight, and I blurt the first thing that comes to mind. "Want something to drink?"

He rakes his fingers through his hair. "Sure. Do you have milk?"

I laugh until a flash of embarrassment flits across his face. "Wait. For real?"

He lets his hair fall over his eyes and walks around me to survey the wall over my bed. It's empty except for a handful of pictures from home and a poster of earnest writing quotes. Finally, West looks over his shoulder. "Or whiskey?"

"You want *milk* or *whiskey*?" I open the mini refrigerator that fits under my loft bed and stare at a half-empty Red Bull that I was rationing for later and the chocolate protein shakes that Amber drinks for every meal. I look back at him. "Shockingly, we don't keep either in our room, unless you want Amber's almond milk. It's expensive, though, so she might kill you."

His shoulders creep up to his cheeks. "I was kidding. Whatever is fine. Or nothing, honestly."

"The girls in 308 always have a stash of something, but they hate me ever since I accidentally left my retainer next to the sink four weeks in a row," I say wryly.

His lips tilt. "It was a joke. I don't even drink."

"Yeah, neither do I when my parents are asking." I flash him a smile, and he lets his bag drop to the floor.

"Do you really brush your teeth in the shower?" he asks as he bends over my desk to inspect a picture of me and a few friends from graduation. Most of them stayed in the San Diego area, but I didn't have the grades to get into any of the UC schools. I doubt we'll still be talking come Thanksgiving.

"Do you *not*? My brothers have done it for as long as I can remember. I thought it was standard."

"Not standard. And not that hygienic, if I had to guess."

"Oh." I bite my lip, standing alone in a shoebox of a room with a guy who thinks I'm gross while my face heats like a solar panel. "I didn't realize that was information I should have guarded with my life. That's even more embarrassing than the quotes on my wall."

He glances up at the poster that reads: The road to hell is paved with adverbs.

"No, it's not. And anyway, my family calls the TV remote a 'genie,' and I didn't know that was weird until I was, like, fifteen. We also howl at the full moon every month."

I blink at him. "Why?"

He shrugs. "I don't know. We thought it was funny, and then we got superstitious about it. One month we didn't do it because it was raining or something, I don't remember, and the *next* day my youngest brother broke his leg. I had to pull him to school in a wagon for six weeks. One day the wheel fell off, so I put him in a wheelbarrow. A neighbor called my mom, and she yelled at me for not telling her about the wagon." He shuts his mouth abruptly and scowls like he regrets telling me all that. "We never missed a full moon again."

"Never?" My real question is implied in my raised eyebrow.

West grimaces. "Never."

I pull the blinds away from my window. "Is it—"

"Not until Tuesday," he says.

"Damn." I suddenly can't imagine anything I want more in life than to see West howl at the full moon. "Well, thanks for sharing the weirdo misery. Glad to know I'm not alone."

"I just told you multiple embarrassing things about my family. You owe me another one."

I climb onto my bed and sit with my back against pillows while I motion for West to sit next to me. "Okay, here's one. When I wanted a snack, I used to eat a piece of Wonder Bread slathered in margarine and white sugar."

"Try harder. That shit was the fancy dessert in my house," West says with a smile.

"I once opened my mom's top dresser drawer—"

He holds up his hands. "I don't think I want to know this—"

"—and it was filled with loose baby teeth. She admitted that whenever she played tooth fairy, she'd drop my and my brothers' teeth in her drawer to save for later, but she never did anything with them. She doesn't even know whose are whose."

"That's worse than I expected, and I expected parental sex toys."

I lean across my twin bed and cover his mouth with my hand. "Don't say that ever again."

His eyes spark, and then he licks my palm. I shriek and rub my hand against his chest while he laughs. "I can't believe you just licked me."

"I can't believe you're surprised. Didn't you say you have brothers?"

"Two older ones. Who are *nice* to me, by the way. How many siblings do you have, and do you torture them regularly?"

He hesitates, like he's not sure of the answer, but finally settles on "Four."

"Whoa."

"Yeah." West ducks his head, letting his hair fall over his eyes again like he does when he's uncomfortable. I didn't realize I knew that about him until now. Just like that, an entire portion of my brain is suddenly devoted to learning the story behind that reluctant *four.* I'll die if I don't find out. I'm going to dream and daydream and write stories in my head until he tells me. I've auto-deleted a mountain of info to make room for this clawing curiosity. The names and faces and histories of any guy I ever had a crush on, for instance. Gone in the bob of his Adam's apple, erased in the slow dip of dark eyelashes against his cheeks.

West looks like he's in agony. He hasn't told me the story yet, but he will. I find the only ounce of patience I possess and change the subject. "You're a horrible distraction. I'm supposed to be doing math homework."

His shoulders slump in relief, and when his eyes catch mine, I see the unspoken *Thank you* in his rainbow irises. "Sorry, I'll stop distracting you."

"I don't mind," I say too quickly. "I can't do my homework, anyway. I don't understand it."

"What are you learning?"

"I don't know."

"You don't *know*?" He picks up my textbook and starts thumbing through the pages. "Where are your notes from class?"

"I don't have any."

A scrap of paper filled with hastily scrawled dialogue flutters to his lap. "I think I've found your problem."

"Inspiration strikes when it strikes, West. It's not my fault that my Greco-Roman-inspired fantasy with an emotions-based magic system and a bodyguard romance is more interesting than trigonometry." Just like it's not my fault that words stay put on the page, unlike numbers, which dance around whenever I look at them.

"You write during class?"

"I write during everything. I'm writing a kiss scene in my head right now."

He chokes on his own breath. "The fuck?"

"What?" I look at his wide eyes and realize he thinks I want to kiss him. His teeth drag over his bottom lip, and it dawns on me that maybe I do. A flush of heat steals across my chest, and for a heartbeat, I'm trapped in his gaze. I clear my throat and tear my eyes away, looking anywhere but at him. I'm going to have to figure out what to do with *that* thought sometime when he's not sitting on my bed. "I'm always writing scenes in my head. You should see the Notes app on my phone," I murmur.

He narrows his eyes like he's not sure what to make of the invitation. After a beat, he continues to thumb through the pages of the textbook on his lap. "Why don't you just drop the class?"

"Because I need a math credit to graduate, for reasons unknown, as if calculators and tax accountants and the nine-times-table finger trick don't exist." I roll my eyes. "The midterm is on Friday. If I fail that, I fail the class. If I fail the class, I have to *retake it in the fall*." I shudder.

"You won't fail."

"I might."

"There are worse things."

I tilt my head to the side. "I'm sorry, I don't understand whatever language you're speaking."

"Having to retake one class isn't the end of the world."

"Sorry, again, my brain just can't compute those words."

He laughs, and it's a sound I want tattooed on my eardrums. "I should have known, based on your reaction to coming in second place in the writing contest."

A loud thud hits my door, and West and I both startle in surprise.

"Is Amber back already?" he asks. Whatever unexamined hopes I had for the evening dissolve like frost.

"Hello?" I yell.

"It's snowing!" comes a loud, giggly response from a voice that's not Amber's.

I'll bet. "Looks like someone raided the neighbors' liquor stash."

"Unless she's telling the truth."

"Well, you tell me, *T-loc*, does it snow in the desert?" I tease, branding him with the nickname given to Tucson locals.

"I'm not a T-loc," he scoffs. "I'm from Casa Grande, which is even worse. And no, it doesn't snow in this dust bowl hell." We stare at each other while the sounds of slamming doors and thudding footsteps echo through the dorm hallway. "Except . . . sometimes it does," he begrudgingly admits.

We slide off the bed, our feet hitting the floor in unison. I grab a sweatshirt from my floor as he opens the door. He grabs my hand and pulls me into the hall as I'm yanking boots onto my bare feet.

Campus is *pandemonium*. Hundreds of students are dancing, running, and screaming in the street in front of the Maricopa dorm. An open window on the third floor next door is blaring music through a speaker.

"No way," I say, my breath clouding in front of me. I hold up my palms and watch wet snowflakes fall softly onto my skin. Of all the things I expected when I decided to go to college in the desert, this wasn't on my list.

We step into the street, then quickly jump back as a group of students in their underwear run past us, soaking wet and shaking from cold. "What's going on?"

"Skinny-dipping in the Old Main fountain," comes the reply.

"Does it count if you're in your underwear?" West asks. I glance up at him; he has snow flurries on his long black lashes. The sight makes me giddy. I'm drunk on cold air. "Has anyone ever told you that you have multicolored eyes?"

"No, just you."

"Really?" I'm shocked. Sometimes I see his eyes in my sleep.

"You're too gullible," he says.

I shove him hard, but he clasps my frozen fingers in the palm of his hand, his gaze hot enough to make me sweat. "Has anyone ever told you that you have a mole right here?" He lightly brushes his thumb over the spot just above my lip.

Most of my features are unremarkable. I'm average height. I have shoulder-length hair that's dark blond or light brown, depending on the light. My brothers tease me for my hazel "Bratz" eyes—they're pretty big—but I could be a walking cyclops, and my mole would still get all the attention. I wrinkle my nose. "Yes. Constantly. All the time. I hate this stupid thing."

West shakes his head. "That's dumb."

"Your hair!" I pull my hand out of his and brush my fingers through his damp hair. Apparently, we're people who touch each other now.

He frowns. "What's wrong with it?"

"It's *curly*!" I don't know why, but the fact that his straight emo bangs curl when wet is the best revelation of my life. "Do you straighten it every day?"

He won't look me in the eye. "Yes."

"Can I convince you not to?"

He groans and covers his face like he's been caught in a compromising position. "No."

A girl from my dorm floor passes me a drink made up of party leftovers. I take a whiff and feel the burn in my nostrils. After a shudder-inducing sip, I offer it to West.

He shakes his head. "No, thanks."

"You sure? It's disgusting!"

"I don't drink."

"You were serious about that?"

He nods.

"There's a story there."

His wet curls are stuck to his forehead as he nods again. Curiosity burns me alive. "Will you tell me about it?"

"Someday," he says easily, and I'm not sure if he's making me a promise or dismissing my question.

We stand in the softly falling snow for a quarter of an hour, doing little besides watching our breath puff in front of us. I don't know if it's the weather or the boy at my side, but I'm frozen to my spot, unable to move. "I'm numb everywhere," I say absently.

West moves to take off his hoodie, but I put my hand on his forearm to stop him. "I'm fine. You keep it. I shouldn't have said anything."

He runs his tongue along the inside of his cheek, considering me for a long moment. Finally, cautiously, he wraps his arms around my shoulders and pulls me into his chest. His long arms cross in front of me and wrap around my torso. "This better?" he asks in a quiet, questioning voice while improbable, magical snowflakes fall around us. I can only nod as the music pulses in my ears and my blood. People pressed on all sides sway and sing and laugh and stick their tongues out to catch the falling snow. My heart feels jittery and floaty, and West's arms are the best jacket that's ever existed. I tip my head back against his chest and close my eyes, and in a shock of realization, it occurs to me that I'm chasing this feeling every time I sit down to write a single sentence on a blank page. This expansive, ballooning, giddy, *oh my god, I could live in this moment forever, but I'll die if I don't know what happens next* feeling.

I jolt out of West's arms. "I have to go write."

"*Now?*"

"Yeah. I know exactly how to finish the scene I've been

stuck on, and if I don't get it out of my head, I'll lose it." I push myself onto my tiptoes and kiss him on the cheek.

He looks dumbstruck, his mouth trying several times to form a sentence before he figures it out. "What about your math?"

I hold up ten fingers and then drop a thumb. "Nine times five is forty-five! What else does a girl need to know?" I slip through the crowd and race back to my room. When I open my laptop, the words have never come easier. I'm powered by the sound of his laugh and the feel of his arms and the sheer biology of my lips against his cheek. I write until my eyes blur, sometime between three and four in the morning, then fall into bed with a grin.

I'm dead tired, happier than I've been in weeks, and blissfully unaware of the consequences of having West Emerson as a muse.

7

Present Day

It's never a good idea to start a conversation with my mother when I'm already in a bad mood, but I'm too irritated by my last interaction with West to give it much thought when her name appears on my phone. I stab the answer button.

"Hey, Mom." I sound every bit as sullen as I feel, sitting on the white steps in front of Old Main. "What's up?"

On the other end of the line, I hear a door closing, and I picture her stepping outside to pace up and down the driveway while we talk. "Did you make it to Tucson?"

"No, sorry, my plane crashed."

She doesn't dignify my snark with a response. "How's the festival?"

Warm and sunny and horrible. "There's a problem with my schedule, but—"

I let the end of that sentence fall off a cliff.

"What problem?" she asks sharply. I fear she's logging in to Facebook as we speak, righteous indignation at the ready.

"It's nothing," I insist, well aware that it's too late. In my distraction, I dipped a toe into the topic I'm always dodging with her. Silence stretches from here to San Diego, but I'm too flustered by the last hour of my life to fill it with anything but the truth. "They have me sharing a stage with someone I'd rather avoid."

"Do they know who you are?" she asks without a hint of irony.

"Mom—"

"No, I'm serious. They're *lucky* to have you!"

"It's not like that."

"It's exactly like that," she exclaims as I writhe in silent misery. Defending me is my mom's favorite (and most problematic) pastime. She thinks everything I write is perfect, and anyone with a different opinion is wrong, as she likes to tell me—loudly—every chance she gets.

I don't give her many chances. I'd rather listen to earned criticism than her empty praise and relentless positivity.

She wasn't always supportive. Daphne says she's overcompensating for her attitude toward my writing when I was younger, but the pendulum has swung too far in the other direction. A few weeks after my third book came out, in the midst of my career implosion, I fled home to wallow in misery and lick my wounds. Instead of, I don't know, buying me ice cream or giving me a hug or venting in private, she used her public social media accounts to argue with readers in the comments of my bad reviews. Like when a guilty party doubles down on her innocence, it made everything worse.

Similar to my recent conversation with Dr. B, I need this one to end. I don't want anyone to be proud of me before I've earned it. "Forget about it. It's not important."

"What about the new book? Are you selling it at the event?"

"No. It's not out yet," I remind her.

"I can't believe you haven't given me an early copy."

"No one got an early copy," I point out. I *could* give one to her, of course, but I can't handle the inevitable compliments. Not until I know whether or not I can trust them.

"But I'm your mom! And I've preordered it from three different stores! Shouldn't that count for something?" she asks.

In the background, my dad yells, "Send your mom a book!"

"Debbie asked if it was going to be an improvement over your last one, so I told her not to talk to me until she understands art. By the way, you never responded to my text about the Page Turner."

I sigh and rub the heel of my hand into my eye. "I forgot." Sensing this conversation is far from over, I stand and walk back toward the lawn.

"I was talking to the event coordinator—Marilyn, have you met her? She blocked off a few dates for you to do a signing with them if you decide to come home this summer."

"I told you my publicist does my event planning—"

"Tell your publicist to book it. I've already told all my friends about it, so you're guaranteed to have an audience."

I sigh. A book signing filled with women who have been guilted into attending might be my final straw. "I don't know when I can next make it home," I say in lieu of the truth, which is that I don't know if I could survive the dissonance of being given a grand homecoming.

"Nonsense. You haven't seen Lucy since she started walking! Oh! Did I send you the video?" Without waiting for my answer, she launches into a story about my niece, and it takes ten more minutes to get her off the phone, at which point I've found Daphne in the outdoor patio section of the authors' lounge.

I sink into the seat across from her and rest my chin on my threaded fingers while I wait for her to remove her AirPods. "You'll never guess who I just ran into." Around us, tables are dotted with authors gossiping and eating and resting between panels. I exchange cursory waves with a handful of people, but events like this tend to be cliquey. If Daphne weren't here, I don't know if I would have been brave enough to show my face.

The crochet hook in Daphne's hand pauses. She studies me for a long moment, and then her eyes widen. "West is here?"

"How'd you know?"

"The look on your face. Fury mixed with . . . well, something I can't put my finger on. Revenge, maybe? It's *intense*," she muses as she resumes stitching a fuzzy pink blob that she claims is two-thirds of a halter top. "Plus, he's local."

I blink in surprise. "When did he leave New York?"

She shrugs. "I don't know. I heard it in passing."

As I sit back to process this, I'm struck by the distinct and unpleasant feeling of being watched. I look around, and unless I'm imagining it, gazes scatter. "Is everyone looking at us?"

"No!" Daphne says quickly, but then she glances around and hesitates. "No," she says again, this time with much less certainty. "What happened with West?"

"We argued. I yelled at him. As expected."

"What'd you argue about?"

I pull my attention from the whispers at the next table. "He was added to my Sunday panel."

The disbelief on her face fills me with smug vindication. "They want you to share a public stage with him?" she asks.

"Can you believe it?"

"Did he even *attempt* to apologize?"

"What do you think?"

She leans toward me, eyes fierce. "What are you going to do?"

The breeze swirls her hair around her shoulders like the palm fronds above us. I tip my head back and close my eyes with a sigh. I swear I haven't felt the sun in four months.

"I thought I could get him kicked off my panel, but my first attempt didn't go well."

"What happened?"

"I asked to speak to the director, and he called me a Karen."

"The director did?"

"No." I sigh regretfully. "I didn't get past the undergrad volunteer. It was West who said it."

"He shouldn't have said that. You have a right to stand up for yourself."

"He shouldn't have said a lot of things, but here we are. I haven't even told you the worst part yet," I add.

"How is sharing the stage with your professional nemesis not the worst part?"

"Because the worst part," I say with my eyes still closed, "is that West thinks he beat me."

I can see his smirk in my mind, can hear his smug voice. *Likewise, Darling.* Darling! He's never called me that in his life. It was always Mars. Occasionally Jupiter.

West thinks he won this round, and I *hate* that. I hate that he knows he got under my skin and that there's not a single inch of this campus that's not colored with memories of him. I hate that without even looking, I know that across the crowded lawn, the library peeks over the tops of food trucks and white vendor tents. I'm surrounded by land mines; anywhere I go, I'm at risk of having my hard-fought peace blown up by something as innocuous as the biography section on the third floor of Main Library.

"Well, what's your plan to show him that he didn't?" Daphne asks.

I sigh again. "I don't know."

"I know an Etsy witch who charges six dollars to put a curse on your enemies."

I snort. "Of course you do. Enough about my drama. How's writing?"

She makes a dramatic dying-animal sound as she slumps onto the table.

"I thought you were doing final edits?"

"Oh, that!" She brightens. "Yeah, I turned those in last week. Now I'm working on something new, and it's going even worse than this." She holds up her lopsided top. "But my editor saved my life by pointing out that my main character needed a stronger motivation for tracking down the killer. I've decided to go with a revenge arc. Should I send her a sourdough starter as a thank-you?"

"Absolutely," I say with a bit too much enthusiasm.

She unpicks a stitch. "How's yours doing?"

"My what?"

"Your sourdough. Did you follow the instructions that came with it?"

I crumble under the slightest interrogation. "It was so many pages, Daph. Why do I need to read so many pages to eat bread?"

Her mouth turns down in the corners. "Is that a no?"

"Regrettably, it's a yes, and this thing has taken over my kitchen and my life and my mental health."

"Well, have you made any bread yet?"

"No! But I don't want it to go to waste, so I keep feeding it, and it keeps growing, and I'm not convinced it won't swallow my building whole while I'm gone this weekend. Say goodbye to Park Slope, because it won't exist by this time next month." I just barely refrain from pointing out that if she hadn't moved to California last year, we would still be roommates in Brooklyn, and none of this would be an issue.

Daphne's spit take soaks our table. We're mopping it up with flimsy napkins when a small voice pulls our attention. "Um . . . excuse me?" Two teen girls in Torcher for Life T-shirts hover just outside the patio. One of them nudges her friend forward. "Your turn," she whispers.

"Are you Margot Darling?" the second girl asks, and it's habit more than anything that makes me wince.

"She is!" Daphne beams. "Nice shirts, by the way. I have the same one."

"Are you signing books?" the girl asks me, and the hopeful note in her voice makes my shoulders relax. Only fans call themselves Torchers—I should have known they came in peace. "I'll be in one of the tents on Sunday morning."

"We're going home today, and we drove two hours just to meet you," she says, still hopeful.

My eyes widen. "Really? Even though I—" *Fucked up beyond measure*, I don't say, because Daphne's foot comes down hard on my toes.

"She'd love to sign them," Daphne says.

Muscle memory takes control, and I usher the girls forward so I can sign and personalize all six books. Then we hug and take pictures, and I feel like I'm floating as they walk away. Meeting someone who loves the thing I made never gets old.

There was a time—right up until about ninety seconds ago—when I worried those days were over.

Daphne shakes her head. "They woke up today and decided to spend four hours driving to meet you."

"Weird, right? They could have watched, like, a hundred YouTube videos in that time."

"Mars. They drove all this way just to meet *you*!"

"My ego is big enough, don't make it worse."

Daphne spins her finger in a circle. "The festival is expecting a hundred and twenty-five thousand attendees this weekend, hundreds of whom are here to see *you*. You're not a Karen; you're Margot fucking Darling! Your book has sold in twenty countries. The movies have made hundreds of millions of dollars. *You* are the star here. If you don't want him on your panel, do something about it. Start your revenge arc!"

"No character jokes," I groan.

"Mars!"

"Fine. You're right. You're right!" I stand up, jostling the table and knocking Daphne's yarn to the ground. I bend to help her clean up, but she shoos me away with the flick of her wrist.

"Go!" she orders.

I nod once, my determination growing and solidifying in real time. "Yes. Good. I'll make West sorry he bothered to show up."

"Good." She nods in approval. "And after you do—stop thinking about him."

"What?"

She gives me a small smile that could be either pity or pride. "You've worked hard to be here, Mars. Don't let him get in your head."

8

13 Years Ago
Freshman Year, Second Semester

"Bad writing day?" West leans over my shoulder.

I snap my laptop closed. No need for him to see the 54 percent I got on my last math quiz. I twist to see his hands braced on the back of the bench. A spring breeze ruffles his straight hair, and you'd never know from the seventy-degree sunshine that it snowed less than two weeks ago. "What are you doing here?"

He nods toward the English building. "Dr. B's class just ended." He drops his notebook next to me, sits on the back of the bench, and swings his legs over. The nails on his right hand are forest green; his left hand is bare. "You look pretty miserable considering spring break just started."

I tip my head back to look at him but find myself squinting into the sun instead. "Not for me. I still have one midterm to go."

"No camping trip for you?"

"Yeah, what's the deal with that?" Amber mentioned it in passing, but I didn't ask for details because, apparently, I'm the only loser with a midterm the Friday before spring break.

"Amber, Kyle, and the crew are driving up to Mount Lemmon in"—he checks the time—"about an hour. They have three blankets, a twelve-pack, and a dream. I give them a twenty percent chance of starting a forest fire."

"Is that all?"

"I wore my Smokey Bear T-shirt this morning as a reminder. Hopefully the message permeated the thick layer of spring break debauchery."

"You're a real environmentalist, Mae West."

He smirks, leaning ever so slightly closer. "I do what I can."

"Does that mean you're not going with them?"

He makes a face. "I don't need to hear Kyle and Amber humping each other more than I already do. Unless you're driving up?"

"As riveting as that experience sounds, I can't think about anything except studying right now. If I fail—"

"The matrix you're living in dematerializes, I've heard. Hey—should you write a story about that?"

"Sci-fi? Not really my thing. But *you* should write a story about that."

He rolls his eyes. "Right."

"Wait, what does that mean?"

He takes my computer and opens it back to my online math portal. "What that means, Mars, is that you've found yourself a math tutor."

~

"What'd you get for *C*?" West drums his pen against his knee while he waits for my answer.

"I'm still working on it." I squint at the triangle on the page. I'm sitting cross-legged on the bench, my back is starting to hurt from hunching for the last two hours, and my brain feels like it's melting out my ears.

"Do you remember how to solve for cosine?"

"*C* squared equals *A* squared plus *B* squared minus two *AB* times the cosine of *C*," I repeat numbly. Memorizing the formula has never been my problem. Making the numbers make sense *within* the formula is the issue. I drop my head into my hands.

"Do you want me to show you again?" West leans toward me, and as his hair falls forward, I inhale a lungful of his woodsy shampoo scent. It's possible the nearness of him is making it hard to concentrate, but I can't bring myself to care. Campus is dead, the sun on my shoulders feels like the first beach day of the year, and I'd rather be doing anything other than trying to make sense of trig.

"I want ice cream," I announce. West looks up at me, a spot of blue on his lower lip. I stare at it a beat too long. "Do you want ice cream?" I force my eyes to meet his.

"I could eat ice cream," he says. I start to smile, but he holds up an ink-stained palm. His left hand is always covered in ink from dragging it across the page as he writes. "Under one condition."

I groan. "Fine. I'll finish this problem first."

"Not that. I want to read the scene you had to run off and write the other night."

This time I can't help my wide grin or the feeling of champagne bubbles in my chest. I've never been precious about my writing—I'll happily give it to anyone who asks, but not that many people ask.

"Done. Are you sure that's the scene you want, though? I have better ones." I'm mentally sorting chapters in my head, weighing the funniest bits of dialogue versus my best world-building versus that clever metaphor I spent twenty minutes perfecting in chapter fourteen.

He makes a show of pretending to consider my request before shaking his head. "That scene or no deal."

West is concentrating. He's a living, breathing Do Not Disturb sign, from the unbroken eye contact with his phone to the plastic soft serve spoon hanging forgotten from his lips as he slowly scrolls his way through my scene. I reached the end of my ice cream a good ten minutes ago and have nothing to do but hyper-fixate on his facial expressions.

"Did you get to the part where—"

"Shh."

"I just want to explain why—"

"Shh!"

I bite my lip and try to count to one hundred. At nine, I break. "What's taking you so long?" This is excruciating. I feel like I'm going to crawl out of my skin.

"It's too bright out here, and I hate reading on screens."

"Should I have transcribed it by hand just for you?"

"That would have been helpful, yes. Now *shhhhh*!"

I inch closer and strain my neck. "Stop reading over my shoulder," he says.

"But I—"

His phone beeps with the sound of an incoming text. The name Bethany flashes across my words. He swipes it to the side without reading it, and I feel like I've won a competition I didn't even know I was in.

"Who was—"

"Mars." He turns to me, our noses inches apart, and takes

the spoon out of his mouth. His next words are achingly slow. "What can I do to make you *stop talking*?"

I swallow heavily. "Let me read something of yours."

Wordlessly, he slides his notebook toward me.

"Which page?" I ask.

"Don't care." I open to the first page, and his hand shoots out. "Wait. Not that." He flips ahead a few chicken-scratched pages and jabs a paragraph with his finger. "That one."

I snatch the notebook before he can change his mind and roll away from him and onto my side. His paragraph is a description of his hometown in the summer, and I can feel the hot windburn on my cheeks and the dust between my teeth as I read. It's spare and stark but still evocative; it makes my chest feel hollow for reasons I don't really understand. I read it three times in a row and wish it were longer. It's *good* (maybe better than the Chia Pet story), and suddenly his opinion becomes even more important. I glance at him in my peripheral and see another incoming text from Bethany. I close my eyes.

"Done," he says.

My eyes jolt open, my heart pounding.

"Who's Bethany?" I ask.

My open textbook rests face down on my stomach. We're looking at shapes in the clouds. A game of Frisbee is happening perilously close to us, but we persist in our laziness. My shoulder blades have sunk into the grass in such a perfect way that it feels like the space was carved for me. The first hints of sunburn sting my forehead, and I don't even care. I'm completely blissed-out.

"Why'd you say her name like that?" West asks.

I turn to see him gazing at me, one arm bent behind his head. "Like what?"

"With such a heavy emphasis on the first syllable. *Beth*-any. It felt pointed."

"I don't like the name Bethany." *I don't like the thought of another girl texting you* is the surprising subtext underneath my lie.

"She's my ex-girlfriend."

My ears perk up. "Oh? Does she go here?"

"No. We dated in high school. I think she wants to get back together."

"Why do you think that?"

He flips over onto his stomach and avoids my eyes as he pulls out a marker and fills in his bare nails. "Her text said that she wants to get back together."

I squirm, my shoulder blades itchy from the prickly grass. I hold my hand up to shield my eyes from the too-bright sun. "That's a good clue."

~

"You already know it's good, I already told you it's good, so stop fishing for compliments!" West laughs.

"But what would you say if we were in Dr. B's class?" I hop onto the edge of the fountain and train my eyes on my feet as I walk around it.

"Why do you wanna know?" He stuffs his hands in the pockets of his jeans.

"Because I care about your opinion!"

"Why?"

"Because your paragraph was good."

He looks like he'd rather jump off a cliff than talk about himself. "There's no plot. Nothing ever happens in my stories. Let's change the subject."

"West—I'm begging! If I'm going to be published before I graduate, I need feedback, and people aren't exactly lining up to read my weirdo magic books. I read a page to Amber, and she *fell asleep*. With snoring! I emailed my brothers my last story, and they never replied. Even my high school English teacher had to clarify that she only had time to read my assigned essays and not the sixty pages of fiction I left on her desk."

"Do you think Amber was faking?" West asks.

"Well, now I do!" I groan and drag my foot through the fountain.

Water splashes his hair, and he quickly smooths it with his fingers. Like the wicked witch, West and his hair. "What's the rush to get published?" he asks.

"Why wait?"

He rolls his eyes and holds his hand up to help me down from the slippery ledge of the fountain. "Fine, don't tell me. Need brain fuel?"

"I could eat."

"Frog & Firkin is right there." He nods to a popular bar a few hundred yards away. "Or Bison Witches on Fourth?"

The sandwich shop is in the funky, artsy historic district a mile away, and since I'm in the mood to procrastinate as long as possible, I choose the long route, and we make our way toward Fourth Avenue.

His elbow bumps mine while we walk, and when I look up at him, I find myself wanting to explain. "I didn't really have friends growing up." He tips his head, indicating that I should continue. "I was weird and introverted, and my brothers both played travel baseball. My parents dragged me all over the state every weekend, and all over the Southwest on every break from school. The number of hours I've clocked in the bleachers watching parents yell at umpires is enough to make anyone a little crazy. I spent all those years with my nose in a book, and then in a notebook, and finally a computer. It's pathetic, but book characters were my *only* friends."

"That sounds lonely."

My cheeks flush, and I realize I didn't have to tell him any of that in order to answer his question. "My brothers both went to school on baseball scholarships. Nothing crazy. Small schools with okay baseball programs but good degrees. One now works in tech in Silicon Valley; the other makes airplane parts in Seattle. My parents told me I needed to get a scholarship, too, but my grades weren't good enough, and I can't throw a fastball, so."

It's actually infuriating, as if they didn't pour thousands into their attempts to turn my brothers into the next A-Rod.

"I needed my parents to help with my tuition, but they wanted me to study something 'practical.' The only way they'd agree to creative writing is if I start paying them back the day after graduation."

"That's why you're in such a rush?"

I scoff. "No. I'll be a barista, whatever. I'm in a hurry to be published because I want to show them that they're wrong for not believing in me. It's my spite goal."

He looks at me sideways. "Hmm."

"What?"

"I don't know if I believe you."

"Why not?"

"I think you love books and writing, and you're ambitious and smart, and you're out to prove something to yourself as much as anyone."

I cross my arms, feeling weirdly transparent. "Even if you're right, I'll do it with or without anyone's help, including yours."

"Kaia needs more internal monologue." He reaches out to push the crosswalk button at the loud and buzzy intersection.

"What do you mean?"

"She likes this bodyguard guy—"

"Felix."

"Yeah. She likes Felix, but I don't know why. What's she thinking when she sees him lie to cover for her?"

"She's thinking that she's shocked that he would break the rules for her, because she's never seen him step a toe out of line, and when she confronts him and they're arguing, she realizes that he's the only person who has ever cared about what happens to her!"

"So put it on the page."

I open my mouth, but nothing comes out.

"Also, Felix licks his lips six times in one scene."

"He does not."

"I counted."

Well, that's humiliating.

West sees my expression. "I don't actually know what I'm talking about, by the way. You get that, right? My writing is—"

"Stop." I hold my hand up.

"Never mind. Forget I said anything."

I pull him out of the flow of people on the sidewalk and crouch next to the window of a tattoo shop. "I need a piece of paper."

He opens his backpack and rips out a blank page from his notebook. He hands it to me with a blue pen. I balance the paper on my knees and scribble the sentences that are appearing fully formed in my head. I don't even have to reach for them. The characters are having a conversation, and I can barely write fast enough to keep up. It's the best kind of writing magic.

I glance up to see West crouched over me in the fluorescent glow of the tattoo parlor's window and admit to myself that I have a massive crush on the tall, skinny boy from my writing class.

He shakes his head in disbelief. "Someday you're going to tell me how you do that."

~

"Do you think I'd look good with a nose ring?" I ask as dinner arrives. We're tucked in a dark corner of the noisy restaurant, sitting on opposite sides of a wooden booth.

"Yeah," West says automatically. "Do you want one?"

I take a bite of my pickle spear. "I'm nose ring curious. I'm writing a character who is covered in piercings, so it seems like I should know what that's all about." I crunch another bite of pickle, and West wordlessly slides his across the table, offering it to me. "I think I'll do it tonight."

"What about studying?"

I wave off his question. "We'll get around to it."

"After dinner?" he suggests.

"Okay," I agree.

He narrows his eyes, and I get the feeling that he's studying *me*. "Why are you grinning like that?"

West wants to study after dinner? Fine with me. This is about to be the longest damn meal he's ever had.

~

I brush the tip of my finger across my nose ring for the tenth time in under a minute. It hurt less than I thought it would, but my skin is tender. It took West and me two hours to eat sandwiches and chips, and when we walked out of the restaurant, I dragged us right into the tattoo and piercing shop. And now I have a ring in my nose, and we've spent the last couple of hours wandering all over campus, avoiding my dorm room and the library at all costs.

Tucson smells like orange blossoms and spring, and I can't recall a time when I ever felt *less* lonely. A few months ago, leaving my room to hang out with Amber felt difficult, but there's nothing easier than spending time with West.

I blink, and we find ourselves walking down Greek row, peering at frat parties from the curb, when three girls stumble down the front porch steps of one of the houses, tripping over their feet and giggling like crazy.

"They're on another planet," West says with a laugh.

"That could be you. You could be halfway through a twelve-pack while Amber and Kyle get freaky in the next sleeping bag."

He pretends to dry heave. "Pass."

"Why didn't you go?" I press, wondering how much information I can pry out of him tonight.

"How many reasons do you want?"

"Because you don't drink?"

"For starters."

"Why don't you?" I ask. He gives me *extreme* side-eye. "It's rude to bring it up but not talk about it!"

"*You* brought it up!"

I put my hand to my chest as I flutter my eyes. "Did I?"

He throws his head back and laughs. "Those eyelashes are out of control."

"Is that a compliment?"

"You look like Bambi."

"You're not changing the subject that easily."

"You are so unsubtle."

"I'm curious!"

"I know. That's why I like you." He avoids eye contact as he passes a hand over the back of his neck, and I wonder how much I should read into his last statement. "It's a boring story, but since you're obviously *dying* to hear it, my dad cheats on my mom."

My stomach drops. "Oh god. How'd you find out?"

"Well, my half sister was a dead giveaway."

"Are you serious?"

West nods. "He had a one-night stand with a woman on a business trip. Claims he was drunk and didn't know what he was doing. Fast-forward nine months, and I had a sister. She's seven now and lives in Boston. Gabbi. She's cute. Sassy. Has a thick accent and already swears like a sailor."

"How did your mom react?"

He blows out a long breath. "She stayed with him and had another kid, so . . . not well, in my opinion. And now he knows he can cheat and she'll never leave."

"West, that sucks. *He* sucks! I'm sorry. I—" Hot, aimless anger churns in the pit of my stomach. "That is *not* a boring story!" I'm worried it's the wrong thing to say until West laughs.

"You can use it in your next book, if it's not too much of a cliché. Don't they all have shitty parents?"

"You're thinking of dead parents. YA characters always have *dead* parents."

"Lucky them," he says dryly. I snort-laugh in surprise, which makes him laugh again, and he wraps his arm around my shoulder and draws me into him. It feels like he's placing a period at the end of a conversation that he's dying to escape, and with his body pressed against mine, every nerve ending sparks to life.

We've almost made it to the end of Greek row when a couple tumbles out of the bushes, straightening their clothes and smoothing their messy hair. West blushes in the streetlight and turns his face away. My stomach riots at the sight of his pink-stained cheeks.

"No judgment on your life choices, but if you'd played things differently today, you could be having a *very* different kind of night," I tease.

His eyes go wide. "What does *that* mean?"

"You could be in the bushes somewhere with *Beth*-any."

He stops us in our tracks and drops his arm from my shoulders. When we make eye contact, I feel like I'm caught in a glue trap. "If I wanted to be with Bethany, I'd be with Bethany."

I'm suddenly aware of all the blood in my body, pulsing faster than before. "Well, what do you want?" I ask brazenly, summoning heretofore unknown bravery.

His eyes flicker across my face as he runs his tongue along the inside of his cheek, thinking. He comes to a decision, and a wry smile appears at the corner of his lips. "Library," he says with deadly precision.

"No!" I protest. "I won't do it! You can't make me. It's too late. I—"

"Library," he says again. "It's close." He tangles his fingers in mine, and I jog behind him, hissing a trail of protests at the back of his head.

"I can't study now. I've hit my limit," I whisper as we step over the threshold and a gust of icy air-conditioning hits my bare skin and the scent of old paper and books fills my lungs. "It won't work. My brain is a black hole." I whine my way up the steps to the third floor, right until the moment West pulls me into the empty stacks and my words die in my throat.

I glance at the shelves next to us—biographies—and register the goose bumps prickling at the back of my neck. West licks his bottom lip. He looks nervous and determined all at once, and it dawns on me that he's not thinking about trigonometry.

His fingers press into my skin as he reaches under the strap of my bag and slides it off my shoulder. It hits the floor with a spine-tingling thud. The air between us is thick with unspoken words, like the moment just before a storm. It's heavy with something inevitable.

"Ask me again," he says in a whisper so quiet I might have imagined it.

Because I'm focused entirely on the shrinking spaces between us, it takes a moment to remember, but when I do, I whisper back, "What do you want, West?"

The amber rings in his eyes are nearly swallowed by his pupils. "I suck at talking. Can I show you?"

I couldn't answer even if I knew what to say. I'm trapped in his gaze, an insistent hum of want stripping me of verbal dexterity. A linguistic blank where my brain used to be.

I can only nod. He takes half a step toward me, and I take half a step back until my spine hits bookshelves. I silently curse my nerves, because now West is looking at me with an arched brow. I'm inexperienced at this and too awkward by half. Exasperated with myself, I exhale a laugh as he watches me carefully. *Waiting*. My tongue darts out to lick my lips, and his eyes follow the movement. I nod again, hoping he understands what the gesture means.

His expression softens in apparent understanding, and his hands come up to rest on the shelves on either side of my head, bracketing me in. He tips his head down, and his lips press lightly against mine before he pulls back. "I wanted to do that," he says, answering a question I asked in a different lifetime. A lifetime where I had not yet been kissed by West Emerson.

He leans in again, his thumb brushing the mole above my lip before he peppers hot, openmouthed kisses against my lips. Once. Twice. Three times. He swipes his questioning tongue across my lower lip, and I realize that he is *kissing* me while I stand frozen. I gasp, opening my mouth for him, and when his tongue slips between my teeth, his left hand moves from the bookshelf to slide into my hair, angling my face up toward him. When he starts to pull back, an embarrassing protest comes from my mouth, and I clutch the front of his shirt and pull him toward me, chasing his tongue with my own.

He exhales a laugh, and I feel his smile under my lips. It only lasts a second before he's kissing me again, his mouth relentless. We stay locked in this position until my fingers ache from grasping his shirt and my spine hurts from digging into the bookshelf, but I won't be the one to break the heady contact, and I don't know how to maneuver us into a new position. My free hand itches to touch him, to run my fingers up his chest and over his throat, but I'm not brave enough to do it, so it hangs limply by my side. I'll give up breathing if it means we get to keep doing this, kissing until we pass out, with West's fingers tangled in the hair at the nape of my neck and his lips firmly on mine.

He pulls back for air, too soon and nearly too late, and heaves in a jagged breath. He rests his forehead against mine as I force oxygen to return to my vital organs.

"You could have done that outside," I murmur, bringing us back to a conversation I barely remember.

Another smile breaks across his face, and I get to see this

one. It strikes like lightning, brief but brilliant. "Not the way I want to," he whispers. This time I'm ready, and I push up to my toes to meet his mouth. My arms wrap around his neck, and his hand drops from the bookshelf. His palm flattens across my lower back, pressing us together. My chest and hips flatten against his body.

"You're not a fan of PDA. Noted," I say, silently marveling at the contrast: the restraint that brought us across campus to this private spot in the library and the utter dissolution of it now.

"I'm a fan of anything that involves you, Jupiter," he breathes between kisses. "I'll kiss you anywhere you let me."

I feel like I'm on fire; West is singeing all my edges. It's the best kiss I've ever had in my life, and that thought has me pulling away with a gasp. "I've been doing it all wrong."

He narrows his eyes. "I really beg to differ."

"Not this." My hand is cupped on the back of his neck, and I apply pressure until my lips are against his ear. "Writing kiss scenes."

His eyelids flutter closed as he presses his lips to my neck, and I shiver against him. He cinches me tighter in his arms and trails kisses from my earlobe down. "Happy to help," he says, and this time, I feel his smile in the hollow of my collarbone before he chases it with a breath of hot air and a firm kiss. And another. And another. I dissolve slowly in layers, melting into him, and when the earth shifts beneath me, I feel like I'm slipping over the edge of something steep.

9

Present Day

Never underestimate how far in life you can get on determination and spite. When I march away from Daphne, I don't have even a hint of a plan vis-à-vis West's continued efforts to ruin my life, but I'm fueled by righteous indignation. That need for retaliation propels my feet forward. My destination is currently unknown, but I'll pace this campus until either West expires under the weight of his own self-importance, like a dying star collapsing in on itself, or I figure out how to deal with him. Whichever comes first. I'm not picky.

I keep to the fringes of the festival, waiting for inspiration to strike. Since I started living in New York City, walking has become my best method for brainstorming. During the drafting of *Shattered*, I walked *a lot*. Every day. Sometimes for hours. Then, when I felt ready, I returned home to write.

Buoyed by my success after so many years of wondering if I'd ever write another word, I preached the virtues of the brainstorm walk to Daphne and dragged her out with me. This usually turned into her helping me with my plot problems; walking does nothing for her creativity, because she does it wrong. The problem with my best friend is that she always has something in her ears, usually a podcast or an audiobook bumped up to 2.5 speed. My brain couldn't untangle anything under those conditions, either.

No, the trick is to stop trying so damn hard and let my mind wander down unexplored paths. I've filled many a plot hole aimlessly trawling the streets of New York, and I expect today's walk to give the same results. A brilliant flash of inspiration, if you will.

It *has* to.

Except it doesn't.

I'm on my fourth lap when I begin to worry.

Relaxing is an issue. My shoulders are tense, my chest is tight, and my mind is loud with the grating sound of West's voice scraping over bone.

Likewise, Darling.

As if *he* has the right to be angry with *me*.

Staying focused is another issue.

Instead of exploring creative ways to exile West from my life or send him to his knees, groveling for forgiveness that I will not grant, my brain is stuck on the same story as always. West and me, how we nearly got it right and then imploded in spectacular fashion. (Perhaps this is where the dying-star metaphor belongs.)

Sometimes, when I'm feeling particularly vulnerable, I wonder if there's a part of my brain that thinks it can outsmart the past. As if history is a plot hole I can rewrite.

Backing away from the dangerous edge of that thought, I pull open a door and step inside, goose bumps pebbling across my skin. I inhale the scent of the library, which is really just an unidentified mustiness that refuses to be romanticized by nostalgia. Independent of a conscious decision, my feet carry me to the third floor. I close my eyes and let my weight sag against the stacks that West once pressed me up against while my mind is hard at work turning worry to despair.

What am I going to do?

No brilliant answers appear. And sometimes brainstorming is like that. Sometimes my first idea is the only one that will really work, and there's nothing to be done but grit my teeth and force the story into submission through sheer will. It's not my favorite way to write, but not every chapter can be driven by mad flashes of inspiration. In fact, most of them aren't.

I need to get West kicked off my panel.

I retrace my steps down the library stairs and back out into the festival. I'm heading toward the admin building when I'm nearly bowled over by a harried-looking woman in business casual. "Oh! Sorry!" she gasps as she stops short two seconds before collision.

"No worries."

She looks up at me then, her face alight with recognition. "Margot! I'm Kate Marsh, one of the directors of events! It's so good to have you with us this year!" We shake hands. "I'm glad I caught you." She gives me a conference schedule from a large stack in her arms. "Have you seen the new schedule? The old one was a mess. Tents were double-booked, and if that wasn't a big enough nightmare, they had to rope some off on the west end because of a bee problem, and now we're scrambling to get the new schedule into everyone's hands. The changes are highlighted in yellow. We're making announcements, and emails have gone out to the mailing list, but I'm worried about the signing event that starts in fifteen minutes. It was moved all the way to the other end of the lawn."

She points to a small list of highlighted names. At the top is West Emerson.

My expression must betray my interest, because she frowns curiously. "You know West, don't you?"

"I actually wanted to talk to you about that. About my panel with him on Sunday."

"We're excited about it, and we appreciate your flexibility. We'd hate to have to cancel." She looks up with a smile, and then back at the schedules. In one hand is a phone from which she's been firing off texts or emails for our entire conversation. "Have you seen him today?" Her question hangs in the breezy, sunny, floral-scented air.

We'd hate to have to cancel.

"I don't know where he is."

She frowns back at her phone. "Well, if you do see him in the next few minutes, will you let him know about the change?"

I blanch. Not only has she booked me on a stage with West, but now I'm expected to run errands for him?

She's waiting for my response. I want to refuse, but *we'd hate to have to cancel* is ringing in my ears. I promised myself that I wouldn't be "difficult" this release cycle.

I sigh. It's only fifteen minutes. It won't even matter. "Sure. If I see him."

"Perfect. See you Sunday!" She nods and hurries off, leaving me once again alone with too many thoughts. Maybe Daphne has the right idea with her endless audiobooks. I could use something to drown out my worries.

I don't make it ten feet before I hear a low voice call my name. "Darling."

Something heavy, and not half as unpleasant as I'd like, drops in my stomach.

"Why are you *everywhere* today?" I grouse, speeding up to make it harder for him to catch up with me. It doesn't help, and he's at my side in three long strides.

"Am I?"

"Yes," I snap, thinking of the library stacks and the orange blossoms in the wind and the schedule in my hand. I can't escape him.

"It's not *my* face on a banner in the bookstore," he says.

I risk a sideways glance to find him staring down at me. "What do you want?"

"I wanted to let you know that I'll save you a spot in my signing line."

"How magnanimous of you."

"There's always space for my biggest fangirls." He winks, and I loathe the way his eyes glitter almost as much as I hate the way my skin itches in response. I will not survive an entire weekend of *this*, but after my failed attempt to speak with Kate, I'm starting to worry that my original plan will not work. If the conference won't kick West off the panel, one of us will have to drop out.

And it's not going to be me.

I notice then that we're walking toward Old Main, though his signing has been moved to the opposite end of the lawn. Something that feels suspiciously like inspiration flickers to life in my veins. It buzzes, growing, refusing to be ignored.

"Did you see the new schedule? I think your event was moved."

"No." West looks at me sharply. "Is that it?" He motions to the paper in my hand.

"There's a bee problem. Very unfortunate. Can't exterminate them without the utter collapse of our food production and ecosystem. And I know how much you like guacamole," I say as I tilt the paper away from his face and pretend to read. "Your signing was moved to Modern Languages. Room 545."

"Inside?"

"Several of the events are in classrooms." Technically, this is true. Just not his.

He glances at the time, and his eyes widen as he realizes he only has a couple of minutes before his signing starts. "Thanks for letting me know." He nods goodbye and jogs north toward the Modern Languages building.

I bite my lip as I watch him go. It's not the cleverest idea I've ever had, but I didn't have much time. With a few hours of planning, maybe I can figure out a way to make his weekend so miserable that he quits.

I remember my conversation with Daphne and grin.

Revenge arc, indeed.

10

13 Years Ago
Freshman Year, Second Semester

Failing a test is a bit like falling down a hill. You trip and lose your footing, and then you're sliding. You put out your hands and scrabble for purchase. You grab for a rock or a tree, anything to stop the momentum. It might feel slow at first, fixable even. If not this question, you'll get the one after. But next thing you know, you're steamrolling hard and fast toward the edge of a cliff, and there are no options left. All you can do is close your eyes and hope you're alive at the bottom.

That's what it feels like when I sit down for my trigonometry midterm only a few hours after I finally drifted off to sleep.

I don't know the answer to the first question. Whatever. It's just one.

I don't feel good about the second one, either, but missing *two* questions never killed anyone.

I'm almost positive that the third question came directly from my study packet, but when I close my eyes and try to see the answer, all I see are West's ink-stained fingers playing with a loose strand of my hair.

After we left the library last night, he walked me to my dorm, where we made out against a column for an unknowable amount of time. Twenty minutes? An hour? All I know is that I was dizzy when I finally stumbled into my bed, drunk on the feeling of West's lips on my skin and his weight pressed against me.

And now I can't concentrate on cosines, because how am I supposed to care what a cosine is when my lips are still swollen and sore from the best night of my life? I press my fingers to my puffy mouth and stifle a yawn; I was up until four a.m. because my hyperactive imagination refused to settle down. I tend to brainstorm in bed, but in the early hours of this morning, I was weaving daydreams about someone real.

Numbers shuffle around on the page. I check the clock—time is moving at warp speed—and set my pencil down. I lean forward until my head hits the desk. I've entered the free-fall portion of the test. I stop flailing and admit to myself that there's no saving this one. I tuck in my arms and legs and hold my breath, praying the ground is soft upon landing.

The bell rings. I turn in my exam and walk numbly through the halls of the math building with new eyes, and it's even worse than I remember. I can't believe I'll have to spend another semester looking at these cold white walls and the backs of frat boys' heads instead of sitting cross-legged in a Socratic seminar with the rest of the humanities majors. I want a TA to write **Impressive** in blue ink at the top of a short story I wrote the night before class. I want to laugh under my breath with West when a classmate's purple prose gets out of control.

I blink dark spots out of my eyes as I step into the sun.

"Mars!" West's voice zaps my heart like a defibrillator. If the test nearly killed me, he's reviving my will to go on. (*Too cheesy. I'd delete that line in revisions.*) West jogs toward me, a coffee in his hand. "You did it!" He wraps his free arm around me and pulls me in for a hug that leaves me speechless. Half of me wants to relax into him; the other half still can't believe what just happened.

He offers me the drink. "I don't know how you like your coffee, so I took a shot in the dark."

I don't like any kind of coffee, but I don't want to hurt his feelings, so I take a sip. As expected, it tastes like burned tar. I make a face, and West grimaces. "Not good?" He runs a hand through his hair, which is still wet from the shower and starting to curl. If I were in a better mood, I'd write a poem about those curls.

"It's, um, I'm surprised that you're here."

His expression falters. "Oh, well, I was up anyway. I thought you'd be in the mood to celebrate."

I take another asphalt-flavored sip. "There's nothing to celebrate, because I failed worse than anyone else has ever failed a one hundred–level math exam. It's shocking how badly I did."

"How do you know?"

"I left half the test blank."

"It'll be okay," West says in the self-assured voice of someone who has no actual skin in the game. "If you get A's the rest of the semester, you can pull your grade up."

"What are the chances of that?"

"I can help you study."

I snort. "That sounds familiar."

His gaze dips to his shoes, and I swear I see pink at the tips of his ears. "For real next time. I won't let myself get distracted by your lips, or your cute snort-laugh, or the freckles you have right here . . ." His eyes find mine again and he traces my cheekbone with his thumb.

My eyes well with ridiculous, unstoppable tears. "West!" I taste salt water on my lips.

His eyes widen in panic. "No! Hey, hey, hey," he says, and I commend the effort, but it doesn't help. When people notice I'm crying, I only cry harder.

I press my fingers to the corners of my eyes. "I have medically diagnosed overactive tear ducts."

He jerks his head back in surprise. "Really?"

"Who's gullible now?" I ask, but he doesn't laugh. "I cry a lot. I can't help it."

He wraps me in a hug while I take several shuddering breaths. "I'm sorry you had a bad morning," he says at last.

"Thanks," I mumble into his tear-soaked shirtsleeve. It occurs to me that it's slightly embarrassing to be crying all over the guy I just kissed for the first time last night, but I'm too sad about my midterm to care.

He pulls back, and I can tell by the way he slouches and hesitates that his burst of confidence is retreating. "So," he says.

I mop myself up and run a hand through the tangles in my hair. "Was there a question in that 'so'?"

His mouth twitches. "Do you have plans today?"

"I'm going home for spring break, so my plans are a six-hour drive and an obsessive rumination on where it all went wrong."

"Sounds thrilling."

"Spoken like someone who has never driven through Yuma." I rub my heavy eyelids. Crying plus sleep deprivation is not the best way to pregame a road trip.

"Call me. I'll keep you company on the drive," West offers.

"You will?"

"What else do I have to do but spend my entire spring break distracting you?"

I hesitate, and he sees it.

"Unless you don't want me to," he adds.

The problem is that I do want to be distracted by him, a little too much. "When are you leaving?"

"I'm carpooling with Burger—"

"The guy with the—" I hold my index finger above my lips.

"The finger mustache tattoo? That's him."

"And the . . ." I mime tapping on cups.

"The annoying habit of playing the 'Cups' song on every available surface? *Yes*."

"Oof. Good luck."

"We're leaving at two, but I'm free until then . . ." He trails off, the invitation hanging unsaid in the space between us, and every bad thought I had about this day vanishes into thin air. Somehow West has magicked me into a good mood.

I twist my lips so he can't see how badly I want to smile. "I can be free until two."

"Yeah?" He doesn't bother to hide *his* smile, and my stomach ties itself in the good kind of knots. Not the failed-your-midterm-and-ruined-everything kind that were demanding squatters' rights just a few minutes ago.

Huh.

I nod, and West leans in for a kiss.

"I think we should just be friends!" I blurt out, my hand on his chest.

He backs off. "Sorry! I . . . it's just . . . you *do*?"

I do? I didn't realize it until I said it, but the instant West kisses me, I'll stop caring about anything else. It happened last night, and I know myself well enough to know it'll happen again. I'll hyper-fixate, and I'll stop studying, stop worrying, stop thinking of anything but him. I might even stop writing. I could easily spend the next nine days texting West from my bed in California, my feet up on the wall and my heart in my throat. Who needs ambition when you have a cute guy who kisses you like the world is ending?

"I do," I whisper.

Something flares behind West's eyes. "Of course. I shouldn't have assumed."

"It's not you! It's . . ." I wince, the cliché dying on my lips. "I need to focus on school."

"Right," he says flatly. "I'll see you around, Mars." He turns to leave, and I call him back.

"I thought we were going to hang out?"

His brow ticks up. "And I thought you were blowing me off."

"No! I want to be . . . friends." The last word takes effort. It's true, but it's so fucking trite. My brain is a math-deficient, cliché-ridden void.

"Usually when people say that, they don't mean it."

"Well, I mean it," I say. He doesn't move. "West, look at me." He forces his gaze to mine, his expression hard. "Do you still want to be friends with me?"

He swallows heavily, and I feel a surge of panic. I want to rewind the last sixty seconds, anything to avoid hearing him say no. But the truth is stuck behind my teeth.

He scrutinizes my face for a long time. "Okay," he says eventually, and just like that, our fate is sealed.

~

Nine days is longer than you'd think. It's enough time to add twenty thousand words to my manuscript, decide I hate it, and start something new. It's enough time to binge the entire first season of *Girls* and wonder if I should move to New York like

Hannah Horvath. It's even enough time to go to a USC baseball game with my brothers, get relentlessly mocked for checking my texts between every pitch, and learn the meaning of the word *regret*.

I'm an idiot! I admit it! It seems that turning down my crush didn't make me think about him any less. The first text from West (Drive safe, Jupiter) set off a ripple of stomach flutters that quickly upgraded to a constant, unavoidable tug. I spent the week with my nose in my phone, either grinning to myself or wanting to delete our whole thread, depending on how long it'd been since he'd replied.

By the time I pull back into Tucson on Sunday afternoon, my stomach is chaos. I've replayed the kiss with West so many times that it's burned itself into my brain, like a person who stares at an eclipse too long and sees crescent shapes for the rest of their life.

Making lunch? *West's lips on mine.* Falling asleep at night? *West's hands on the small of my back, pressing me closer.* Standing in a steaming-hot shower? *West's breath on my neck, a shiver tracing my spine.* I don't want to do anything else until I've kissed him again.

I drop my clean laundry in my room and walk straight to West's dorm. No one answers when I knock, so I sit on the floor with my back against his door and wait. I jump to my feet when the door to the stairwell opens, and every muscle in my body draws taut in anticipation. West steps into the hall and does a double take.

"Mars?"

I smile. His nails are hot pink, and his hair is straightened within an inch of its life, and I'm officially obsessed with him. "Hey."

He props the door open behind him, and a pretty girl with short blond hair steps into the hall. Her mouth turns into a frown when she sees me. She glances quickly up at West's deer-in-the-headlights expression before looking back at me. "Who are you?"

I blink at her in surprise, wondering when and how they met. If she knows him from class. If she has a crush on him. If she knows that he likes *me*.

"I'm Mars."

She tilts her head and adjusts her thick black frames. "Like the planet?"

West flinches, and I feel it in my bones. I swallow heavily. "Like the Roman god of war," I tell her, my eyes on West. When he doesn't crack a smile, I know it's over. "What's your name?"

"I'm Bethany."

"Like West's ex-girlfriend?"

She wraps her arm around his waist. "Like his *current* girlfriend."

11

Present Day

Not all book signings are created equal. Some are filled with what I call BDE, or Big Debut Energy, a term I've coined for new authors who are so optimistic about their book signings that they go all in on props for their table. Giant banners, bookmarks, costumes, stickers, character art, and table games. And when all that fails, candy to lure in unsuspecting passersby. (As someone who is too anxious to eat actual meals before events, I love sitting next to a candy table.) I sigh wistfully as I observe the hopeful setup in front of me.

I miss who I was before this job made me cynical.

West's signing tent is two-thirds BDE, one-third MIA. The table on the far left is holding the most intricate model pirate ship I've ever seen, next to a bowl of candy, and the table in the middle is occupied by a woman in a black velvet cloak with a crystal ball and tarot cards. She promises a free reading for anyone who buys a copy of her book. And then there's West's table on the right, empty except for a stack of books and a picture of his face. His author photo looks exactly like I would expect from a pretentious literary upstart: dark and moody, with a Chris Evans cable-knit sweater wrapped around his unfairly broad shoulders.

I pretend to browse photoprints from a local artist while I keep an eye on West's lonely stack of books. I wonder if he's sitting alone in an empty classroom right this minute. When he eventually realizes that I've set him up, he'll curse, sprint down five flights of stairs, trip in his haste, and tumble ass over teakettle all the way to the bottom. He'll lie on his back and stare up at the ceiling, tears running off his whiskered jaw, and rue the day he agreed to join my panel. Realizing his mistake, he'll withdraw from all festival events.

I hope he goes home to lick his wounds and think of me.

I smile at my farfetched little daydream. If even a fraction of it comes true, I'll go to bed a happy woman tonight. But I won't know for sure until I see what kind of mood he's in, which is why I'm waiting around for him to show up instead of downing margaritas at a campus bar with Daphne at this exact moment.

My eyes wander again to his empty table, and curiosity draws me toward the stack of untouched hardcovers. I edge my way toward them and have just opened to the dedication page when a hand reaches out and snaps the book shut. I wrench back and look up to find a pissed-off West towering over me, his fingers steepled on the cover of his novel. "That'll be twenty-eight dollars. Should I make it out to you?"

I blink up at him, my brain trying to process his words. Something about *I* and *make out* and *you* in the same sentence has me seeing spots. "What did you say?"

He drops his bag at his feet. "Has it really been so long that you've forgotten how it's done?" he asks drolly.

"Excuse me?"

He flips the book open to the title page. "I write my name here"—he points and speaks slowly—"and your name here. Or I can save you the time and make it out directly to the garbage can of your choice."

My brain catches up, and I'm annoyed at the way my tongue feels too big for my mouth. *Am I really in such a dry spell that the words* make out *are enough to send me into a tailspin?*

"I'm good," I say before letting my eyes drop to his shoes. Time to regain the upper hand. He's the one who should be flop-sweating his way through this conversation.

I gesture to the swaths of empty space in front of his table. "It's a shame you couldn't even be bothered to show up to your *busy* signing line on time. It seems like *someone* in charge should know how unreliable you are before they trust you with the keynote."

His eyes narrow. "You did this on purpose, then," he says flatly.

"Did what?" I bat my eyes innocently and am assaulted with a memory of him from a lifetime ago, laughing and calling me Bambi. I kibosh the fluttering.

"You knew the location of my signing and sent me to the wrong place?" He grinds the words out, the tension between us drawing taut.

I'm surprised that *he's* surprised. I thought our earlier conversations made it clear where we stood with each other. I decide to remind him. "I hadn't planned on it, but then I saw you, and inspiration struck. What can I say, West? You've always made the best muse."

He steps toward me, crowding me against his table. "What the fuck, Mars?"

I have to crane my neck to look up at him. "Drop out of my panel."

"No."

"Then I'm not sorry for what I do next."

"Do you have someone else to antagonize right now, or is it only me?" He smirks like he knows something I don't as he helps himself to my personal space. He angles his mouth close to my ear, hot breath misting over my neck. "Don't tell me that you're still obsessed with me after all this time. You don't still sleep in that Fox Caldwell shirt, do you?"

I'm suddenly aware of my heartbeat in places very far from my heart. I push him away, unable to make eye contact. He's infuriating, but I only have myself to blame for bringing up the word *muse*. "I'll leave, but only because you have so many adoring fans waiting to have their books signed." I direct my attention to his still-empty signing line. "Oh wait."

His knuckles turn white on the edge of the table, and I know I've won this round.

I spend the next half hour pretending to browse photography in the adjacent tent, watching West's spirits fall further and further into hell. The author next to him has pulled at least a dozen tarot cards, and try as he might to entice people to his table, West's dark glower is chasing everyone away. A mom with two kids stops by the pirate ship table, and the children both have candy clutched in their fists as they approach West. He forces himself to smile—terrifying the boy with his wolfish expression. I don't blame the child one bit when he hides behind his mom's legs. She rushes them away as West shouts miserable apologies in her wake.

I snort, and West's head whips toward me. We lock eyes, and damn it, I'm hit with an unwanted flash of survivor's guilt.

If I ignore the years that I spent writing books alone in my bedroom, I'm the closest thing publishing has to an overnight success. *Torched* hit bestseller lists the week it was published, and because of that, I never had to wonder if anyone cared about my story. I'm haunted by other insecurities—whether I deserve my success, whether I'm a bad writer who got lucky, whether I'll ever redeem myself in the eyes of my readers—but I never had to sit in an empty signing line, wondering if anyone cared.

I regret what I'm doing before I even do it. I order my feet to stop walking. To pivot and buy a book from Tarot Card Lady, just to make steam come out West's ears. I should do anything other than what I'm about to do, but I'm propelled by a feeling I can't quite name.

"I'll take a book," I tell West in a bored voice.

He rubs a hand over his tired eyes. "Please go away."

"Just give me one," I snap.

His expression turns wary. "What are you going to do with it?"

I sigh, irritated that he's dragging this out. "I don't know, West, what do people do with books?"

He cocks an eyebrow. "Read it again?"

"Definitely not." I bristle at the suggestion. "Do you take credit cards?"

He shakes his head. "You'll have to buy it from the bookstore."

"Fine." I grab the book and stomp to the bookstore, my entire body flushed with annoyance. Only after I've paid for it do I let myself look at the cover.

Drought.

Set in the Southwest, then. His stuff always is. *Was*, I remind myself. I don't know anything about who he is or what he writes anymore. Familiar curiosity flickers to life behind my rib cage, but I'm back within eyesight of West's tent, and I don't want him to see me flipping through the pages or even reading the back-cover synopsis, so I hold the book loosely in my grip, forcing my eyes not to focus on the orange blossoms on the spine. I wait in line as West signs books for two outrageously pretty girls, both of them way too young for him, and I'm annoyed all over again. I didn't even need to buy this stupid book; he sold two on his own.

The girls leave, and I step up to the table. I slap the book down hard enough that everyone within twenty feet looks at us. West swears under his breath and quickly signs the title page. He closes the cover and pushes it toward me.

"I hope you find it illuminating," he says, which strikes me as a stupid thing to say. But I can't fault him too much, as I say stupid stuff at my events all the time.

"I can assure you I won't," I say with an acid smile. I turn to leave, but West calls me back.

"Oh, and, Darling?"

Hearing my name on his tongue is like hot lava flowing down my spine. "Don't call me that."

He stands up and leans his weight on his hands. His gaze is a wrecking ball of intention. "I will get you back for this, *Darling*."

12

12 Years Ago
Sophomore Year, First Semester

"Honey, we're home!" Amber's voice carries from the front door to the small sunlit kitchen at the back of the house, where I've been deleting and writing the same paragraph for the last half hour.

"Who's 'we'?" I yell back. When Amber asked if I wanted to live with her this year, I jumped at the chance. I hit the roommate jackpot with her; not only is she easy to live with and spends half her time at Kyle's frat, but also her parents bought a house close to campus over the summer, and they're only charging me a couple hundred bucks in rent.

I'm confident that Amber and I wouldn't have been friends if we hadn't been roommates—she likes to party, and I like to spend my weekends talking to people I made up in my head—but the forced proximity and shared trauma of watching *Grey's Anatomy* every week in a two-hundred-square-foot dorm room really bonded us together. She doesn't let me get away with being a hermit too many days in a row, and I inexplicably make her laugh every time we meet someone who asks *Like the planet?* She never gets tired of my bit, and I love that about her.

The moment I knew our friendship was going to last, however, was the night we couldn't fit microwave burritos in our freezer because of the frost buildup, so we dragged it down the hall and defrosted it in the shower. Something about the shower spray mixing with our tears of laughter made our friendship permanent.

The door slams, and Amber's sandals thud against the tile floor as she kicks them off. "Me and Kyle," she says as she enters the kitchen. "And West," she adds as he trails after them, ducking to fit under the low archway.

"Hey." West nods and runs a self-conscious hand through his hair. Bethany convinced him to buzz it over the summer, and now it's too short to straighten *and* too short to fully curl, so it's this fluffy sort of in-between that looks like it would feel like silk under my fingers. Last time I saw Bethany, she was bugging him to cut it again because *it looks better short*, and I had to wire my mouth shut to avoid telling her that her opinion sucks.

"We need to talk," Amber says as she scans the pantry and then the refrigerator and emerges with a tub of questionable hummus and a half empty bag of pita chips. She offers the hummus to Kyle to sniff. He makes a face but then takes a bite anyway.

"I think it's expired," I say.

"Tastes fine," he says.

Amber shrugs and takes a nibble. "We need to grocery shop."

"Soon," I agree. We've been saying it for the last five days, though, and I doubt today is the day either of us will make it happen. It's getting dire, and Kyle's presence isn't helping, but I'd be an idiot to argue with two-hundred-dollar rent. "What do we need to talk about?"

She drops the pita chips dramatically on the table and fixes me with a serious face.

"If this is about the dishes in my room, I swear I'm going to—"

"Halloween party," she cuts me off. "Tonight. Rishi's house. We're all going. Plus Bethany, right?" She turns to West for confirmation, and when he nods, she looks back to me for an answer.

I never imagined that West and I would hang out with Amber and Kyle as much as we do, but Kyle was iced out of his fraternity after he reported them for hazing and thus found himself with more free time this year. He's not so bad. "Okay."

She frowns. "That's it?"

"Sure."

"You don't have to stay home and study?"

I click to one of the dozens of open tabs on my laptop and tilt it so she can see my trigonometry grade. I'm four weeks away from finally passing this class and saying goodbye to math forever. *Hallelujah*.

West leans over Amber's shoulder and grins when he sees the B-minus. He reaches across the table to give me a high five.

"That was anticlimactic," she complains. "I had a whole speech prepared and everything. It was about being young and hot and how few Halloweens we have left to celebrate before we get too old to dress like slutty nurses."

"Aren't you planning to go to nursing school?" West asks.

"Yeah, babe. If you dream hard enough, you can be a slutty nurse every day," Kyle says earnestly.

Amber ignores the men. "If my speech didn't work, West was going to talk you into it."

"This is news to me," West says.

"Why do you want me to go so badly?" I ask.

"Because Connor is going to be there tonight."

"Connor who?"

"Rishi's friend. English major. He was in your Pop Culture and Politics class."

"He was?"

"Yes. And we sat with him at the improv show in the Modern Languages building that one time."

"*Riiiight*," I say, though I've blocked most of that night from my memory. It was the first weekend that we all hung out with West and Bethany while she was in town, and I was trying exceptionally hard to act like a girl who didn't know what it was like to grind on her boyfriend in the library stacks. I was nervous that if she didn't like me, West and I would have to stop hanging out. "What about him?"

"He's going to be at the party tonight," Amber says.

"And?"

"He thinks you're hot," Kyle says through a mouthful of expired hummus.

"Oh!" My spine straightens. Three pairs of eyes watch me with interest; what I say next will get relayed to Connor before the party tonight. I avoid looking at West, because even though it's been six months since our one and only make-out session and neither of us feels that way anymore, it's still awkward that he's here for this conversation. "Cool."

"Can we tell him you'll see him tonight?" Amber asks. When I confirm, she squeals her approval and then disappears into her room with Kyle.

West takes the seat next to me while Amber's Slow Jams playlist filters through the thin walls. "You don't remember that Connor guy at all, do you?" he asks.

"I do!" I protest while West laughs.

"What does he look like?"

"He has blond hair."

West shakes his head.

"Brown?"

"Wrong again."

"The redhead," I say, finally putting a name to the face of a guy I've seen in Kyle's Facebook pictures. And in the seat in front of me in Pop Culture and Politics. And apparently at improv night.

"He'll be flattered to know how well you remember him."

"No need to tell him."

West laughs—until something about my expression makes him pause. "Wait. Are you interested in him?"

"Maybe." I shrug, and an uncomfortable silence settles around us. West and I are the kind of friends who talk about everything—except who we're dating. I don't ask about Bethany, and he doesn't ask about my love life.

"I emailed you notes an hour ago. It's your best one so far," he says, opting to forcefully change the subject.

"You always say that." I roll my eyes, though I'm secretly pleased. A West Emerson compliment is like a good hair day; there's no such thing as too many.

West started freshman year as a history major, switched to psych halfway through second semester, and is now flirting with the idea of coming over to the English Department. Every day, he gets a little bit closer to admitting that he loves words almost as much as I do.

After that surprising, snowy night during freshman year, I started to wonder if my growing crush on West made him my muse. Thank god that's not the case. West's impact on my writing is entirely separate from the brief period of time when I wanted to kiss him. He hasn't even looked at me since he got back together with Bethany, but he's always first in line to read whatever fantasy worlds my brain conjures up.

"It's always true," he says casually, and my stomach flutters to life with the familiar praise. "When you're famous, I get to say I was your first fan."

I pick up the pad of blue sticky notes next to my laptop and write **Margot Darling's #1 Fan**. I sign my name at the bottom with the signature I've been practicing since I was thirteen years old and stick it to his forehead. "When I'm famous, that'll be worth money." I grab the strap of his backpack and tug it toward me. "Do you have anything for me to read this time?"

He snatches the bag to his chest.

"C'mon! It's only fair."

He throws his head back with a groan. I know he's working on something new because of the way he shielded me from seeing what he was writing last week at the library. He almost failed Dr. B's final because he was so reluctant to turn in his short story. "I'm new to this," he grumbles.

"So?"

"It's not as good as yours."

"Bullshit."

He grimaces. "Mars—"

"Please!" I beg, pouting my lips and batting my eyelashes.

He mutters something that sounds like "Bambi" under his breath and turns to a dog-eared page near the back of his notebook. A rush of satisfaction zips through me.

He rolls his eyes as he hands it over. "Don't look so smug. It's basically fifteen hundred words on *rain*."

"I love it already," I tell him seriously as my eyes fall to the first sentence.

"I can't be here while you read that," he says.

"I know." My nose is already buried in the pages, my attention slipping from West to his writing. "I'll give it back at the party tonight."

"And leave you with my notebook? Not a chance. I'll wait outside."

"Do you want to watch TV?"

"I can't even be in the same house with you while you're reading that." He shudders and nearly trips over his own feet as he leaves the room. When the screen door swings shut behind him, I take it as permission to dive back in.

The thing about West's writing is that it always makes me feel something, even if it is fifteen hundred words about a summer storm and even if he has run-on sentences or fragments or whatever. For some reason, he gets away with breaking the rules that I can't, and damn if it doesn't hit me square in the chest every time. His writing transports me right out of Amber's parents' off-campus house to the inside of West's brain.

I don't ask myself why I like it there so much.

13

Present Day

The high of my sabotage mission has worn off by the time I arrive at Gentle Ben's a few hours after West's signing, the buzz in my veins giving way to apprehension. All I managed to do was slightly annoy him and part with twenty-eight bucks—a percentage of which will go toward paying off his advance. It's not the first time I've spent money on a book of his that I'll never read, but I don't plan to make a habit of it.

"Here are your drink tickets." The hostess hands me two paper tickets. With West's warning hanging over my head and an author mixer in my immediate future, I have a feeling I'm going to need them. "You can order at the bar upstairs or down; rooftop access is that way."

I follow her direction and take the stairs to the rooftop bar, where a gust of wind almost blows off my hat. I clamp my hand down on it and scan the crowd for Daphne's red hair in the shoulder-to-shoulder crowd.

I circle the rooftop three times, growing steadily more desperate with each loop. I text Daphne and grab us the last empty table while I wait for her to arrive, one hand still glued to my stupid hat. My nerves about this evening led to a wardrobe crisis in my hotel room, which led to this influencer-core wide-brim hat perched precariously on my head. Despite packing more than enough outfits for the weekend, when I dumped it all on my hotel bed, I hated everything. It was all too . . . bookish. Cardigans and funny T-shirts and jeans at least three years out of style. The next time West sees me, I want to make him sweat. Not because I care what he thinks of me but because making him uncomfortable is my current drug of choice. After years of daydreaming about revenge, it starts here. With this little vintage sundress that I purchased on Fourth.

The only flaw in my plan is the hat. Tucson's hard water wreaks havoc on my hair, so when I saw a hat near the register, I made my second impulse purchase of the day. Between West's novel and this hat, I'm collecting things I hate at a rapid pace. And now I'm committed to the bit.

My phone rings with a call from Daphne. "I saved us a table! Are you close?" I ask.

"I accidentally took a three-hour nap. The jet lag hit hard"—she yawns—"but I'm coming." She's been on the road doing events for three weeks; it's no surprise that she's exhausted.

"Where are you?" I glance at the street below the bar.

"In my room, but I'm coming, I promise."

"Daph—"

"I'm putting my shoes on," she mumbles in a sleepy voice.

I run a hand down my green dress and imagine how much easier it'd be to skip this evening than pretend I feel braver than I do. "Go back to bed."

Tap water runs in the bathroom, and she makes a garbled sound. "Teeth brushed. Shoes on. What am I forgetting?"

"Go back to sleep, Daph. I'll be fine."

She hesitates. "Are you sure?"

"At this point, I'll be mad if you show up," I say, already planning my exit strategy. If I walk quickly, I can be watching Bravo from my hotel bed in thirteen minutes.

A sense of being watched tickles the back of my neck as I make my way from one side of the bar to the other. I duck into the bathroom and check for toilet paper on my shoe or tags that I forgot to bite off my dress, but nothing about my outfit strikes me as embarrassing (other than this cursed hat).

I swish my dress around my legs one last time in the mirror, check the pockets for my phone and hotel room key, and step back onto the rooftop. A pair of eyes cuts away from me, and paranoia creeps into my lungs.

I make eye contact with Sabrina Lowe, an author who debuted the same year as I did. When I smile, she nods before elbowing the man next to her. He looks at me curiously before turning to whisper something to Sabrina.

I'm not imagining it, then. People are talking.

My knees feel like jelly as I approach the bar. "Two shots of whatever will make me forget this night." I pass my tickets to the bartender.

I hear a scoff over my shoulder, and when I turn, West's eyes are cold. "The more things change, the more they stay the same, don't they?" He tips his beer in my direction, and I see the exact moment his gaze catches on my bare thighs. He does a double take, his eyes tracing the line of my dress up to the low neckline that fits snugly against my chest. "Nice dress."

He doesn't sound insincere, but I shift under his heavy gaze, suspicious of the compliment. I cross my arms. "Get on with it."

He pushes his tongue into his cheek, calculating his next

move. "Not a day goes by that I regret leaving New York. I saw that there's a freeze warning this weekend," he says casually.

I narrow my eyes, waiting.

"Warm tonight, isn't it?" he continues.

Not particularly. A chill has swept over me as the sun sets, and I've been regretting not bringing a jacket. West must feel differently, because he shrugs his off, revealing the T-shirt he's wearing underneath. I pause, too stunned to react. He tilts his head, his eyes roving over my face like searchlights—hungry, eager for my reaction.

Finally, after several seconds in which I can only blink numbly at his chest, I snap out of shock and grab his forearm. I open my mouth to tell him off when I see the blank skin where his tattoo used to be. A second shock. I drop his arm like I've been burned.

"Take your shirt off," I hiss, low and panicky.

"Now? You don't want to go somewhere more private?" He lifts the hem of his shirt, revealing a sliver of his flat stomach that nearly gives me vertigo. Blazoned on West's T-shirt is a picture of the actor who plays Fox in the *Torched* movies. He's wearing honest-to-god *merch*. The words Fox Caldwell Fae King are written across the shirt in bold type.

"Not here!" I grab his shirt and yank it down, mortified at my heady response to two inches of bare skin. My knuckles brush against the hard planes of his stomach, a sensation that steals all my focus until a gust of wind carries my hat and the last of my sanity off the rooftop. "You have to leave," I demand as the bartender slides two shots my way. I shudder as the cinnamon whiskey hits my tongue.

"Have you met my friends?" West gestures to a loud group occupying a table at the edge of the bar. "I'll introduce you." His hand presses on the small of my back, and if my stomach feels like hot coals have been dropped inside, it's only because of the Fireball.

I lock my knees like a petulant teenager. "Everyone is looking."

"We're old news, Darling. No one gives a shit about us."

"Then why did you wear *that*?"

His lips quirk. "Because I knew you would hate it." My knees buckle as I let him steer me across the bar, and this time I know I'm not imagining the whispers or the stares that follow.

His hand presses firmly on my shoulder until I find myself on a bench seat. My dress slides up my legs, revealing a distressing amount of skin, and he drops next to me and scoots close. His thigh presses against mine, and when he leans back and stretches his arm out on the railing behind me, goose bumps scatter across my chest.

"Take this," he says, offering his jacket. A familiar scent tickles my nose.

"No, thank you."

His eyes dip—briefly—to my chest, and I remember that I'm not wearing a bra. He lays the jacket across his lap, and when a gust of wind reveals yet another inch of thigh, I snatch the jacket and spread it over my legs.

He smothers a laugh. "Everyone, this is Mars Darling. Mars, this is Bryan, Jo, Mario, Durfee, and Liza."

Jo leans toward me, resting her chin in her hands. "I *have* to tell you that you're the reason I'm a writer."

"I'm so sorry," I say, reaching for an easy joke that gets a laugh every time.

"So, it's brutal out there for everyone, not just me?" Mario asks as he looks around the table.

"Here we go." Jo laughs.

"My publicist told me I should be posting five TikToks a week, as if I don't already have a full-time job *on top* of writing," Liza says, holding her glass up.

"I can't even tell you how many agents claimed that the market for gay Latino romances is 'too small,'" Mario says with an eye roll.

West points at him. "*Fuck. Them.*"

"Amen!"

"Let's see." Jo turns her glass in her hand. "I was tagged in a review that said my book made them want to gouge their eyeballs out, *and* I can't afford health insurance."

"Hear, hear!" Glasses clink again, and then all eyes shift to me. It's my turn to join the horror story swap, and Lord knows I have a lot to choose from, one of which is pressed against my side, his eyes fixed on my face.

I lick my lips. If possible, West's thigh presses harder into mine. "BuzzFeed once called me 'everything that is wrong with YA fiction,'" I say at last. Jo pushes a pitcher of beer toward me. I pour myself a glass.

"Why do we do this again?" Bryan asks.

"Not writing isn't an option, so I may as well get paid for it," Jo says.

"Unfortunately, it's the only thing I'm good at," Mario says with a laugh.

I open my mouth to commiserate, but the words stick in my throat as West reaches across me to grab a bowl of pretzels from the other end of the table, his muscles flexing under his too-tight Fox merch. The woodsy scent from earlier overwhelms me, and I feel an antsy, aching need and press my thighs together to make it stop. When West settles back into his seat, his foot rests against mine under the table. I kick him to let him know that I'm *me*, not a piece of furniture. His neutral expression doesn't waver as he quickly shifts away.

The table splits into several side conversations. I glance sideways as West pops a pretzel into his mouth and chews slowly. I watch him lick the salt and dust off his fingers. "Something to say, Darling?" he finally asks, turning to catch me staring at him.

A million things run through my head. *I hate you. I hate your shirt. It looks terrible on you. I never even think about you anymore. I want to ruin your life.*

With a heavy sigh, I tilt my face up to the darkening sky. "Daphne told me not to let you get in my head." I'm quickly inching my way into tipsy. I wouldn't have let that slip otherwise.

"And? How's that working out for you?" he asks on a quiet breath.

"Not great so far, but I never lose the capacity for hope."

West barely manages to conceal his amusement. Annoyed with both him and myself, I lean back until my shoulder blades brush his arm, and I realize immediately that I've made a capital-M Mistake. I bolt upright. "Sorry! I didn't—I wouldn't—that was an accident!"

"You're fine." Twin flickers of surprise and confusion replace his previous delight.

I pour myself another drink.

Even when I hate West, I can't help but react to his touch. It's been imprinted on my DNA since the very first night we kissed, and not even a decade and a World War III–size grudge can make me forget. Of all the things he's ever done, making me fall in love with him when I was nineteen might have been the worst.

West's eyes search my face. "What's wrong?"

"It's an open mic downstairs!" Jo drains what's left in her glass and stands. "Prepare yourselves for some slam poetry."

I nudge West off the bench and step out of his orbit. Now that I don't have to smell him or touch him or even look directly at him, my brain sharpens. "Congratulations, et cetera. You won this round, but I'll beat you next time."

"A bit of a cliché, don't you think?"

"I'm serious."

He motions to his shirt. "We each got a shot in, and now we can drop it. We're even."

"Nice try, but it's not even close."

Downstairs, a crowd of mostly drunk writers gathers in front of a small stage. West leans against a wall in the back and quietly fumes. I'm sure I'd be able to ignore him if not for that infuriating shirt. My eyes are drawn to it every twenty seconds, my heart tripping over itself.

Jo performs a poetry slam that both is technically good *and* gives me secondhand embarrassment. When another author gets onstage to recite a (mercifully non-slammable) passage from his book, a perfect idea drops fully formed into my half-drunk lap.

I take my place at center stage and reach for the microphone. "This one is for Fox Caldwell's number one fan." The audience hoots and hollers, plastered but supportive. I'm surprised. I spare a quick glance at the statue formerly known as West. His stare is heavy and blatant. It feels like hot water down my spine, and my fingers tremble slightly as I flip West's book open to a random page. I clear my throat. "I'll be reading a passage from West Emerson's new novel, *Drought*."

West and I haven't been close in years, not in any way that really matters, but the part of me that's always been connected to him pulls tight across my ribs. Anger radiates off him in nuclear waves, and I feel it blistering in my veins. There's nothing West finds more excruciating than listening to his own writing, and now he has to do it in a packed house full of colleagues.

I don't want to look at West again, but I can't stop myself. His face is half in shadows, but his expression is undeniable.

Don't.

Please.

His eyes beg me not to, but I forced myself to stop caring about what West Emerson wants a long time ago.

My throat tightens. I thought this moment would feel like winning, but instead it feels like holding a match to something precious.

Well, that's stupid. I shake off the thought and clear my throat again, buying myself a few extra seconds before doing the thing I swore I never would—reading a West Emerson novel.

It goes like this:

The main character's car breaks down as he's trying to leave Arizona in the middle of a scorching heat wave. West's writing paints a vivid picture, as always. The character gets lost in the desert. Dehydrated and desperate, he stumbles onto a fairy garden.

I pause—something about the scene feels familiar.

My eyes track back over the last few sentences. It's unclear whether the man is hallucinating; it's left ambiguous by design.

Someone in the audience coughs. Voices murmur. I look up just in time to see the door swing shut behind West's retreating figure, which can only mean one thing.

I won this round.

The victory doesn't feel quite like I thought it would.

14

11 Years Ago
Junior Year, Second Semester

The first sign of trouble between West and Bethany came at a bonfire in the desert. A guy I'd just met had his hand on my knee when their fight started, and by the time he leaned in for a kiss, the ice coming off both of them was enough to douse the fire.

The second sign was at a game night in January. I watched the couple have an entire silent fight with their eyes over a game of Cards Against Humanity because West wasn't picking her cards to win.

The third time is when I'm sitting on the floor in West's room, scrolling through Facebook instead of writing, and I see that Bethany has posted an old picture of them with a long caption about how much she loves him—aka the relationship death rattle.

I glance at West. He's sitting on his bed playing video games, *The Canterbury Tales* abandoned on the floor. We don't spend much time at his apartment, but Amber's dad is making repairs at the house, so we ended up here, hiding from West's roommates and their intense game of Dungeons & Dragons at the kitchen table.

"What are you doing this weekend?" I ask. We have no classes on Monday, and West usually makes it a point to visit his girlfriend at cosmetology school in Scottsdale if he hasn't seen her for a few weeks.

His expression is pained. "Gabbi's visiting for the week. My mom wants me to come home and do the happy family thing . . . but I don't know."

"Is your dad still . . . ?"

"An asshole? Yes." He sighs and scrubs a hand through his hair. "She wants me to forgive him, but I don't know if he deserves it."

"Hmm." I click through Bethany's most recent photo album.

"You're ruminating."

"Only a little."

"About what?"

I bite the inside of my cheek, trying to figure out how to word this without sounding like I am defending West's stupid dad. "I guess I don't think you forgive someone because they deserve it or they've earned it or something."

"Then why would I do it?"

I shrug. "Because you love your mom. And you love him."

After a pause, West says, "I don't know if I do love him."

My heart squeezes. "You don't have to."

"It's not Gabbi's fault, but I hate him *more* when she's around, because she deserves better than a cheating dad who flies her in once every few months and an older brother who doesn't want to be around her. I lied and told her I was busy this weekend, so if you're keeping score, I'm not exactly treating her any better than my dad is."

"You're nothing like him."

"I'm trying not to be," he mutters.

"It wouldn't be a lie if you visit Bethany this weekend." I'm careful to put the same amount of stress on each syllable, and as a result, I've been saying her name like a robot for two years now.

His eyes flick quickly away from mine. "Nah."

Nah? He doesn't know me at all if he thinks I'm going to be content with that answer.

"Is everything good with you two?"

He blinks in surprise, and I wonder if he thinks I haven't noticed the way he's been uncharacteristically sleeping in and missing classes or zoning out when we're together. I'll catch him looking at me with a strange expression, and it's clear his mind is somewhere else entirely.

He dies on-screen. "Yeah, why?"

"No reason." I close out of Facebook and pull my Word doc up. That's enough internet stalking for me.

"Maybe I can convince my mom to bring Gabbi and the others down here this weekend," he says.

"Gonna take them on a tour of Greek row?"

He tilts his head to the side. "Gabbi's never been to Kartchner Caverns. She'd like that."

"What is it?"

"An underground cave filled with limestone formations. You've never been?" When I shake my head, his eyes light up. "You should come with us. It's pretty cool, and I doubt she's seen anything like it on the East Coast." He smiles for the first time all day, and my stomach tugs strangely while I watch him plan an afternoon for his sister. An afternoon he wants to include me in.

"What about you?" he asks, stretching out on his bed with his arms behind his head, a chewed pen cap appearing in his mouth from who knows where. His shirt pulls up, revealing a strip of skin above his boxers, and the room shrinks by half. "Do you have big plans for the long weekend?"

"Just cave exploring, apparently, and this." I hold up my laptop. What started out as a spite goal (to prove my parents wrong) quickly turned into self-preservation. The minute I tell someone that I'm a creative writing major, I get a scoff or a sneer or a condescending lecture that boils down to one point: *How are you going to make money doing* that?

It's not like I'm a theater major!

My parents cloak their disapproval in concern for my future, but they're the only ones. Strangers, classmates, and friends have zero filter when it comes to my job prospects, and I figure the best way to make them eat their words is to have a book on the shelves by the time I cross the stage in a cap and gown.

Huh, maybe it *is* still a spite goal.

Or maybe I just love it.

Either way, I had to move the goalpost at the start of junior year. I'm nowhere near ready. My new goal is to finish a book and find a literary agent before the end of next year.

I've written hundreds of thousands of words in the last half decade, but none of them felt good enough. After I finished my latest novel, I planned to take a two-week break. Two days later, everything changed. One minute, I was curling my hair, thinking about what to eat for dinner, and the next, these characters were in my brain. A fae king, the mortal girl who falls in love with him, and their fight to protect his kingdom against warring creatures. It's magical and whimsical and deeply romantic. Or it will be, once I've transferred it from my brain onto the page. Small details.

"Are you working on something new?" West asks, and it's the closest we've come to broaching the subject in months.

"Yes, and I'm so obsessed with it that I can barely sleep."

"What's it about?"

"Magical teenagers. What else?"

"Another weird story that should never be published?"

Oh. His words are a sucker punch. When it comes to my writing, I have my guard up around nearly everyone *except* him.

West takes one look at my expression, and his eyes widen in alarm. He rolls to his side and pushes his weight up onto his elbow. "Wait, hey, no—"

"Nice to know how you really feel." I try to laugh it off, but my words come out hoarse and wounded.

"No! It's a quote! Robert Pattinson said it about *Twilight*. You read it to me the first day we met."

I swallow the lump in my throat. "Did I?" I don't remember that at all.

"*Yes*," he insists.

We stare at each other as the silence around us rises in volume. His expression is one of forged steel.

"Okay," I say eventually. He looks relieved as he flops backward. I want to believe him as badly as I want to believe that I'm not delusional for writing every chapter with his reaction in mind. But it might be too late for that.

Last semester, I asked if he had time to proofread a short story (emphasis on *short*) for my Young Adult Lit class, but for the first time ever, he was too busy. He hasn't asked to read anything of mine since, and the thought that he might have grown sick of my silly magical teenagers makes me feel like the oxygen is being sucked out of the room.

"Remember when you used to color your nails with Sharpie?" I ask suddenly.

"What about it?"

"Just thinking about freshman year."

"Do you ever miss it?" he asks.

"Your emo nails? Full offense, but no."

He rakes a hand through his hair, eyes still fixed on the ceiling. "Living in the dorms. Hanging out on campus between classes because we had hours to kill and nothing else to do. I didn't have a job or any stress or a—whatever." His head falls to the side and our eyes meet.

Something close to longing crosses his face, and a small, chronically curious part of me wonders what he almost said on the other side of *whatever.*

I avoid the place in my brain that still feels the weight of West's gaze on my lips or his hands on my waist. I don't think about the days following spring break, when I cried my eyes out over a boy who went running straight into the arms of his high school sweetheart, and I sure as hell don't romanticize what could have been. West made his intentions very clear: If he wanted to be with Bethany, he would. Two years later, he still is.

"I miss it," I finally admit. My whisper might as well be a shout. His gaze grows pensive as our eye contact holds for longer than I understand, and I worry we're tipping into territory that we can't ignore. "But this year is good, too."

He turns his head, and the moment is gone. I'm relieved and disappointed and flushed with feelings I don't want to feel.

"Are you hungry? I'm hungry," he announces. Always good for an unsubtle change of subject, he is.

"I'm good." I type a nonsense sentence as he leaves the room.

I tip my head back against his wall as a nostalgic kind of melancholy drips down my spine. I breathe deeply, count to ten, and browbeat my emotions into a manageable shape.

By the time West returns with a protein bar and starts another game, the weird tension between us has evaporated, and I'm back to writing. The main character is meeting her love interest for the first time. I'm giddy with anticipation, but I'm also at a roadblock; it's time to describe what he looks like, and I suck at description.

I type the first thing that comes to mind. He has a nose. Two eyes. And a mouth. In a hot way.

I groan and delete it. *What do people even look like?*

"I need help," I announce when my fingers have been hovering over the keyboard for the time it takes West's on-screen character to die and come back to life and then die again.

"Nine times five is forty-five," West says without skipping a beat. I snort. *Now that's a callback I remember.*

Hands still frozen, I study his face: long black eyelashes and a crooked nose. Without my permission, my fingers move. *Fox Caldwell is born.*

15

Present Day

I follow West out of the bar and chase him down University, annoyed at myself the whole time.

"Wait!" I call, and I'm mad when he does.

He turns dramatically on his heel (how very *Fox* of him), surprise quickly melting into suspicion. His narrowed eyes match the expression on the actor's face on his T-shirt. I wish he'd take it off.

I huff an exasperated sigh. "Relax, I'm not going to *jump* you." *Why did I say it like that?* "'Jump' as in 'rob.' I'm not going to rob you," I clarify. "I wasn't meaning 'jump' as in 'jump your bones.' Sexually." I cross my arms, irritated. What possessed me to use the word *sexually*? Am I still buzzed?

Even now, with the stench of weed swirling around us and undergrads spilling out of bars, West looks exactly like the kind of guy you write a book about. Tall. Brooding. Just the right side of dangerous. My stomach is doing those pleasant swirly loops that lead to bad decisions. He's a decade-plus virus that I can't sweat out.

He crosses his arms over his chest, mistrust dissipating into amusement. "So, to be clear, you *are* here to jump my bones?" he deadpans.

"Hilarious."

He drags his fingers through his curls, his shirt riding up again. I try not to watch. "What's up? You didn't torture me enough tonight?"

"Is that what it would be?" I put a hand on my waist and cock my hip, all bravado. It's fine to joke about something that will never happen, right?

He tenses, his expression steely. He chooses his next words carefully. "What are you doing here, Mars?"

I drop my hand. "You still can't read, talk about, or listen to your own book, huh?"

"Something like that," he says flatly.

I feel a small, obnoxious urge to apologize. It's easy enough to ignore. "You forgot your jacket," I say quickly, relieved to have found an excuse for standing under a streetlight with him.

"Okay." West nods.

He blinks. Patient. Waiting for . . . *Oh.*

Goose bumps streak across my chest as I slide the jacket off. My nipples harden under this ill-advised sundress. I wonder if he notices.

West's eyes are dark as they dip low for a fraction of a second. "Keep it. You're cold."

Question asked and answered. My body flushes hot, desire gathering between my thighs.

I pull his jacket tight over my chest and hold it closed with one hand. "This stupid fucking dress."

"*No,*" he says abruptly. When I raise my eyebrows, he clears his throat, looking suddenly uncomfortable. "I meant what I said at the bar. It's a nice dress. Green is . . . um . . . you look . . ."

"Don't bother," I say when it's clear that he'd rather cut his tongue out than say something nice about me. I motion to his jacket. "When will I give it back to you?"

His expression turns wry. "Do you really think we've seen the last of each other, Darling?" My face must give something away, because he asks, "Why do you hate it so much when I call you that?"

"Because it implies that we're friends, which we haven't been for a while." Maybe it's the alcohol, or maybe it's just the way he's looking at me, but my tone has lost all of this afternoon's bite. I don't have it in me to open more old wounds tonight.

"Huh," West murmurs cryptically. "Are you hungry?"

"I would do something illegal to get my hands on a slice of Mount Lemmon pie."

"The café closed down."

My shoulders fall. "What? When?"

"A few years ago."

"Oh." I feel sadder than the situation warrants.

"I'd bet there's another establishment in Tucson that sells pie," he offers.

"It wouldn't be the same."

"I guess."

"What else changed?" I ask, suddenly curious about how many of my memories this town has erased.

"Not much. Casa Video still rents DVDs, but now they have a craft beer bar where they screen films on the upper level."

"Do they still have the velvet curtain with the adult titles behind it?" West and I were freshmen the first time we stumbled upon that room, and I giggled uncontrollably for twenty minutes straight.

He raises his shoulders in an exaggerated shrug. "I wouldn't know."

I gasp. "West Emerson! Tell me you are *not* renting nineties porn!"

He laughs. "I have no idea if the velvet curtain still exists. I promise."

"Mm-hmm," I hum, suddenly giddy.

"Seriously."

"Okay."

"Is that a real 'okay,' or are you humoring me?"

"Whatever you say."

He levels me with a pleading stare. "Please tell me you believe me."

"Fine." I twist my mouth so he won't see me grin. "I believe you. Happy?"

"Yeah. Now c'mon, I'll walk you to your hotel."

"You don't have to do that. Seriously. I'm fine. I used to haunt this campus after dark."

"*We* used to haunt this campus," he corrects, "and you're not as sober as I'd like you to be when you're walking alone after dark." His jaw flexes, a stubborn line forming on his lips. It doesn't seem worth it to argue.

I give him the name of my hotel and fall into step by his side. There's a faster route, one that doesn't involve cutting through campus, but the ghosts of our past can't leave us alone tonight, and walking next to him feels less complicated than it did this afternoon. The darkness tends to do that. When I can't mark the passing years by the faint traces of smile lines around his eyes, it's easier to chase the shadows of our old selves.

The wind swirls my hair in every direction. There's no hope for it. If I move my hands from my skirt, West will know the color (light blue) and cut (cheeky) of my underwear.

"Speaking of people who aren't sober . . ." I tilt my chin up to look at him. His large jacket slips off my shoulder again, and the chill cuts straight to my bones.

"Is there a question under those ellipses?" he asks dryly. I laugh. West knows as well as anyone about my deep and abiding love for ellipses.

"Not if you don't want to answer one."

He glances up at the sky, weighing his words carefully. "The older I get, the more I realize that nothing is as black-and-white as I thought when we were twenty-two."

We.

My stomach hurts.

"Because of my dad, I saw alcohol as bad, sobriety as good." He glances sideways, and I can't bring myself to meet his eyes. An old, sickening feeling settles heavy on my chest, but he continues, unfazed. "Eventually I realized that I don't want to make my decisions based on his mistakes. I refuse to give him that level of control over my life. And once I loosened the grip on my own anger, he stopped taking up so much real estate in my head." He turns his empty palms to the sky. "I gave myself permission to stop fighting my past."

His confession shocks me. I inspect his profile under the blue glow of a campus emergency light. Gone is the anguish that used to surround him when he talked about his dad, and in its place is a hard-fought peace. He looks settled. Confident. Steady.

He grew up, I realize with a start. The sensation of guilt quickly makes room for something different but equally as alarming. *Pride.* I shouldn't be feeling either in relation to West Emerson.

"I'm happy for you, West," I say, and the look he gives me in return is so unguarded that it terrifies me. I need to redirect this conversation away from soul-baring confessions and toward something lighter. "Friday night and nothing is happening. Other than the café, Tucson hasn't changed at all, has it?"

"It's not so bad."

"I'll never believe it. This city has always been sleepy."

"Because there's so much to do in New York?" he asks darkly.

We stare at each other in silence, the absurdity of his question hanging between us.

"Don't say anything. I heard it," he mutters, before furrowing his brow in thought. "Are you still willing to do something illegal in the name of sugar?"

"I will always, at any time, do something illegal for dessert."

West nods toward the Student Union food court. The lights are off and the doors are locked. "Prove it, Darling."

Ugh.

I roll my eyes and follow him into the dark.

16

10 Years Ago
Senior Year, Second Semester

Amber was relentless, and West was game, so we spent our sophomore and junior years seeing art-house movies at the Loft, getting high and hiking in Sabino Canyon, sneaking into apartment complex swimming pools after dark, and driving all the way to the café at the top of Mount Lemmon for overpriced slices of pie. I studied *just* enough to pass my classes, and by the time senior year rolled around, I'd done everything there was to do in Tucson. You can only get drunk in the desert so many times before the city starts to close in around you.

"There's nothing to do in this fucking town" was our new motto. In every class, the conversations revolved around making plans to get out. And since I'd only ever had one plan, my nights were once again spent alone, tangled in crumb-filled bedsheets, with an overheated laptop perched on my thighs.

And then, on a random Tuesday afternoon outside Modern Languages, I type the words The End and feel the world shift. (I later hit backspace seven times; novels don't announce their conclusion.) This book is different from all the ones I've written before—I know it in my bones. Fox Caldwell and Juniper Devereaux feel more real than my own life.

I give it a title (*Torched*) and start the email-driven search for a literary agent. After months of obsessing over this book, my obsession reroutes to my inbox. Who needs TV—hell, who needs books or a social life or a boyfriend—when you have the thrill of watching the clock and refreshing your inbox each time the second hand hits twelve? It's entertainment that doubles as torture, and the fun part is the stakes. At any time, an agent could email me to say that they want to make all my dreams come true. *Or*—and this is where the true mind fuck happens—they could send a rejection detailing all the ways in which my book is unsellable garbage. It's a toss-up!

I don't see West as often as I used to. His grandma was diagnosed with dementia in July, and his family needs help with the medical bills, so before the fall semester started, West withdrew from his classes and gave his tuition money to his family. I panicked when he told me, afraid it meant he was leaving Tucson, a thought that filled me with dread that I didn't know how to express. But instead of moving home, he quit his job at the soft-serve counter and took one with a pest control company in Tucson that doubled his pay and gave him triple the hours.

It's a warm day in February when I refresh my inbox again with a sigh. Nothing. Typical for a Sunday evening. Typical for most days, but I can't break the habit, even on weekends and holidays and while I'm asleep. I once woke up with my phone in my hand and my thumb on the Gmail icon. My sanity is slipping.

I slide off the bed that doubles as my desk and walk to the

kitchen, only to stop short when I see Amber and her new boyfriend, Patrick, cooking spaghetti with horny music playing in the background. She dumped Kyle in a loud blaze of glory one morning in September, throwing him out of the house after she discovered another girl in his DMs. This was followed by a month of crying and long runs, and then one day around Thanksgiving she told me about a cute guy from her nursing program named Patrick. I've never seen her happier.

"Don't worry, I'm leaving." I skirt around them to the pantry and grab a bag of popcorn.

"We have extra!" Amber says as she prods meatballs with a wooden spoon. Patrick stands behind her with his chin on her shoulder and his arms around her waist. The simple intimacy of it makes me ache for something I've never had.

"Thanks, but I'm going to my room. I haven't tried sweet-talking my inbox yet—maybe if I give it compliments it will repay me with good news."

"It'll happen! I haven't read a book in five years, and I read yours in a day. That should tell you something," she says.

"That you should read more?" I call over my shoulder as I leave them to their honeymoon-stage date night and crawl back under my covers, knocking three books to the floor in the process. I don't know why I bothered; I'm in the reading slump from hell. I've been too anxious to do anything but daydream about seeing Fox and Juniper on the shelves of a Barnes & Noble.

I open my inbox. Refresh. Text West. Scroll Facebook for five minutes. Refresh. Ten minutes on Twitter. Refresh. Five minutes on Instagram. Refresh. Text West again. Re— My fingers pause before they hit the button; my email has refreshed itself, and there's an unread message sitting in my inbox.

> I love the sample pages . . . your voice jumps off the page . . . hooked from the very beginning . . . already in love with Fox . . . dying to find out what happens . . . please send the full manuscript . . .

My body goes numb with shock.

I reply with my full manuscript attached. The send time between her email and mine? One minute. Hopefully she doesn't think I'm at home on my bed refreshing my email like the obsessed weirdo that I am. My fingers shake as I slide my feet into sandals and grab my keys. "I'm going out!"

Amber takes one look at my stunned expression and my day-five unwashed hair and frowns. "Everything okay?"

The door shuts behind me before I know what to say. I'm jittery the whole mile and a half to West's apartment. His roommate answers the door with a hand over his gaming mic.

"Is West here?"

"In his room." He nods for me to step inside.

My stomach flutters with nerves as I knock quietly on West's door. When he doesn't answer, I knock again. Unintelligible mumbling filters through the wood.

"It's me," I say.

There's a pause. "Just a sec." His voice is sharper now. I hear his feet hit the floor, and when he opens the door, he's shirtless, basketball shorts slung low on his hips. He squints at me.

"Did I wake you up?"

"It's fine." He shakes his hair out of his eyes. "What's up?"

"An agent wants to read my book."

His lips part in surprise. "What?"

"An agent requested my full manuscript. She might want to represent me."

"Mars. Holy shit." He wraps his arms around me and pulls me in to his bare chest. I stiffen, too surprised to react. He tugs me into his room and shuts the door behind us, letting his arms drop away from me. "Why didn't you tell me that you were looking for an agent?"

I pick up a Rubik's Cube off his dresser and mindlessly rotate it to avoid having to make eye contact. "You've had a lot going on." The bigger truth is that I wasn't sure if he'd care. He hasn't expressed interest in so long.

I glance at him out of the corner of my eye just in time to see his frustrated expression before he blinks it out of existence.

"Can I read it?" he asks.

"Do you want to?"

He winces before taking a deep breath and looking up at me from under his long, dark lashes. "I want to."

It feels almost like a dare. I use my phone to forward him the manuscript. "Done."

"Thanks." He scratches his nose. "I'm working twelve-hour days this week, so it might take me a while to get through it."

"No pressure."

He stares at the floor. I put the Rubik's Cube back on his dresser. We stand in silence for an excruciating moment. "Have you been working on anything?"

"No time." He shakes his head.

"Yeah. Of course." I want him to say something—anything—to make this less awkward, but he leaves it up to me to bail us out. "I should go."

"Okay."

"Well, see you around, I guess."

He nods. "Right."

"Right." I place my hand on the doorknob.

"Hey, Mars?"

I turn back hopefully. "Yeah?"

"Congratulations."

Back at the house, Amber and Patrick are watching a movie on the couch. "I was about to send out a search warrant," she says.

"Am I not allowed to leave the house?"

"You usually don't," she counters. "And you look spooked. What happened?"

I fill them in on the request from the agent—stopping every other sentence to explain to Patrick how publishing works. Amber shrieks in excitement and declares that we need to celebrate immediately. But because she's starting her OB rotation in the morning and can't stay up late or get drunk, she sends Patrick out to pick up fruit slushies from Eegee's. When he leaves, she corners me in the kitchen.

"What are you going to tell West?"

"About what?" I spear a leftover meatball with a fork.

"If the book gets published?"

"That's *years* away."

She looks at me like I'm a very simple idiot. "What if he wants to read it?"

"He does. I sent it to him tonight."

Her eyes widen. "You're pulling off the Band-Aid. I didn't think you had it in you."

I pause with the meatball halfway to my lips. "I have no idea what you're talking about."

Amber blinks at me. "Fox is West."

"What?"

"Fox Caldwell is West Emerson. They're the same guy."

"Amber." I say her name like *she's* the very simple idiot. "Fox is immortal. But most importantly . . . *he's not real.*"

"Black hair. Long eyelashes. Jacked-up nose. Those freaky multicolored eyes. The fidgeting. How he's tall, tall, tall. So damn tall, it's mentioned on every other page." She ticks the similarities off on her fingers as icy dread slithers up my spine. "His obsession with loyalty. His protectiveness over his sister. The way his fingers are smudged with charcoal—"

My fork falls to the floor. Marinara sauce splatters like blood on the tile. "Oh no. No, no, no, *no.*"

"You really didn't do it on purpose?"

I grip the edge of the counter as my mind jumps back and forth over things I wrote in the book. *Humiliating* things about Fox's lips and his body and the kissing scenes . . . oh my god . . . the scene with the knife against her neck . . . and the one where they have to share a bed. "Do you think he'll notice?" I wheeze. I'm having trouble breathing. I might be dying. I'm looking at Amber through a fish-eye lens.

Her expression turns sympathetic. "The main character's name is Juniper. West is the only person on earth who calls you Jupiter."

Fuck. There goes my plausible deniability. "I swear I didn't mean to. I don't even know what I was thinking or why I did that."

She tilts her head. "You don't?"

"No!" *It was an accident. Coincidence. Temporary insanity.*

Her eyes widen in surprise. "Mars—it's because you're in love with him."

Denial: googling can you unsend an email?

Anger: stonewalling Amber for the rest of the night after she had the audacity to point out something painfully obvious.

Bargaining: writing a text to West and begging him not to read my book. I delete it before pressing send, afraid that acting like a weirdo about it will only make him *more* curious.

Depression: vowing to never get out of bed again because a person as oblivious as me is a threat to themselves and society at large.

Acceptance: rereading my manuscript with a new perspective and admitting that it's basically West-and-Mars fan fiction.

I cycle through these stages at warp speed, and by Monday morning, my life suddenly makes a lot more sense. Hearing Amber say the words out loud broke the spell I'd put myself under, and I have no choice but to admit that I'm in love with West Emerson.

It's why I rarely feel the need to date or make out with anyone else and why West's face appears in my head every time I sit down to write. It's why his opinion is the one I care about most and why I'd rather spend time with him than anyone else.

It's likely the reason that Bethany is annoyed by my mere existence.

And if West didn't know before, he will once he reads my manuscript. My only hope of surviving this situation with my pride intact is that he gets too busy or loses interest or suddenly forgets how to read. I don't know how I'll *ever* look him in the eye again, but unfortunately, I find out sooner than expected.

West is sitting on a bench outside the languages building when I leave my afternoon Creative Nonfiction class, his elbows on his knees and his head down. The whole campus smells like orange blossoms, and when I leave Tucson after graduation, I'll miss West first, and I'll miss this smell second. It's intoxicating, making me feel drunk on spring and sunshine.

I stop in my tracks and flash back to the first time I met West in this exact spot, with his skinny jeans, his colored nails, and his refusal to let me ignore him. He was tall, he was funny, and he didn't know it yet, but we'd spend the next four years revolving around each other, creating worlds out of thin air. *How could I not fall in love with him? And why is he sitting in front of me?*

"West?"

He rises slowly to his feet, his thoughts masked behind a neutral expression.

"What are you doing here?" I glance around, looking for context that doesn't appear. "Are you taking classes again?"

"No."

"I thought you had work today."

"I called out."

A beat. "Are you going to tell me why, or make me guess?"

He lets out a ragged exhale. "I read your book last night."

That's—hmm. That's less than ideal. "All of it?"

"Yes."

I nod. Swallow. Choke on air that goes down like sandpaper. I forget how to breathe, think, move. I'm trapped between fight and flight, so I choose the third *F*: fucking lie.

I cross my arms to prove that I'm casual, that this is *fine, thanks for asking*. "What'd you think?" I ask calmly, as if my body isn't malfunctioning in every capacity.

He studies me for a long moment. Judging by the pained look on his face, he's here to let me down gently. "I think we should talk."

Oh god. The cliché of it all doesn't make it hurt any less. I am *heartsick*. Four years later, I finally understand the gravity of the word.

I take slow, even breaths and keep my eyes trained on his, determined to salvage as much dignity as possible. "Cool. About what?"

He frowns. "It was great, obviously . . ."

"But?"

He runs his tongue across the inside of his cheek. "Fox seems a lot like me."

"You think?" I pretend to consider this; meanwhile, I'm in a full mental spiral. "I mean, I guess so. I didn't do it on purpose."

His expression flickers. "You're telling me it's a coincidence?"

I shrug as blood rushes to my face. It's not fair that he knows I love him; I just barely found out myself. I didn't even get a full day to love him before having it crushed under his heel.

"Sorry. If you hate it, I can change him in the next draft. I'll give him two blue eyes like every other boring character."

"I'm not mad; I just want to know what you were thinking."

"I don't know. When I was writing, you kept popping into my head."

He steps toward me. "And what does that mean, Mars?"

"It means nothing. It doesn't have to be a big deal."

"Is that what you want?"

"What else is there?" I throw my hands up in surrender, and a shadow crosses his face. If I didn't know better, I'd think it was hunger. "Isn't that what *you* want?"

"Last night I drove to Casa Grande to see Bethany."

Damn, what a swift return to reality. "I hope you both had a great time." My voice is hoarse as I try not to cry.

"Not really. I broke up with her."

Time stops.

My heart beats deliberately against my ribs, like someone knocking at the door to be let in. "Why?"

He takes another step toward me, backing me up against the brick. We're close enough to touch, but instead he rests his forearm on the wall above my head. "Why do you think, Mars?"

I shake my head, too afraid to hope. If I can write three hundred pages that bleed the same sentiment, he can say it once out loud.

His gaze sharpens. "Because I can't stop thinking about someone else."

My breath turns shallow as his tongue darts across his lower lip. "If her name is Juniper, you should know she doesn't exist."

Amusement ghosts over his features. "And if my name is Fox?" He tips his head lower, until the tip of his nose brushes mine.

"Don't flatter yourself," I murmur.

He laughs softly. "It's always been you, Mars."

"Don't lie." I turn my head; he backs up just enough to give me room to breathe. "Things between us have been different lately. Weird."

He nods. "I had to pull back, because every time I read one of your stories or watched your eyes light up in excitement, I knew I wanted you. It was shitty to Bethany and shitty to you, and I got so fucking sick of myself I could hardly stand it."

I've never been so close to what I want and so scared of having it disappear. "What changed?" My voice shakes in time with my knees.

"I couldn't lie to myself anymore. And you're *brave*, Mars.

You're going to get everything you've ever wanted in life, and I'm . . . what? Not going to be there to see it happen? Too scared of my own feelings to read your book?" He shakes his head. "That's not the guy I want to be."

"Who do you want to be?"

He drags his fingers slowly from my shoulder to my wrist, his hand collecting goose bumps as it moves. "I'll be whatever you want, Mars Darling." Two fingers pause on the inside of my wrist. His mouth hitches up into a wolfish grin as he measures my pulse. "Interesting."

I'm tachycardiac. Drenched in endorphins.

His hand slides to my waist and urges me toward him until our bodies are flush. My breath hitches in disbelief. *This can't be happening*.

His eyelids droop to half-mast, and the aching need in my stomach spreads out, traveling lower. My blood is hot, and my skin is tingling, and if he doesn't kiss me soon, I might collapse. He leans in until our lips are touching. "Admit that I'm Fox."

My eyes are closed, but I feel the smirk against my mouth. I nip his bottom lip with my teeth as he groans. "Never." My fingertips slide over his stomach and up to his chest as I enunciate the word slowly, but I barely get it out before his mouth is on mine, muffling my response. He reaches up to cup my face in his hands, his fingers spread across the sides of my neck and up to my jaw. His lips catch mine, slow and questioning. He inhales through his nose as his chest shudders, and then his tongue sweeps once over my lip before he pulls back. He is completely still, attention rapt as he gauges my reaction.

Desire courses through me, hot and impatient. I need contact. I twist his shirt in my hands and pull him back to me, molding my lips to his. This time, he presses me hard against the wall, pinning me with his hips as he kisses me. His hands slip to my waist, his thumb brushing under the hem of my shirt, and suddenly I need him closer. I open my mouth, and his tongue brushes over mine as I slide my hands up to his jaw, feeling it move as we kiss like we invented it.

This kiss is chaos and fervor and speed, and I can't get enough.

I lose sense of where I am as he rolls his hips against mine, the sensation making starbursts appear behind my eyelids. I arch against him and thread my fingers into his hair, pulling a moan from both our lips. His mouth works its way to my neck, lips traveling greedily over my skin until he finds a spot below my ear that makes me squirm under the heavy weight of him. His hands skirt over my body as we kiss like we're making up for lost time, but I don't even care about any of it. I would do the last three years over the exact same, because it brought us to this moment, with West's hand slipping under my shirt, his fingertips searing the small of my back.

"For a guy who doesn't like PDA, you keep kissing me in public." I gasp as he presses a kiss to the underside of my jaw.

"And for a character who isn't based on me, Fox is a hell of a lot like me," West retorts, his lips turning up into a smile against my mouth. My feet leave the ground, and I scream in surprise as he lifts me up and walks out of our empty courtyard with my legs wrapped around his waist.

"What are you doing?" I laugh until I snort, and West's eyes shine as he grins up at me.

"You don't want me to kiss you in public? Looks like we need to find somewhere more private."

"Now?"

He pauses. "Now. Tomorrow. And the day after that."

I slide through his arms, my curves dragging over his body until my feet touch concrete. "Do you mean it?" I whisper.

West leans down and presses his lips to my forehead before tracing his nose over the length of mine and parting my lips with his tongue. He pulls back, his eyes nearly black. "I'll kiss you for as long as you let me, Mars Darling."

17

Present Day

West pulls a small tool out of his pocket and picks the lock to the food court with a quick flip of his wrist. He opens the door, checks to see if the coast is clear, and then holds it out so I can enter first. I throw him a quizzical look as I slip inside the empty building.

"Um, we're definitely going to talk about why you carry a lockpick," I whisper.

"Up there," he says, pointing toward a staircase leading to the second level. We pass a handful of fast-casual restaurants, all of them locked up for the night, and take the stairs in silence.

The top level is an open cafeteria, and West strides confidently across the tile floor. He hops over the stainless steel counter with the remembered ease of a former employee.

"What are you doing?" I whisper as he fiddles with the buttons on a large machine. He ducks under the counter, tears open a bag, and pours it into the top.

"No one is going to hear us," he says at full volume. The machine hums to life, and West turns to me, satisfied. "Fifteen minutes until soft serve."

"They sell soft serve on University."

"Bougie stuff that comes in flavors like charcoal and mocha."

"I like mocha."

He shakes his head in mock disappointment. "Who are you, and what have you done with Mars?"

"You're not the only one who's changed," I say. I hop onto the counter and scoot to the ledge, crossing one knee over the other, once again wondering why my dress is so short. It feels like the hemline shrinks another inch every time West's eyes slide to my thighs. Now, though, his attention is squarely on my face as he leans against the counter across from me and crosses his ankles. His corded forearms are too visible in the dim light. I feel vaguely like I've been abducted from my own life and dropped into an alternate reality.

I clear my throat. West's face is impassive. I don't want to be the one to break the silence, but neither does he. I tilt my head, and he matches the gesture, his lifted brow the only testament to his burning curiosity. I can't help but wonder how long he can last. My twisted mind picks up the innuendo in that thought, and I flush molten hot.

"Fine, you win." I lift my hands in surrender.

"Were we playing a *game*, Darling?" His tone betrays the smirk lying beneath neutral features.

I hum noncommittally.

His hands grip the countertop, fingers twitching with the restrained urge to drum them against steel. My eyes travel up his arms to his face, where he's staring at me hard.

He's dying to say something. I can read his restraint in every muscle.

"Just spit it out, West."

He presses his tongue to the inside of his cheek—his thinking face—and I wonder if he's sorting through his options, deciding between the hundreds of things he wants to say.

Or maybe that's just me.

"You were blushing a minute ago. Why?"

I swallow heavily. "It's hot in here."

He huffs a laugh that sounds like frustration. "You've always been a bad liar."

"I wish I could say the same about you," I say, my tongue lazy in my mouth.

His smirk slips sideways, his mouth flattening into a hard line. "Why did you read that passage from my book?"

My shoulders relax. An easy one. "To piss you off."

"Because you still hate me."

"Yes," I say, a bit too late to be convincing.

"Even after reading it."

I roll my eyes. I'm not nineteen anymore. I'm not going to fall in love with him because of a few pretty words on a page. "You haven't given me a reason not to."

He searches my expression for the lie and doesn't find it. He nods slowly, pain flashing in his eyes.

The timer dings. West shakes himself out of his trance and rifles through shelves until he reappears with two spoons and a giant bowl. He pulls the lever on the soft-serve machine and fills the bowl with chocolate-and-vanilla swirl. It's lopsided and near collapse, like a mountain in a Dr. Seuss book. He presents it to me with a self-directed grimace. Off-kilter due to his proximity and resigned by way of sugar, I exhale the very last of my fight. It's a losing battle, anyway, when he's determined to be kind.

"Losing your touch," I say as I lean in for the first bite of his messy creation.

He swats my spoon away with his. "Patience, Darling," he admonishes. Reaching under the counter, he produces a ten-pound bag of chocolate sprinkles.

"I forgot about these!"

West looks smug as he shakes them over the top before looking to me for approval.

"More."

He doubles the number of sprinkles and wordlessly pushes the bowl toward me.

"I still don't see why we couldn't have purchased soft serve like the non-felons we are." I dip the spoon into the bowl and bring it to my mouth, flipping it so the cold ice cream lands on my tongue. I groan in surprise. "Never mind. You're right. This is what soft serve should be."

The ice cream slips down my throat, and I feel a sick swoop of nostalgia that makes my eyes burn. I can't count the number of swirl cones I ate in my four years here. Breakfast, lunch, dinner, the memories all mixed up with my memories of West. Objectively, I've had better desserts. But this one is my favorite.

West ducks his head, a self-satisfied smirk playing at the corner of his lips. He digs his spoon into the bowl and comes away with a large bite.

"If you did this to prove to me that Tucson is better than New York . . ." I trail off, unsure how to end my sentence.

He leans a hip against the counter's edge. "Why would I need to do that?" He closes his lips indecently around a large spoonful.

Blood rushes feverishly to my cheeks, and I have to look away. "It's no contest."

"I agree."

I drag my spoon through the ice cream to avoid looking at him. "I haven't been back since graduation—" I wince at my own mistake and push forward, hoping he doesn't notice. "This city feels like another lifetime. I don't know how you can live here without constant reminders." My face flushes again, and I wonder why I'm dancing so close to topics I'd rather avoid.

"Who says I do?"

My eyes snap up to his, and *oh no*, have we been this close this whole time? He's leaning sideways against the edge of the counter I'm sitting on, his body fully turned to face me, and his hips are inches from my crossed knees. I swallow and see his eyes track the movement. My eyes fall to his lips, a spoon dangling loosely from them, then his hands. His fingers rest on the counter, dangerously close to my thighs. We're not touching, but I've never been so *aware* of not touching someone. The absence of it is nearly corporeal.

As if reading my thoughts, West pushes away. He takes the empty bowl and holds it up expectantly. I blink at him. He reaches across my lap to gently pry the spoon from my clenched fist before turning around, and I watch the muscles under his shirt stretch and tighten as he washes the dishes.

When all traces of us have been erased, West dries his hands on his jeans and turns to face me once again. "Time to get you home for real."

With proper breathing air between us now, I can think clearly. "I'll go alone. I'm totally sobered up, and I could walk that route with my eyes closed."

"You think so?" He rakes an unsure hand through his curls, and I realize he's torn. He wants to be a gentleman, but he'll let me leave if I don't want him around.

"Maybe not. I've forgotten some things." I surprise myself with the lie. As hard as I've tried to forget, this campus is spilled across my memory like permanent ink. Even with the vast benevolence of thirty-six inches of space in which to make good decisions, I don't want to walk home alone.

West narrows his eyes, curiosity warring with doubt. "I bet you didn't forget the library," he says.

I remember hands in my hair. My spine against a bookshelf. His tongue on my neck.

A beat passes. "Because you were always writing," he adds.

"Not always," I protest.

"You were single-minded."

"I was fun!"

The lines around his eyes crinkle when he laughs. I like it more than I should. "You know you're fun when you have to say it out loud."

I childishly kick my feet in annoyance, knocking them back against the shelves, sending a metal bowl clattering to the floor. I lean forward, but West touches me just above the knee, wordlessly stilling my movement.

The sensation registers between my thighs.

A bad idea, this dress. It's tricked my libido into thinking this is a date.

He bends down and returns the bowl to its place, and when he stands up, he's positioned between my knees. My dress is criminally short. If I move closer, he'd be between my bare thighs. A bolt of repressed heat shoots through me.

His eyes are intense as they sweep over my face. They trace the outline of my mouth before dipping lower and then back up again. If he's as surprised as I am, it doesn't show.

There's a cacophony happening inside me. All the warning bells are blaring: a five-alarm fire. Without permission from my brain, my body inches toward him. His hands relax heavily on my upper thighs, his fingertips lightly brushing the hem of my dress.

I nearly stop breathing. His expression is so clear I can practically hear him.

Your move, Darling.

I glance down and see a hard swell against his jeans. Heat blooms in my belly and spreads out. Into my chest, making it burn. Below my waist, making me ache. I'm jittery and nervous and lightheaded. If he weren't pinning me to this counter, who knows what I would have done by now. Hooked my leg around his. Slid myself to the edge of the counter until I felt him pressed against my inner thighs. My thoughts run wild, and I fear that they're all over my face.

West's throat works, his gaze as steady as his hands. I can feel him inside my head. He knows exactly what I want.

My throat goes dry. "Admit it, West. Sometimes I was fun."

He leans so close I feel the scrape of whiskers against my jaw. "You were more than fun, Mars." He moves slowly, pauses. His hands tighten on my thighs—a question. I tilt my head, and he presses a kiss under my ear, right where he knows I like it. Fire licks down my spine. "You were the best fucking thing about this town," he whispers, scattering goose bumps across my skin.

I skim my shaking hands up his arms and take a deep breath. If I turn to the side, even an inch, he'll kiss me.

He's in my head again. *Your move, Darling.* It's shocking that after all this time, I still know him so well. Like fluency in a dead language.

I bite my bottom lip and consider my options, thinking about what could be waiting for me on the other side of a kiss. But then he exhales a hot breath against my ear, the sound misting through me, and I'm adrift, swept up in his tide; it no longer feels like a choice.

My nose brushes against his whiskered jaw as I turn and press my lips to his. Something deep in my chest shifts and unlocks. We're both unmoving; it's hardly even a kiss yet. It feels more like a return.

There you are, I think.

What took us so long? his mouth says in return.

We're still motionless, but his lips are warm and soft, and his kiss is resolved. Like kissing me is a decision he made once and never looked back from.

Stunned by the implication, I gasp. His tongue presses against mine, his mouth pulling oxygen from between my teeth. His hand leaves my thigh, and once again, the absence of him is physical, but then it threads through my hair and tilts my jaw up to give him a better angle. His hair tickles my forehead, and I want to brush it back, want to grab it between my fingers, want to touch him in so many places, but he is everywhere, crowding me, surrounding me, taking control of this kiss, which I hadn't planned to want but am desperate to continue. He's broader and stronger than the last time we were this close. I can't think. Can hardly breathe as his lips work over mine.

Kissing the man in front of me contains shades of our history but is also completely different and infinitely better than it once was. Heat rushes to my core, pulsing painfully. A tangled frisson of pleasure and desire weaves under my skin, remaking me into a new version of myself. Building me a different set of bones.

The sensation of his tongue on my lips and my teeth and my neck is the most catastrophic thing I've ever felt. If I had the capacity to think, I'd realize that I'm careening toward ruin.

There's a buzz against metal, sending my thoughts ricocheting in every direction. I wrench away from him, and we both look down, our breaths jagged and desperate. The noise is coming from his phone, in his front pocket, pressed against the edge of the counter.

"Answer it," I say. I need a minute to catch my breath. To *think*.

West adjusts himself with a wince and reads the text. As he's reading, his phone buzzes again. He looks at the caller and I catch a glimpse of the ID photo—she's smiling, she's gorgeous.

My new bones crumble to dust, carried away with the breeze.

He grimaces. "Sorry, I have to take this. I'm really sorry."

"It's fine." I barely choke the words out as I scoot back and cross my legs. My dress slides up. I tug it down, mortified.

"Everything okay?" West says into the phone.

I hear a woman's voice on the other end of the line, but it's too faint for me to decipher what she's saying. I tilt my head closer, shameless. I hear a string of swear words, but the voice doesn't sound upset. If this is West's girlfriend, she probably doesn't know that I just felt his erection against my leg. That I could look at it now, if I wanted to. (*I don't want to!*)

"Yeah. Mm-hmm. Call if you need anything. Don't forget to send a pic." He ends the call and slides his phone in his back pocket. Whatever *pic* she's sending, he's saving it for later.

"That was my sister," he says quickly, and I delete the sarcastic remark about nudes from the tip of my tongue.

"Gabbi? Little foul-mouthed Gabbi?" I reach my hand into his back pocket and grab his phone. West watches with amusement. "How old is she? I want to see a picture!" He unlocks it and swipes through recent photos, showing me a stunning young woman with dark skin and curly hair.

I snatch the phone out of his hands to inspect it closely. "Wow. She's gorgeous!" I place his phone on the counter. "It sounds like you two are close now?"

He nods. "We got closer when we were both on the East Coast; I talked so much about this place that she decided to come."

I shake my head in awe. He really did it. He became the man he didn't think he could be. "It's a good thing you came back, isn't it?" I ask quietly.

His face is full of feelings, but this time, I'm not sure which ones. He dips his chin in silent confirmation. "I have regrets. That's not one of them."

He opens his mouth to speak again, and I panic about the potential destination of this conversation.

"What's Gabbi up to these days?"

"She's an undergrad. Engineering major. *So* smart. She gives me shit constantly—"

"I bet you deserve it," I cut in.

His mouth quirks up fondly. "I'm sure I do. She has a date tonight. Some guy from an app. She called to tell me where they're meeting, what they plan to do for the evening. She'll send me a picture of his ID and let him know that her older brother will hunt him down if necessary."

I *knew* he looked like a hit man. "What better way to scare off creeps than to threaten them with her six-foot-four, problematically jacked older brother?"

I've never been so thankful for the full moon shining through the window, because it means I get to see West blush. "What's problematic about the way I look?"

"You look like you belong on an oil rig, not behind a typewriter."

"You know I don't use a typewriter, right?" He's gorgeously indignant, his eyebrows a dark slash, his curls a work of art. I should have written them into my book. They deserve to be memorialized.

"I know when you're lying, Virginia."

"Virginia?"

"You changed *my* nickname," I challenge.

"That one's just bad, though."

"What about West Nile Virus?"

"What about no."

"WestJet? North West?"

He cocks an eyebrow. "Wild Wild West."

I pretend to gag.

He rolls his eyes. "I *used* to own a typewriter, but I left it in New York when I escaped Dimes Square."

I put my hand on his forearm. "*Oh my gosh*, can we talk about that whole situation?"

He recoils at the thought. "Too soon."

"The Doc Martens–to-typewriter pipeline is undeniable. It's your Tumblr culture."

West barks a surprised laugh, and my mood soars. I retreat from the touchy subject of our past and return to safer ground.

"Gabbi does sound smart. Taking pictures of their IDs and all," I say.

"Don't tell me you date *without* doing that." His tone is full of disapproval.

"Dating in New York is . . ." I trail off, unsure how to describe the hellish, postapocalyptic landscape of NYC dating apps, where no one ever gets together, because the promise of someone hotter, smarter, and richer is only a swipe away. "Let's just say I've been off the apps for a while. I prefer to meet men the old-fashioned way."

"Such as?"

Falling in love with him at nineteen, letting that relationship ruin your life, and never getting over it.

"To be determined."

"Well, if you ever get back on the apps, you can send me pictures of your dates. I'll threaten them, too."

I huff a laugh. "Funny thing to say for a guy who just had his tongue in my mouth."

West scrutinizes my face, but in a different way than he did earlier. Before, I knew he wanted me. Now he looks calculating. Assessing.

I shrug out of his jacket and shove it back into his hands, feeling stupidly transparent. I cross my arms over my chest. I've written enough love scenes to know when the moment has passed; if West wanted to kiss me again, he wouldn't be mentally sending me on dates with random dudes.

I'm an idiot, and I should have known.

"Um, thanks for the ice cream, I guess. I'll walk the rest of the way on my own." I tuck my hair behind my ears and slide off the counter.

He steps closer, crowding me until my ass hits metal. "Don't leave. We still need to talk."

I roll my eyes. "I must have misunderstood what we've been doing all night."

His grips the counter in frustration. His phone screen illuminates, the vibration rattling against steel.

I don't mean to look, and I *certainly* don't mean to read the notification on West's lock screen, but it's second nature: Hear a phone buzz, look toward the sound. When my eyes land on the name of the sender, the air seeps from my lungs.

In a blink, I digest the subject of the email. It's only three words, but it snaps me back to reality. Like waking up from hypnosis.

Noon on Sunday?

A shock runs through me. "I'm an idiot."

"Mars, no."

I step around him, too stunned to speak. "You're speaking with *her* this weekend? That's not a coincidence. It can't be." I glare at him, daring him to contradict what I already know is true.

West hesitates, a wolf caught in a trap.

I let out a disbelieving laugh. "I can't believe I thought you changed. I can't believe I *kissed* you!" His expression flickers to one I recognize but can't name. "Don't follow me." I turn on my heel to do the thing I should have done an hour ago—*run*.

West's voice trails after me, but I don't stop until I'm safely off campus and away from our memories.

For one shining, nostalgic hour, I tricked myself into thinking that West and I could outrun the things we did to each other, but I was wrong. It won't happen, and I was a fool to believe it could.

It's only later, while I'm staring at the ceiling of my hotel room, that I put a name to the emotion on West's face as I fled.

Heartsick.

I could weep for the irony of it, but I don't. Instead, I laugh as tears run sideways down my cheeks, mad as hell that I can't tell the only other person who would understand the joke.

18

10 Years Ago
Senior Year, Second Semester

It's official; I have an agent for my West-inspired faerie novel. (Weeks later, my face still flames with embarrassment when I think of the Fox-West parallels. West's ego has never been bigger. It's a fantastic disaster. An absolutely humiliating dream come true.) In the span of one month, I went from an *aspiring* writer to an *agented* one. Danielle is smart, experienced, and almost as obsessed with Juniper and Fox as I am.

When I finish my revisions based on her notes, she plans to send the book to every major publisher in New York. No sale is ever guaranteed, but her confidence makes it hard to keep my hopes from spiraling wildly out of control. It starts with daydreams about book signings and launch parties and hitting bestseller lists and ends with me booking plane tickets to New York. Sure, I *can* be a writer from anywhere, but if Hannah Horvath taught me anything, it's that grad school sucks, and why would you live in the Midwest when you could live in Brooklyn instead?

It's almost midnight, and my heart is racing when the train

spits West and me out into Penn Station. I'm hopped up on Red Bull, disgusting airplane coffee, and the incomparable high of blasting "Welcome to New York" through my headphones as the city came into view. We drag our suitcases up the steps and emerge into a cold night in Midtown. It's spring break in Arizona, but it still feels like winter here. Goose bumps race across my bare legs, and my breath puffs in front of me.

I glance at West as he messes with the strap of his bag, swearing lightly under his breath as he struggles with it. He's finally letting his hair grow out, and the East Coast humidity has unearthed a loose curl above his ear. The urge to run my fingers through it is stronger than ever, and my head feels a little buzzy. After so many years of schooling my heart and my hands into submission around him, it's wild to know that I can touch him whenever I want.

My eyes trail from his stern profile to the busy midnight street, and cold spring air expands like champagne bubbles in my chest, fizzing with the promise of dreams I've been carrying for more than half my life.

"You ready?" I ask.

He slings his bag over his shoulder and nods. "How do we get to the hotel? Cab? Subway?" He surveys the dark street with wide, apprehensive eyes. West has never been to New York, and I plan to wield my vast experience over his head. (I spent four days here with my family the summer before fifth grade. If West needs to know what the inside of the Statue of Liberty looks like, I'm his girl.)

I bounce on the balls of my feet to stay warm. "We walk."

He drops his arm around my shoulder and rubs his hand against my skin to warm me up. We walk a few blocks to a Koreatown hotel wedged between a liquor store and a hair salon, and

I've never felt as grown-up as I do standing at a hotel check-in counter with my boyfriend. The moment West palms the room key, however, my nerves catch up with me. He might be a New York virgin, but I'm an *actual* virgin, and this week we'll be staying together, in a hotel room, in the same *bed*.

I didn't set out to be a twenty-two-year-old who has never had sex, but it never felt right with anyone else. (Likely because I was in love with West. Obvious only in hindsight, if you can believe it.) It's been about a month since West kissed me in our spot outside Modern Languages, and it's getting harder and harder to say goodbye when he pulls himself out of my arms at night. Until now, we've been taking our time, tiptoeing over lines that were once carefully drawn, finding new places to touch, new ways to make each other gasp.

We come to a stop in front of a door, and I take a deep breath, knowing that I'm finally ready. West grins down at me like there's a thought bubble above my head, tucks one finger into the waistband of my jeans, and pulls me in to him. I blush hot, and he sweeps his thumbs over my heated cheekbones before trailing a familiar path over my mole, across my jaw, down the side of my neck. I turn my head to press a kiss to the inside of his wrist. Eyes shining bright, he swipes the key card to unlock our room. I push the door open in anticipation and dissolve in a fit of laughter.

It's so tiny that West could stand in the center and touch both walls, but that's not what gets me.

He follows me into the room with a strangled groan. "Bunk beds?"

We stand in front of the rickety furniture and eye each other warily. We might need to rethink our plans. I don't even know if we can both *fit* in one of those beds.

"They really said if we're going to pay like broke college students, we're going to sleep like broke college students."

"To be fair, some of us are broke college *dropouts*," West deadpans as he places his duffel bag on the floor. My stomach tightens at the remark.

"Well, in a couple of months, we'll both be broke, and college won't have mattered at all."

"You're about to sell your book for a million dollars, but okay."

I roll my eyes. "No one gets million-dollar book deals."

West slants his eyebrows. "You sure about that?"

"Fine, *almost* no one, and definitely not me."

He crosses his arms and leans against the post of the bunk bed with a sardonic smile. "I can't wait to say I told you so. Top or bottom?" he asks, changing the subject so abruptly that my mind returns to the daydreams I was having in the hall.

"What?"

"Top or bottom?" he asks again slowly, one side of his mouth curling up. "Where do you want to sleep?"

My cheeks flush. "Top."

"Perfect. This arrangement will be good inspiration for you," he says, his eyes glinting in the dim light.

I smell a setup. "How so?"

"You can start planning book two while you're lying in bed, staring at the ceiling, pining for me."

"I hate you."

His smirk transforms into a wide grin as he pulls me into his arms. I yelp in surprise when he cuts me off by planting a kiss on my lips, and my embarrassment melts into desire.

As he pulls away, I nip his bottom lip with my teeth. "You'll be the one dreaming of me," I joke.

He looks at me through half-moon eyes, which makes my

throat dry. "I always do, Jupiter." He kisses my forehead and then leans toward the window to pull back the curtain. "Check it out."

I stand over an ancient radiator, and my breath fogs the glass as I stare at the glittering Empire State Building. "Should we go out?" It's late, but we're still on Pacific time, and I'm so loaded with adrenaline that I don't think I could sleep in these shitty bunk beds if my life depended on it.

West wraps his arms around me from behind and rests his chin on the top of my head. "Sure. This is your trip, I'm just along for the ride."

I frown. I don't want him to think of it like that. I want him to *want* to be here. I crane my neck back to look at him. "What do you think of New York so far?"

He nudges my face back to the window, and I watch his eyebrows raise in the reflection of the glass. "I think I need to see it before I form an opinion, but I'm not worried. If you love it, I'll love it."

I spin in his arms and peer up at him. "Do you mean it?"

His eyes heat as he tucks a lock of hair behind my ear and cinches me tighter against his chest. He opens his mouth, grimaces, closes it again. "All these years later, I still have a hard time finding the right words around you," he says, an edge of frustration bleeding through.

"What do you mean?"

He rubs the back of his neck. Looking at war with himself as he considers what to say, he finally reaches a détente. "I hope you get everything you've ever wanted, Mars, starting with New York."

I wrap my arms around his neck and tug until his lips are on mine. The kiss surprises him, and we're both knocked off balance, stumbling sideways. I grab his shoulders and pull him again, harder this time, until we're lying flush against each other on the bottom bunk, his body pressing into mine. He shifts until his weight is half-balanced on the mattress, one leg thrown over mine, pinning me with his hips. He bends his head and kisses me with brain-melting, aching slowness, but after several hazy, lazy minutes, I am unmoored with want. His unhurried, careful, exploratory kisses aren't nearly enough. I need all of him, right now.

"I'm ready," I whisper against his lips.

He pulls back in surprise. "What?"

"I'm ready," I say again as I reach for his belt buckle.

"Now?" He looks slightly horrified.

"Now," I confirm as I slide his belt out of his pants. I drop it to the floor and reach for his button.

His eyes rove over the walls of the dingy room, halting on the bunk bed only a foot above his head. "Here?" he asks weakly. "I wanted something less . . . dreary than this for you. For us." If I weren't horizontal, the rasp in his voice would have buckled my knees.

"West," I say, drawing his attention back to me. "Are you really going to make me say it again?"

His pupils grow, black swallowing amber, and his careful restraint snaps. He presses his thigh up between my legs and rocks into me, overwhelming me with the exquisite gift of friction. My eyelids flutter shut as he parts my lips with an insistent tongue and presses his body into mine, bracketing my head with his forearms. "One day," he says, peppering me with frenzied kisses between each word, "I'll find the right words."

I take his face in my hands and pull his mouth reluctantly from my collarbone. "Sometimes words aren't enough," I say, hoping he comprehends what I mean. I don't need him to say the perfect thing, because I already know. As he presses his forehead to mine, I think he understands. I lift my arms as he pulls my shirt over my head, and we spend the rest of the night trying to tell each other how we feel without ever saying anything at all.

On our second full day in New York, West uses my phone to take my photo under the elm trees at the Central Park Literary Walk. As I scroll through the hundreds of nearly identical pictures, I try to imagine my face on the inside of a book jacket. I'm smiling so hard I look like I've got a secret that I'm bursting to tell, and with the golden-hour sun on my face, you'd never know that I was shivering the whole time.

"How'd I do?" West asks, blowing into his hands to warm them up while I survey his work.

I delete a handful of pictures that really emphasize the vein in my forehead and keep scrolling. "If this writing thing doesn't work out, you can become my full-time Instagram boyfriend." I maximize a photo where the breeze has picked my hair up just right and save it in my favorites.

"How long do we have until we meet your agent?" he asks in a tight voice. He's stuffed his hands in his pockets, and his nose is turning red. We need something warmer if we're going to survive the rest of the trip.

We have a couple of hours before drinks with Danielle, so we kill two birds with one stone by walking to Times Square and finding a gift shop with cheap hoodies. West clasps my hand in his as we walk, and while I chatter about the cute shops and my favorite neighborhoods and how if I moved here, I'd have to buy a whole new wardrobe, West is quieter than usual. He doesn't say more than a few words until we pass a piercing and tattoo shop advertising a flash tattoo event. "Remember when you got your nose pierced on our first date?" he asks as he draws us to a stop in front of the window.

I touch the ring in my nose as I smile up at him. "You consider that night our first date?"

"Obviously." West's eyes darken with the twilight sky. "Do you remember what we did in the library?"

I press my cold hands to my warm cheeks. "I still don't think you can call that our first date."

"Why not?"

"Because it took you two and a half years to ask me out again."

He rolls his eyes. "And whose fault was that?"

"*Beth*-any's," I declare with a grin, unable to stop myself.

West laughs, but then his smile fades as his eyes rove over my face like he's trying to memorize the pink tint dusting my cheeks.

"Any particular reason you're thinking about that night?" I prod.

He runs his fingers through his hair with a sigh. "School's almost over, and, I dunno, I'm upset about all the time that we missed."

"What are you talking about? We have nothing *but* time," I insist, although the future is looming in front of us, wild and heavy, hard to ignore and even harder to see. We don't talk about the specifics of it.

He drums his fingers on his thigh, looking more nervous than I've ever seen him. "Maybe."

I wonder if he knows that I'm in love with him. We haven't

said it yet, and this moment doesn't seem like the right time. But I want him to know that I'm all in. I don't know how to picture a future without West.

"Let's get tattoos!" I point to the flash designs in the window, my finger landing on a small orange surrounded by flower blossoms. "It's kismet." All of campus smelled like orange blossoms on the night of our first kiss, and now I can't think of anything else when I smell them.

West narrows his eyes. "Aren't matching tattoos bad luck? What if you break up with me?"

"Please." It's my turn to roll my eyes. "If you break up with me, I'm going to have bigger problems than an orange tattoo."

"Such as?"

"Such as a character known as Fox Caldwell, remember him? I still have at least two books to write, and I need the inspiration, so you're stuck with me." I nudge him playfully to distract myself from the painful thought of losing him. "Not to mention I'd be devastated."

His eyes bore into mine, steady but wary. "Me, too."

I pull open the door to the tattoo shop, and an hour later we walk out with orange blossoms on our inner forearms. I can't help but stare at mine as we walk side by side in the dark, and I like how permanent it feels.

West hates Times Square. He doesn't say it, but he scowls as we shoulder our way through the crowds and moves closer to me, his fingers tightening on my waist every time we nearly collide with other tourists.

"I think most New Yorkers avoid Times Square at all costs," I shout to be heard over a band of street performers. I wonder if he picks up the subtext beneath my words: If I lived here—if *we* lived here—we wouldn't be tourists anymore. Over the last forty-eight hours, I've been unable to stop myself from imagining a life here. Every coffee shop we pass could be the one where I write the sequel to my book. Every train stop could be *my* stop. It feels like a puzzle piece clicking into place.

"I can see why" is all West says, and my heart dips. We stop for a selfie and get scammed into tipping five dollars to an unknown character who photobombed us. Minutes later we come face-to-face with a wall of I ♥ NY merch, and West's scowl deepens as he dons his new beanie and gloves. "We look like a gift shop threw up on us."

"We look hilarious. Danielle's going to laugh." I glance at my phone, looking for the fastest train to take us to the Lower East Side.

"Are you sure it's not weird for me to be there?"

"Why would it be weird?"

He pinches the bridge of his nose. "Because I'm not her client."

"I told her you're coming, and she said it was fine," I say, regretting it instantly. "More than fine. She's excited to meet you!"

"I'm worried I'll feel out of place," he confides, which is exactly what I've been trying to avoid. "I can hang out here until you're done." He gestures to the famous red stairs in the center of the square, and I know instinctively that if he sits here for the rest of the evening, his opinion of the city will have fallen into hell by the time I return.

"I *want* you there," I say. He presses his lips together, thinking. "I always want you where I am," I tell him seriously.

"That might not always be possible," he says, as if my skin isn't still sore from my fresh tattoo, as if we didn't just do something to permanently cement our relationship. He shakes his head like he's shrugging off a bad thought. "Ignore me. I'm coming. I can't wait to meet Danielle."

"West's a writer, too!" I tell Danielle an hour later as we sit in a booth, an expensive and foreign cocktail in front of me. The dark and bustling bar has an industrial feel. The walls are exposed brick, and pipes and beams are visible where the ceiling should be.

"Barely," West says quickly before taking a big gulp of his soda.

Danielle is shorter than I expected—barely five feet—with a mane of curly brown hair. Her size and Southern accent are immediately disarming, and I can see why her other clients refer to her as a "shark in disguise." She is charming and friendly, and after the past few months of phone calls and emails, we fall into an easy conversation about my book, how excited she is to submit it to publishers, and her recommendations for the best pizza in the city. West has been polite but uncharacteristically quiet, and he's resisted all my attempts to pull him into the conversation.

"He's being modest, but he's an *incredible* writer," I tell Danielle.

"What do you write?" Danielle asks him.

"Nothing worth talking about," West says quickly. Under the table, I nudge him with my foot. He shifts in his seat. "Fiction. Um . . . literary, I guess." He grimaces, and I feel a twinge of annoyance. Writers pay good money for the opportunity to pitch their books in person, and he's wasting this chance.

I shoot him a curious look before turning back to Danielle.

"He blurs the line between fantasy and reality in a really beautiful way that always leaves you guessing what's real."

West fixes his eyes on the table, and I remember how uncomfortable he gets talking about his own stuff. Luckily, I'm here and can do it for him.

"His writing inspires mine so much. I can't even tell you how good he is. He was always the best in our writing classes."

"Do you have a manuscript?" Danielle asks.

West clears his throat. "I've been working on something, yeah. It's sort of like a coming-of-age thing."

"I'd love to read it when it's ready," Danielle says, and I nearly jump out of my seat in excitement.

He looks stricken by the offer. "Oh. Um, thank you, but no," he says abruptly. I shoot him a look. *Why is he being so rude?*

"I mean, it's not even close to being done. I'm not as fast as Mars," West adds.

"When you are, it's a standing offer," Danielle says. I squeeze his hand under the table. He takes another long drink. Danielle flashes me a hesitant smile, and I force one in return. This is not going at all how I thought it would.

"How are you liking New York?" she asks West, trying again to make friendly conversation.

"I don't think it's for me," he says bluntly.

"It's not for everyone," she says diplomatically. "Fortunately, you can be a writer from anywhere. I have a client who lives in Noorvik, Alaska. We've sold three books together, but she's never once stepped foot in New York."

"Lucky her," West says flatly.

Danielle raises her eyebrows at me, and my stomach squirms in embarrassment. She excuses herself to use the restroom. When she's out of earshot, I turn to West.

"What is your problem?"

"What do you mean?"

"You're being rude to Danielle!"

"Why do you care?"

I grit my teeth in frustration. It's not like him to be purposely obtuse. "Her opinion is important to me."

"And she likes *you*. Who cares what she thinks of me?"

"I do. I vouched for your book, and you're acting like you're too good for her request."

"I didn't ask you to vouch for me!" he snaps.

I draw back, shocked by his sudden burst of uncharacteristic anger. "I don't understand what's happening right now," I say. My chest is tight, and I feel the familiar, awful sensation of burning tears. I blink up at the ceiling and pray that Danielle doesn't come back for a long time.

"I'm gonna go," West says.

"What?"

"I'll wait in the bookstore across the street. Come find me when you're done." He takes a final swig of his soda, thumps it down on the table, and stalks out of the bar.

I lie to Danielle and tell her that West had to take an important phone call outside, and even though it's obvious I'm lying, she glosses right over it, and we chat for another thirty minutes before saying goodbye. I text West to meet me at the nearest subway stop, and as he approaches me with his hands in his pockets and his head down (I 🥨 NY announcing his arrival from a hundred yards away), I fight another wave of tears, confused about how we went from matching tattoos to utter disaster in the course of one evening.

"Hey," West says dully as he comes to a stop in front of me.

"*Hey.*" If it's possible to make a single syllable sarcastic, I've done it.

The glow of the streetlight illuminates his defeated posture. "I'm sorry I ruined your night."

"What the hell happened back there?"

"I don't need your pity," he says.

"Good, because you don't have it."

He sighs, looking frustrated. "I mean it, Mars. I don't want you to bullshit your agent and say things about my writing that you don't mean."

"I didn't."

He scoffs. "One minute, I'm destined to be your Instagram boyfriend 'if this writing thing doesn't work out,' and the next, you're acting like I'm Jonathan Safran Foer. Which is it?"

"First, that was a joke. Second, I wasn't talking about you! I was saying if writing doesn't work out *for me*."

"It *is* working out for you! You're going to sell your books and move to New York and be wildly successful, and you'll deserve it, and I'll be happy for you."

"But?"

He sighs, a puff of breath appearing in the cold air. "*But* I don't know if that's in the cards for me."

"Says who?"

"Look at my life, Mars. I'm from a small town no one's ever heard of, I'm a college dropout, and my family has no money for me to fall back on if I go out into the world and fail."

"Why do you think that you're going to fail?"

He starts to speak but cuts himself off with an aggravated sigh as he scuffs the toe of his sneaker against the ground. Finally, he straightens his shoulders and looks me in the eye.

"You're moving here after graduation, aren't you?" It's not an accusation, exactly, but somehow it feels like one.

"I haven't decided yet," I say, tasting the lie for what it is. I hadn't fully admitted it to myself yet, but I think a part of me knew that I'd be moving here ever since I booked my plane ticket.

"Yeah, you have. I can see it in your eyes."

"Yeah, I have," I admit.

West nods, and I suddenly understand what he meant earlier about wasted time. He thinks moving to New York means the end of us. I step toward him and wrap my arms around his neck. He eyes me warily, but I hold his gaze steadily until his expression softens, and he snakes his own arm around my waist and pulls me tight against him. He closes his eyes and presses his lips to my temple.

My heart plays a staccato rhythm in my chest. "I'm in love with you, in case you didn't know."

I feel his nerves as he swallows. "That's convenient, given the tattoos. I've heard they're a bitch to remove."

I make a noise of protest and try to pull out of his arms. He cinches them tighter and tilts my chin until my eyes meet his. His expression is soft, if a little scared. "It's also convenient because I'm wildly in love with you, and I'd rather not return to my emo phase."

My heart explodes. I nearly laugh. I'm *so* happy.

He kisses me. It's slow until it's not, tender until the heat of our argument turns it into a deep, hard kiss that leaves us both blinking stars out of our eyes at the end of it.

I swallow, steeling myself for a moment of bravery. "I want you to move here with me."

"What would I do in New York?" he asks wryly, a smile playing at the corner of his lips.

"Hang out with me."

He raises his eyebrows and runs his hand down my back, tucking it into my jeans pocket, giving my ass a squeeze. "How will that pay rent?"

"I don't know," I say truthfully. "We'll be baristas or servers or bartenders or whatever it takes until someone pays us to write. We'll be poor until we're not, and it won't matter, because we'll be here together. With proper coats, away from Times Square." I tug his beanie over his eyes, which makes him laugh, and then he tries blindly to kiss me again. I laugh and squirm away as he pushes the beanie out of his eyes.

He grins at me, the planes of his face awash with affection. "Okay, Jupiter. Let's move to New York."

19

Present Day

Daphne knocks on my hotel room door with Cafe Maggie coffee in one hand and a bag of croissants in the other. Against all odds, she's wearing yesterday's crochet project. "Would you believe me if I told you I saw a dead body on campus this morning?"

"I'm going to need the coffee." I reach for the cup as she breezes past me and paces the room. "Start from the beginning." It's barely seven a.m., and I slept like shit.

"My presentation is in two hours, and I want to talk about starting your book with a strong hook."

"And telling everyone you saw a dead body will be *your* strong hook?"

"I'll come in a few minutes late, crying hysterically, stumble to the microphone, and yell that someone needs to call the police." She pauses for dramatic effect. "Too much?"

"Depends, are you a good actor?" I take a sip of my drink, and my eyes widen in surprise.

"Peanut butter mocha," Daphne says by way of explanation.

"The pretty barista talked me into it. But to answer your question, I played Satine in my college's production of *Moulin Rouge!*, *and* I can cry on demand."

"Then you have to do it."

She sits on the still-made bed next to mine and bites into a croissant. "How was last night?"

"A shit show."

Her face falls. "I should have been there."

I shake my head, letting her off the hook. "It's not your fault; it's *his*. I just— I really— He's so— *Why* do I keep giving him the opportunity to hurt me?" I fumble my way through the question, my once-strong command of the English language nowhere to be found.

Her mouth opens in a small O of surprise. "West?"

"Who else?"

"He hurt you?" Seeing my pointed stare, she amends her question. "*Recently?*" Daphne studies me curiously before straightening and brushing croissant crumbs off her lap. "What happened? Start at the beginning, and don't leave anything out."

I drop my head into my hands, unsure if I have the emotional wherewithal to recount the circumstances that led from the bar to soft serve covered in sprinkles to my knees around West's waist and my dignity in tatters. "It was bad, and then it was . . . surprising, and then it was *horrible*."

She squeezes my hand gently. "I know you hate exposition, but I do need more than that."

"He wore a Fox Caldwell T-shirt to the bar."

She sits back in surprise. "Huh."

"I expected a little more righteous indignation."

She shrugs. "Couldn't that have been his way of, I don't know, being supportive?"

"He was screwing with me."

"Like you're screwing with him?"

"Why are you defending him?"

"I'm not. What happened next?"

"As payback for the shirt, I read a passage from his book at the open mic."

She wrinkles her nose. "How is that payback?"

"If you knew him, you'd understand."

"If you say so." Every syllable is heavy with skepticism. "Was that the surprising part?"

"No. That happened later."

"Go on."

"After we left the bar—"

Her eyes widen. "You left together?"

I nod. "After we left the bar, he— Well, no, if we're being pedantic about it, *I* kissed *him*." Daphne's jaw drops. I hold my hands up before the questions building in her mind explode all over the room. "It was a horrible idea that I regretted immediately."

She exhales, probably relieved that she won't have to talk me through my insanity. "The kiss was bad?"

I groan inwardly. "I wish it was."

"That's a lot to process, Mars."

"I can't. Not yet. If you could let this drop for now, I'd appreciate it," I say with a level of cool detachment that I don't feel.

She nods, casting her eyes about the room for a change of subject. "Remind me what his book is about?"

I roll my eyes. It's not the hard pivot I was hoping for, but it'll do. "Oh god, I don't even know." I rack my brain for the passage I read last night, but that's when I was at my tipsiest, and

I can't remember anything other than a man, a desert, and a vague sense of familiarity that probably comes from knowing West's voice so well. "Let's find out, shall we?"

I scan the room for my bag from last night, but I don't see it on the nightstand or the desk by the window. I can't find it anywhere. "We have a problem."

"What's wrong?"

"I lost my bag." I hadn't noticed because my phone and room key were in the pocket of my dress and I was so emotional coming back, but I've lost my wallet with my ID and credit cards. My conference badge and credentials. My Kindle. The book West signed for me.

"Did you leave it at the bar?"

I run my hand through my hair and attempt to recall the non-West events of last night. "Maybe? Probably? I'll stop by later and check."

"We have time now. I'll come with you."

"But your presentation—"

"Isn't until nine. We'll be fine."

I shoot her a grateful smile as I make my way to the bathroom to change. "Thanks. You can help me brainstorm ways to screw up West's panel this morning."

"You're still doing that?"

I lean out of the bathroom. "Have you had a personality transplant since yesterday? What is going on?"

She shakes her head and then surveys me with a critical eye. "Is that what you're wearing?"

I look at my GIRLS JUST WANNA HAVE BOOKS T-shirt. "What's wrong with what I'm wearing?"

"I crocheted this dress that would look really cute—"

I disappear back into the bathroom.

Unbothered, she calls through the door. "I assume you were awake devising a sabotage plan all night?"

I should have been, but instead I spent the night tossing and turning, stuck between awake and asleep, my mind wandering through my past, visions of West and me disappearing before they fully materialized.

"I have one vague idea, but I don't know if it's possible. I'd need to recruit help."

"I'll see what I can do."

Bright lights glow behind Gentle Ben's locked door. Ignoring the Closed sign and the empty dining room, I knock until a manager answers. She has a stack of receipts in one hand and a pen tucked behind her ear. "We open at nine."

"I think I left my bag here last night. Would you mind checking the lost and found?"

"What does it look like?" she asks as we follow her to the bar.

"Tote bag. Covered in books," I say as she crouches down to look in a small box.

She laughs. "You might have to be more specific."

"It's black-and-white. It says 'Waterstones' on it."

"Bingo!"

I open the bag and exhale an immediate sigh of relief when I see my wallet and Kindle. I take inventory as I stack my possessions on a barstool. Sunglasses, conference badge, two paperbacks, a notebook, three pens, and a handful of snacks.

A pit grows in my stomach. "I'm missing a book."

"You sure?" She eyes the books already on the counter.

"Yes. It's a hardcover. It has oranges on the spine."

She shrugs.

I lean over the counter, trying to see into the box. "Can you check again?"

She pulls the box to the bar top and lets me look through it myself. "I know it was here," I insist, my eyes combing through the room and across the small stage. "Can I check the rooftop?"

I search every inch of Gentle Ben's, including the restrooms. Daphne watches me with a curious expression, checking her watch every few minutes. She's getting impatient, but I can't bring myself to stop. I bite my lower lip, trying to replay last night in my mind. *I was reading from the book, West left, and I ran after him.* I must have dropped it on the stage or put it on the corner of a table on my way out.

"You can get a new one today," Daphne says.

"I want *that* one." I'd sooner publish a first draft than ask West to sign *another* book for me, and for some reason I can't let this one go. "What if someone else finds it and sees my name in it?"

Daphne represses an amused smile.

"Never mind. I just want it." The manager is sitting in front of a pile of receipts at the corner table, and she looks less than thrilled when I approach her. "Is there anywhere else it could be? Anyone else who would know?"

She sighs. "I have a bartender who's one of those BookTok girls. She might have borrowed it from the lost and found."

"When can I talk to her?"

She rolls her eyes. "You're persistent, aren't you? Evie isn't on the schedule today, but you can come back tomorrow. During business hours."

Strange amount of attitude for someone who just admitted that her employee might be stealing from the lost and found. I smother the fluttery panic that is bouncing off the walls of my stomach. "I'll be back tomorrow."

The sky is overcast as we leave the bar and walk to the festival. Daphne throws me what she thinks are stealthy sideways glances the entire time. "Is everything okay?"

"Peachy."

She raises her brows. "Want to try a more believable answer?"

"Sorry." I blow out a breath and try to shake off my inexplicable anxiety. "Thanks for coming with me. Are you ready for your performance? Do you have a description of the dead body locked and loaded?"

She glances at our feet, only to look back at me seconds later, tears pooling in her eyes. When the first one slides down her cheek, she swipes it away and gives me a self-satisfied smile. "How'd I do?"

"You're going to kill it, Daph. I'll have to sneak out the back of your talk ten minutes early to make it to West's panel, though."

"Text me the play-by-play."

"Your friend agreed to help?" I ask, reviewing the plan in my head. Of everything I've done to ruin West's weekend, this is the one thing most likely to backfire, but Daphne insists her friend is down to help. From what I understand, she lives in Tucson and is big in the improv scene.

"I had to promise signed copies of *Torched* for her nieces, but yes, she's down to help."

"Thank you. Thank *her*."

Daphne eyes me pensively. "Are you sure you want to go through with this? The last time you let yourself get distracted by him, it ended pretty badly for *you*."

"I'm not scared of him. He should be scared of me and my revenge arc."

A beat of silence.

"Right?" I prompt.

Daphne throws her head back and laughs. "Yes, Margot, you're very scary."

20

10 Years Ago
Senior Year, Second Semester

I knew life would change after graduation, but I never could have predicted such a harsh line in the sand. The call comes when I'm in my navy cap and gown, queued up alphabetically with the rest of the College of Social and Behavioral Sciences majors waiting to file into the auditorium. Danielle's name flashes on my phone, and as I step out of line to answer it, my stomach churns with excited, anxious nausea.

Life rarely hands you such an obvious life-altering before-and-after moment, but as I answer Danielle's call with sweaty palms and a medically concerning heartbeat, I know that this is the biggest moment of my life thus far. I'm ten minutes from my college graduation, but fifty years from now, when I think about today, this is the moment I'll remember.

Our call is quick, and when I retake my place with the rest of the graduates, no one around me knows about the tectonic shift that has taken place under my feet. My book sold at an auction between eight publishing houses. The amount of money makes my head spin, second only to the emotional vertigo that swallows me whole when I realize there will be a book, with my name on it, on a bookshelf.

I can't believe it.

The guy in front of me turns around with a scowl, and I realize I must have uttered that out loud. "What?" he asks.

I shake my head, trying to bring myself back to reality. "I can't believe we're graduating," I say, because this random man will not be the first person to know that I achieved the goal I've worked toward for as long as I can remember.

"What's your major?" he asks, and I can't help but laugh. Hopefully this is the last time in my life I'll have to answer that question.

"Creative writing."

He chuckles a bit too much for someone also graduating with a liberal arts degree. "What are you going to do now? Write the next great American novel?" His casual condescension would bug the shit out of me on any other day.

"Something like that." The ceremony starts in ten minutes, but I risk slipping away again. I text West to meet me, and a minute later, I crash into his arms outside the doors of Centennial Hall.

"What's going on?" He grabs my shoulders and holds me at arm's length, his eyes roving over my face.

"My book sold. I'm going to be a published author."

His face splits into a grin. He wraps his arms around me and spins me until my feet are off the ground. When he sets me down, his eyes are shining with tears. "I'm so fucking proud of you, Jupiter."

"I couldn't have done it without you."

He shakes his head. "This was all you." He bends for a kiss. "The graduates are going in. You don't want to miss it."

"I don't really care, to be honest."

"You're not skipping graduation."

"C'mon, West. I just got hired at my dream job! Why do I need to walk?"

"Because your parents are inside waiting to cheer as you cross that stage. We'll celebrate after, I promise." We kiss again, and he squeezes my hand as we enter through the glass doors and separate: I join the graduates, and he sits with my parents in the auditorium.

I don't absorb a single word of my graduation ceremony, but it doesn't matter.

I did it.

I can finally stop running.

My parents take me to a late lunch after the ceremony, and they've settled into a lecture on the cost of living in New York when I tell them the good news. As soon as I get my first check, I'll not only be able to afford my half of rent, I'll also be able to pay back their tuition money.

I've never seen my mom speechless. It's *so* satisfying.

They have a million questions. Am I sure it's not a scam? *Yes*. Do I have a backup plan if the book doesn't do well? *No, but thanks for the vote of confidence.* Do I plan to branch out from YA and write a "real book" next?

I don't dignify that with a response, but I *do* order an extra-strong drink.

After lunch, my parents come to the house and help me pack everything I own. Amber is keeping all the furniture, so it's just a matter of throwing clothes and shoes and books into boxes and drinking old margarita mix from the fridge in order to tolerate my parents.

By the time they're on the road to San Diego, the sun is setting, I'm weary from their passive-aggressive remarks, and I'm itching to get out of the house. I don't know why I expected them to have a better reaction to my book deal, but their surprised and skeptical faces when I broke the news kind of crushed me. All I want to do now is celebrate with West. I text him to meet me at the house and then change into a white off-the-shoulder dress that I've been saving for a special occasion. I'm sitting cross-legged on the bathroom counter, touching up my curls, when I hear a knock on the front door.

"Come in!" I shout, and a few seconds later, West's face appears in the mirror.

"Whoa," he says, his eyes traveling over the stack of boxes pushed into the corner of my room.

"Weird, right? How'd packing go at your place?"

"I don't have much stuff."

"I mean, same, if you don't count the books. My parents took four boxes home with them." I release the last curl, run my fingers through my hair, and spritz everything with hair spray. "Sorry my parents stayed forever, but you could have come over sooner."

He leans against the doorjamb with his arms crossed and watches me reapply my makeup in the mirror. "You don't get to spend much time with them."

"Thankfully. I only need five more minutes and then I'll be ready. What should we do? Dinner to celebrate? Can you *believe* we're finally leaving?"

"Dinner sounds good." He stuffs his hands in his pockets as

I attempt winged eyeliner with my nose two inches from the mirror.

"And then Rishi is having a grad party, if you want to go?" My hand slips, and my right eye wings out way too far. I run a Q-tip under the tap and fix it.

"Eh," West replies. "I didn't graduate. Might be weird."

"What? No. These are your friends, too. I'm on the fence. It'd be fun to say goodbye to everyone, but we'll probably get on the road faster if I'm not majorly hungover in the morning. Did we decide if we're leaving tomorrow or the next day? We get the keys to our apartment on Wednesday, so it just depends on how we want to split up the driving, where we want to stop for the night." I swipe on a matte red lipstick and lean back to survey my face. The eyeliner is still uneven, but whatever. *I'm going to be a published author!* Who cares what my makeup looks like?

I knock over an open bottle of foundation as I'm climbing off the counter, and I meet West's wary expression in the mirror. "Oops." I quickly wipe it up with cotton balls. The counter is covered in makeup and hair stuff, and West looks thoroughly unimpressed. "I'll be cleaner when we share a bathroom." West is cleaner than I am—this has always been obvious by the state of our bedrooms—and I don't want to get off on the wrong foot when we move in together.

He steps out of the way to let me pass. In my empty room, I slip on a pair of comfy sandals. "When we live together, I'll be different. I'll do my dishes and take out trash and whatever else clean people do—" The corners of West's mouth are turned down, his brow furrowed. "What's wrong?"

He swallows heavily. A prickling sense of foreboding settles over me as I watch his throat work. I step toward him, faltering when his body tenses.

"I can't go to New York."

"Tomorrow? That's okay. We can leave Sunday."

"No, Mars." His voice is rough enough to bruise. "I'm not moving to New York."

I blink, convinced I heard him wrong. "That's not funny, West."

He presses his lips together, waiting for something. For me to understand what's happening, maybe? I glance at the open door over his shoulder, looking for—I don't know what. Someone to tell me why he's saying this. But the hall is empty, and it's just him and me, and he's looking at me with puppy dog eyes that are begging me not to hate him.

Panic builds in my throat until I'm halfway to asphyxiation. "What are you talking about? We found a place. You're my *roommate*." Yes, that's good. Focus on that. Losing a roommate is a lot fucking easier than losing the love of my life.

He stares at the floor. "You won't have trouble making rent."

My breath is tight in my chest. *Oh my god*. He's jealous. "Is this about my book deal?"

"*No*," he says with blistering force. "I shouldn't have said that. I didn't mean it. This has nothing to do with you."

"Then I can't wait to hear the reason."

"My family needs me. My grandma is getting worse by the day. My mom can't take care of her and all the kids."

"You're moving back home?"

"Maybe." He sighs heavily. "I don't know yet."

If this were entirely about his family, we would have talked about it before now. There's something else going on; his words don't match the tragic look in his eyes. "Is this about Bethany?"

"No." He steps toward me, but I duck around him and out of my room, mind reeling.

I need fresh air. I need to not be here anymore. I need to know what the hell is going on.

I turn, and West is right behind me. "Are we breaking up?"

His head rears back in surprise. "If—if that's what you want."

"I want to move to New York with my boyfriend, but I guess that's not an option. So it looks like you're calling the shots. What do you want?"

His face falls. "I don't think long distance ever works." There's a jagged edge to his voice that triggers something deep inside me.

I straighten. "Got it. Okay. You can leave," I say woodenly. For the first time in my life, I'm too furious to cry.

"Mars," he says, and then thinks better of it. "*Jupiter*." It's a bolt of pain straight through the heart. He grimaces as he rubs the back of his neck. "I thought we could still go out for your last night here."

"Are you kidding me?"

"This isn't happening the way I wanted it to."

"Same." My voice cracks.

He swallows heavily, his eyes lingering on my face for long enough that my chest shudders. He grips the countertop, his knuckles turning white, and he looks like he's restraining himself. It's chemical, this thing between us, and even when he's breaking my heart, I want to let him step closer to me and drag his mouth over my skin. "This is the most exciting day of your life, and you deserve to celebrate."

"You're right," I say. His expression turns hopeful. "And I will. Without you."

His shoulders fall, but he leaves without argument, and it's salt in the wound. He didn't even fight for one last night.

I walk nearly a mile to Rishi's in the dark; by the time I get to his house, I'm stone-cold sober in a way that requires immediate attention, because if I think about how West just torpedoed our future in five minutes, I don't know what I'll do. I let myself in the front door, and I'm early—the party is a dozen people sitting around a coffee table debating the ending of *Breaking Bad* over empty take-out containers. In normal circumstances I'd join the debate, but right now, I need a different energy.

"You didn't need to wait for me to have fun," I announce, one hand on my hip as I survey the room, looking for the nearest bottle. Rishi, Improv Connor, and a combination of English lit nerds and engineering nerds say hi, and when they ask where West is, I tip back a shot instead of answering.

"Couldn't make it" is all I say, and I see Connor and Rishi raise their eyebrows at each other across the room. Whatever. Let them speculate. After twenty minutes and two more shots, I force the antihero conversation to a close and convince everyone that it would be the best idea in the world to turn the lights down and the music up. By the time Connor turns to me, I'm past the point of being pleasantly tipsy and have careened straight into drunk.

"Hey!" He tips his mouth closer to my ear so I can hear him over the music. "Are you okay?"

"Why wouldn't I be?"

"You seem different."

I giggle even though it's not funny. "That's because I am.

Can I tell you a secret?" I ask, and when Connor nods, I crook my finger, and he leans over the arm of the couch until our faces are close. The strap of my dress slips down my shoulder, and I see Connor's eyes tracing the fabric. "Today, my wildest dream came true."

"What's that?" he asks, and I realize I don't want Improv Connor to be the fourth person in my life to know about my book deal.

"I actually can't say. Top secret." I mime zipping my lips.

Connor pouts, so I boop him on the nose with my fingertip and am drunk enough that I don't care how weird that is. "Lucky you, though. You're the only one in this room who knows that today is the happiest day of my life." Maybe if I say the words out loud, it will make them true.

"You don't seem that happy," Connor says. When I don't respond, he goes in for the kill. "Why are you here alone?"

I shrug again and then leave to refill our drinks before the ghost of West ruins the mood. When I return, Connor's arms snake around me and pull me into his lap, sloshing vodka soda across my thighs. He swipes his bare hands over my skin, and I relax back into his chest and let him. And when he leans in for a kiss, I'm so fucking miserable having the best day of my life that I kiss him back.

I know something's wrong before I open my eyes. And then Connor's toenail scratches my calf under the sheet, and my stomach churns. Not something, but *everything.*

I jump out of bed and knock over a glass of water that is sitting on the floor as I grab my dress with shaking hands.

"Mars?" Connor squints at me, his red hair sticking out in all directions.

"I have to go." I need to get out of this room and this house and as far away from this mistake as I can.

I search under dirty clothes and discarded blankets for my sandals and eventually find one under the bed.

"Do you want me to drive you home?"

"No!" I yelp, my voice tinged with hysteria. "I'll walk." I straighten my dress and bolt out of the room, one shoe in hand, the other left behind. Connor half-heartedly calls out for me to wait, but I let the front door slam behind me without another word. I wince as I sprint through the rocky front yard, sobbing giant tears as I rush home under a periwinkle sky.

I don't have my house key or my cell phone, but Amber left the back door unlocked for me, so I let myself in and trudge through the quiet house. I catch a glimpse of myself in a mirror as I walk through the hall; mascara is smudged down my cheeks, my eyes are puffy and red, and my curls are flat and snarled at the same time. I drop my sandal and trudge to my room.

My eyes widen at the sight of West asleep in my bed.

I blink, shuffling through a mixture of shock and joy and devastation so quickly it leaves me nauseous. I sprint to the bathroom and puke into the toilet. Even when I'm sure there's nothing left to come up, I stay hunched on the tile floor, unable to face what I've done. When soft fingers pull my hair out of my face and hold it behind my head, I want to die.

I slowly push myself up, turning to rest my back against the side of the tub. West lets my hair slip through his fingers and sits on the floor across from me, his arms resting on his knees.

He takes a deep breath, and I wince in anticipation of his anger. "I'm sorry," he says, like they're the only two words in the world. "I never wanted to break up with you."

"West—" My voice cracks on his name. I never thought it'd be painful to say, but I never thought we'd end up here.

He holds his hands up to stop me. "Let me get through this. I can't follow you to New York. Not until—" He rakes a hand through his hair. It's as long as I've ever seen it. It's the best he's ever looked. "I have some stuff I need to get sorted first. But we can make this work, Mars." He scooches closer until our knees are touching. He puts his hands on my thighs, and I want them to stay there forever. "I need you. I don't know who I am without you. I've never loved anything or anyone the way I love you."

"I had sex with Connor last night." I wipe tears off my cheeks, but it doesn't stop them from coming. I wrap my arms around my knees and squeeze to keep myself from splintering apart, shocked at how this has become my reality, when twelve hours ago, West and I were about to start our lives together. His hands drop away from my thighs.

A coil of dread tightens in my chest, binding my lungs until I can't breathe. "I'm so sorry and I love you, too. It meant nothing, less than nothing. I hate that I did it. I feel sick. I never would have done it if you hadn't—if we hadn't—I was drunk, West," I say desperately.

The light in his eyes flickers out, a torch snuffed. In that moment, I become a stranger to him.

"That was always my dad's excuse, too."

My stomach pitches. A fresh wave of nausea hits. "I'll stop drinking. I'll never do it again."

He pushes himself to his feet and walks out of the bathroom. I follow after him, crying and pleading and making promises as he walks out of my house and my life without another word.

One hour later, with all my shit thrown in the trunk of my car, I leave Tucson.

21

Present Day

West is sitting on a makeshift stage under a big tent in dark jeans and a thin forest-green sweater. I frown at him from behind my giant undercover sunglasses. Why does he need so many sweaters? It's not like he still lives in New York. Between this and the photo on his book jacket, he's practically drowning in wool. When I knew him, he didn't own anything but short-sleeve band T-shirts and skinny jeans. I feel vaguely provoked by the sight of him up on a stage, in front of a crowd, looking exactly like the man I imagined he would become. His hair is unruly, his jaw sharp, his shoulders squared.

My eyes sweep impatiently over his body, looking for evidence of nerves. But unfortunately for me, his feet are still, and his ink-stained fingers are clasped on the table in front of him. He is completely unruffled. I bet he got a great night of sleep.

Ugh.

My stomach dips when I realize how little my schemes have affected him. I wish he were sitting up there stewing in misery, thinking of me in my short dress, but instead he's saying something under his breath to the author sitting next to him. She's laughing, and he's smiling.

I've been trying to ruin his weekend, but he is unmoved.

Well.

Good thing I'm here to make him move.

Almost every chair under the tent is filled. It's perfect. One hundred people are about to watch West have the most frustrating hour of his professional career.

My stomach tightens with anticipation.

I take a seat in the last row of the audience as the moderator is introducing the two people onstage with West—Ayesha and Rowan, both literary writers who, I do admit, I feel a little sorry for. Hopefully when they receive invitations to present at the *Los Angeles Times* Festival of Books in their inboxes next week, it'll make up for today. (I still have enough connections to make that happen, at least.)

"—and finally, we have West Emerson, whose debut novel, *Oasis*, was nominated for a Young Lions Fiction Award and whose highly anticipated novel *Drought* was released last month. Thanks for being here, West."

"Thanks for having me, and for not telling the audience that I'm the one who slipped the words 'highly anticipated' into my bio."

The moderator explains that this will mostly be a Q&A panel, which I knew from reading the description online, and as soon as she asks the panelists to introduce themselves and their books, a hand shoots up in the front row.

I bite back a smile.

The hand remains steadfastly in the air while Rowan and Ayesha speak, and then it's West's turn.

"I'm West, and I—uh—" He stumbles over his words as the

hand begins waving frantically back and forth. "I write books that my mom calls 'depressing,' and—uh—I guess we'll just start the questions." He nods to the woman in the front row. She takes a microphone out of the moderator's hands. "I just wanted to say that I think it's really cool that you are all writers, and I want to be a writer, too."

West blinks at her. "You're in the right place."

Halfway back, another hand goes up. The microphone is passed to a middle-aged white man. "My question is more of a comment," he says, and I see warning bells go off in West's head.

When Not-a-Question Guy finishes his five-minute ramble on why the push for diversity in publishing is "regressive, actually," West's jaw is clenched tight. He exchanges eye contact with his fellow panelists, and Ayesha says, "I think we all disagree with your take. Next question?" I'm impressed with how she handled it. Better not to give those comments more attention than they deserve.

Front-Row Woman has her hand in the air again, and when no one else raises their hand, she happily takes possession of the microphone. She asks a question about filing for a copyright on her unpublished manuscript and claims that the idea of *Dora the Explorer* was stolen from her.

The rest of the hour continues in the same fashion. Whenever there's a five-second lull, Front-Row Woman blurts out another question without waiting for the microphone, and the moderator has given up trying to control it.

Rowan and Ayesha try to help him, but it's tough when every question is prefaced by the same statement: *This question is for West.*

"How much did you get paid for your last book?"

"Do you feel like a creative sellout because you're not self-published?"

"What is your favorite young adult novel?"

"Do you believe in muses?"

When she finally relinquishes the microphone, she shifts ever so slightly and gives me a subtle thumbs-up. *Thank you*, I mouth silently. She tips an imaginary hat. Daphne is unbelievable for making this happen; I should try harder with the sourdough. She'd appreciate it.

The microphone is passed to a young woman in the third row who introduces herself as a U of A student. West sits back in his chair, looking relieved to get a break from the onslaught.

"I recently started querying my novel and am wondering if you have any advice for dealing with rejection."

"Alcohol," Ayesha says immediately. The audience chuckles. "Wait, how old did you say you are?"

"Twenty-two."

"Alcohol or antidepressants. Don't mix the two. I can also recommend ice cream, crying, and venting to your friends in a private group chat," Ayesha says.

West's eyebrows skyrocket. "You mean my method of bottling up my feelings and refusing to talk about them isn't a good idea?" he asks. The audience laughs again, and an old wound reopens in my chest. I know he's talking about career rejection—not us—but it hits a little too close to home. "In all seriousness, being an author means dealing with a truckload of rejection. It sucks, especially in the beginning, and unfortunately nothing any of us can say will make it suck less."

"So we're not even going to try," Rowan quips.

"I still remember my first brutal rejection," Ayesha says. "I was sick over it."

"I have parts of mine *memorized*," West says.

"Do you really?" Rowan asks.

"It's framed in my bathroom. Hanging next to my *New York Times* book review." The audience loves this. "Have to keep myself humble somehow." He winks, and I'm annoyed that even after that hellish Q&A, he's still charming the crowd.

"I think it would make us all feel better to hear what it said," Ayesha prompts, and it's not that surprising that she'd ask. Writers like to swap rejection stories like badges of honor.

"Nice try." He shakes his head, but the woman in the front row yells "C'mon!" and then someone else shouts "Please?"

West rolls his eyes good-naturedly. "Let's see what I can remember." He runs a hand over his jaw, and my stomach tightens. It feels unfathomable that he went through something so monumental and I don't have any idea when it happened or what book it was in response to or how he reacted in the moment. I don't know anything about his journey other than what's in his author bio. It's just weird.

West's eyes reach a spot in the back of the tent, and I slouch lower in my seat, grateful for the sunglasses. "This agent isn't working in publishing anymore, but at the time, he was extremely well-connected and respected. He wrote 'Dear Mr. Everson'—yes, he got my name wrong—'You are not ready to be querying. You are nowhere close. Go back to high school and stop wasting my time with this insipid drivel. Ten years from now, you might think you're ready to try again. If you are, don't query me.'"

My chest caves at the thought of him opening that email with excitement and then reading . . . *that.*

I wish the circumstances had been different.

I wish I'd been there.

"What a bastard," Ayesha says.

West runs a hand through his hair, a wry smile on his face. He's good at this. Confident, calm, funny. Meanwhile, I'm out of practice, riddled with anxiety, and desperate to succeed. Is there anything less likable in the eyes of the public than a woman who's a try-hard? At our panel tomorrow night, West will be charming, and I'll be drowning in flop sweat. I've spent the last twenty-four hours spinning my wheels to make him feel like he doesn't belong in this world, but the joke of it all is that he's more at home here than I am.

"That is uniquely brutal," Rowan says.

"At twenty-two, I wasn't mentally prepared for that level of rejection."

I frown, positive I misheard him. West wasn't trying to get published back then.

"You were a Wildcat then, weren't you?" Ayesha asks.

"I'd dropped out by this point, but I read that letter on the day of my would-be college graduation."

I shift uneasily. He never told me that.

"You think that's bad?" West continues. "That email's not even the worst thing that happened to me that day." He laughs as if he didn't just rearrange my entire past with one careless sentence.

I'm frozen in my seat.

Our eyes meet. It's hard to breathe. Like there's cement drying in my windpipe.

The missing piece of a decade-old story clicks into place.

I lean against a tent post as West slowly descends from the stage. He takes his time chatting with everyone who stops to introduce themselves. I watch, tapping my foot and listening to a rush of blood in my ears. Eventually he runs out of admirers, and he braces himself as he approaches me.

"I learn something new every time I come to one of these things," I say with a bright, fake smile before stepping closer. "Why didn't you tell me?" I demand under my breath.

"Not here," he growls. West wraps his hand around my elbow and turns, running us straight into Dr. B.

"My star pupils!" the man booms. "Can't say I'm surprised to see you two together again." His eyes drop to West's hand on my arm, and I wrench it out of his grasp.

"Thanks for coming, Dr. B," West says.

"You should be extremely proud of yourself, Mr. Emerson." He claps West on the shoulder. West nods his head in silent thanks. "Readers are going to really respond to this one." His eyes twinkle with something I don't understand as West stiffens slightly.

Dr. B turns his attention to me. "Don't forget about your promise!" He winks at me again as he walks away, looking entirely too pleased with himself.

I frown at his retreating back when I feel the heat of West's chest crowding me. "*Ugh*, stop looming." I glare over my shoulder at him.

He barely manages to suppress an eye roll. "Don't act like you don't love it. You wanted to talk?"

"I do. Move." I grab him by the biceps, sighing heavily when he flexes, and spin him. I shove him lightly between the shoulder blades.

"Where are we going?"

"Koffler." I push him again, and we march to the front door

of a large cinder block building that vaguely resembles a wildcat. He opens the door and waves me through, his hand brushing over the small of my back. I lurch away from him, pretending to hate that he's touching me, and then immediately invalidate this by grabbing his hand and pulling him into a large lecture hall.

Inside, he leans against a desk at the front of the room and drums his fingers on the edge. It reminds me so much of last night that a welcome anger builds in my chest. "Why didn't you tell me?" I ask again, bringing us back to the reason he refused to go to New York with me all those years ago.

"When would I have told you?" he sneers.

"Before you dumped me would have been ideal."

His expression hardens. "Do you really want to do this now?"

"Should we wait another decade, you think?"

"I was trying not to make *your* day about me and *my* fucking insecurities."

"And look how well that turned out."

A storm burns in his eyes. "I *tried*, Mars. I screwed it up, clearly, but I was in love with you! I would have done anything."

"Except tell me the truth!" It's a physical pain to hear him say that word for the first time in ten years. I went to Rishi's party that night thinking he didn't.

"I wanted to. I realized almost immediately that I screwed up. Ten minutes after you kicked me out, I came back to wait for you. I *slept in your bed* while you were—" He grits his teeth, the absence of the words almost more painful than hearing him say it.

I tortured myself for years, wondering what would have happened if I'd stayed home. Had nothing to drink. Kidnapped West and made him come to New York with me anyway.

"You lied when we had drinks with Danielle in New York, didn't you? About not looking for an agent yet?"

He tips his chin in silent acknowledgment.

"Why?"

He scrubs his hands over his face. "I needed to succeed on my own, and I knew you would try to help me—"

"Because I *loved* you!"

He lifts his hands, exasperated. "I know! I know I should have been honest. But I was twenty-two and a fucking idiot!"

"It would have changed everything, West." My voice cracks. I press my tongue to the roof of my mouth and blink like my life depends on it. "Everything could be different between us right now."

His face softens, his eyes lighting with something that looks deceptively like hope. "Do you want everything to be different between us?"

Sometimes I think I do. Hating West is exhausting. Nothing about it comes naturally. Sometimes, when the fire burns away, it leaves a dull ache that I've never been able to fill. Not with other men. Not with bestselling books. Not by throwing darts at West's picture or pretending that when I'm near him, I don't feel a chain connecting us, handcuffing our fates until we're both miserable.

For a minute last night, I wanted things to be different, and then I got slapped in the face with a harsh reminder of why they can't be.

I close my eyes, fighting memories of months spent in bed, death threats in my inbox, a career on fire. It's enough to make me nauseous with anxiety, even now. And none of it would have happened if it weren't for him.

If I'm being honest, though, I could get over *that*. But my pride won't ever let me be with someone who humiliated me the way he did.

I shake my head in answer to his question. "No. You'll do your interview, I'll leave, and with any luck, we'll never have to speak to each other again."

22

9 Years Ago

Leave it to Amber to be the first person from our old friend group to get married. If living alone in New York hadn't shoved me headfirst into adulthood, receiving her wedding invitation would have done the trick. And even though the idea of getting married at twenty-three feels impossible and foreign, like something that only happens in the stories I write, I can't pretend to be surprised. Amber and Patrick are good for each other. I'm unbelievably happy for them.

The fact that *I* haven't managed to cobble together anything resembling stability says more about me than it does about their relationship. I threw myself into the deep end when I moved to the city more than a year ago, and every day since has been an exercise in not drowning. In loneliness. In insecurity. In the fear that I've tricked people into believing I'm capable of something that I'm not, and that when they figure me out, it'll all be taken away.

Their wedding venue is close to Patrick's family and nestled in Redwood National Park in California.

When my flight lands, I tuck my laptop and my notebook into my carry-on bag, not sure why I bothered to pretend to work. I'm barely writing under the best of circumstances, let alone at thirty thousand feet in the air, hurtling toward a collision with my past. The sequel to *Torched* is due to my editor, Whitney, next month, and every morning when I open my laptop, I stare at a blank page and relearn the meaning of the phrase *existential dread.*

What if I can't do it?

What if Torched *was a fluke and I'm a fraud?*

What if I only ever had one good book in me?

My brain is a noisy bitch pretty much all the time.

The scenes between Fox and Juniper are the worst. Their dialogue is too cliché, their movements too wooden. When I think of my looming deadline, a pit the size of a baseball sits in my stomach. I have a constant nagging feeling that I'm waiting for something, but I don't know what, and I don't know how to make it go away. I feel stuck and impatient and frustrated.

I always thought that writing would get easier the more I did it, not harder. And that living my dream would feel different from crying alone on the subway.

Life in New York feels at times both unbearably small and unbelievably unmanageable. I go entire days without leaving my apartment or speaking to other people. I've considered looking for a roommate, but the risk of ending up with someone who is a bad fit feels scarier than continuing to live alone. I haven't yet figured out how adults who work from home make friends. The internet tells me to join a coed sports league, but I'm not that desperate. *Yet.* Give it another winter. Next spring I might be lacing up my nonexistent cleats.

The city is big, but my world is small. Writing my second

book gets harder every day I put it off, and emotionally I'm a wreck, due in large part to *Torched*'s impending release. I don't know how I'll handle the pressure or the reviews or having my love letter to my ex-boyfriend available for critique. It's no wonder I've forgotten how to write a love story. I've been lonely and anxious and devoid of inspiration for far too long.

The morning of the wedding, I dress alone in my hotel room while Amber and her bridesmaids get ready together in the bridal suite. I might have been with them if I hadn't dropped off the face of the planet when I went to New York, alone and depressed and letting phone calls and text messages go unanswered. I sent my congratulations later than I should have, and while Amber says she understands that I was going through a brutal breakup, I still feel guilty that we now mainly communicate through "happy birthday" text messages and in the comments of our social media profiles.

My dress is an emerald-green maxi with gold accents and a V-neck so deep, not a bra on this planet would work with it. I'm leaving all my faith in sticky tape and the universe. I curl my hair into loose waves and painstakingly apply makeup, and when I survey the results, I can't help but think it's the most effort I've put into my appearance in more than a year. Before I leave, I slip a small notebook and pen into my clutch just in case inspiration strikes.

In case he's there.

Stupid, really, but old habits die never, I'm starting to fear.

I arrive at the outdoor wedding with only minutes to spare, stepping over moist green moss, fallen needles, and soft ferns as I make my way to the wooden benches on the bride's side of the aisle. I scan my surroundings with my heart in my throat. Golden beams of light filter through the canopy of ancient trees, and an earthy fragrance fills my lungs. I drink it in, enchanted, even as part of my brain is focused on something else entirely.

He's not here.

Well, that's okay. It's good, actually. Now I can give my full attention to the wedding.

I smooth my hands over the stupidly expensive dress that I bought just for this. As the last few guests take their seats, I wave to Amber's parents and some people I know from school. Finally, the wedding party enters, the groomsmen in white shirts, bow ties, and suspenders and the bridesmaids in shades of rust, walking arm in arm across the forest floor toward a circular clearing of trees—a redwood fairy ring. When the music swells, it's Amber's cue.

In unison with one hundred guests, I turn to watch her big entrance, and my stomach pitches violently. Sitting on the edge of the very last bench is West.

His hair is short again, not a hint of a curl in sight. It's a small mercy, but I realize immediately that I have never, not once in the five years I've known him, seen West Emerson in a suit. He's wearing black pants, a black jacket with no tie, and a crisp white shirt with the top button undone at the neck. He could not look further from the emo boy in guyliner and Sharpie nail polish I met when we were both eighteen. It's almost like looking at a stranger. His head turns in my direction, and I nearly give myself whiplash whirling around to face the wedding party. I bunch my hands in the fabric of my dress, cheeks burning, heart racing.

The wedding is beautiful, and I don't hear a word of it. I can't distinguish the vows from the blood rushing in my ears. I cheer and clap when Amber and Patrick kiss, but my own lips have gone numb. I've thought about this moment for so long, but now that it's here, all my wires are crossed, the signals short-circuiting.

Amber and Patrick are quickly whisked away for photos, leaving the guests to enjoy cocktail hour on the deck attached to the rustic banquet hall.

"Mars! Are you famous yet?" I'm pulled into a circle of old classmates and am bombarded with questions about my book deal. I've never made as extreme eye contact as I do now. My neck aches from how actively I am *not* looking at West, but the problem with avoiding someone is that you have to know where they are at all times; when I'm offered a fruit skewer from a passing server, West is on the left side of the room chatting with Patrick's best man. By the time the prosciutto-wrapped figs make it to me, I can *feel* him standing by the bar. It's like he's the moon, and I'm the tide, constantly tugged in his direction. It takes restraint I didn't know I had to act like I don't care that we're breathing the same air for the first time in sixteen months.

It's almost unthinkable that we haven't talked in that time. A few months after the move, I sent him a long, groveling letter of apology, but I don't know if he ever read it. We had no last conversation or moment of closure; one minute we were together, and the next he changed his mind, and I lashed out, and by the time the dust settled, we lived on opposite sides of the country, and there was nothing to force us together.

It didn't take long after our breakup for me to block him on Instagram. Eventually, determined to hurt my own feelings, I created a fake account so I could check his profile without being caught—but, of course, he never posts. When it comes to the details of his life, I'm a dog with a bone.

Cocktail hour ends, and Amber and Patrick join us to thunderous applause in the twinkly banquet hall for dinner. I find my assigned place at a table near the back of the room, and it gives me a perfect view of West. As I watch him sip from a glass, too far for me to know if it's alcohol or water, it occurs to me that any idea I've had about his life over the last year could be dead wrong. Every time I picture him, it's just a story made up in my head. I don't know where he lives or what he does for work or who he texts as he's falling asleep. The thought makes my chest feel like a drum: hollow but loud, my heartbeat thumping steadily against my ribs.

The chicken arrives, and as I'm taking my first bite, I realize the awful restless, waiting feeling is back with a vengeance. I glance at West and find him watching me, his mouth turned down, his eyes guarded. I wave, tentative and awkward. He nods, his eyes dropping to his plate.

My hands are frozen on my knife and fork, impatience clawing its way up my chest. I realize, *finally*, what that persistent feeling is all about.

The speeches are nice, Patrick's best man only eliciting a few groans from the audience. The way Amber and Patrick gaze at each other during their first dance makes my eyes well with tears. While I still can't believe any of us are old enough to be getting married, they look wildly happy together. The dance floor opens for everyone else, and by the time I'm pushing my chair back from my table and walking toward West, I'm already emotionally wobbly.

He makes eye contact as I weave through chairs, his Adam's apple bobbing. I expect him to drop his gaze with every step I take, but he's locked in; I'm holding him hostage with my stare.

"Hey." I stop at the empty chair next to his, placing my

hands on the back of it. "Mind if I sit?" I pull out the chair and sit, scooting it a couple of inches closer to him. "Nice suit."

He yanks on the sleeve of his jacket. "This stupid fucking suit," he mumbles, looking uncomfortable. I wonder if it's the first time he's ever worn one, and the fact that he did for Amber's wedding makes my chest warm. Not even the groomsmen are wearing jackets. He looks better than all of them.

"No, I mean it. You look nice," I say. He grimaces, and I feel the urge to lessen the impact of my compliment. "Although . . ."

"What?" He looks himself up and down.

"Would it have killed you to wear some eyeliner?"

He rolls his eyes. "I'm emo for *one* year—"

"Two," I interject.

"Two years of eyeliner and fake nail polish and no one lets me forget it." He tries to hide his smile, but it hits like a drug. I've been in withdrawal this whole time. No wonder everything hurts.

He studies me with guarded eyes, his jaw working. "You look—" He cuts himself off. *Pain on top of pain.* He tries again. "You look beautiful. How've you been?" He frowns like he wants to take back his words, snatch them out of the air and stuff them deep in his pockets.

"Oh, you know . . ." Tears are imminent. It's been a hundred years since someone asked me that question and meant it. How boring for me to cry right now. I was crying the last time I saw him. I don't want him to think it's all I do. "I'm good, I think? New York is not what I thought it would be, but most things aren't."

Except you, I think with a dull ache. *You are so much more than I thought you'd be.*

He's leaning toward me, his elbows resting on his knees,

and I'm close enough to see the wince when I mention New York.

"How are *you*?" I ask, too earnest by half.

He leans back, looking mildly alarmed by the question. "I'm really good. Happy for Amber and Patrick. They're great together." He motions toward the dance floor, and I can feel his attention slipping away. The pressure that's been building in my chest reaches a breaking point.

"Dance with me?"

A host of emotions play out on West's face, and I recognize them all. Hesitation. Fear. Desire. "Mars—" he says in a measured voice.

"One song."

"Dance with her, man!" urges a vaguely familiar voice to my left. I don't turn to see who it is. I'm afraid that if I look away, the moment will dissolve entirely.

We walk toward the dance floor, side by side but not touching, as "YMCA" starts playing. West raises one singular, judgmental eyebrow.

"Maybe we wait for the next song," I say.

He backs slowly onto the dance floor. "You said one song."

"I didn't mean this one!" I protest while he lifts his arms in a Y shape.

He has the audacity to laugh, his eyes lighting with amusement. "Sorry, Jupiter, not my problem."

It's the nickname that kills me. That's all it takes, and my feet are moving in his direction, accepting the excuse to be in his orbit for a little while longer. Amber sees us and shrieks with excitement, joining us for thirty seconds as we scream-sing and jump and dance before she moves on to another group, but we keep dancing, our arms flailing wildly. It's the silliest and happiest I've felt in recent memory, and when the song fades and transitions into something slower, I can't help but feel disappointed that it's over. Without meeting West's eyes, I turn to leave.

He catches me by the elbow. "One more?" This time, I don't recognize any of the emotions on his face. His eyes are serious, but his voice is casual, like he's entirely unaffected by his skin on mine.

"Okay." My pulse trips over itself as his fingers slide from my elbow to my hand, my skin burning with awareness. He pulls me in to him, his other hand settling lightly on my waist. I touch his shoulder like we're at a seventh-grade dance, but he inches me closer until you can no longer fit an *Oxford English Dictionary* between us.

I am breathless. Sweaty. Questioning all my life choices. West's eyes are on something or someone I can't see, his face giving away nothing. "Am I really the only one who's dying right now?" I exhale, immediately showing all my cards. I spent three years secretly in love with him, but I can't keep my cool for the length of one dance.

He sighs and looks down at me, heat kindling in his eyes. "I'm always dying when I'm with you, Mars."

A hot shiver rattles down my spine. We stare at each other about a dozen beats too long. It's wonderfully unbearable. Strangers don't make eye contact in New York, and everyone in New York is a stranger to me. But doing this with him feels like the most obvious thing in the world. When West is in the room, why would I look at anything else?

He looks away, the tension intolerable.

"How's your family?"

"We're holding it together," he says, and I worry that means *he's* holding it together for them.

"I'm sorry," I whisper.

"Please don't," he says tightly.

"It never should have ended like that."

"It's fine." He moves his hand off my waist to pinch the bridge of his nose.

"It's not, though, and it's killing me, West. Did you know I can't write anymore? Of course you don't, because we don't know each other. Isn't that messed up? You're wearing a suit, and your hair is all short again!"

"What does that have to do with anything?"

"It surprised me!"

"And? What's your point?"

"I don't want to be out of the loop on your life, West! Your hair might be short again because you're with *Beth*-any and that's how she likes it, but I wouldn't know."

His jaw clenches, and I realize belatedly that I lost the right to talk about his love life. "I'm not." He grinds the words out.

"I know, but only because I stalk her on the internet and she posts pictures with her new girlfriend!"

He huffs an annoyed laugh. "What do you want from me, Mars?"

"I want you to forgive me, because I want you in my life. I don't know what to do with myself in New York. I don't know how to be an adult. It's awful." My eyes well with tears. "I want this stupid nightmare of a fight to be over."

He presses a kiss to my forehead, stopping my meltdown in its tracks. I freeze, too stunned to move. I blink up at him through wet eyelashes, and he swallows heavily, looking shaken to his core. "It's fine, Mars," he says, his rough voice scrubbing away the worst layer of our history. I wonder if he downed a shot of whiskey when I wasn't looking. "I forgive you. It's really not that big of a deal."

"It's not?" How could it not be? It's the reason we're not together.

He shakes his head. He *laughs*. "No. We're good."

"Oh, thank god." I let my head fall to his shoulder and my body sag against him. His frame catches my weight; we're touching nearly everywhere, and it feels perfect. We never should have stopped doing this.

Too soon, West straightens and brings us back to middle school–dance position. His hand stiffly on my waist, our arms held out wide, and a familiar foreboding clings to my skin like smoke. "We're good? You're sure?"

"Yes." He nods decisively, but the warning bells are loud in my head.

"So, we're friends now?"

His brows crease. His eyes full of pity. "You're in New York; I'm here. It doesn't make sense."

"But you said we're good." I hate how small and unsure my voice sounds.

"It was college, Mars." He shrugs. "Nothing that happened then matters anyway. I've moved on. You should do the same."

It's only later, after he's dropped my arm and walked off the dance floor, that I realize I selfishly said all the wrong things.

I *want you to forgive me.*

I *don't know what to do with myself in New York.*

I *don't know how to be an adult.*

When what I really meant was *You were my best friend, and*

hurting you is the biggest regret of my life, and you deserve to get everything you've ever wanted.

Even if that isn't me.

~

I cry every mile from California to New York. The flight attendants exchange worried looks and silently pass me tissues as they walk by. I hoped to fix things with West so badly I didn't even admit that I wanted it. Like if I kept it a secret from myself, it couldn't hurt me.

By the time I return to my apartment in Brooklyn, I'm jet-lagged, dehydrated, and exhausted. I haven't slept in twenty-four hours.

I drop my bag just inside the door and fall into bed with my laptop.

Six days later, I email my editor the sequel to *Torched*.

23

Present Day

I spent a lot of my mid-twenties in hotel rooms, and for a few years, it was extremely fun. Traveling to new cities, visiting bookstores across the country, meeting readers, visiting movie sets. Being an author on tour is the best level of famous because absolutely no one knows or cares who you are except for your own fans. I was almost never recognized in public, but my readers were thrilled to meet me at a signing or a conference. And after an event, there is nothing better than coming back to a hotel room, taking off my bra, and eating delivery while watching HGTV.

Tonight, my bra is off, a half-eaten poke bowl rests on my lap, and real estate porn is on mute in the background. Unfortunately, I can't appreciate any of it. I toss a paperback to the end of the bed, where it joins a growing pile. I've read the same page five times, and I couldn't tell you if I'm reading a mystery or a romance.

I stare at my Kindle. It's taunting me from the nightstand. If I open it, I won't have the self-control not to download

Drought, and I don't think I can handle that tonight. Now that I know the reason West refused to go to New York, buried guilt threatens to claw its way to the surface. The fact that he was drowning in fear and self-doubt while I was having sex with some guy I didn't care about is a brutal thought. The last thing I need is to crawl inside West's head and look around.

I groan and pull a pillow over my face.

My mind skips easily from *if* to *if*: If that agent had waited one day to send the rejection. If West had told me about it. If I'd not left the house, not gotten drunk, not tried to hurt West to get back at him for hurting me.

Ugh.

Now is not the time to fall into a depressive spiral. Tomorrow is too important. This book and this tour and this second chance are too important.

I need a distraction. Books aren't cutting it. Reality TV isn't cutting it. Not even a doomscroll is enough to get me out of my own head and my mind off West. I've got one thing left to try, and it's the thing I tend to do when I'm desperately bored or incurably sad.

I redownload my dating apps.

I swore them off six months ago, after I spent an hour getting to Manhattan for a date only to be stood up, ghosted, and blocked without ever meeting the guy. But desperate times and all that.

I open an app that's location based. I don't want to meet anyone in Tucson—heaven forbid—but I'm so burned-out on the wannabe stand-up comedians and finance bros who are inescapable in the city. With any luck, the men of Tucson will be interesting enough to keep my mind off West for the night.

I spend the next hour numbly swiping through the profiles

and am devastated to realize that bad dating profiles aren't unique to New York.

Some things are different in the Southwest: I swipe left on too many pictures of men holding fish, men holding guns, men in the driver's seat of a truck, wearing sunglasses that hide their entire face. There are also way too many guys who can't be bothered to fill out their bio and ones who are looking for their "partner in crime." I'm constantly surprised by the number of men who apparently need someone to rob a bank with. Don't they have friends?

Eventually, I drift to sleep, and hours later, my phone is still open on Josh, 34 (Just ask) when a shrill alarm wrenches me from sleep. Instinctively, I check the phone still clutched in my hand, but the noise is coming from somewhere else. My brain plays catch-up as I blink sleep from my eyes. The alarm is blaring through the hotel, and I'm out of bed with my feet in sandals before I realize there's a fire. My brain turns to autopilot; my body moves without direction. I race seven floors down the smoky stairwell and don't stop running until I get to the crowded parking lot.

It's chaos. People are everywhere. Parents clutch sleeping or crying kids in their arms. I'm weaving through the crowd in search of red hair when my phone lights up with a text from Daphne.

Sidewalk across the street.

I breathe an enormous sigh of relief. When I get to her, she quickly folds me into the blanket wrapped around her shoulders. We huddle together and watch smoke billow from the hotel.

"You're a lifesaver," I say, breath misting in front of me. I didn't consider the nearly freezing weather when I left my room in a thin tank top and sweats, and my teeth chatter from a mixture of cold and adrenaline. Daphne clutches my hand as screaming fire trucks pull onto the scene. Ambulances follow closely behind, but soon enough, word spreads that no one is hurt, and some of the tension in the air dissipates. The fire was contained to several empty conference rooms, and aside from checking out a few people for smoke inhalation, the EMTs stand around without much to do.

Daphne and I sink to the curb and wait, adrenaline draining nearly as quickly as it arrived. She leans her head on my shoulder and drifts off. After what feels like hours, a man from the fire department gathers all the displaced guests and tells us that because of smoke damage, no one will be allowed back inside for several hours.

"Make other arrangements for the night," he concludes.

Daphne yawns.

"Should we start calling hotels?" I ask.

"Doubt we'll have much luck," she says, gesturing to the people around us. Most of the families called other hotels immediately, and we hear loud groans and low mutters of "fully booked." The city is packed due to the book festival; it's not going to be easy to find an empty room in the middle of the night.

"I'll call our mutual sabotage friend Jazz," Daphne says. The phone rings until it goes to voicemail.

"We're old now, Daph. No one we know is awake at this hour." I drop my forehead to my knees and breathe into my hands to stay warm.

"I'm texting her. I'll keep trying."

"If nothing else, there's a twenty-four-hour Waffle House down the street."

"I can't," she says.

"Why not?"

"I'm wearing a crocheted nightgown."

"Cute. Can I see?"

"It's covered in holes."

"As most crocheted things are."

She opens the blanket, giving me a view of her chest.

I press a hand to my mouth to keep from laughing. "You're right. Even for the Waffle House at two a.m., it's too much nipple."

"And that's only the top half." She cinches the blanket tighter around us. "What now?"

"I don't know." My ass is numb from cold concrete.

"What about your old roommate?"

"Amber moved to Oregon a few years ago." I scrub my hands over my face. "If I'd been better about keeping in touch with people from college, we'd have more options."

"Well, we have at least *one* option." She stares at me pointedly.

"No."

"What else are we going to do? Sit here half-naked and turn into Popsicles for the next six hours?"

"I knew you'd understand."

"I absolutely don't."

"I can't, Daph," I whine.

She pulls the blanket from my shoulders and wraps it snugly around herself. "You owe me." I start to protest, but she continues. "For helping your ill-fated revenge scheme and for not even *trying* with your sourdough starter."

I knew that sourdough would come back to bite me in the ass. "Fine! I'll try, but I can't promise he'll answer."

She rolls her eyes. "He will."

West answers after one ring, his voice sounding shockingly coherent for the middle of the night. "What's wrong?"

I walk out of Daphne's earshot. "My hotel caught on fire."

"What?" he barks.

"I'm fine."

He swears under his breath. "Lead with that next time."

"Sorry."

"You need somewhere to stay?" Mercifully, his intuition saves me from having to ask. I wonder absently if he's in bed. If *his* pajamas are appropriate for Waffle House.

I'm in so much trouble.

"Daphne and I both do."

"On my way."

I squirm at the thought. "We can Uber. Text me your address and leave a key under the mat. We'll find a couch to crash on."

"I'm already in the car." The timbre of his voice tells me he's rolling his eyes *hard*.

"Are you wearing a shirt?"

He swears again, this time exasperated instead of annoyed. "I'll see you soon," he says in a low, gruff voice that sends a shiver down my spine. For some reason, his words register like a warning.

I rejoin Daphne under the blanket. "He's on his way."

"I could tell. You had that smile on your face."

"The smile that means we're not going to die of hypothermia?"

"The smile that means you're thinking about West. Your eyes get kind of big and crazy, too."

"Sounds flattering," I say dryly. After a few minutes, I turn to her. "Do you really think my revenge scheme is ill-fated?"

"Do *you* think it's going well?"

That's enough conversation for now, I think.

Less than fifteen minutes after our phone call, West pulls his pickup truck parallel with the curb. Daphne and I stand, and I wonder what her plan is, blanket-wise. Does she care if West sees her nipples?

Do I?

(*Yes. Yes, I do.*)

West steps out of his car as a yellow Volkswagen Beetle pulls up to the curb behind him. "I think that's Jazz," Daphne says, and my relief is staggering. Jazz leans across the empty passenger seat and waves.

"Perfect! We'll go with her! Sorry for bringing you all the way out here," I tell West as he holds the passenger door open. He's wearing gray sweatpants and a white T-shirt, with slippers on his feet and glasses on his nose. It's a combination of choices that makes my throat dry.

Jazz rolls the window down. "Who's coming with me?"

"Both of us!" I'm emphatic, leaving zero room for discussion.

"I hope you don't mind sharing the couch," she says.

"Nope!"

"Or cats. I have four."

I tug the blanket toward the Volkswagen.

"You're allergic to cats," West says.

"No, I'm not!"

"Yes, you are," Daphne says.

"I'll take a Benadryl," I say tightly.

Daphne turns to me. "I love you, Mars, but not enough to be the big spoon, and especially not enough to wake up every thirty minutes and make sure your throat hasn't closed up."

I blink at her. "I'll take the floor."

She presses her hands together, pleading. "It's the middle of the night, we're both freezing, and there's an obvious solution here."

"But—"

"I'm not above begging, Mars. I can barely keep my eyes open."

I glance over my shoulder at West. He's leaning patiently against the open door with his arm draped over the top. He raises one eyebrow in a move that feels like a dare.

I exhale heavily. "Okay."

Daphne pulls the blanket off my shoulders and pushes me toward West. "Don't give me a reason to hate you," she warns him.

"Another reason," I remind her.

"Hmm?"

"You already hate him. You don't need *another* reason."

"Don't worry. I don't bite," he says as I slide into the front seat. He rests his palm on the top of the doorframe and leans in so only I can hear him. "Hard."

West shuts the door with an ominous thud. There's no going back now. I inhale slowly as I buckle my seat belt, the scent inside the truck making my head swim. It smells like I crawled into West's lap and stuck my face in his neck.

He turns the heat up, puts his hand on my headrest, and angles his body toward me as he backs up the car. "So, you really didn't want to go home alone with me, huh?"

I'm in dangerous proximity to his forearm. "Not really."

"Just so we're clear, I was joking about biting."

"So, it *will* be hard?"

I expect him to take a shot back, but his expression sobers. "I want you to feel comfortable tonight. It won't be a repeat of last night."

I roll my eyes. "That's a very honorable speech, but it's not you I don't trust."

"Oh?"

I squirm in my seat, suddenly on fire. I might not trust West with my feelings, but I fully trust him with my safety. He wouldn't do anything that I don't want him to do. The problem is, he might do some of the stuff I *do* want, and that's not a good idea. I press my knees together and crack the window open to get some cool air.

"Was that the woman who asked a bunch of awkward questions at my panel this afternoon?"

"Yep."

"And she's friends with Daphne?"

"Mm-hmm."

Unbelievably, the corner of his mouth quirks up. "Got it."

"It sounds insane when you say it out loud."

"I wonder why that would be."

I suppress a laugh. He's not even mad. Daphne was right; I have no future in revenge.

I shift toward him and lean against the headrest, staring shamelessly. The silence settles, and I suddenly have the alarming thought that I could stay like this for the rest of the night, breathing his air and watching the way streetlights create shadows on his crooked nose, his sharp jaw. I can't get enough of him. It feels like making up for lost time. In lieu of the last ten years, I'll accept a few stolen minutes in a dark car.

His fingers flex on the steering wheel. "You know how to make a guy self-conscious, Darling." His hoarse voice makes my blood hum.

"I won't mess with you anymore," I say.

He throws me a cautious glance. "Why not?"

I shrug. "I'm not very good at it."

He laughs loud enough to indicate his agreement.

"*Even so*," I continue, the words pulled out of me by the late hour and the small space, "it was petty. And it doesn't feel right now that I know what I know. I'm sorry."

"Now that you know I used to be a tragic, insecure loser who was scared of your success?" he asks.

I don't know if he's being sarcastic or serious, so I let the comment drop. It's too late to relitigate the past tonight, and I want to stay a little longer in this bubble with him, pretending that a small but very vocal group of chronically online Torchers wouldn't find it outrageous that I'm on my way to sleep at his house.

"I didn't mind when you were messing with me," he says after a long stretch of silence, and I wonder if he's as sleep-deprived as I am. Maybe he's delirious.

"How quickly you've forgotten that you showed up to the bar last night in my book merch."

"I like knowing that you're thinking about me."

"What else is new?" He's never going to let me forget that I was once so obsessed with him it inspired a half-billion-dollar franchise.

West turns off the main road into a neighborhood with charming tree-lined streets. We pass Whitman, then Elmwood, then Burns. He turns onto Poe Street and pulls into the driveway of a redbrick mid-century modern home with a black front door.

"Tell me the truth. Did you buy this house because it's on *Poe* Street?" I ask.

West turns the car off. "Welcome to Poet's Square."

I laugh, no longer sleepy. I haven't pulled an all-nighter

since I was on deadline for my second book, but I'm feeling the same lightness in my chest that used to hit around this time. "That's cute. Did you come up with that?" Regrettably, I love it.

He laughs. "It's the name of the neighborhood, but I won't pretend it wasn't a contributing factor toward purchasing this home. C'mon. Let's go inside."

"Full moon tonight?" I ask as we walk up the stone path to his door.

"I think so, why?"

I pause, hands on my hips. "Have you done the thing?"

"What thing?"

"West!" I gasp, grabbing his arms. "You have to do the thing!" I tip my head back and howl at the moon. When I lower my chin, West is watching me in awe.

"I haven't thought about that in so long."

"Your turn." I squeeze his biceps, and his pupils double in size. We howl together, too loud and too silly. By the time he unlocks the door and I'm lurching inside, tears of laughter are streaming down my cheeks.

The hall is dark, illuminated only by moonlight, and the door clicking shut lands like an anvil in my ears. West crosses his arms, lifts one foot, and presses it against the door, staring at me intently.

My throat goes dry. I hear nothing but my own shallow breaths.

His soft shirt clings to his body, his sweatpants low on his hips in a way that makes it hard to look anywhere else. I want to curl his eyelashes around my finger and trace the shape of his nose. I want to run my thumb over his lips, then follow it with my tongue.

"So, this is it, huh?" I ask, breaking eye contact. "I wonder where you stash the typewriters."

He flips on a light and leads me into the kitchen. In the bright overhead light, I remember that I'm braless, in pajamas, with smoke in my hair and clinging to my skin.

"Can I get you anything?" he asks as he pours a glass of water and sets it on the counter in front of me.

I drag my fingertip over the rim of the cup. "Just somewhere to sleep, and then you can pretend I'm not here."

"Not possible," he says in a low voice that stirs something inside me. "My bedroom is this way." He points down a long hall just off the kitchen.

"*Your* bedroom?" I ask sharply, my pulse jumping to wild conclusions.

He scratches the back of his neck, looking nervous. "It's the only bed in the house. I'll show you." He leads me down the hall to a room that is clearly his office. It's empty with the exception of a small desk, a laptop, an open notebook, and a handful of blue ink pens.

"Were you writing when I called?"

He confirms, thus quashing my daydream of him jumping shirtless out of bed.

The next room contains a set of weights and half a dozen moving boxes pushed against the wall. I look at him with a raised eyebrow.

"I haven't been here that long," he says defensively.

"Where are you going to sleep?" I ask dubiously. "A couch?"

He shakes his head. "I don't fit. I'm too big." His words hang in the silence between us as we make eye contact for a bit too long. I slap my hand over my mouth to suppress more giggles.

"Get your mind out of the gutter," he scolds. But when he turns away, I don't miss the smirk he's trying to hide. "I'm too tall, and it's murder on my back. I'll blow up an air mattress in here."

"Oh, I can take that."

"Not happening." He motions for me to follow him. We stop at the open door of West's bedroom. I survey the large bed with white sheets and a dove-gray comforter. The room is tidy but lived-in, a jacket draped over the back of a reading chair in the corner, a water bottle by the bed, a stack of books on the floor.

I put the back of my hand to my forehead and pretend to swoon against the doorframe.

"I forgot that you get a little weird when you're tired," West says.

"You have a headboard! And pillowcases!"

"Doesn't everyone?"

"I once hooked up with a guy who kept a bottle under his bed that he would pee in when he was too lazy to get up."

West looks deeply disturbed.

"I was in a situationship for nine weeks with *another* guy who had a mushroom growing in his shower the whole time." I double over, giggling at the disgusting memory. "And then *he* ghosted *me*!"

"Fucking hell, Mars!"

"What? I'm giving you a compliment! You should learn to take it!" I shove him lightly on the shoulder.

His eyes follow the path of the hand that touched him. "Why would you settle for that? Surely you know that you're—" He snaps his jaw shut. The muscle works. "You deserve better than a condemned building," he says somewhat lamely.

"I know. That's why you don't see me with any of them now. But the city, my job—it's lonely." I shrug as the words tumble unexamined from my lips. "And most of the guys who ask me out still act like boys. But look at you." I gesture to the room, the house, him. "You have your shit together. You're an adult. A *man*."

Heat crawls up my spine. *What the hell was that?* I meant it as a general acknowledgment of the passage of time, but one look at West's gobsmacked expression tells me that my diatribe sounds as bad as I fear. Like I'm measuring West against the people I date, and he comes out on top.

Trouble left the station a long time ago. I am well and truly fucked.

"I don't know why I said that," I say in a quick breath.

West's eyes darken as the air between us shifts, stretching taut, pulling us together—though we don't move. My slaphappy mood sobers, and desire melts through me, dripping slowly, pooling, gathering, simmering until I'm molten. Want reaches every part of my body. Tightening my chest and gathering between my thighs and making my toes curl. I worry my bottom lip between my teeth and suddenly remember West's words. *I don't bite. Hard.* Another flush of my skin, and impossibly, his gaze grows hungrier. His intent is familiar, but the intensity is new.

I glance over my shoulder at the bed, and when I meet his eyes again, all the corded muscles in his neck and arms are visible. His hand flexes on the doorknob for the length of time it takes to build an empire and watch it collapse.

"If you don't say something right now, I'll walk to Jazz's house and take my chances with the cats," I say in a voice much huskier than I intended.

His expression is tortured, and I can't tell if my outburst has horrified or intrigued him. I take half a step toward him at the exact moment West tears his eyes away. The tension defuses.

He clears his throat and points toward the connecting bathroom. "You'll find clean towels in the linen closet. T-shirts are in my dresser."

Horrified, then. Good to know.

I blink at him, unsure how I misread the situation so astronomically.

"I, uh, assume you want to get out of your smoky clothes."

"Thanks." I don't trust myself to say more.

"If you leave your clothes in the hall, I'll wash them so you have something to wear in the morning."

"You don't have to do that."

"But I will," he says, leaving no room for debate. I nod once.

West stands in the space between the hall and the bedroom for another minute, looking like a man desperate to confess his deepest secrets, but with a final clench of his jaw, he says, "Night, Darling," and backs slowly away.

I watch him retreat to the room across the hall and pretend the feeling in my gut isn't disappointment. For a few heart-stopping seconds, I thought he'd finally found the words he promised me a decade ago. The *right* ones, whatever that means. Logically, however, I know I'm better off with his silence. The right words no longer exist between West and me.

Showering in West's bathroom is as weird and wonderful as I expected. I can't help but pick up and inspect everything: his razor, his shaving cream, shampoo, conditioner, bodywash. I huff them all until I get high off the scent of him for old time's sake, letting myself do what twenty-year-old Mars could only dream of.

I've been tiptoeing into dangerous territory all night, but now I fling myself in headfirst.

I wear one of his soft T-shirts, which hangs to my knees. No underwear. His shirt feels indecent as I slide the cotton over my skin. The hem brushes against my bare thighs, and I have a hunch that I'm going to feel the imprint of the soft stitches for a long time.

I approach West's bed on cautious tiptoe, though I'm not sure what I'm scared of. I kneel on the floor and inspect the stack of books. I've only read a few of them. My heart thunders as I slowly slide open his bedside drawer. The scrape of wood is as loud as church bells. I hold my breath and wait to be caught snooping, but the house is quiet, and I resume my excavation.

The drawer is nearly empty, aside from a handful of condoms and a small stack of papers.

I make a promise to myself that I won't read anything as I pick up the stack and thumb through it quickly. There are a few cards. A letter. West's passport and birth certificate. What looks like the closing documents for this house. Sticking out of a corner near the bottom of the pile is a piece of bright blue paper that catches my eye. I flip to it, and there's a brief moment of confusion as I stare at my own signature below a scrawled note that says **Margot Darling's #1 Fan**.

A joke I made in another lifetime. A throwaway moment that I haven't thought about since.

Quiet footsteps pass the door. I dump everything back in the drawer and jump to my feet, heart pounding recklessly in my chest. By the time I slide between West's sheets, I'm wide-awake, vibrating with sensory overload, unsure I'll survive the night.

24

9 Years Ago

I wake up criminally early on the day *Torched* is published. I'm an antsy little kid on Christmas morning, too excited to sleep. I lie in bed and comb through my social media comments, congratulations pouring in from my family, friends, and anyone my parents have ever met. My parents are deeply concerned about the way these "damn millennials" are buying too much avocado toast and moving back in with their parents, but now that I've survived a year and a half in New York without once asking for money, they've finally accepted that they can brag about me to their friends—without caveats that my book would be published *eventually, someday, no really!* As of today, I'm no longer a jobless menace to society. I'm an author. Even better, a *novelist*. They are so supportive. They are so *proud*.

I'm outside the Barnes & Noble in Park Slope when they open up the store, and I'm greeted by a table of my books at the front of the YA section. I wonder if this is the part where I cry. It doesn't happen, but that's okay. Happy tears have never really been my thing. I take a hundred pictures, and they all look awful; bookstore lighting is a crime. I post online with captions that I drafted last week, and I check the clock.

With more than ten hours until my launch party and no other plans for the day, I walk to Trader Joe's and carry my groceries back to my apartment. I repost every story that I'm tagged in. I write Thank you!!!!! one million times. I abuse the black heart emoji.

I sit on my bed and wait.

I check my phone again, again, again. He doesn't contact me.

I'm signing books on a small stage at the back of my local independent bookstore. Bookshelves have been cleared out to make room for about thirty folding chairs, only some of which are occupied. I hoped for more, but apparently no one comes out to see an author until they already know and love you, and that takes time. I invited my parents and brothers, but they couldn't make the trip. I assume I'll see them in San Diego on the last stop of my eight-city tour, but maybe not.

"I've been excited to read your book for months."

I look up from the pen in my hand to a tall, stunning redhead. I blink in surprise. "Really?"

She nods eagerly. "I've seen it everywhere online. I can't wait to read it."

My chest prickles with a warm feeling. "Thank you. Do you want the book made out to you?"

"Please. My name is Daphne. I'm a writer, too!" she confesses as I write my name in big, swooping letters across the title page of *Torched*.

I glance at her again. She looks about my age. "What do you write?"

"Everything. Lots of stuff. Historical right now, although it's hard with my roommate. She and her boyfriend fight a lot. They're screamers."

A small bell chimes as the door at the front of the store opens. My eyes are drawn to the dark curls of the man entering. For one heartbeat, I stop breathing, but then I exhale—it's not him.

"Sorry, what?" I turn my attention back to the redhead.

"Can we take a picture with the book?" Daphne asks.

"Sure! Of course!"

Her friend holds the cell phone and snaps a picture, and when she turns it to us for posting approval, I lay eyes on the ugliest picture of myself I've ever seen. "Looks great!"

"I'll tag you!" she promises before she turns to leave.

"Wait!" I cry. When she looks at me over her shoulder, I take a chance. "Do you want a new roommate?"

The store locks its doors behind me. I go home alone, where I drink a glass of wine and watch a rerun of *Grey's Anatomy*. Same thing I did last night. Same thing I'll do tomorrow night.

When I close my eyes, I think of a man with dark curls ducking into the bookstore. This time, he has multicolored eyes.

Just over a week after *Torched*'s release, Whitney calls to tell me that I've hit the *New York Times* Best Seller list.

Again, I wait for tears that don't come, and this time I wish they would, because I don't know how to process this information.

The predominant feeling is a free fall of relief.

I can finally relax. I can stop worrying.

As it turns out, publishing a bestselling book series is pretty fun.

Everyone wants to be friends with me. My inbox is filled with messages from authors I've been obsessed with for years. I'm booked to appear at conferences that require an exclusive invitation. I'm added to group chats with names that make me blink twice when I see them. My follower count increases every day. Unbelievably, I'm in the Cool Kids of Publishing club.

The crowds at my signings are getting a little bigger at every stop, and girls are showing up in homemade Fox Caldwell T-shirts. They beg for the sequel. The bookstore near me can't keep *Torched* in stock for more than a few days at a time. Oh, and did I mention the movie? A production company in Hollywood snapped up the film rights, attached a director, and started production in record time.

I've moved on from West. I joined the apps, I swipe right, and I send flirty messages to my matches. It hasn't led anywhere yet. It's hard when I'm traveling so much. When I told one guy that I'd be out of town for the next few months, he hit me up for nudes to keep him busy while I was gone. *Blocked*. Another guy accused me of lying about my job after he googled me. His bio said he was a writer and musician. I'd told him I was a writer, too, but he took that to mean I was a work-from-home SEO content machine. When he saw a feature on me in *Slate*, he blocked *me*. After he called me a bitch.

I don't think about West anymore, except when I do. When it's one of those nights, I can't help but wonder what he thinks of all this. If he sees my name online. If he walks around with a smug expression, knowing he inspired an "instant cultural phenomenon" (*Slate*'s words, not mine). I get asked all the time where I got the idea for the book and who inspired Fox. I always give some dumb, vague answer about "the power of imagination." I feel ridiculous every time I say it.

The second time I hallucinate West in the audience, it's at my hometown bookstore in San Diego. My parents seized the opportunity to show me off and invited every person they've ever met. The mailman? Yes. Their local Trader Joe's cashier? Yes. (He *came*. I'm mortified.) They invited their old college roommates and the parents of all my high school acquaintances and the HOA board members my mom has been feuding with for a decade.

It's standing room only, and I'm melting under the scrutiny of fluorescent lighting and people who've known me since I was a baby. I'm jet-lagged, and I'm hungry. It's probably the hunger that does it. I really should have eaten something. I see a flash of dark hair, the collar of a jacket pulled up against scruffy cheeks. I blink and he's gone. My face is hotter than ever, and this Q&A session feels never-ending.

“How did you come up with Fox?” asks a girl in the audience. She has braces, a fox-ear headband, and hearts in her eyes.

I snap my focus back to the crowd. “I’m sorry, can you repeat your question?”

“Was he inspired by anyone you know in real life?” she asks as my eyes stray to the back of the store. I squint against the bright lights.

“And how can I meet him?” another voice asks. Everyone laughs.

I could have sworn it was West.

“Margot?” The moderator prompts my response, and I drag my attention back to the Q&A, searching for the answer I’ve given at least a dozen times.

I can’t find it.

They’re staring at me, and I can feel myself bombing. My mom is sitting rigidly in her chair, hands clenched. Her eyes slide around to her friends, and I realize I have to say something or risk embarrassing her in front of the people whose approval she needs the most.

“Yeah, yes. West—I mean Fox—he was inspired by the boy I was in love with when I was in college.”

“Oooh,” my moderator croons, sounding excited. “What happened to him?”

I turn to her, wondering how I got myself into this situation. I can’t tell a room of my mom’s friends that I got drunk and had sex with someone else.

I swallow heavily, searching for the simplest truth. “He’s the one that got away.”

25

Present Day

If I thought that West's truck smelled like him, it has *nothing* on his bed. My head is on his pillow, and I might as well be drowning in West Emerson pheromones.

It's *torture.*

A message to anyone looking for cruel and unusual forms of punishment: Drop your subject into the bed of their smoking-hot ex who is also a professional rival and sometimes asshole. For maximum agony, do it after he's rescued them in the middle of the night. Bonus points if he's been holding on to an artifact from their past.

Waffle House is looking pretty good right about now.

I punch West's pillow, annoyed that it's the perfect amount of squashy. His sheets feel clean, his blankets soft, his bed comfortable. This is a nightmare.

I'm overtired, overstimulated, and can't stop tossing and turning, my mind switching between the hunger in West's eyes when we stood on the threshold to this room and the email that I saw on his phone from the one person who he knows would hurt me the most. Either West is playing games with me, or I tragically misunderstood the look on his face earlier. His expression could have been exhaustion or frustration or annoyance. Or maybe my own hormones were clouding my judgment, making me see phantoms where none exist.

I cross the room and crack the door open, hoping to hear the sound of West's deep, even breathing in the room directly across the hall. Instead, his door is also propped open, and I hear him fidgeting on the air mattress. Startled, I sprint back to bed, mortified by the idea that he can likewise hear my erratic breathing and comically loud heartbeat. He's going to think I'm getting hot and bothered in his sheets, and he'll be half-right. I'm bothered, but I won't let myself get hot for him. Not when it's less than twenty-four hours after finding out he set me up. *Again*.

I unlock my phone and mindlessly open the same dating app from earlier. I'm mindlessly swiping left after left after left when I stop myself just in time. I sit upright, my heart pounding.

West, 32

I zoom in on West's profile picture and slap my hand over my mouth to keep from laughing at how bad it is. West in real life is melt-my-clothes-off hot, but it's impossible to tell that from this faraway, slightly out-of-focus picture of him hiking. He's squinting into the sun, half his face covered in shadows from his hat.

Whoever told him this picture was a good choice is praying on his downfall. I'll send a gift basket.

My thumb hovers over the screen, indecision pulling me in

both directions. In the end, curiosity about the rest of his profile threatens to eat me alive. I swipe right.

We match.

Across the hall, West curses just loud enough to reach my ears.

I'm drenched in endorphins as a chat bubble appears on my screen. As always, any clever thought I've ever had evaporates. There's nowhere that I'm less charming, less funny, less knowing-how-to-put-words-together than a first message. There's also nowhere I'm more judgmental; I half hope that West sends me a generic *How's your day been?* or an even worse *Hi*, because it will be my solemn and sworn duty to unmatch him.

I lick my lips, waiting.

He's taking too long, and I get impatient. My fingers fly over the keys. Before I can hit send, a message appears.

U up?

I laugh loud enough that he must hear it.

I respond with my prewritten message.

Congratulations on your first match!

How'd you know?

Your profile picture.

Ouch.

Move your third picture to the top spot.

The one in the sweater?

In the third picture, he's alone at a table with a stack of papers in front of him. He looks like a sexy, disheveled English teacher. Hair in his eyes, red ink on his hands. I'm blindingly jealous of whoever took it.

I don't want to stroke his ego too much, so I keep my reply simple.

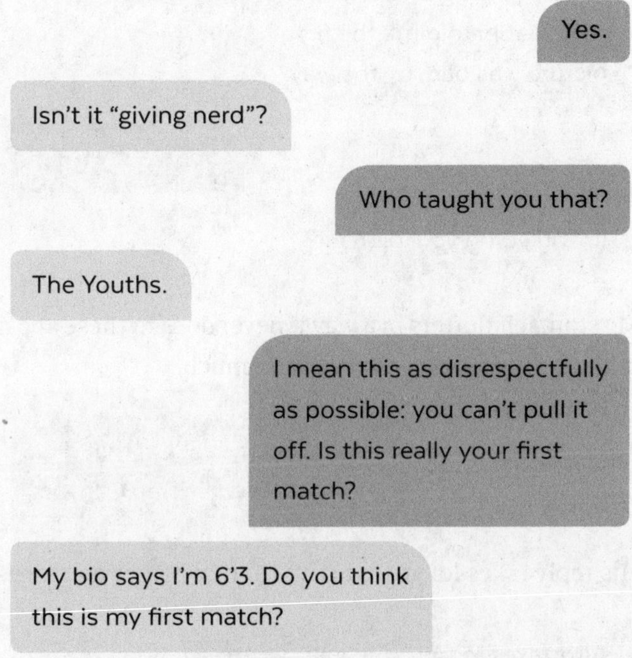

Damn. He's right. I know girls who would swipe right on the grim reaper if he were tall with a jawline.

Life for tall men must be so easy.

You forgot sexy.

Says who?

You like me in a sweater. I read between the lines.

Don't let it go to your head.

I'm afraid it's way too late for that. Gabbi told me the first picture was bad, by the way.

She's not wrong.

It worked on you, didn't it?

My stomach flutters in a way it never does in these app conversations. I'm enjoying this *way* too much.

It was the sexy saguaro that did it. I always loved Sabino Canyon.

His reply takes longer to arrive than his other messages.

All it takes to turn you on is desert landscaping and pillowcases? You've set the bar in hell.

I bite my lip and switch to a more relaxed position, settling in. I pull West's comforter up to my chin as I type.

New York beat the hope and romanticism out of me.

I don't believe you.

I'm serious. I'm jaded and cynical now.

Hence the swooning over my headboard.

I hear the words in his dry voice and flip to my other side as warmth spreads through my body. This is headed in a dangerous direction.

My swooning made you look like you were going to be sick.

That's not what it was.

Do tell.

I'm baiting him, and awaiting his response is pure, everlasting agony.

I've been waiting 10 years to get you in my bed, Darling. No, I don't want to hear you talk about other guys.

I blink open-mouthed at my phone. *What am I supposed to say to* that?

I put the screen to sleep and drop it on my chest, trying to make sense of this information. I lie in darkness, save for the faint glow of his phone slipping through the crack in my door, until mine chimes with a new message.

Too much?

Yes.

No.

When I saw West at Amber's wedding, he made it crystal clear that he'd moved on. And later, it became painfully obvious that he wanted nothing to do with me. But now he wants to pretend that he's been pining for me or some bullshit?

I just don't believe you.

Even after last night?

Was it the bickering in the bar that was supposed to convince me or the fury in his eyes when I read his book onstage? Clearly, he means the kiss, but I'm not a lovesick undergrad anymore. One nostalgia-and-hormone-fueled moment is not enough to rewrite our history.

Especially after last night.

Across the hall, West's phone blinks off.

26

8 Years Ago

Two and a half years in the city, and I still don't know how to dress for cold weather. I have boots, gloves, and a coat that doubles as a sleeping bag, but when I duck into a bookstore fourteen blocks from home, I've lost all feeling in my nose. My cheeks are windburned and stiff. My eyelashes are chipping off like icicles. When I get home, I'm buying the biggest Lenny Kravitz scarf I can find and wrapping my face like a mummy. I'll be nothing but a pair of eyeballs until spring.

As I enter the shop, the bookseller tells me that they're closing early because of the storm, but I can stay inside and warm up for a few minutes while they close out the register and clean up. I visit *Torched* first and sign stock while the bookseller tags the covers with cute little Signed by the Author stickers. After that, I browse the rest of the YA section like I'm visiting my friends, and then I check historical fiction for Daphne's novel.

Daphne did tag me in that horrible photo on Instagram; I

DMed her to tell her that unfortunately, my vanity would not allow me to remain tagged. She came to look at my apartment the next day, and a few weeks later, she moved into the spare bedroom. And then one day, without realizing it, I had a new best friend. She's a nanny for a wealthy Upper East Side family, but she moves through the world like she has spare hours stuffed up her sleeves. She writes, gets an agent, sells her novel. Every time I blink, she has a new tattoo. She starts an herb garden in our kitchen before quickly abandoning it. Her resolution for the New Year is to learn to crochet; she's already stockpiling yarn on every flat surface available. When I'm in town, she walks with me to the coffee shop on her mornings off, and when her historical fiction novel is released, we celebrate together.

I am *so* much happier at her book launch than I was at mine.

Her book isn't selling well, and she's bummed about it. I look for it in the store, hoping to snap a picture and send it to her to cheer her up, but it's not in stock. Almost no store has it in stock, which is half the problem. How is anyone supposed to read a book they don't know about?

"I'll be finished in about five minutes," the bookseller calls. I weave my way through tight shelves toward the front of the store, stopping at an endcap labeled Local Authors. I scan the dozen titles; once again, Daphne's is nowhere to be seen. I make a mental note to ask the bookseller to order a copy to add to their display on my way out. I'm walking away when I stop and do a double take. Sitting on the bottom row, only inches off the floor, is one copy of a little black paperback with a white title. *Oasis*. Small letters under the title spell *West Emerson*.

I blink several times.

I slowly pick up the book. There's no author photo, but there is a short bio on the back cover.

> West Emerson *was born and raised in the Southwest but now lives in Manhattan.* Oasis *is his first novel.*

The store lights turn off. "Are you ready to leave?"

"Coming!" I yell. My heart is pounding feverishly. I hear the front door open and a whoosh of cold air and snow flurries swirls into the store. "Can I buy this book?"

"Sorry, the register is closed."

I open my bag and dig for cash, but come up empty-handed.

"I can hold it behind the counter for you," she offers. I'm disappointed, but she tucks the book under the front counter and locks the door behind us.

The city is blanketed in snow for the rest of the week. After that, I'm preparing for tour, and then it's the holidays, and I'm unable to make it back to the bookstore for a few weeks. By the time I do, the sidewalks are covered in a completely different layer of ice and snow. I was paranoid that an employee would reshelve West's book, but they assured me over several phone calls that they wouldn't.

I pay for the book with jittery hands and walk home in record time. Inside my apartment, I stand frozen for a solid minute, my fingers wrapped around the spine. I'm momentarily paralyzed by indecision, but then my fingers thaw, and reality comes into focus.

I'm about to go on tour for my second book, and I can't get wrapped up in the idea of West again. I'm finally emotionally disentangled. I have a third date tonight with a cute guy I met on an app. His messages are a little dull, and when I caught a glimpse of his apartment last weekend, it was filthy, but he's nice to me. He always messages first. I have a good feeling about him.

I slide *Oasis* next to a copy of *Torched* on the bookshelf in my bedroom and promise myself that I'll never read it.

27

Present Day

I thought time would fade West from my memory, but it didn't happen like that.

It happened like this.

I close my eyes and remember. I hold on to everything. I preserve him in resin. I fall asleep and trace the crooked line of his nose. I run the pad of my thumb over the swoop of his lashes. I lick the divot above his lips.

Tonight, he stumbles into the darkness of my room, and it's achingly familiar. I've imagined his hands on me more times than it happened in real life. I feel the drag of his fingers over the bare skin of my hip before they slide forward, flattening over my stomach. I roll onto my back, desperate for contact. His hand slides to my ribs and stops. I arch into him, groaning in frustration. His touch has me in shambles.

His face is over mine now. He's shirtless, in the same gray sweatpants he was wearing earlier. His thumb brushes against the underside of my breast, and I wriggle against the sheets, looking for friction I can't find.

His lips fall to my neck. The scrape of his whiskered jaw against sensitive skin makes me shiver. I run my hand down his chest to his waistband. He swears loudly and collapses to his elbows, his weight pressing me into the mattress. It feels so good I almost pass out. He drags his tongue from my collarbone to my ear, and I'm panting.

"Can I touch you?" he rasps. He sounds like he swallowed a fistful of gravel.

"Yes," I beg. I press my hips against his, the shock of contact threatening to burn me alive.

He slides his hand down to the inside of my thigh and nudges. My knees fall apart.

"But I thought you hated me." I hear the smirk in his voice.

"I do." I grind out the words. My eyes fly open, and I catch a glimpse of chest, forearms, muscles, before he rolls off me and flips me over. I'm on my stomach, my hands scrabbling for purchase.

He presses a line of kisses down my spine and then traces back over his work with his tongue. He settles his chest against my shoulder blades, crushing the air from my lungs so perfectly I want to ask him to do it again. I bite my lip to keep quiet as his mouth ghosts over my ear. "Do you want me or not, Jupiter?"

"I don't know," I pant.

I feel the whisper of his hands everywhere. "I'll have to help you decide," he promises. I don't know if it's a vow or a threat.

I wake up, sweaty and flushed, West's sheets twisted around my ankles and damp heat pooling between my legs. I don't dare reach down and feel, knowing I won't be able to stop myself from finishing the job. I bite my lip and screw my eyes shut tight while my heart slows and I try to repress the feeling of

West's weight pinning me into the mattress. *His mattress.* The one he claims he's been waiting to get me on.

I need to get out of here.

I pull myself up and make West's bed look less like I had a sex dream about him. When I find my clean pajamas folded on his nightstand, I ignore the possibility that he might have walked in *while* I was having a sex dream about him. I step softly into the hall and stop in my tracks at the soft murmur of voices. *Plural.*

I tense for whatever I'm about to walk into, but a smile blooms on my face as I enter the kitchen. "Gabbi?"

"Hey, Mars." She looks up from her phone. She's wearing a matching orange workout set and has two neon star-shaped zit patches on her chin. She's folded up comfortably in one of West's kitchen chairs. He's standing over the stove, stirring something in a saucepan. He glances over his shoulder at us, his eyes sparking with interest, but he doesn't say anything.

"You remember me?" I ask Gabbi.

"Sure. We went to those caves that one time, and you bought me one of those black velvet souvenir bags filled with shiny rocks."

I lean my hip against the counter. West wordlessly hands me a cup of coffee, which I accept without taking my eyes off his sister. I need more distance between the dream and the next time I look at him. "I did?"

"I think I still have it somewhere. I fucking loved those things."

"Wow. Good for me," I say. West chuckles.

Gabbi's eyes dart to her brother before she looks back at me with an apologetic grimace. "I didn't realize you'd be here when I came over."

"It's fine," I assure her quickly. "It's not what it looks like. I'm just crashing here because of a fire in my hotel."

"I know," Gabbi says.

"Oh." I tuck my hair behind my ears, feeling West's eyes on the back of my neck.

"Why, what did you think I meant?" she asks.

"West and I aren't, we're not—" I'm searching for the words to emphasize that nothing is going on between her brother and me when he stretches across the counter and gently removes the mug from my hand. His arm brushes mine as he lifts the mug to his lips. He takes a long sip and wordlessly hands it back to me, as if to say *We are.* I blink up at him, dazed as his tongue darts out to lick a drop of coffee off his lower lip.

Gabbi watches with raised eyebrows, and any plausible deniability I had goes right out the window. I swallow, my knees a little wobbly after West's naked display of intimacy. "So, what are you up to this morning?" I ask Gabbi.

"Just stopping by to borrow West's lockpick. I locked myself out when I went for a run this morning." She rolls her eyes at herself and lets out a colorful series of swear words.

"Hey, since you brought it up, is your brother a serial killer or something? I can't think of another reason he'd own one of those."

West glances up at me over the bowl he's cracking eggs into. "It's for late-night break-ins." He throws me an easy smile, and I have to repress false memories of his mouth doing other things, the dark scruff on his chin scraping wonderfully against my skin.

"It's for me," Gabbi interjects. "I'm a fucking idiot, and I lock myself out all the time."

"Was a spare key out of the question?"

"If I had a nickel for every spare key I've given him, taken back, and then lost, I'd have at least two nickels. Now he keeps a lockpick on hand because he's worried I'm leaving keys all over the city."

"I wonder what it's like," I muse.

"What?" Gabbi asks.

"To know the version of West that's thoughtful. Kind. Not an asshole. I've heard rumors of his existence, but . . ." I shrug and take a sip of coffee.

Gabbi laughs, and West gamely ignores the insult. "There's oatmeal with brown sugar on the stove. I remember you used to like that. Scrambled eggs will be ready in a few minutes. Or feel free to raid the pantry. You can have anything you want." His voice is still hoarse from sleep, and when his eyes flit to mine, a flash of last night's dream comes back to me.

Gabbi stands and stretches. "He wants you to have the oatmeal, though."

"Gabbi." West's tone is exasperated, with maybe a hint of warning?

"He went to the store at seven a.m. to buy it," Gabbi says with a gleeful smile. "Okay, bye!" She scoops up West's lockpick from a key bowl and jogs down the hall and out the front door.

His fingers find a pen on the counter. He spins it in a circle. "She can be a lot."

"She's a little sister. Torturing our older brothers is our birthright."

"I deserve it, probably. She's actually pretty cool." He picks up the pen and taps it against granite.

Adult West is less fidgety than the boy I met at nineteen, but it's still there inside him, emerging when he's not keeping it carefully restrained. He almost looks *nervous*.

"What is the rest of your family up to these days?" I ask.

"One brother is a forest ranger in Idaho, another one is on a cross-country biking trip at the moment, and the baby of the family is still living with my parents. They're all doing well. I don't go home that often, though."

"Still?"

"I'm not angry anymore. I just know what's good for me and what's not. After my grandma passed and my brothers all got a bit older, my mom didn't need as much help with them."

I nod as five hundred follow-up questions appear in my head unbidden. "I should leave."

"Now? You don't want to eat?"

I look at my dead phone. I can't contact Daphne, I have no hotel room to return to, and I *should* eat before my signing this morning. I can spend another thirty minutes with West, right? What's the worst that could happen?

"Do you have a charger?"

He shows me where to plug in my phone, and then I cross the kitchen and hop onto the counter next to the stove while he scrambles eggs in the pan. I don't want to give him a trophy for doing the most basic cooking task, but too many of the guys I've gotten into situationships with in New York treat food delivery apps like their own personal chef and taxi service.

I lean my head against the cupboard while I watch West and wonder if this is what we would have had if he'd come to New York with me. And if we had spent Sunday mornings making breakfast together, would it have lasted, or would his self-esteem and my career have blown it all up anyway?

"You're ruminating," West says.

"A little."

"What about?"

"I haven't seen any gaming consoles in your house."

"*That's* what you're thinking about?"

"That and the stack of papers on your table." The pile of papers with a red pen sitting on top has been in my peripheral vision since I entered the kitchen. "What are they?" I hop off the counter and scoop oatmeal and brown sugar into a bowl.

"Student essays." West serves himself eggs and toast before sitting across from me.

"What students?"

"Mine."

I choke on my oatmeal. "Hit men have students?"

"First assignment: ten thousand words on how to hide a body."

"What's the second assignment?"

This stumps him. "Assassination?"

"Practical."

He laughs. "I'm a high school English teacher, Mars. These are essays I need to grade."

"I was kidding when I called you a sexy English professor."

He arches a brow. "When did you call me that?"

Oops. Must have been in my head.

"So, high school, huh?" I ask.

"Kinda crazy, right?"

I feel a welcome rush of irritation. "As in teenagers?"

"Yes," he says slowly, perhaps sensing a trap.

"For how long?"

"This is my second year. I moved back here to get my teaching certificate and have a more stable job, as fun as it was having four roommates and no money in New York."

"Do you like it?" My mind sketches a portrait of West with reading glasses perched on his nose, chalk dust in his hair, and elbow patches on his tweed jacket. It fits.

"I do. I mean, no one wants to need two jobs, but until I'm making real money from writing, this isn't a bad gig. Dr. B wants me to get a master's degree and teach in his department, so that's an option, too. The kids are awesome, but every single day they come to school and say the most unhinged things I've ever heard in my life. Last week, one of them looked me in the eyes and said I'll never get a girlfriend because I dress like his dead grandpa. They give *zero* fucks."

"You don't terrorize them into respecting you?"

"You can't terrorize this generation into respecting shit."

"Well, there goes my last theory."

"About what?"

"Why you're so jacked. I was sure you were something scary like a hit man or a gravedigger. But between two jobs and all the macros you must be counting—"

"I don't do that." He looks offended.

I laugh and turn my head to the side. I drop the teasing lilt and drag my spoon through oatmeal. "I'm surprised you and Gabbi are so close," I say, trying to keep the conversation in neutral territory and *not* on his muscles.

He scoffs. "You made that clear when you told her I'm an inconsiderate asshole."

I bite the inside of my cheek. I cast West as the villain in my life so long ago, it's difficult to accept that without a time machine, he could be anything else.

"You're right, I'm sorry. You're one of the good guys, but you make exceptions for me."

West sets his fork down and pushes his plate out of the way as he leans toward me. His gaze is piercing. "Is there a world in which you forgive me? Ever?" he asks in a voice that makes the hair on the back of my neck stand up.

"This is a pointless conversation."

A muscle in his jaw works. "You're telling me there's nothing I can do to fix things between us?"

The oatmeal turns to sludge in my stomach. "Correct."

He drums his fingers on the table as he stares at me, his expression scrutinizing. "Give me your worst."

"What do you mean?" My voice wobbles.

He waves his hand for me to get on with it. "I'm serious, Mars. Get it all out of your system. All the scathing words you've written in your head over the last decade. I want it all on the record."

"Why?"

"I need to know what I'm up against."

I close my eyes and take a breath. It doesn't matter what he says now, because it can't change the fact that he never loved me the way I loved him, and all it ever got me was pain. I don't hate myself enough to try to make it work for a third time.

"Nothing we had is worth salvaging, West."

"That's bullshit and you know it."

"What am I supposed to think? You see me for a few days and get lost in college memories and think you want something more, but we've been here before. This isn't the first time we've done this dance!"

He folds his arms, his eyes narrowing. "This is different. *I'm* different now," he insists.

"Do you still have that interview scheduled for today?"

"Yes."

"If you cared about me at all, you wouldn't." I don't bother to hide the thickness in my throat as tears burn my eyes. I push back from the table and grab my phone from the charger, quickly requesting an Uber.

West pushes to his feet with a pained expression. "I'm trying to fix this, Mars, but I need a little more time to show you. Give me time," he pleads.

"You had a decade! A decade in which you did not show up, did not care, and pushed me away every chance you got. Time's up, West. It's too late."

28

7 Years Ago

Fox Caldwell is the internet's favorite book boyfriend, and I have no one but myself to blame. I've created my own personal hell. The fact that I based him on an ex-boyfriend becomes a fandom fixation; I get comments every week asking who he is.

I thought *Torched* was popular, but the sequel exploded to a degree I couldn't have fathomed. Book sales are in the millions. Fox fever is sweeping the nation. Multicolored contacts are flying off shelves.

I've never had more money or attention in my life. I've also never been so creatively stuck. My third book was due months ago. The deadline came and went. Emails from Whitney started out gentle and understanding, but now they've adopted a panicked tone. She says that I should just send her what I have, that she trusts my vision for this series. That's her first mistake. I don't even trust myself anymore.

The only thing I know for sure is that the series needs a happy ending. Millions of readers are invested in this love story, and I can't imagine a world in which I write anything *other* than a happy ending. It would be a betrayal. Fox and Juniper are supposed to end up together, but I don't know how to get them there. I can't open my laptop without crumbling under the weight of reader expectation. It was easier to write when there was the possibility that no one would ever read it.

The *Torched* movie premieres on a warm weekend in September. I take photos with the absurdly beautiful cast and wave to the screaming fans who are waiting in the rain. Every time someone tells me they can't wait for the next book, I bite another nail down to the quick. By the end of the evening, all of my fingers are bleeding.

It's in this condition that I run into West for the first time in two years.

My red-eye from the premiere took me straight to Boston, and I'm standing with my luggage at Ground Transportation outside Logan Airport when I feel a tap on my shoulder. I yelp in surprise and spin around. West Emerson is standing in front of me with a backpack slung over his shoulder, saying something I can't hear.

"Hang on." I take out my AirPods. "What'd you say?"

"Sorry for scaring you! I was just saying hi."

"Hi." I'm in shock. West leans toward me, then rethinks, and I kind of lean in but not really, and it's awkward, and we both laugh. "Hug?" I ask. He nods and wraps his arms around me for the world's briefest hug.

After I found out that West moved to New York, I was on edge for weeks, thinking I'd run into him on the street or in the subway. I can't believe that when it finally happens, we're in Boston of all places.

"What are you doing here?" I ask. He's wearing joggers and a hoodie that he's owned since college. His curls are brushing the tops of his ears.

"Waiting for a bus."

"But what are you doing *here*? In Boston."

He runs a hand over the back of his neck. "I'm, uh, on my way to a work thing."

"What are you up to these days?"

He hesitates. "I'm kind of a writer now. *Barely*. Not like you."

I shake my head, frustrated that he still feels this way about himself. "Don't do that. Don't minimize it. Your book is called *Oasis*, right?"

"That's right," he says. If he's surprised that I already know, he doesn't look it.

"Congratulations. I'm happy for you."

"Thanks, Mars."

"You live in New York now?" I confirm, and West nods. Again, he doesn't seem surprised that I'm up to date on his life. "What are you waiting for? Tell me everything! What's the book about? When did you write it?"

He searches for something in my expression. I hold my breath, but after a few moments, his features slide into something more neutral. "Maybe another time. It's not that interesting."

"It *is*, though! You did it, West." Regret strikes me suddenly. I should have contacted him the day I saw his book. I wonder if he also spent his publication day waiting for a text that never came.

He exhales a hollow laugh. "I don't know about all that. My publisher is basically three guys and a dog. I think my novel sold twelve copies total."

"What does the dog do?"

"He's our emotional support and mascot. Also proofreading," he says dryly.

I laugh. "You're here for work?"

"I might have used the term 'work' a little too loosely. I'm staying in a house on Martha's Vineyard with some friends for the week; we'll be writing."

My eyes widen, and then I burst into nearly hysterical laughter. I blame my overtired, jet-lagged brain.

West watches with amusement. "Care to share with the class?"

"Do you want to hear something crazy?"

"Crazier than a dog who proofreads novels?"

"I'm also on my way to Martha's Vineyard to stay in a house and write for a week."

"Do you know Tristan Rossiter?" he asks incredulously.

"Who?"

"His parents own the house."

"Never heard of him, but my roommate was invited last minute and she's dragging me along."

"Do you think we're going to the same place?"

"Nah, I'm sure we're both on our way to two different writing retreats on the same island at the exact same time."

"Really?"

I give him a look.

"Sarcasm, got it." He rubs the back of his neck, and I want to say anything to make our conversation last.

"Do you want to hear something ridiculous?"

"You don't have to keep asking me if I want to hear things. You can assume that I do."

"When I was little, I thought Martha's Vineyard was Martha

Stewart's own private island. I've never been able to separate the two in my mind."

He laughs as my Uber driver pulls up to the curb and rolls the window down. "Margot?"

I look at West. If we separate now, we probably won't meet back up until we're under the same roof. It's a long car ride to the ferry terminal in Woods Hole. I'm low on sleep, high on energy from the premiere, and feeling reckless.

"Do you want to ride together? It's faster than the bus."

West picks up the duffel bag at his feet and slings it over his shoulder. "Let's go, Margot."

I throw him another look as I heave my suitcase into the trunk of the car. "Who the hell is Margot?"

It's early when West and I arrive at the house, and we've both been undersold by a lot. Our lodging for the week is a three-story Victorian mansion with a wraparound porch. The house is white with black shutters and a blue front door that sounds like old money when we open it.

I whistle under my breath as we walk into the quiet house. "Your friend Tristan is *rich* rich."

"'Friend' might be too strong a word," West says.

I smile at him over my shoulder as I walk into the large kitchen. "You just don't want to admit that you're running with rich kids and nepo babies."

He rolls his eyes in confirmation, and my stomach turns over. I feel like I've stumbled into a treasure trove of information about West. We spent the entire car and ferry rides catching each other up on our lives, but meeting his friends is another level entirely. He was pretty quiet about what he's been up to since college, instead asking me question after question about publishing and traveling and the movie premiere. He wanted to know if I had any say in the cast (no) or the script (some), and he had specific notes for the actor playing Fox. (*Why does he look so pissed off in the movie trailers? Tell him to stop scowling so much!*) Through slaphappy middle-of-the-night laughter, I promised to pass his thoughts to the director. Eventually I nodded off and was embarrassed to wake up with my head on his shoulder.

The kitchen is littered with evidence of a party, the large stone island covered in empty cups and vapes, a stack of pizza boxes piled high next to the trash can.

"When your friends say they're getting together to write, is that an excuse to party all week?"

"They're *new* friends," West stresses.

"Take a guess."

He runs a hand through his hair as he surveys the mess in the kitchen. "I'd guess they'll sleep until two, hang out until six, 'create' until ten, and then party until five."

I'm not loving his use of the word *create*. If I'm stuck in this house with a bunch of wannabe influencers, it'll be a long week. "Drugs?" I ask.

"Some," he confirms.

"Huh." Maybe he's changed more than I thought. "Well, I'm in danger of missing yet another deadline, so you don't have to worry about me." I grab my suitcase and head toward the stairs to find Daphne's room. At the very least, I need a shower and a power nap before I start working.

"What does that mean?" West's voice stops me.

As much fun as we had on the ferry, I can't forget that the last conversation we ever had was him blowing me off. Not to mention the fact that I need to buckle down and write; if I don't have something to send to my editor by the end of this week, my publishing date will be delayed *again*.

"I know you didn't plan on me crashing your trip with your friends. I'll stay out of your way," I say. He blinks in surprise, and I can't stop myself from saying the next thing. "I've *moved on*."

It feels like shots fired. Like launching a grenade into our otherwise-peaceful conversation. Until now, neither of us has even alluded to the fact that we used to be in love or that we set fire to our entire future in a handful of hours.

West fixes me with a hard look. I make a mental note to tell the actor playing Fox that his scowl is perfect. No notes.

"I've said and done a lot of regrettable things in my life. I guess it's too much to ask that you don't keep a catalog of them all in your head," he drawls.

I exhale the tension from my body. He's right. If he's not holding the past against me, I should give him the same courtesy.

"Truce?"

"Truce," he agrees, and with an official armistice in place, I drag my suitcase up the stairs.

29

Present Day

Karma has a twisted sense of humor. Thanks to a hotel fire, a tense breakfast, and a last-minute stop to purchase a second dress from a shop on University, I'm late to my signing. It feels like cosmic payback for making West late to his.

It's another overcast day, the sky filled with slate clouds that promise rain. I'm worried it'll keep people at home, but by the time I arrive on campus, the festival is buzzing. Signings and presentations and panels are in full swing for the last day of the event, and it's a stark reminder that my joint panel with West is tonight. If this crowd holds, there will be a lot of people around to see us share a stage.

My stomach roils with anxiety. I'm starting to think this entire weekend was a mistake. I should have been one of those authors who kept my identity a secret, like Elena Ferrante. Daphne always jokes that she'll know she's "made it" as an author when she can delete her social media. Right now, that doesn't sound like a bad idea.

The closer I get to my assigned tent, the more my stomach

tangles up in knots. They loosen when I arrive and see that my signing line stretches to the back of the tent and snakes through the grass past several vendor tables. I spot two people in Fox shirts and one in pointed fae ears, and I can't help but smile. It's not the biggest line I've ever had, but it's a relief. It's good. It's not embarrassing. That's what this weekend was supposed to be about before West showed up and screwed with my head.

This book *will* succeed, even if it kills me. (Sometimes it feels like it might kill me.)

I uncap a Sharpie and wave forward the first person in line. She's wearing a Wildcats shirt and holding a stack of my books. When I see her smile, I let myself breathe.

She's nice; the next person in line is nice; they're all nice. They say all the things I never thought I'd hear again.

You're my favorite author.

Your book saved my life.

I started reading again because of you.

I have to pretend your third book doesn't exist.

So maybe they aren't all nice, but I've heard worse.

I scrawl my name in black ink, my energy draining with each signature. I look up at the line, sweat forming on my brow as it grows. It's not like me to have my social battery zapped by an event; I usually end a signing with enough energy to power a small city, but today I'm dragging, and I'm frustrated. I've spent too many years clinging to this career by my fingernails. I clawed myself out of a depressive valley for moments like this, and instead of feeling happy or accomplished or proud, I don't feel anything.

I sign the last book, cap my marker, and take stock of my situation. I have a new book. I have fans who haven't abandoned me. No one said anything openly hostile. This is the moment I fought so hard to get back—so why don't I feel better?

A vision of West appears at the edge of my tent. I blink. I'm either hallucinating or dreaming again, because not even he is dumb enough to show up at my signing after our fight this morning. But as he walks toward me with determined strides, he doesn't look like a hallucination. He doesn't smell like one, either; the scent he carries with him is exactly like the soap I tried to inhale last night.

"Take your BDE and leave," I say as I pack up my pens.

West lets out a surprised laugh. "Excuse me?"

"Big debut energy. It's the spark you see in the eyes of a new author. Unlike me."

He frowns. "You have a spark."

"No, I don't. Publishing beat it out of me a million years ago. And I'm off the clock."

West drops a heavy backpack on my table and points to his watch. "You have one minute left."

"Fine." *Sixty seconds.* I fix him with my blandest expression and pretend it's a chore. It's decidedly not. Even when he was the skinny emo kid in eyeliner, I couldn't stop looking at his face. *I saw the vision.* If West and I were together now, I'd feel like a genius, like people who bought Apple stock in the nineties.

West unzips his backpack and pulls out a stack of books. *My books.* He pushes them wordlessly toward me.

"What are you doing?"

He opens the beat-up copy of *Torched* and stabs the title page with his finger. "You write my name here"—he points to the top of the page—"and your name here." He speaks slowly, an almost word-for-word repeat of the conversation we had two days ago. But my brain can't compute any of it, because West is somehow in possession of three very worn copies of my novels.

I pick up *Torched* with trembling fingers and thumb through the pages. It's a librarian's worst nightmare—full of highlighted passages and notes in the margins. It seems like half of the pages are dog-eared, and the spine is cracked.

This is a book that has been read. *A lot.*

"Where did you get this?"

West looks confused. "My house?"

I flip through the other books, and unbelievably, they're all in the same condition. No matter how West's opinion of me has shifted over the last decade, I can't accuse him of being indifferent. "Why?" I say, unsure what question I'm really asking. *Why did you read them? Why are you asking me to sign them? Why does it suddenly feel like there's not enough air in this open tent?*

"I went to your event at the Page Turner," he says abruptly.

"What? When?"

"Right after *Torched* came out. You were wearing a black dress with stars on it."

I've done so many bookstore signings and events that most of them have faded to gray, but then it hits me. At the first event my family attended, I was distracted by a man who looked like West at the back of the room. "I saw you there! You disappeared." My brain scrambles to make sense of this new information. "Why were you there?"

He throws his arms wide before letting them fall to his sides. "Why do you think?"

A beat passes in which we blink at each other in surprise. Before I can get another thought in, he changes the subject. "Will you get lunch with me?"

He leans his weight on his hands as he splays them across

the table, the taut lines of his arms mirroring the tension in his brow, his jaw, his mouth. Without thinking, I uncap my Sharpie and slowly color in the nail on his middle finger. If it weren't so supremely weird of me, I'd do the rest. Anything to keep touching him.

"Why?" I ask again. Apparently, I can't say anything else.

He looks at his hands for a long time. "We need to plan for this evening."

I narrow my eyes; somewhere buried deep in the forgotten recesses of my mind—deeper even than all the events I've nearly forgotten about—is the sensible, responsible version of me, and she's screaming at me to say no. But there's something about seeing West's handwriting in the margins of my book that makes my world tilt. It's like I've been looking at life through a fun-house mirror and he just shattered the glass.

I sweep my markers into my bag and stand up, acting braver than I feel. "I'll go to lunch with you, but I have to run an errand first."

His eyes flash. "I'll come with."

"You'll miss your interview."

"No. The interview is off."

My eyes fall to his copies of my books, knowing it's too little, too late. But I find myself unable to turn him away.

We walk together to Gentle Ben's, and the air around us is different. We're both being so cautious. Watching what we say. Staying far enough away from each other that our elbows won't bump. I feel like a freshman on a walk with my brand-new crush. It's disorienting, like time has cast a spell on West and me in a way that allows us to be every version of ourselves at once. I miss him, and I hate him, and I'm over him, and I want the back of his hand to brush mine at least one more time.

Gentle Ben's is busy with the lunch crowd. I tell West to wait for me outside, and I navigate through the tables back to the bar, where an unfamiliar face in a bartender's apron asks what he can get for me. He has brown hair pulled back in a bun and tattoos down both arms.

"I'm looking for Evie. I was told she'd be working today," I say.

"She called out sick."

I swear under my breath as I sit on the stool to think. He leans across the bar toward me and lets his eyes rove obviously over my body. "I mix a better Aperol Spritz than she does. Want one?" He reaches for a large wineglass.

"No, thanks. I just really need to talk to Evie. Do you know any way that I could contact her?"

"Are y'all friends?"

"She helped me out the other night while she was working and held on to something important. I was supposed to pick it up today because I have an early flight in the morning." I figure it doesn't hurt to tweak the story to make me sound less like a stalker going off a vague hunch that she might have stolen my book.

He grabs a napkin and a pen from his apron and scribbles two phone numbers after glancing at his contacts list. "Evie's and mine," he says with a suggestive wink. "In case you're looking to work up a sweat tonight."

"What a charming offer." I snatch the napkin out of his fingers and hightail it out of the bar.

I sit on the curb while I dial Evie's phone number. West's eyebrows skyrocket when he sees both phone numbers. "Who's Evie? And who's *Zach*?" he asks, his expression darkening.

"Don't worry about it." Evie's phone is ringing.

"This was the errand you needed me for? Copping phone numbers?"

His tone makes the hair on my arms stand up. "Calm down." I roll my eyes as Evie's phone sends me to voicemail. I hang up.

"Was that bartender hitting on you?"

"Yes."

"And you took his number?"

"Yes."

He grinds his molars, looking possibly more annoyed than I've seen him all weekend. I type a text explaining the situation and send it to Evie. She responds in less than a minute with confirmation and an address. I stand up as the first raindrop hits the sidewalk.

"What now? Do I get to help you get ready for your date?" West asks dryly.

"No. But you do get to take me for a drive."

The address Evie sent is in the foothills on the north side of town. As we drive out of downtown Tucson, the landmarks turn from university buildings and housing developments to cacti and mountains. Even with the drizzly sky, it's stunning. "I forgot how pretty the desert is."

I feel the weight of West's gaze on my profile. "Would you ever move back?"

I laugh in surprise. "Why would I?"

"Just making conversation, Darling."

By the time the road begins to rise in elevation, the rain is coming down steadily. West's fingers are drumming on the steering wheel, and I take sick pleasure in knowing that he's stewing over the napkin in my lap. I stare at it and pretend to contemplate giving Zach a text, but eventually the pretending stops, and I *am* contemplating it.

He's cute. He's interested. It'd be easy. I could stop by the bar tonight and flirt a little. Maybe more. I could have one night of uncomplicated fun before going back home, and I've never wanted anything less.

I glance sideways at West, who is tense and frustrated and more than a little annoyed that I've dragged him here with zero information. We have about eighteen hours left until my flight leaves, give or take. Eighteen hours until we slip seamlessly back into our lives and this weekend becomes another footnote in our history. Since the first day West kissed me, it's felt like I've only ever had him in brief moments. And I realize now that I'd rather spend the rest of this weekend with him than waste even a minute of it with anyone else.

"I didn't *ask* for his phone number," I say at last.

West's shoulders relax marginally. "Are you going to tell me where we're going?"

I wave the napkin in the air. "I left something at the bar, and this employee has it."

"That's it?" He eyes me skeptically.

"That's it."

He presses his lips into a thin line and lets the subject drop.

The rain is coming down in sheets as West pulls into the driveway of the address Evie sent. "I'll be back in two minutes," I say.

Evie's mom answers the door and hands me the book. I shove it in my bag and run to the car. "Let's go," I say as I shut the door behind me and buckle in.

West is pulling his sweater over his head, revealing a white button-up stretched tight across his chest, and I'm momentarily stunned by the movement. He hands it to me. "You look cold."

"Thank you." I pull it on and wait. "You ready?"

The car is still in park, and West is in no hurry. "As soon as you tell me why we're here."

"What? No."

"I drove you all the way out here. I want to know why we made the trip."

"Are you serious?"

He turns the car off and pockets the keys. "I've got time."

"Ugh, you're annoying. And this forfeits your right to lunch, by the way." I unzip my bag and retrieve my signed copy of *Drought*. "It's your book, okay? Can we go now?" My hair drips water on the pages. As a booklover, it pains me. As someone who wants to get under West's skin, I let it happen.

Lightning flashes over the nearest mountain peak.

He starts the car, and we pull onto an empty road, the rain making it hard to see more than a few feet ahead of us. "You've got to help me out, Mars," he says quietly.

I swallow heavily. "With what?"

His eyes fall to the book grasped tightly in my fingers, and I know I've been caught. If he asks why I care so much about it, I'll have no defense.

I glance up as a coyote darts in front of the car. "Look out!"

West swerves. The car lurches off the road and spins into a ditch.

30

7 Years Ago

West's friends are exhausting, but Daphne and I discover pretty quickly that they're so up their own asses it's easy to stay out of their way. Petra, a girl I can only describe as pointy—from her nose to her winged eyeliner to the hip bones jutting out of the top of her pleated miniskirt—is in Daphne's Soul-Cycle class. The two got to talking, and when Petra found out that Daphne was a writer, she invited her to spend the week at this retreat. The instructor yelled at them to be quiet before Daphne could get more details.

When I ask Daphne if Petra is a writer, Daph admits that she *thinks* she's a podcaster who also might be writing a play and running a Kickstarter to fund her online zine. In the short time we've been here, I haven't seen Petra write anything except a string of "hot take" tweets crafted to go viral. But who am I to judge? I haven't done much writing lately, either.

This cohort is young and beautiful and dressed in clothes that are both expensive and insane. As West predicted, they sleep late and appear at dusk like a coven of malnourished vampires. They unironically claim to be creating "art" while writing their Instagram captions. They spend the evening basking in their own cleverness and cloaked in vapor. Every conversation is buried under three layers of irony. As soon as we meet, they "casually" mention that a reporter from the *New York Times* Culture Desk is visiting at the end of the week to write an article about them and the "microneighborhood" they haunt. They call it Dimes Square, which is basically a concrete triangle at Canal and Division Streets in New York. When I ask if that's just gentrified Chinatown, they raise their eyebrows at one another meaningfully.

Simply put, they are delightfully insufferable. Whenever we have the misfortune of being harangued by them, Daphne and I leave in stitches, grasping each other for support as we laugh. We could try harder to avoid them, but pointy Petra might just be Daphne's muse. Their endless self-righteous conversations about everything from international politics to woke internet culture hit Daphne like a truck, and soon she's twenty thousand words deep into a bloody thriller about a group of unlikable nepo babies getting murdered.

We create a schedule that looks like this: While they sleep, Daphne and I enjoy our WASP cosplay as we write on the wraparound porch. When the sun sets and the temperature dips, we all eat dinner together on the back deck. As their night is ramping up, Daphne and I head back to our room to gossip in between writing sprints.

Writing hasn't been this easy in years. The words finally start to flow, and I credit the unbroken roar of the ocean in the distance and the salty sea air.

The porch swing.

Daphne's encouragement.

Anything other than the fact that West and I are breathing the same air again. It's not because of the way my chest hurts when he looks at me from across the dinner table or because we brush our teeth side by side in the mornings. On the first morning, he caught me wearing a Fox T-shirt as pajamas. The smirk on his face was catastrophic. We've been sidestepping each other for two days, never in the same room for more than a few minutes. He rounds a corner, and I quickly retreat. My palms are permanently damp.

Dinner tonight is a mountain of oysters and three lobster rolls to share between the eight of us. (Tristan was high as a kite when he ordered and just hit buttons.) I'm not an oyster girl, and if I'd known this was dinner, I would have skipped with Daphne, but I'm starving, and she's in a trance. She's already written ten thousand words today with no signs of stopping.

Tristan, Petra, and a DJ named Blake are at the table when I sit down. (No, I don't know why a DJ is on a writing retreat. Yes, I asked.) Blake and Petra are debating religion—Scientology and Catholicism, respectively. I tune them out while I nudge an oyster onto my plate and stare it down.

"You squeeze the lemon juice on top," Tristan says.

"Yeah, I know."

"You looked confused."

"I wasn't."

He waves his white napkin and exchanges a look with Blake. "Forgive me, I didn't mean to mansplain."

They laugh while Petra rolls her eyes. "Ignore them," she says as she takes a hit off her vape. There's an untouched lobster roll on her plate. My stomach growls. She tips her head back to blow blueberry-scented vapor into the sky before looking at me. "West said you're a writer?"

"She wrote the book that that movie is based on," Tristan says.

"No, no, don't waste your words," Petra drawls.

"What's it called? *Fire and Flame and Third Cliché Here*?"

"Don't be rude," Petra says, the corner of her mouth curling up. "She's my guest."

"Actually, I'm here with West," I say. I can't help myself. The lie is worth the puckered confusion on Petra's face.

"You know Emerson?" Tristan asks, appearing genuinely interested in me for the first time all week.

"Since college."

"Is it *Torched*?" Blake's staring at his phone. He missed the change of subject.

"Ooooh. Cinematic!" Tristan says.

Blake angles his phone so they can watch the trailer together. I sit opposite, watching them watch. Petra elbows Tristan in the side when he laughs at the dramatic climax.

"Cute!" Petra croons when it's over.

"If I was in it for the money, I'd write something like that," Tristan says. "Like taking candy from a baby."

I care too little of his opinion to be upset by it. "I bet it's easy not to be in it for the money when your parents own this house."

Scientologist-slash-DJ Blake laughs so hard that sauvignon blanc squirts out his nose as West emerges from the house with damp hair and bare feet.

"I don't think your friend Mars likes us," Tristan says, and drains his glass. "We have too much *privilege*."

"Don't be an asshole," West says.

Tristan turns to Petra. “Is ‘privilege’ the buzzword of the day? The insult that’s supposed to hurt us the most?”

“We should record that for the podcast,” Petra says.

“Now?”

“Now.”

“Don’t come inside for an hour,” she warns me and West. “Ambient noise will ruin the recording.” She, Tristan, and DJ Blake take their smoke and their post-woke, wannabe-edgelord humor inside the six-thousand-square-foot Martha’s Vineyard beachfront mansion.

“They get off on shocking people,” West says apologetically.

“I can tell.”

He sits in the vacant seat next to mine. His eyes look tired.

“So . . . your friends *suck*,” I say.

“Yep. Yeah. I’m increasingly aware.” He nods.

I lean toward him. “West, what are you doing here?”

“*You’re* here.”

“Because there’s something cultish about SoulCycle and Daphne is bad at saying no. What’s your excuse?” I rest my chin on my hands and wait.

“I know,” he says with a sigh, running a hand through his damp hair. “The guy who owns the press that published my book is part of all of this.” West gestures to the house.

“Okay. And?”

“And what? I’m in kind of deep with them.”

“Why? Because you sold them your novel for—and I’m guessing here—a fraction of its worth? They published it, the deal is done. You don’t owe them anything.”

“They have connections, Mars. They have a reporter from *The New York Times* coming to talk to us. That could be big for me.”

"You don't need them! You have more talent than all of them combined."

He looks surprised, and then uncomfortable. "You don't know that."

"Yes, I do."

"How?"

"I remember." I turn sideways to face him and tuck one leg up under me. We're treacherously close. The butterflies in my stomach wake from hibernation.

I remember, but I don't know if he does.

When I'm feeling emotionally fragile, I sometimes wonder if I made it all bigger in my head. If, in the process of writing Fox and Juniper, I've mythologized our own history in a way that was outside of reality and then bought into my own lie. Maybe what we had is better on the page than off.

West's gaze is searing. His hand lands on my bare skin, just above my knee, and silent acknowledgment passes between us. The set of West's shoulders and the weight of his palm say the same thing: *It was real. You didn't imagine it.*

I look down at his hand. Heat is building in all my dangerous places.

The glass pocket doors at the back of the house slide open. West withdraws his hand, seemingly unbothered. Meanwhile, my heart pounds like we've been caught by our parents. A bearded guy with no shirt on sticks his head out the door. I can't remember his name.

He stifles a yawn. "Food?"

"Depends. Do you want oysters for breakfast?" I pick up the oyster from my plate and gag it down. It's disgusting and unsexy. *What a move.*

"Pass." Beardman vanishes back into the house.

West looks at the table. "Are you going to eat this?"

"Not if I don't have to."

"We could make dinner?"

I pretend to gasp. "Think of the ambient noise!"

He laughs, and I grin, feeling nineteen again.

"There's nothing edible in the kitchen anyway. Except the edibles," I add.

Under the table, West's foot nudges mine. It feels like a question. I nudge back. A silent negotiation. What the outcome will be, I don't know.

He takes a bracing breath. "Want to walk with me to town? Grab dinner? You can tell me more about how you hate all my friends."

I sink my teeth into my bottom lip, tempted to tell him that I'd go anywhere he wanted. I'd put up with his awful friends for as long as it took. "Deal."

The next morning, West joins Daphne and me for our writing session on the porch. At lunchtime, her hands are cramping, but she refuses to come up for air, so West and I take bicycles out of the garage and ride along the boardwalk. We order fried shrimp and carry it to the beach, where we eat with our toes in the sand and swap stories about life in New York as we watch the tide drag in and out.

I worried that dinner last night would be stilted or awkward, but I should have known better. Even when we can't get anything else right, talking to West has always been easy. He quiets an inherent restlessness in me, settling my anxious thoughts like snow in a globe.

A breath of disbelieving laughter escapes me when I realize

that the settling effect is what spooked me so badly when he first kissed me freshman year. I've always thrived on the agitation in my brain. Believed that I would never achieve anything without the constant pressure to do more, achieve more, prove myself. At nineteen years old, West made me content in a way that was *terrifying*.

"You're ruminating," West says. Not exactly a question, but an offer to listen.

I hug my thighs to my chest and drop my cheek to my knees. "Can I ask you—"

"Yes."

I survey his profile, my tongue loosened by the lack of eye contact. "Are you happy that you didn't move to New York? Back then?" After our conversation last night at dinner, I know that he moved back in with his parents for two long years and helped his mom with his siblings while she took care of her mother. By the time his grandma passed last year, his siblings were older and life was calmer, though I get the feeling the responsibility continues to weigh heavily on him, and his eyes still cloud in anger every time he thinks of his dad.

"I can't bring myself to regret it. It was the right thing to do," he says, wonderfully predictable.

"If things had been different with your family—"

"But they weren't. They needed me," he says firmly. I think he's going to let it drop there, until he adds a quiet confession. "I wasn't ready yet." He scowls as his fingers drag forcefully through the soft, warm sand. I recognize his expression of internalized frustration.

"What I'm trying to say, badly, is that I wasn't good enough yet. I still don't know if I'm—" He rakes a sandy hand through his windblown hair, as curly as I've ever seen it thanks to the salt air. "I would have held you back," he says, though he looks unhappy with his own words.

I feel a bruise bloom below my rib cage in a spot I thought I'd protected well from West's influence. Just moments ago, I was wondering if I'm better off because he didn't come with me. Hearing him echo that sentiment, however, makes me ache. He thinks he would have hindered me by not being good enough, when I know the real reason is because I loved him too much. He made me too content.

"That's not true," I whisper, and when he grimaces at the water, I match his expression.

We spend an endless stretch of time watching the tides, lost in memories, until eventually West stands and pulls me up by the hand. "What a tragic pair we make today," he says dryly.

"Not tragic," I argue.

"No?"

"No," I confirm as I throw a leg over my beach cruiser. "In progress."

His eyebrow ticks up with curiosity. "I thought our story ended a while ago, Mars."

I shrug and pedal away from him, tossing one last comment over my shoulder. "Haven't you heard, West? I like sequels."

"Are you seeing anyone right now?" West asks that night as one of his friends snorts a line off the porch railing in my periphery. His question is abrupt, but after our trip to the beach, I've been waiting for it.

My mind flashes to my most recent ex. He was smart and

kind, and when drinks turned into one date, which turned into two, which turned into eight months, I initially felt I'd done the impossible. I'd found one of the good ones.

In the end, I needed more than smart and kind and good. I needed *heat*.

"No. Not for a couple of months now."

"Why'd it end?"

I push my feet off the brick porch, swinging us higher. Do I tell West that I broke up with my last boyfriend because I didn't feel anything when he touched me? That during sex, my mind wandered to my to-do list more often than not?

West narrows his eyes. "You can't smirk like that and not tell me."

"He didn't inspire . . . well, much of *anything* . . . in my writing. Or me," I say. West's brow lifts impossibly high. "What about you? You were always the boyfriend type."

"Was I?"

"You were in a four-year on-again, off-again relationship with your high school sweetheart."

"If you want to think of it like that."

I roll my eyes playfully. As if it wasn't *exactly like that*. "And when I saw you at Amber's wedding, you were dating someone."

"No, I wasn't."

"You said you'd moved on."

"I was lying." He outstretches his hands in a what-can-ya-do gesture.

"And now?"

"Recently single," he confirms.

It's impossible to deny the vibe shift after that, and for the rest of the week, West claims the spot next to me on the porch swing. It is both motivating and distracting to have him so close. When he drums his fingers against his thighs, my thoughts scatter.

As the week goes on, matchsticks collect behind my belly button. One for the time his knee rests against mine. Another for the minutes we pretend not to notice our arms brushing against each other while we work. A third for when he silently passes me an AirPod and we take turns adding songs to the world's most chaotic playlist. It's terrible for my focus, but listening to the songs West selects for me is another struck match, each one held dangerously close to a pile of kindling.

As twilight descends on our last evening in the house, Daphne stretches and announces that she's done. As in *done* done. Wrote-an-entire-novel-in-a-week done.

"I'm headed to town for celebratory sugar," she says. There is no group dinner tonight because everyone else is out on a chartered yacht.

"I hate you."

"Will I see you before you go?" she asks.

I'm leaving in a couple of hours to catch a red-eye for the London premiere of *Torched*. "No, but go celebrate. You deserve it. I'll see you back in New York."

She waves goodbye and bounds down the stairs, brimming with the kind of joy that can only come from knowing you never have to write that first draft again.

I lean my head back on the porch swing with a contented sigh. The sky slowly turns from purple to navy, stars winking into sight. The push and pull of ocean waves drones in the distance, covered only by the clacking of West's fingers against his keyboard. I wouldn't mind if this were the soundtrack of my life. My head is quieter than it's been in years. "Should I move to Martha's Vineyard?"

"Hmm?" He's focused but trying to pretend he's listening to me.

"No wonder rich people are so happy." I'm talking more to myself than to him. I want to carve this moment on stone tablets. I want it to survive a nuclear fallout and outlast the cockroaches.

"Rich people aren't that happy," he muses before adding, "Aren't *you* kinda rich?"

I glance sideways to find him with a chewed pen between his lips, and I'm pretty sure I want to kiss him. It's a feeling so familiar it's almost hard to identify. Wanting to kiss West is like the sound of the ocean's tides on this island: a constant hum in the back of my mind. I'm so used to it that I've allowed myself to pretend it isn't there.

The pen falls to his lap, blue ink staining his bottom lip.

"You're still doing that, huh?"

"What?" he asks, his eyes still scanning the document on his screen.

I reach across him and run my thumb over his bottom lip.

His fingers pause over the keys.

I withdraw my thumb and hold it up so he can see the ink, and time stops. I have the worst sense of déjà vu: *I've written a book, and he knows that I'm in love with him. I'm begging him to go to New York with me, and he's saying no. We're dancing at a wedding, and he's moved on.*

I jump to my feet. "I have to go."

"Mars, wait." West follows me to the front door. His hand grasps the crook of my arm, and in one fluid motion, he pulls me back toward him and presses his mouth to mine. I barely have time to register my surprise before he pulls away. "I hope that was okay." His eyes are dark, and there is a hint of pink on his cheekbones, but he doesn't look half as shocked as I feel.

I swallow heavily. "It was."

"Good." He nods, running a hand over his jaw. "I usually try to ask first."

"It's fine."

"Good. But if you want me to kiss you again, I'm going to need you to say it." As his eyes sear into mine, my loosely held matchsticks fall. All I feel is sizzling heat, burning me from the inside out.

"West—" My breaths are uneven, but my voice is steady. "Take me inside."

The words aren't even fully out before his hands are under my thighs and my legs are around his waist. He crushes his lips to mine as his hands find their way under the bunched-up hem of my dress to my ass. He tightens his grip, holds on. I suck air through my teeth.

"Did I hurt you?" he asks.

It's pleasure that's right on the brink of pain. I shake my head as he backs me into the house and up the stairs, his demanding mouth pulling breathy whimpers from behind my teeth. We stumble through the door to his room, and he kicks it shut with his foot. The thud makes my bones rattle.

He sets me on the edge of his bed and pulls back, cupping his hands around my face. He kisses me one more time, slow and lingering. "If you change your mind, tell me to stop," he says, his voice raspy.

"I'm not going to change my mind."

His eyes darken with focus. "Then tell me what you want."

Embarrassment washes over me. I've had a million fantasies

of this moment, and I can't say a single one of them out loud. "Anything."

The mattress dips on either side of me as his hands press into it. He leans over me with another drugging kiss. In a blink I'm on my back, scrambling on my heels as the mattress dips again under his knees. A steady hand runs up under my dress and wraps around my hip bone, a thumb brushing over lace.

Before he exposes another inch of me, I'm greedy to see him. I reach for the hem of his shirt, but he makes quick work of it, grabbing the back of his collar and dragging the shirt over his head in one fluid motion. If this were a different sort of moment, I'd trail my fingertips along the contours of his stomach, savoring every inch of him, pressing a kiss everywhere my palms touched. But time is short, and our patience is gone, and every lick and touch and graze of teeth is a frenzy. His mouth traces a line of kisses down to my collarbone while I struggle to remember how to breathe, my fingernails scraping across his shoulder blades while he curses into my skin, so soft I almost don't hear it.

After an agonizing stretch of time, he runs his fingers under the strap of my dress and lets them linger, his thumb rubbing soothing circles on my skin where his teeth just were. He looks up at me with hazy eyes. I nod, and he slips the dress down my torso. I lift my hips as he pulls it off. When he looks at me in just a bra and underwear, the furor slows.

"Mars—" His voice is raw, barely stitched together with awe and longing.

"I know," I agree on a rasp. I'm not sure what I'm agreeing with, because his fingers are tracing slowly over my bra and across my soft stomach, stopping when they meet lace again. He dips one finger under the fabric and brushes lightly. My breath stutters as my eyes fall shut, preparing for sensory overload.

His hand retreats as he laughs softly. It retraces its path back over my stomach and up to my chest, where he slowly rubs his finger over my nipple. Then he lowers his mouth and pulls me in, his tongue flicking against fabric. I'm hit with a rush of endorphins, a heavy downpour in my veins. I press my knees into West's side and bring his mouth back to mine. I feel like I'm out of my mind. I can't move fast enough, can't touch him everywhere at once, can't stay still, can't stop myself from arching into him. I do, and it doesn't offer enough friction. I hook my fingers into his belt loop and pull him down until his full weight collapses on top of me.

"I need you to touch me," I gasp, starting to feel lightheaded. His mouth moves to my neck, his tongue relentless as he gently bites then licks the sensitive spot below my ear. His hand squeezes my breast as I suck in air, trying to clear my head. He rolls his hips against mine, his cock dragging over my clit, and we both moan.

"West," I whine, grinding my hips harder.

"Patience." He playfully admonishes me with a nip of teeth on my collarbone, then shifts his weight to one forearm. Just when I think I might actually beg, he finally tugs my underwear to the side. I press my forehead to his shoulder as my knees fall open. I'm soaked, and I know the exact moment he feels it, because his mouth curves into a wicked smile. "Already, Darling?" He brushes a featherlight finger over me, gathering moisture before circling my clit. I inhale through my nose and sink my fingernails into his arms to stop myself from coming too quickly.

"West—" I nudge his shoulder up. He looks at me with dark, drugged eyes. "Do you have a condom?"

"I can get one."

I check the clock and groan. "I have to leave for the airport soon."

He presses a kiss to the hollow of my throat and circles my clit again. "There are things we can do without a condom."

A door slams downstairs. "Emerson! Now!" West and I freeze. "Emerson!" Tristan roars.

West grits his teeth and rolls onto his back. "I'll tell him to shut up."

I pull my dress back over my head, combing my hair with shaky fingers as my breathing slowly evens out. "I'm flying to London tonight."

"Emerson!" Petra's footsteps patter up the stairs.

I push up to my knees and lean into West for a last kiss. "Where will you be after London?" he asks as I pull back.

Petra knocks on the door. "Emerson, the reporter from the *Times* is here. You coming or not?"

"New York."

West rakes his fingers through my hair and holds the back of my head steady as he kisses me again. "You'll be in New York, and I'll be in New York."

"Looks that way."

"Emerson?" Petra yells.

"I'll call," West promises, and I know he's committing to more than a phone call. When we're both in New York, he wants to try again. He wants to be together.

I don't have a single reason not to believe him.

31

Present Day

"Are you okay?" West's low voice is halfway to panic as he unbuckles his seat belt and leans over the console to check me for injuries. He runs his hand over my forehead and down my neck, where it settles.

"I think so. Just a little out of breath."

Curls fall across his brow as he leans closer, looking disturbed beyond belief. His hand stays heavy on my neck, like he's afraid that if he moves it, I'll disappear.

"I swear I'm fine. The airbags didn't even deploy."

"Are you sure? You could be in shock." He holds my chin between his fingers and gently turns my head left and right.

"Hey." I rest my hand on his cheek until his eyes meet mine. "If anyone here is in shock, it's not me."

He closes his eyes for a moment, and he almost looks like he's in pain. Just when I'm starting to worry, he opens them again and blows out a breath, shaking off his alarm and entering problem-solving mode. The rain is still coming down heavily, and the truck is stuck in a ditch. The front end hit a saguaro, which I'm pretty sure is a crime, but it seems like a bad time to mention it. From inside the vehicle, it's hard to tell how badly the truck has been damaged.

West braves the storm to check it out and comes back a few minutes later, soaked from head to toe. "We have two flat tires, but other than that, the damage looks cosmetic. I'll call a tow truck."

The operator tells him that because of the storm and our location, it might be a few hours before someone can come out to help us. West decides to change one of the flats out for his spare and see if he can flag down someone who will lend us another just long enough to get the truck to the nearest repair shop.

"Can I help?" I ask.

"Do you know how to change a flat tire?"

"I can't even remember the last time I drove a car."

"New Yorkers." He shakes his head. "Hang out in here. Hopefully it won't take long."

I pick up *Drought* off the floor. "At least I have something new to read. Or I can use it to defend myself against the next coyote."

Confusion flickers in West's brow. "What do you mean?"

"Your book is a brick."

He frowns.

"That's not an insult. It feels substantial and oh so very serious. I know that's important to you lit-fic guys." I recklessly inch closer to our unspoken past.

"You haven't read it?"

"It was stolen goods, West. What was I to do?"

"No. I'm talking about before. I thought . . ." He shakes his head. "I thought there was a chance that you already had."

"No. Um, not yet."

"What about the first one?"

I wish he hadn't asked. It's a unique kind of embarrassment to find out in real time that a person you thought has read your book hasn't bothered. "I mean, I kind of hated you." The past tense slips out.

He laughs harshly. "Believe me, *I know*. But you met me at our spot, Mars. And when I tried to tell you about *Drought*, you seemed like you already knew."

I blink in surprise at the way he characterizes that chance encounter when I first got to campus for the festival. "I *ran into you* at our spot. I needed privacy for a phone call, and it was the first quiet place that came to mind."

As West's eyes flicker in comprehension, I can't recall a time I've ever regretted the truth more. His crestfallen expression presses on an old bruise in my chest, one that never quite healed. "Yeah. Of course." He opens the door, and rain whooshes inside the car. "That makes sense. I'll change the tire now."

I watch him duck out of the car, and I'm more confused than ever—about his book and our spot and what one has to do with the other.

I glance at the clock. The day is half-gone, our panel starting impossibly soon. The weekend is nearly over, and for reasons I don't understand, my throat swells around tears I don't want to shed. With nothing else to do and no excuse not to, I open the cover of *Drought*.

I exhale a soft sigh as my fingers absent-mindedly trace the pages. It's a beautiful book, with endpapers the color of rust and a tiny fairy illustration hanging from the *g*. It strikes me as unusually whimsical.

I turn to the dedication page.

If you're reading this, you know who you are
Thank you for changing my life
I'm sorry

Every nerve ending in my body heightens, and I mentally scold myself. There's no need to freak out over an anonymous dedication. It could mean anything. It could be directed *toward* anyone.

The sharp twinge behind my ribs calls me a liar.

I swallow my fear and turn to the first page.

A career in books has made me a speed-reader, but I don't think I've ever read anything as quickly as I tear through the pages of *Drought*. I read with my heart in my throat, and I can't deny the truth for long.

This book isn't just dedicated to me. It's *about* me.

It's a love story. For some reason, I didn't think it would be. I've been writing the same type of story for more than a decade now, and I assumed that West's book would be a continuation of his college work. Stories about coming of age and complicated families. Feelings of resentment and fear. Life in a small town. And to be fair, this book has all of that. But mostly, it's a love story.

The main character is a young man who has spent nearly his whole life trying to leave his small desert town, only to end up back there over and over again through some inexplicable combination of fate or magic or despair, each time coming face-to-face with the woman he's been in love with for years.

Every time, they meet at the same spot. *Their spot*.

Her name is Luna, and she's me in all the ways that Fox

Caldwell is West. We have similar features: brown eyes, honey-blond hair, a smattering of freckles across our nose. We're not identical, though, and I have to wonder if West thought the similarities were too obvious and tweaked a feature or two at the last minute.

I imagine him sitting in his chair at two a.m. the night before copy edits were due, frantically trying to scrub me from the page. Inserting comments that would annoy everyone on the editorial team. *Make her hair longer! Add a tooth gap! Grant me plausible deniability!*

It's an easy scene to sketch, because I did the same thing. After I turned in my final edits for *Torched*, I called Whitney in a panic and told her I simply had to remove the excessive references to Fox being tall. (*That'll fool 'em!*)

I choke on my own laughter when I find out that Luna's arms are covered in fairy tattoos. (Fairies because I wrote a fae book. I suppose he wasn't aiming for subtlety after all.)

My shock increases with every page. It's like reading West's and my history, our memories and inside jokes splashed on the page, cloaked in beautiful prose and disguised as fiction. It's overwhelming. My skin overheats. I pull off West's sweater.

When he returns to the car more than an hour later, hair dripping like a black labradoodle, my heart is pounding like *I'm* the one who changed the tires in the pouring rain. "No luck finding a second spare. I think our best option is calling for backup. The rain's slowed down a lot. Should be safe to drive again."

His attention snags on the open book on my lap. I've nearly reached the midpoint of *Drought*, and my thoughts run unchecked. I feel everything all at once. I don't know how to reconcile the discordant emotions in my body. I'm stunned and confused and heartsick all over again. My fingers curl around the edges of the book. "What did you do?" I whisper, gazing up at his profile.

He stares out the windshield, his numb expression completely at odds with the bubbling outrage I'm trying to contain. He sighs heavily and pinches the bridge of his nose. "What do you want me to say, Mars?"

"I don't know. Try something and see what happens."

He gestures to the book. "It's all in there."

"When?" I demand.

He looks at me sideways, brow furrowed. "Always?"

I scowl at his nonanswer. "When did you write this?"

"I worked on it for a while," he hedges.

"For fuck's sake, West. Before or after Martha's Vineyard?"

"Does it matter?"

Maybe not. It's infuriating either way. I latch on to that feeling and sink in, because it's right at the surface, and it's easy to understand. "Yes."

His teeth clench around the answer. "After."

I close the book slowly and lean toward West. When he finally looks at me, apprehension bleeds around all his exposed edges. I press the book into his chest. "You know what, West? *Fuck you.*"

32

7 Years Ago

West does call, but New York is five hours behind London, and by then it's too late. Fox Caldwell's European fans have already read the article.

I sleep in. Between jet lag and the string of movie events I've attended over the last seventy-two hours, I barely know what time it is. The story I dreamed up in college is the biggest movie in the world, and it's a surreal feeling that I don't have words for. My brain wasn't built to process something on this scale.

I finished writing my third book on the flight here. I'll email it to Whitney next week, but for now I'm lying groggy and happy in a hotel bed. When my phone buzzes, I wonder if it's a text from West. I haven't heard from him yet. I'm not sure why, but it feels like we're waiting to be on the same continent. I won't believe this past week really happened until we're together again.

It's a text from Daphne, asking if I've been online.

I tell her no, and ask why she's awake.

Pulling an all-nighter revising this book. You need to go online. And then call me.

I start with Instagram, and I have so many notifications that the app crashes. I scroll and quickly realize that something is off. I sit up in the hotel bed, no longer groggy. A spike of acidic adrenaline has perked me right up.

I've been tagged in dozens of comments, but most of them seem to be talking *about* me instead of talking *to* me. They're defensive and angry and written in all caps.

FUCK YOU @WestEmerson. @MargotDarling deserves better than this.

I'm tagged in another post with a link to an opinion piece in *The New York Times*.

The article starts as an explainer about the emerging scene at Dimes Square and introduces the online debate about whether or not this microneighborhood is worth caring about. There seems to be no love lost between the author and Tristan's band of wannabe misfits, although she stops short of outright roasting them for claiming to be at the forefront of New York's art scene from the kitchen table of a Martha's Vineyard mansion. West isn't mentioned at all until the last third of the article, in which the interviewer describes him as "charmingly bookish and distractingly handsome."

I bite my lip, anticipating West's cocky grin when I return

to New York. It'll inflate his ego worse than the first time he read *Torched*. He'll suffocate under his own cloak of arrogance.

I keep reading.

It's Emerson's kaleidoscope eyes that draw my attention, as heterochromia is having a pop culture moment thanks to the popular fantasy novel (and movie by the same name) *Torched*. This runaway hit series has captivated readers around the world, and eagle-eyed fans have discovered that the book's heartthrob, Fox Caldwell, is inspired by none other than West Emerson, the ex-boyfriend of the novel's author, Margot Darling. Fans claim that at an early book signing, Darling admitted that her ex had sparked the creation of the character Fox, who is beloved for his captivating charm and fierce loyalty.

If you're willing to go far enough down the *Torched* fandom rabbit hole, you'll find old photos of Emerson and Darling together during their time as students at the University of Arizona, as well as theories that the book's heroine, Juniper, is based on the author herself. A source close to the pair states that they were "very serious" and "madly in love" before their sudden split. They did not confirm where Emerson and Darling stand now, although online sleuths have deduced that the two do not seem to be in contact. For fans of the book, the revelation has added an extra layer of intrigue as they try to unravel which parts of Fox and Juniper's story could be inspired by real-life events.

Interestingly, Emerson himself is an author. His debut novel, *Oasis*, was published last year through

Underlight Press, one of the many creative endeavors to come out of Dimes Square. While Emerson has yet to replicate his ex-girlfriend's commercial success, *Oasis* has received critical praise, and Emerson appears poised on the cusp of making a name for himself in the literary fiction scene. Today, he is eager to discuss his work, but when I bring up his connection to Darling's *Torched*, he does his best to redirect the conversation.

Rossiter does not let that happen. He begs on hands and knees for the backstory, so I give it to him. By the time I finish, Emerson's friends are volleying insults across the kitchen with alarming ease. When I ask how it feels to have his name connected to the biggest YA fantasy series of the year, Emerson is visibly irritated. "I'd rather be kept out of it."

"Why?" I can't help but press the issue. "A connection to *Torched* could only help your career."

He bristles at the perceived insinuation that he needs to hitch his wagon to Darling's star and insists that he writes serious books. When I ask if that means he doesn't take Darling's work seriously, he seems to shoot from the hip. "It's a love story for teenagers. It's never going to be taken seriously."

"I know a few million people who would disagree with you. I believe they call themselves 'Torchers,'" I counter.

Emerson laughs along with his friends. "Do you think I care about anyone who calls themselves a 'Torcher'? Those people need to get a life."

The honesty catches me off guard. *Torched* has a passionate fan base, and insulting them won't do Emerson any favors. I ask him to be clear—is he *denying* the rumors that Fox Caldwell is based on him?

"I haven't seen Margot in half a decade," he says, a statement that garners audible scoffs from the rest of the group. Seemingly unwilling to allow his friends to speak on the topic of Darling, he continues without pause. "If I was some sort of inspiration to her, and she's still writing about me all these years later, wouldn't that be kind of pathetic?"

It's not exactly a denial, but it is a rebuke. One thing is clear: West Emerson has no interest in being cast as anyone's muse.

When West finally calls, I block his number.

I spend the day in my hotel bed. The YA faction of every social media platform is the car crash I can't look away from. Just when I think it can't get worse for West, it does. He's the main character of the day, and they're tearing him to shreds on behalf of me, my readers, and the entire YA community. Uninvolved parties emerge from internet obscurity to contribute their two cents. And as usually happens, everyone has the same two cents: West is a judgmental, untalented, bitter snob. He doesn't respect teenagers. He doesn't respect women. He doesn't respect YA readers. He doesn't respect fantasy as a genre. He doesn't respect romance.

He doesn't respect *me*.

By the time the West Coast is sitting down for their morning coffee, the review-bombing has commenced. West's previously under-the-radar novel gets spammed with one-star reviews.

I feel sick. The man in that article is not someone I know. I should have seen his friends for the glaring red flag they are instead of blindly believing he's still the same person I fell in love with. I wanted it to be true so badly that I ignored common sense.

By evening, I'm trembling with unspent energy. It has taken every ounce of my self-control not to vomit my feelings all over the internet, but that will only make me look wounded, and what was the word West used? *Pathetic.*

I refuse to give him the satisfaction.

In search of a distraction, I open my Word document to read my manuscript one final time before sending it to my editor.

As I review the painstakingly chosen words, anger spills from my fingertips. It strikes me as absurd that Fox is so attractive. It's not realistic! Before I know it, I'm making small changes here and there. Suddenly, Fox is a little less hot, a little less perfect. Instead of flawlessly tousled hair, I give him a bad haircut, and feel a small hum of satisfaction. What kind of masochist was I to immortalize my college boyfriend in paper and ink? The injury is too much, and there's only one hope of fixing it.

When I stumble across a line of romantic dialogue that makes my stomach clench, it *hurts*, so I delete it. Human boys don't ever say the exact right thing at the exact right time. Why should an immortal king be any different?

When Juniper waxes poetic about how much she loves Fox, I frown. Am I sending teenage girls a bad message? Should I let my heroine be a little more independent? Is she sure that Fox is even worth all this trouble?

Driven by West's betrayal, I charge carelessly through revisions. I edit with the reckless abandon of someone who has nothing to lose. By the time I get to the final act of the book, I'm knee-deep in blinding anger and unbearable hurt. I delete the last three chapters and rewrite them. I kill Fox Caldwell.

No one gets a happy ending. Not Fox, not Juniper. Not even their adopted magical wolf. He dies with Fox. It's revenge and misery and gloom all the way down.

As the sun is rising over the Thames, I email the manuscript to my editor. She calls in a panic a few hours later. "None of this works. Especially not the ending."

"It's the ending I want."

"Don't betray your readers," she begs. I tell her that nothing else feels honest. To the bitter end, West is the muse I can't shake. I take perverse pleasure in knowing it's a title he hates. When this book is published, headlines will be written with both our names in them. He can screw me and then screw me over, but he'll never be able to escape me. He wants to be removed from this conversation? *Too bad.* With this ending, it's impossible.

Whitney asks me to take a week to reconsider. She offers to brainstorm with me. But when the week is up, the sting of betrayal is still too fresh to consider anything else, and we both know that we're out of time. The book goes to print. It is what it is.

At least it's not boring.

By the time the final book in the *Torched* trilogy is released, I realize that *boring* would have been a blessing. Readers can forgive boring. My sins are much greater, and there is no shortage of critics eager to catalog them all.

Each review reads worse than the one before it, and despite Daphne's insistence that I stop reading, I can't. I feel cursed. Addicted. I wake up in a cold sweat in the middle of the night and reread the tangible proof of my failure. I memorize the lines that hurt the most and let them play on a loop.

> . . . an insult to both its genre and the intelligence of anyone brave enough to finish it . . .
>
> Comically misguided.
>
> Bestselling author Margot Darling strips the heart from a genre that deserves so much better.
>
> Darling takes the very essence of YA romance and shreds it, leaving readers with a soulless imitation.
>
> . . . leaves me wondering whether Darling understands the genre she is trying to exploit . . .

I assumed the book would be polarizing, but I've never been further off the mark. The entire fandom has rallied together under the same cause: hating me.

I receive my first death threat two days after the book is published. I read it with shaky hands before sprinting to the bathroom. Daphne holds my hair back while I puke up breakfast, and then she helps me forward the message to my publisher and report it to the authorities. Half a dozen death threats later, I stop bothering with the formality, although my body trembles every time I open my email.

If possible, social media is worse. My accounts attract an onslaught of angry comments.

You owe me a refund and several hours of my life back.

BRB, burning all of your books

A dumpster fire from start to finish

Did you really have to kill the dog?

(Why the hell did I kill the dog?)

Last book of yours I'll ever touch

Go die

Two weeks after the release, Daphne pries my phone from my fingers and deactivates all my accounts.

My publishing team cancels my tour.

A complete reworking of the book pops up on a fan fiction website. I read it, and the truth is humbling; the story treats my characters with more respect than I did. It's more fun, more satisfying. It's *better.*

On a long, sobbing phone call with Danielle, who has been more loyal amid the shitstorm than any agent should have to be, I promise to write a new book and have it ready to sell by the end of the year. She advises me to slow down, take a breath, give myself time. I don't want time, but at the end of the day, it doesn't matter what I want; it only matters what I'm capable of. And that includes very little except lying in bed, numb to the world. Daphne tries to help, but she's out of her depth.

In the span of six months, my entire life and sense of self fall apart. I can't write. Can't read. Can't get on the internet.

Can't leave my apartment. I have always defined myself by my success, and the idea of redefining myself without it is unfathomable. My brain becomes a dark, desperate place, and when I drill down to the center of it, I find West Emerson.

He ruined me, and I'll never forgive him.

33

Present Day

I slam the door to West's truck and barely think as I charge across rain-soaked asphalt. "Mars!" West catches up to me too quickly. "Where are you going?"

"I'm storming away!" I'm not ready to face him yet. I'm still fuming.

"Why?"

"It's called a dramatic exit, and you're ruining it." Nature has provided all the drama an author could ask for: mountains and desert and a traffic-stopping thunderstorm. If West would've just left me alone, this would have been an extremely cool, cathartic moment.

Instead, his long strides easily keep pace with me. His height is pissing me off. *Why does he have to be so tall?*

"Mars." He catches me by the crook of my elbow and turns me toward him. "Please talk to me." His expression is bewildered, and if I had any sense at all, I'd stomp away and leave him wet and miserable and confused.

I hate myself a little when I don't.

I want him to beg me on his hands and knees to stay.

I want it to hurt when I leave.

And the fact that any of that still matters to me is the reason I stay. If I had *ever* been capable of walking away from West, we wouldn't be in this mess at all.

"I read your book."

"I gathered." West's eyes are heavy with unspoken words that make me feel too many things. I drop my gaze to the raindrops sliding over his lips. *No.* I look at his chest. His shirt is plastered to every groove and hard line. My eyes slide back up to his face, and my rib cage feels like it's been cracked open.

I grit my teeth. "It's not fair."

He nods, relieved that I've decided to stay and hash this out. "Which part?"

"You can't write about me like that."

His eyes narrow, his focus sharpening. "Like what?"

"Like you're in love with me!"

West looks genuinely surprised. "I know *you* of all people aren't trying to argue that art can't be inspired by real life."

"Not yours!" I step closer to him. "You lost the right to be inspired by me or write about me or even *think* about me the second you sat down with that journalist. If you think my books are trash—"

"You've seen what I think of your books, Darling." His stern voice knocks me off-kilter. He read and reread and marked up my books like scripture, and I don't know how to handle the cognitive dissonance this gives me.

"You had an interview with that same journalist scheduled today," I accuse.

"I've been trying to schedule that interview for months, but she's been giving me the runaround. She's the one who canceled today's call. I've been trying to publicly apologize for everything I said in the first article."

I narrow my eyes. "Like when you said you didn't want to be associated with me."

Pain and regret are etched in every line in his face. "I need you to believe me when I say this: I was an idiot back then. I've been an idiot a lot, unfortunately, but especially during that time, with those people. What I said was awful, but if you walk away from this weekend with anything, I need you to know that I did not mean it. Not then, not now, not ever."

"Those thoughts didn't come from nowhere, West."

He squares his shoulders. "Have you ever had a thought you didn't believe?"

Every time I've told myself that I hate you, I can admit, but lying to myself is not the same thing as humiliating someone in public. "If you have something more to say, just say it."

He presses his lips into a hard line. "Okay. I've been waiting seven years to explain this to you, and I don't want to mess it up, but I hardly know where to start." He paces back and forth on the road, his body restless as he sorts his thoughts. Finally, he rolls his shoulders and faces me again, fixing me with a determined, naked expression.

"I was so fucking insecure, Mars. Full stop. It's embarrassing, but it's the truth. From the moment you signed with Danielle, if not sooner, I knew that you were going to take over the world."

I roll my eyes in disbelief, but he's not having a second of it.

"Doubt me all you want, but your success was never even a question to me, Mars. I met you, and I fell in love with you, and I saw your path so clearly that it made my future all the more laughable. Who the fuck was I, to think I was good enough for you? I dropped out of school. I broke your heart when I couldn't go to New York. I was replaced in a matter of hours—"

"West—" My voice rasps.

"Let me finish. I felt replaceable and discarded, and it confirmed all the insecurities that were already suffocating me.

"I stockpiled rejection letters. I wrote, and I wrote, and I wrote, while the walls of my parents' house closed in on me, but I didn't let myself write about you, because I knew once I started, I'd have to take a hard look at my life and my choices, and they would be found wanting." He is a man possessed, confessions pouring from his lips like honey.

"So then finally, *finally*, I make it to New York with an expanded version of a story I wrote in Dr. B's class. It tanked—it wasn't that good—but in exchange for hanging out with the worst crowd on the planet, a journalist was going to talk to me. About *my writing*, Mars. The one and only thing I had going for me. God, was I naive. I thought I'd done something worth talking about, but in the end, all she cared about was *you*." The softness in his voice matches the tenderness in his eyes. His next words are a reverent whisper. "And how could she not? You are spectacular, Mars Darling."

My head spins. "West," I say again, not sure what's on the other side of that plea.

He's not done. "So she asked me about you, about us, and in a matter of seconds, I was reduced to a juicy bit of gossip. I'm not proud of it, but it brought back every doubt I'd ever had. About myself, about my career, about why you would want to be with a man who is a footnote in your biography. Years of pent-up self-loathing and frustration erupted. Frustration at my god-awful friends and with the journalist and with the fact that right when I almost had you, you had to leave for your own movie premiere! I was convinced that you'd land in London and realize that you'd made a mistake in letting me touch you again. I just . . . snapped," he finishes at last. His eyes fall closed, and his shoulders relax with the unburdening.

I never got the impression from the article that West was losing his temper, but I forgot about his capacity for restraint. "Thank you for telling me." I exhale the words, unsure if they're the ones he wants to hear.

He steps close enough that I can see the raindrops clinging to his eyelashes.

I close my eyes and swallow the hard knot in my throat. It'd be so easy to lean into him and let him put his arms around me. "I wish I hated you more," I whisper.

He cups my face in his hands and brushes his thumb over my cheek, wiping away either rain or tears. "I'm sorry for the article. Thinking about it makes me physically ill. And mostly I'm sorry that I ever let you or anyone else believe that I have not been amazed by you since the day we met."

"Why did it take you so long to say that?" My voice breaks. I'm afraid the time apart has done us no favors.

"You blocked me on everything," he points out. I start to protest (*email exists!*) but don't get the chance. "I wrote you a letter. Several, actually, but I trashed them all until that last one."

"I didn't get a letter."

"I didn't send it. I still have it if you want to read it. I carried it with me for weeks, convinced every day that *this* would be the day I was brave enough to send it."

"Why didn't you?"

"It was a bad letter, full of excuses and self-sabotage and groveling."

Despite myself, my mouth twitches. "I don't mind a little groveling."

He breathes a laugh. "Maybe it wasn't so bad, after all. But the words felt wrong," he says as one or both of us closes the last bit of distance. We're so close now, trading air, inhaling each other's syllables.

"Telling you that I was sorry was never going to be good enough. I needed to *show* you, but I didn't know how. And then, after I'd had some time to reckon with what I'd done, the truth became painfully clear. I needed to fix my own shit. I needed to get out of New York and write something I was proud of. I needed to grow up. We wouldn't have survived if we'd gotten together seven years ago, Mars. I wasn't ready then."

His words hang in the barely there space between us.

"And now?" I'm in a trance. Dazed by his proximity.

"I already told you: I've been waiting ten years. Just say go." His husky voice scratches my skin like sandpaper. It's almost enough to make me forget.

"How do I know this time will be different? That you don't think I'm *pathetic*?" My voice cracks as I step away from West.

His eyes are wild and desperate as he pushes his hand through his curls. "Because I never have. I was upset, yes, but I was also terrified of your fans, Mars. They are relentless. I wanted to get rid of the connection between Fox and me so that no one on the internet would care if you and I tried to make a real go of it."

"We're not famous! We're *not* Fox and Juniper. No one would have cared."

"Maybe you're right. But they combed through our history. They saved our college pictures and made the online equivalent of one of those crazy FBI string boards." He drags a hand over his face. "It freaked me out, Mars. When I said all that, I just wanted them to *go away*, and I wanted them to see how invasive they were so that we could figure out how to be together without any eyes on us." He's dangerously close to groveling, just like I thought I wanted. I feel nauseous about all of it.

"Do you understand how that article destroyed me? How it flattened me so thoroughly that I blew up my career because of it? How am I ever supposed to forgive you for that?"

I'm not sure how it happened, but we're standing inches apart again, forever doomed to orbit only each other.

He looks away as he rubs the side of his jaw. "Do you want to forgive me?"

"It doesn't matter."

"It's the only thing that does."

I swallow past the tears that threaten to overwhelm me and brush past him. "If you want me as much as you claim, you would have apologized," I say over my shoulder.

"The book is the apology!" he shouts, forcing me to come face-to-face with what was clear from the first page. I stop walking.

For seven years, I've operated under the idea that West hates me. The article is the evidence, and cutting him out of my life was the conclusion. It was painfully easy to draw a line from *A* to *B* to *C*, until *Drought* came along and upended the premise. If none of my carefully drawn lines make sense, what does that mean for the one I'm keeping between us?

"I was trying to speak your language, Jupiter. *Our* language. The way we did from the very beginning. I was trying to get the words exactly, perfectly right, because I knew I'd only get one more chance. I didn't contact that journalist before my book was out, because at the time, a public apology felt like a cop-out.

It would have been too easy. I wanted to give you the apology that you deserved, and that wasn't with some online statement that you had no reason to believe. It was only once I'd finished *Drought* and put it out into the world that I thought there was even a chance you'd forgive me."

I close my eyes and take a bracing breath. West is wrong about one thing. There were days I was so sad and months that were so dark I would have accepted a public statement or an email or a note sent by carrier pigeon. Instead, he wrote me a whole damn book. A love letter on every page. He devoted the last several years of his life to apologizing the best way he knew how.

I turn toward him, one foot on a tightrope, unsure which way the wind will blow.

He takes a shuddering breath. "I don't know if I deserve your forgiveness, but you once told me that's not the reason to give it."

My chest squeezes until I can't breathe. Heat and fear and longing coil tight in my center.

I look at the strong lines of West's jaw and the broad planes of his shoulders, and it's hard to see the boy I fell in love with underneath the confident, determined man standing before me, but there are traces. In the rhythm of ink-stained fingers tapping against thighs. In the slow dip of dark lashes against his cheeks. In the way my brain settles when I'm with him, if only I can stop fighting instinct. And forever in the way he looks at me, and how I savor the heat of his gaze all the way down to my bone marrow.

Truth after truth piles up in my brain like a mudslide until I'm left with one question: *Am I willing to make myself miserable just to prove a point?* I find the answer in West's eyes, and it's the same as it was a decade ago.

I lick salt and rainwater off my lips. "Go."

A whisper of a word crosses his features before he steadies himself and nods. *Heartsick*.

"If that's what you want," he says, and takes a step back.

"*West*. I'm saying go."

He stares at me for a few breathless seconds, but when my meaning registers, he pounces. He reaches me in three strides and threads one hand through my hair until his palm rests on the back of my head. With his other hand on the small of my back, he pulls me in to him and holds me tight against his body as he bends his face to mine. His tongue sweeps over my bottom lip, and my mouth opens for him as I struggle to keep up. He is tall and hot and hard, his body firm against all my soft curves. Our clothes are soaking wet and paper-thin, and I press and press and press, needing him closer.

He kisses with abandon, his jaw working furiously, his tongue sweeping across mine. I tip my head back as his lips fall to my neck, then scrape my nails through his hair, pulling a low groan from him that crackles hotly at the base of my spine. "I've waited so long—so fucking beautiful—wanted to tell you—" He mutters words I barely comprehend as he marches me backward toward the car, his hands still firmly in place, his body steering me, holding me upright when my knees threaten to buckle.

We reach the truck, and he presses me back against the cab. He catches my bottom lip between his teeth and pulls, dragging slowly until it pops free. I'm drowning in sensation and the aching need to touch him everywhere, but my hands are shaking with nerves and years of anticipation. My breaths come out shallow and fractured.

Without breaking the delicious, wet contact between his lips and my neck, West gathers my wrists in his hand and holds them steady against his chest. "Breathe with me."

I drag air through my teeth and exhale through my nose, and I *cannot believe* I'm getting this worked up over a kiss, like it's the first time I've ever been touched. "Should we talk about this?" I gasp nonsensically.

"Respectfully, I'm tired of talking." West drops my wrists and wrenches the back door open. "Get in," he demands in a hoarse voice. It's the hottest thing I've ever heard. It's a torch pressed against sensitive skin. A swallowed match. I'm smoking, melting, turning to molten lava. I put my heel up on the running board and lift myself up into the back seat. He sees something on my face that makes him smirk.

"What?"

He shakes his head and puts his hands up on the doorframe. When he leans in for a kiss, I hold a finger to his lips. "Tell me."

He presses his lips together, still fighting a smile. "In the past, I've asked you what you want. Now I know you like it better when I tell you." He breaks into a wicked grin.

"West!" I shriek.

He tips his head back, laughing. All these years later, it still makes my insides glow. I still want to tattoo it on my eardrums. I lean in and press my lips to the hollow at the bottom of his throat. His laughter turns to a low groan. I flick my tongue against skin, and his hand shoots up to my thigh, under the hem of my dress. He swears under his breath.

I do it again, and he shakes his head, even as his tight grip holds me in place. "Wait, Mars."

I pull away in surprise. "What?"

He grits his teeth as his chest heaves with the effort of holding back his wandering hand. "Help. On the way. If I— If we start—I don't know if I'll be able to stop."

"Okay. Right. That makes sense," I say through deep, shuddering breaths, even as my face grimaces. I writhe against the seat. I'm so turned on it's almost painful.

He exhales through his nose and makes a quick decision as he pulls me out of the truck. Like before, he presses me against the cab, this time bracing his thigh between my legs. The noise that escapes me would be mortifying if I had the means to care. "Don't move," he says as his hands settle low on my hips and he shifts me farther up his leg until I'm in a position to grind against him. He pulls his head back. We make heated eye contact, electricity gathering in me like a storm cloud. After several motionless breaths, his hands slowly and deliberately roll my hips over his thigh.

He raises an eyebrow. *Can I? Will* you*?* he asks silently. I nod, and when he does it again, I gasp and scrabble for contact, sinking my fingers into his forearms. "There, yeah?" His mouth tilts up in a cocky grin. On the third press, my head falls forward to his shoulder. He gradually increases the pressure and pace until my hips are moving on their own, grinding down hard as he murmurs unheard words into my drenched hair.

A hysterical laugh bubbles out of me. "I can't believe I'm grinding on you like a teenager," I gasp between whimpers.

West flashes his wolfish grin. "I feel perpetually nineteen around you, Darling. I can't help myself." His fingertips sear into my hip bones as instinct takes over and my movements become desperate and jerky.

"That's it, come on," he says, the rasp of his voice enough to drag me to the edge. The tension coiling tight inside me becomes almost unbearable. "Come for me, Darling," he whispers, and the exquisite friction, combined with his coaxing plea, is my unraveling. My orgasm hits hard and fast, and I bite my lip to keep from crying out as I muffle my face in West's neck.

With one hand on my nape and one on my lower back, he holds me to his chest as the aftershocks subside, and I slowly melt into him. It takes a long moment for my breathing to settle, but when it does, I hide my grin in his chest. "Nineteen again, huh?"

"Fuck, Mars. I'd forgotten what it's like with you." He laughs in joy and disbelief, then presses a kiss to the crown of my head.

I glance between us, stomach fluttering again at the sight of his cock straining against his jeans. I move my hand down, but he stills it with his own as he reaches to smooth my dress over my thighs.

"Keep that thought, but not yet." I'm about to ask why when he nods over my shoulder at the approaching truck. "Help has arrived."

34

Present Day

I choke back my surprise when Dr. B parks his truck on the side of the road and climbs out with a knowing smile as he looks at West's sweater, which is once again swallowing my small frame. "I heard my star pupils need help?"

West nods, looking shockingly at ease as he helps our professor unload a tire from the bed of his truck and roll it into the ditch. Words elude me as I watch them work silently side by side until Dr. B brushes his hands on his cargo shorts and hooks one end of a rope to the hitch on the back of West's truck and the other end to his own.

Minutes later, the rescue mission is complete. Dr. B claps West on the shoulder and mutters something low that I can't hear before giving me a hearty wave and a promise to see us soon at our event.

"What was *that*?" I ask when we're back on the road.

West shrugs easily. "I spoke to his class a couple of months after moving back, and he sort of took me under his wing after that."

"*Why?*"

"Is it so impossible that someone would want to spend time with me?" West asks dryly, but the spark in his eyes betrays his amusement. After a beat of silence, he relents. "It didn't escape his notice that every story I ever wrote included an absent or shitty father. I assume he knew I was lacking in that area."

Impossibly, my fondness for both men grows.

"He's going to call in that favor, isn't he?"

West laughs and tugs on the sleeve of his sweater meaningfully. "He is after seeing you in this."

We drive to the festival in our damp clothes, and the large auditorium is already jam-packed when we arrive. The time for planning or brainstorming is gone. We spend the hour chatting about writing, publishing, and our time as Wildcats, and for all my anxiety leading up to it, it might as well be any other event. My fear was completely unfounded. No one says anything weird or rude. No one brings up the past. The questions for the Q&A are pre-vetted, and when it's over, I'm dizzy with relief. All that worry was for nothing, and the panel was the least eventful part of my weekend.

West and I sneak out the back door, stopping only for Daphne to pull me into a tight hug and drag me away as she whispers "We *will* be talking about this" with a gleeful glance at West.

"How did you— When did you—?"

"I read his book the first night we were here. Enough of it, anyway. That man is hopelessly in love with you. Judging by the smile on your face, I'm guessing you two worked it out."

My mouth dries as I look at him over my shoulder, leaning against the door with his hands in his pockets and a hungry expression.

"*Go.*" Daphne pushes me toward him.

"That went well, right?" I ask as West drives. My suitcase, which we rescued from the hotel, is in the back seat.

He throws me a quick smile before fixing his attention back on the road. "It was great."

"I hope people liked it. I didn't want to talk about my new book too much."

"Why not?"

I shrug. "I just want to give readers what they want."

I've learned the hard way what happens when I don't. I couldn't go online for a year, my publishing team resented me, and the movie studio refused to green-light the third installment of the series without a different ending. No one trusted me to write it, so Fox and Juniper's theatrical fate is now in the hands of the producers and a scriptwriter I've never met.

"It's your career. You shouldn't feel obligated to talk about anything you don't want to," West says with a frown.

"I wouldn't have a career if it weren't for the success of those books. And without my success, no one would care about anything I have to say."

"I would."

"You know what I mean. Being an author is the only thing I've ever been good at."

West's frown deepens. "You know you're worth more than your accomplishments, right? That the right people will love you even if you fail to live up to your own impossibly high standards?"

I'm on the cusp of agreeing with him when I reconsider, unsure if I actually *do* agree with him. "It's normal to define yourself by success. You do it, too."

He runs a tongue along the inside of his cheek before speaking. "I disagree. I defined myself by my failures."

"Two sides of the same coin."

He dips his chin in silent acknowledgment. "But I worked hard to stop, because it turned me into the worst possible version of myself."

I survey his inscrutable profile before sweeping a hand to gesture from my head to my toes. "And is this a bad version of Mars Darling?"

West pulls the truck into his driveway and cuts the engine. "I'm afraid I'm too biased to answer that question."

"Oh?"

He shifts in his seat so we're facing each other. His hair is mussed, the shadow on his cheeks darker every day. The top two buttons of his white shirt undone. He looks perfectly wrecked. "It's true. I met you at the impressionable age of nineteen, when my frontal lobe was still developing, and you burned yourself into my synapses. I'd have to reroute them to change the way I see you. I'd have to tear down the very foundation of myself and rebuild, brick by brick of wishful thinking, for even the chance of ridding my psyche of you. To my mind, there *is* no bad version of Mars Darling."

"*Oh*." Breath rushes from my lungs. What a liar he is, to have spent so long bemoaning his way with words.

His eyes are sharp and focused on mine. "As long as you're happy, I'm happy."

A warm, contented feeling brushes against sensitive skin. West's simple statement is the sincerest thing I've ever heard, which makes my next thought all the more worrisome. *What if the only way* I *know how to be happy is through success?*

I push the notion down, burying it deep enough to avoid, at least for tonight.

"Hey, West?" I lean close.

"Hmm?"

"You're better at the whole talking thing than you give yourself credit for."

His half-moon eyes drag down to my lips, and my mouth goes dry. He smirks. "Does my lexical prowess turn you on, Mars?"

I can only nod. The space inside his truck shrinks, and my limbs feel suddenly heavy. I shiver.

"Are you cold?"

"A little." Unlike West's, my long hair is still damp.

"Do you want to come inside?"

"Where else would I go?"

"You know what I mean."

"Yeah, I do."

We get out of the truck, and West walks around to the passenger side to take my hand. I glance down at our intertwined fingers as anarchy brews in my stomach. I've written so many West-and-Mars scenes in my head. The ones where we're driven together by dramatic circumstance and the ones where I yell at him and the ones where we fall into his bed, but I imagined fewer of the in-between moments. With his sweater on my body and my hand in his, this suddenly feels very real.

He unlocks the door and lets me in first, and now that it's not dark and I'm not flustered into oblivion, I use the moment to move slowly through his home, taking it all in. He has pictures hanging on the refrigerator and built-in shelves filled with books and succulents and knickknacks. The living room has a *rug*.

"You like living here, don't you?"

West hangs his keys on a hook by the door. "I do."

Those two words crack something open in my chest.

"Was that the wrong thing to say?" he asks.

I shake my head, even though it was. I wanted him to say that he hates the desert and he's coming back to New York with me.

West sits on the small couch in his living room and pulls me down until I'm sitting next to him. "What are you thinking about?" I ask.

He shoots me a suggestive glance.

"Other than that," I say.

"There's very little room for anything other than that," he says. He shifts me until I'm sitting on his lap facing him, my knees straddling his waist. He grips my thighs in his hands, and his thumbs trace small circles over my dress that make it hard to focus on anything else. I inch closer, my fuse lit.

I drag my fingers through his hair, scraping my nails lightly against his scalp. His head lolls back as his eyes fall shut. His fingers are nearly bruising my thighs now, and it's the best feeling of my life. I run my hands over his chest and arms and trace his edges, resting a thumb in the notch between his collarbones. I brush my nose against the line of his throat, feeling his heavy swallow. He's patient as my fingers and eyes rove over him, but the corded tension in his forearms betrays him. "Either kill me or put me out of my misery, Darling."

"I need a minute to get used to the idea that this is real," I say.

I can hear the rush of blood in my ears and count the beats of my unsteady heart. It's hard not to wonder how many heartbeats I have left in this limbo before West and I fall into something that will change everything. I shift my weight and feel him under me, and his eyes fly open. His fingers tighten, searing through the fabric of my dress. The burn of his eyes on mine tells me that, like it or not, everything has already changed.

I kiss him. Not a first kiss, but one that feels like a daybreak all the same. When I realize this, I draw back, but he catches my chin in his hand and pulls me to him. When our lips touch again, it's like slow-dripping molasses, his tongue unhurried and exploring, licking promises against mine with every stroke. His hand slides to the back of my neck and holds me there, and for the span of a few heartbeats, I think I could spend the rest of my life kissing West like we're in a hazy, slow-motion daydream.

My hands slide down his arms. I brush my thumb across the skin where his tattoo used to be and pull my mouth away, resting my forehead against his as I inhale a shaky breath.

I lift my eyes to his, and he understands the question without my having to ask.

"It's still there if you look closely," he says. I raise his arm and see that he's right. It's faded, but buried under layers of healed skin is the faintest outline of an orange blossom tattoo that matches mine. "I had it lasered a few months after the article came out, when my self-loathing was at its peak. I changed my mind after a couple of sessions, though. Decided to write us a different ending."

I nod, the riot of emotion in my chest making it hard to speak.

"Anything else you want to know?" he asks, and I know that if I decide to ignore the heat simmering in my blood, West will sit with me on the couch and answer my questions until the sun comes up. But the tension between us is nearly at a tipping point, and West's hands are wandering, and our collective patience is a rubber band stretched beyond its limit.

I shake my head. "Is there anything *you* want to know?"

He traps my lips with another long, slow drag, worrying my bottom lip between his teeth. He releases it and then soothes the tender spot with a swipe of his tongue. "Can I take you to my room?" His voice is a low rumble that makes me want to press my hand against his chest and feel it.

"Please," I beg.

His hands slide up my sides as he walks me backward down the hall and into his bedroom. I lift my arms, and he pulls his sweater over my head and throws it to the side. "Your dress, too," he says.

If possible, I flush even hotter as I slip my dress down my shoulders and let it puddle at my feet. West's eyes darken as his gaze wanders over me. I feel his attention everywhere, the weight of it dancing over my skin like popping firecrackers. A spike of heat here, a crackle of energy there.

He curses softly as he drinks me in, and it occurs to me a beat too late that perhaps I have a reason to feel self-conscious. He's seen me like this before, only now there are added years and pounds and scars on my frame, telling stories that he doesn't yet know. I hear the whisper of a learned instinct to hide my body, but it's quickly smothered by the dark heat in West's eyes.

His face creases with longing that I'd recognize anywhere; it's the same sensation that lances through me every time I see him. It's hot and demanding and unrelenting, and when he looks at me like that, I feel like tissue paper held over a fire. Like he's singeing me from the inside out, burning me up until I'm ash.

"I can't stop looking at you," he breathes.

"Let me look at *you*." I'm in nothing but scraps of lace, and he's fully dressed, which won't do at all. I cross the scant space between us and undo the first button on his shirt.

He lifts a brow as he watches my hands move lower. With each button, I press a kiss into the hollow of his neck.

"Careful." His voice is a low warning that makes me want to do dangerous things just to hear him say it again. "A man could get used to being undressed like this."

"That's the point. I never want you to undo a button again without thinking of me," I say, pulling a bark of surprised laughter from him. I push his shirt over his shoulders and press a soft kiss right over his heart. Lips still against his skin, I tip my head up and lock eyes with him. I snake my tongue out and lick up his chest in a slow drag, and West decides in that moment that he's had enough.

I gasp as he lifts me and sets me on the edge of the mattress.

"On your knees," he rasps, looking drugged and desperate. He puts his hands under my elbows and pulls me up to my knees, a move that brings us eye to eye again.

I rake my fingers through his perfect curls, reveling in his unraveling. "Did you know I had a sex dream about you in this bed last night?" I screw my eyes shut tight as his teeth find my earlobe.

He exhales a sharp curse near my ear. "Did you know that I touched myself thinking of *you* last night?"

I press my hand to my mouth to trap the mortifying sound I feel coming.

He pulls it away. "Let me hear you," he demands as his lips work their way south.

He presses an open-mouthed kiss to my ribs. The inch of skin beneath my bra. With each kiss, I feel starbursts in my bloodstream.

"How many first kisses have we had?" I wonder aloud, partially to keep myself from fully giving in to the breathy whimpers clawing up my throat.

"Too many and not enough," he says at last, his attention narrowing to the fabric between my legs. He drops to his knees and peppers a trail of kisses up my thigh to the triangle of lace, pauses, then leans in and presses a hot kiss against the fabric. My fingers tighten desperately in his hair. I would do anything to keep his mouth where it is, but after that torment disguised as a kiss, he diverts his teasing attention to my breasts. I'm already writhing in wonderful misery when he pinches my nipple through my bra. My head falls back as a lightning bolt cracks through me.

We meet for another long kiss, and then his eyes light with renewed intensity and astonishment as he brushes his thumb over my lips and across my mole. "You have no idea, Mars, how long I've thought about this. How much I—" He cuts himself off, pained. "I want you anywhere, for as much time as you'll give me," he vows.

"Prove it."

West's pupils flare, and I have one second to drink in the breathtaking, restrained sight of him before the bars on his self-made cage well and truly break.

"Mars, *darling*. Bra off. On your back." His voice is a low rumble that threatens to topple my foundation. I comply, and West curses roughly under his breath as he watches. He lowers his mouth to my chest, and when he flicks his tongue over my nipple, my back arches to meet his mouth. When he flattens his tongue and starts to suck, I nearly black out.

The inkwell of our long-suffering patience has officially

run dry. He whispers incantations into my skin as I undo his belt and his jeans with eager, clumsy hands.

His words are interchangeably filthy and sweet, murmured spells that make promises and demands, and it's the single most arousing moment of my life. It's so hot it's almost worth the decade without his mouth on me; he never used to talk like *this*.

He pulls off my underwear and utters "Look at you" in a way that makes me painfully, achingly aware of the pulse between my thighs. He settles between them and moves my leg over his shoulder, pressing a single kiss to my calf. My breath stutters, and when he gently rests his whiskered jaw against my inner thigh, I stop breathing completely. When our eyes connect, I nod, and I can't quite make out the string of words that roll off his silver tongue in the seconds before he presses it against me.

I fling my forearm over my eyes and pant as he drags his tongue slowly over me in life-ruining licks. When I tilt my hips to expedite the process, he reaches up and presses a large palm across my lower stomach, pinning me to the bed. My breaths become shallow as he finds a blinding rhythm, and I dig my heels into his back, wondering if he'll bruise.

"West." His name falls out of my mouth without intention, but he hears meaning in my voice anyway.

He lifts his head, looking at me with glassy eyes. "Tell me," he insists.

"More pressure."

Like any good writer, he takes notes like a pro, dipping his head and sucking my clit firmly into his mouth. Before long, the pressure sliding up my spine is hurtling toward the brink, dragging me with it. My fractured breaths alert him to my unraveling, and he releases his strong grip on my leg to find my hand and thread our fingers together while I fall apart on his tongue.

He wipes his chin on his wrist as he sits back on his heels, hair utterly destroyed, eyes bright, smile wicked. "You taste fucking perfect. I fear you've just given me another decade of inspiration."

"You're good at that," I say hoarsely, my throat dry, my head dizzy.

"That's because you inspire *art*, Mars Darling." He winks, and I sink my head into a pillow and laugh.

"Did you just call yourself an *artist* at going down on me?"

He grins at me like he can't believe his luck as he moves up my body, coming to rest with his hands braced on either side of me. "Is it unjustified?" A cocky tilt of his chin has me laughing again. I lace my fingers around the back of his head and pull him toward me, pouring the words I'm not saying into a long, searing kiss.

I love you and *I love you* and *I love you*.

Everything after that is a perfect, frenzied blur of strong hands and quick kisses and hushed exclamations, broken prose spilled from his lungs into my hair, my lips, the crook of my neck.

When he finally pushes into me, his eyes screw shut, and his features melt into an expression that rides the line between pleasure and pain, his mouth a tight grimace. We hold perfectly still for an unbearable length of time until his eyelids flutter open and we look at each other in shock. Curls falling around his face and arms corded with tension, he doesn't have to say the next words aloud.

There you are, his body says.

What took us so long? mine replies.

It is a returning and a discovery. As we move together, West finds my gaze and holds on, hardly daring to blink. I trace his lips with my finger, mesmerized by his slow undoing. He slides his hand between our hips, his thumb tracing circles that quickly pull another sob from my throat. He swallows my cries with his mouth, chasing my release with his own before falling onto me, crushing the very last of the air from my lungs with a desperate huff.

He flips us, his arms snaked tightly around my back as he pulls me in to his side. I settle my head on his chest and listen to his runaway heart as he drags my leg over him.

"I'm never leaving this bed," I promise.

His deep laugh vibrates against my ear. "Convenient, because I wasn't planning on letting you."

Spellbound and spent, I watch West trace his fingers over the soft slope of my hip and down my side. I shiver under his touch, my mind already dashing away with the moment. I want to save it, hide it, tuck it in a place I'll never forget.

"How did you do that?" I breathe.

West lifts my hands and twines our fingers together. "How'd *we* do that?"

"Fluency in a dead language," I whisper.

He kisses the back of my hand. "Never dead, just lost for a while."

35

Present Day

West's room is dark when an alarm goes off, the first hint of periwinkle light bleeding around the edges of his curtains. His hand is under the shirt I'm wearing (his), splayed across my stomach. "Don't go," he murmurs into my hair as he draws me closer, his sleep-raspy voice scattering goose bumps across my neck. I relax into his chest, remembering my half-baked plan to wake up in this bed for the rest of my life. A pretty thought in the afterglow of two mind-bending orgasms, but hours later, it hasn't lost any appeal. In fact, I only want it more now that I know what it's like to wake up in his arms.

"What about my flight?" I mumble through bee-stung lips, my eyes already slipping closed again.

"Skip it. Stay here."

"What about your job? Think of the teenagers who will be disappointed not to see their sexy professor."

West lays a scratchy kiss on my shoulder. "That's weird. And it's spring break."

I snuggle deeper into the crook of his arm, bewildered by

the good timing. Is it possible that the goddess of fate and timing is on our side for once? He has the week off, and I have a long stretch of days before my book tour launches in tandem with the premiere of the third *Torched* movie. A week at least. Two if I move some prelaunch appointments.

"I don't have enough clothes," I pretend to protest.

"You won't need them," he promises, and my body warms. Eyes still closed, I smile into the pillow as West brushes a featherlight kiss against my neck. When his hand wanders north and he rolls my nipple between his fingers, I surrender with a happy sigh.

I will not be making that flight.

~

Our plan to live and die tangled in West's sheets is thwarted by the need for food. I grin stupidly at him over a bowl of oatmeal, and he doesn't even try to hide his pleased smile as he watches me. As soon as my spoon hits the empty bowl, he pushes his plate away and knocks my chair sideways with his feet. He pulls it toward him until we're sitting face-to-face with my legs draped over his. His large palms rest on my thighs, just below the hem of the baggy shirt I'm wearing.

"Hi, Mars." With his wide smile, floppy curls, and bright eyes, he has very little in common with the brooding character on my shirt.

"Hi, West."

The air shimmers between us with an intoxicating mixture of anticipation and certainty.

"What do you want to do today?" he asks. My eyes slide to the fingers drumming on my bare thighs. "Other than *that*," he clarifies, reading meaning in my glance. "Obviously we'll do that." He leans in and kisses me, pulling back with another grin.

God, I could look at him like this forever.

"I met this cute guy once," I say, and West's fingers tighten as his smile slips off his face. "He claimed that Tucson is better than New York."

"Oh?" His smile has returned, but I lean forward and kiss him as an apology for chasing it away, even briefly.

I shrug. "Seems like now is his chance to convince me."

West squares his shoulders as he internalizes the challenge. He presses his tongue to his cheek and thinks. "Okay," he says finally. He taps my thighs twice. "Get dressed. We're going out."

"I was mostly joking. You don't have to . . ." I wave my hands in the air, trying to express an emotion I'm not fully conscious of.

"Have to *what*?"

"You know, impress me or show me a good time or whatever. I don't care about *Tucson*. I'm only here because of you. It could be Chernobyl out there for all I care."

West's mouth curls in distaste as he sits back in his chair. He pulls his hands into his own lap.

"Wait. What's wrong?"

He turns his head, frowning out the window. "Nothing."

"West." Reluctantly, he faces me again, still grimacing. I shuffle out of my chair until I'm in his lap, straddling him. He watches warily as I rest my hands on the back of his chair, bracketing him in so he has nowhere to look but at me. "As I learned last night, you are very good with your words when you want to be. Use them. Tell me what just happened."

He releases a frustrated sigh. "It's nothing. I'm being unrealistic."

"About what?"

His jaw clenches as he searches my face. A moment later, the tension bleeds from him. He kisses my forehead, then tilts my chin with his finger. "If you think there's a chance in hell that I'd have you for a week without trying to impress you, I worry that *Drought* didn't land the way I intended."

I tilt my head in question.

"We'll talk about it later," he promises as his hand smooths a path up my spine. I push off the chair, but West grabs my waist, trapping me against him. "Where do you think you're going?"

"You told me to get dressed," I remind him as he shifts my hips closer to his, lining my center up against him in a way that makes my breath hitch. I brace my hands on his shoulders as my eyes flutter closed.

"Did I?" he asks as he sucks the skin below my ear. I nod breathlessly against his mouth. "You have to get undressed in order to get dressed. Might as well kill two birds with one stone." He runs his hands under my shirt and draws it over my head, leaving me naked in his lap.

West packs a picnic, and we hike Saguaro National Park, hopping over streams formed from the weekend rain and winding among the cacti. When he sees how giddy I am from the blue sky and the sun on my shoulders, he takes it upon himself to do a live reading of New York's weather forecast. He sits me down on a large boulder, clears his throat, and delivers his line: "Forty degrees and rain for the rest of the week." I suppress a shudder.

We stop for fruit slushies at Eegee's after our hike, and the nostalgia sugars my blood as we pull the car over on Tucson's Astro Trail and eat them lying in the bed of his truck with pillows and blankets. West tells me that the trail is named for its proximity to observatories, planetariums, and national parks. It's designed for stargazing on clear, dark desert nights like this one. He positions me between his legs and pulls me back against his chest, and I enjoy the silence as we wait for the stars. By now most of the surface conversation has been scratched away, leaving us both with the understanding that we have bigger discussions in our future. I'm in no hurry to move out of the bubble we're in now, however.

"Why did you think I was there to meet you at our spot on the first day of the festival?" I ask, slowly putting together that first conversation now that I have more context.

West removes a spoon from his blue raspberry–stained lips. "Just a thought I had," he says cryptically as another pleasant quiet settles between us. "Do you have to work this week?" He drags his fingers deliciously through my hair.

"Hmm, not really. I should stop neglecting my inbox sooner or later. And I have emails to send, appointments to reschedule. It'll only take a couple of hours."

He nods. "Use the office. I'll clear out a space for your things."

"Don't bother. I can send emails from anywhere." I rarely work at a desk even at home. I write from my bed as often as not.

His chest tenses against my shoulder blades. In a blink, he's relaxed again. "I'd like to take you on a date tomorrow."

I lift his arms and wrap them around my middle as I fight an inevitable smile. “That can be arranged. Under one condition.”

“Name it.”

“I get to plan Wednesday.”

“You’re on, Darling.” I settle my head against his chest under a canopy of stars, and we watch the sky turn from purple to navy to black, my fingers tracing lightly over his forearms while his draw lazy swirls down my neck, across my thighs, and under my shirt.

“I haven’t seen stars like this in years,” I say, mesmerized by the glow above us.

“I thought that might be the case.”

“Thank you, West. I’ll miss this view when I’m back to freezing my ass off in the city.” I can’t remember the last time I felt so content. My brain is usually taken up by an endlessly repopulating list of things I should be doing. *Drafting. Editing. Reading. Promo.* Here, my mind is blissfully quiet, and the only thing that dampens my mood is the regret I already feel that this perfect, stolen week will have to end.

He motions between us. “Is there anything about our new situation that makes you nervous or unsure?”

I lift my chin and press a kiss to the underside of his jaw. “Right now? No.” He hums lightly in response. “What about you?” I ask.

“Fuck yes.”

“What?”

“Next week,” he says bluntly, tiptoeing right to the edge of one of those big conversations.

I cinch his arms tighter around me, and we quietly watch the stars for another hour, neither of us daring to ruin the perfect moment.

When West knocks on his own bedroom door the next evening, my nerves are out of control. I kicked him out after our joint shower so I could get ready without the distraction of his hands and his mouth and his body, and in sixty short minutes I became a wreck. *How does one go on a date with the man they've been in love with for more than a decade?*

West picks up a lock of my hair and lets it slip through his fingers. "I could get used to this."

"What?"

"Picking you up for a date from my bedroom."

I search my brain but can't find a response. When West knows what he wants, he is not a subtle man. And I understand where he's coming from. We've always been all-or-nothing, and neither of us wants to lose more time when we've already lost so much.

After a beat too long, he says, "I have something to show you." He moves into the room and opens the drawer to his nightstand. He ruffles through the stack of papers inside the drawer, and my already-nervous stomach squirms uncomfortably.

"I went through that drawer the night of the fire!" I blurt. He looks over his shoulder, mouth quirked. "I'm sorry. I didn't read anything. I was just so curious about you and your life. I wanted something tangible or . . . I don't know. I also touched everything in your shower and used your razor." I slap my hand over my mouth as West laughs.

He pulls a letter from the stack and hands it to me. "What's this?" I ask.

"Read it."

I unfold the paper, and my heart drops when I read the first line.

Mars,

I'm sorry. I love you. I'm so, so sorry.

It's the apology he wrote seven years ago and never sent.

West shoves his hands in his pockets and waits. I fold the letter and hand it back to him. "I don't need to read this."

"Why not?"

"I've already forgiven you."

He frowns. "I would feel better if you read it."

"I don't need you to grovel, West. Not even a past version of you."

He sighs, looks strangely defeated. "Will you at least take it with you when you go back to New York?"

"I told you, I don't need this to know that I"—my eyes widen at the words that almost slipped out. As if it wouldn't be crazy to admit forty-eight hours into this thing—"that I've already forgiven you. I'm ready to move on."

"You think that now, but there's every chance in the world that when you leave, you're going to remember that I ruined your life, and you'll slip away again, despite the fact that I'm trying desperately to hold on to you this time. If you have this letter as a reminder, I might stand a fighting chance."

"Hey, that's not going to happen." I grab his wrist.

He looks down at where I'm holding him, his hand still tucked in his pocket. "What *is* going to happen when you leave?"

I tug his hand out of his pocket and slip my fingers through his. "Take me on that date, West."

He tucks the letter into my suitcase on our way out.

"Being here makes me feel old." I hook my ankle around West's under the table at Bison Witches as he wordlessly slides his pickle toward me, just like he did on our first date. West and I are without a doubt the only people over thirty in the entire bar.

"Try teaching high school. I feel like I've got one foot in the grave."

"It is still so weird to me that you're a teacher."

"You don't trust me to educate the young minds of America?"

"Please. I bet you're the best teacher that school has. It's just odd that one of the most important aspects of your life was unknown to me until a couple of days ago."

West nods. "I feel like I know everything and nothing about you at the same time."

His statement lands uncomfortably. I hate thinking of him as a stranger. "Don't say that. It makes me sad."

"Nonsense. That's what the date is for." He knocks his foot against mine, a reminder that we're in this together. We don't have to spend another day of our lives as strangers if we don't want to. "Tell me the stuff I don't know."

"Like what?"

He tilts his head side to side. "Off the top of my head . . . Is Daphne still your roommate? How do you take your coffee? What time do you wake up in the morning? How many hours a day do you write? Do you write with music on? TV in the background? Total silence? What do you do when you're sad? How are your parents? Do you visit? Do they visit you? Where do you live? Do you own your apartment? Do you like living in the snow? Where do you spend Christmas? What makes you feel better when you're sick? What's the last perfect book you read? Do you want any more tattoos? A pet? Kids?"

I throw my head back and laugh. "*That's* off the top of your head? Holy shit, West."

"I want to know you, Mars. Sue me."

When I realize he's being sincere, I reach across the table and take his hand. "Where do you want me to start?"

36

Present Day

I work very hard to keep my eyes from straying to West at the back of Dr. B's classroom. As I speak to the students, however, his gaze weighs on me like a physical presence, like his hands are pressed to my shoulders, demanding my attention.

He looked skeptical when I steered his truck toward campus earlier today. "I want you to know there's more to Tucson than our old college campus," he said flatly.

"We can go anywhere you want tonight, even the roped-off room at Casa Video," I said with a wink that earned me a laugh. "But I have a promise to keep first."

He broke into a grin when he realized that I was leading him toward Dr. B's classroom and settled happily in a desk in the far corner to watch me speak to a class of undergrads.

Dr. B knew I was coming, but he chuckled with delight when I showed up hand in hand with West. "My star pupils! Together at last."

I'm starting to think he says that to all his former students, but I don't care. My heart warmed to a worrying degree to see the proud smile on West's face as he greeted our old professor. West has an entire life for himself here—a life he can't pick up and transfer as easily as I could. With Daphne in California now and a job I can do from anywhere, I don't have many physical ties to New York.

But we haven't had that conversation yet. It's too early to even be *thinking* about that conversation. Or at least that's what I tell myself when the constant flutter in my stomach threatens to overwhelm me.

I open the class up to questions for the last few minutes, and as much as I'm sure Dr. B wants me to focus on writing and publishing, most of the questions are about the *Torched* movies.

"Any other questions? Anything *not* related to whether I can give you the phone number of a certain famous actor?" I ask.

A few students laugh, but a lanky blond boy sitting in the front of the room leans forward over his desk. "I have a question."

"Go for it," I say as I pack my bag to leave.

"Do you know that you're blowing up online?"

"Like I said, if it's about the movie, that has very little to do with me."

"It's not that. Everyone is talking about you and your boyfriend back there." He jerks his chin in West's direction.

My hand pauses. "What?"

"Apparently, he's persona non grata. Made himself some enemies a few years ago. Especially with *your* biggest fans."

"*What?*" I lock eyes with West at the back of the room before focusing again on the blond boy. "What are people saying?" Too distracted in my bubble with West, I haven't been online in days.

Dr. B claps his hands, drawing the students' attention. "We're out of time. See you Friday."

In seconds, West is next to me, pulling my phone out of my hand and lacing his fingers through mine. He tugs me out the door, and I walk just slowly enough for him to know that I'm annoyed about it.

I reach for my phone. "Hang on. I just need to check—"

He slips my phone into his pocket. "Let's go."

"Wait, West."

"Not here."

"Give me my phone." I tug on his arm as cold dread crawls up my throat, making it difficult to breathe.

He faces me in the crowded hall and places his hand on the side of my neck, his thumb brushing across my jaw. "Please, Mars," he says softly. "Come with me to the truck, and I will relinquish my possession of your phone."

I nod and let him lead me through campus. True to his word, he hands my phone over the moment I fasten my seat belt. It feels heavy in my palm, and my fingers tremble with an old, familiar feeling. West frowns when he sees the tremor. "I don't suppose you'll listen to me if I tell you that this is a bad idea."

I clear my throat. "I can't avoid it forever."

He exhales a sharp laugh. "You *could*, though. It's just the internet. Nothing that happens on social media is real."

"I don't know, it felt pretty real when I was getting death threats and my fans were calling for book boycotts," I say sharply.

West winces, memories of last night's conversation still painfully fresh. After I answered all his questions, he asked me to tell him about my life after the article was published. The color drained from his face as I recounted the shitty aftermath of my book's release and the period of depression that followed. He tried to shoulder all the blame, as if he'd personally opened my Word document and torn it to shreds.

I scroll silently for several minutes before turning to West. "The internet has decided that we're together."

His brows furrow as he studies my face. "Based on what?"

"A picture of us from the panel. It's fairly obvious that I'm wearing your sweater. And we're looking at each other."

He scoffs. "We're not allowed to *look* at each other?"

I sigh and scrub my hands over my face. "It's the *way* we're looking at each other."

Like we're in love. He stares at me like he's holding vigil. I gaze at him like I'm falling into the sun.

It started with the picture, which led to comments linking to the old article about West, which led to posts and videos and more comments. They all boil down to the same thing: West is problematic, therefore I'm problematic by proximity. Doing the panel with him is implicit support. I'm platforming a misogynist. I'm *dating* a misogynist. I'm disappointing. I'm disrespectful to my fans.

Everyone has a take; everyone wants a pat on the head for joining the conversation. For calling out the bad guy. There's nothing the internet loves more than a dogpile. I read DMs from readers I've known for years. Profile pictures and names I recognize and interact with regularly. They beg me to make a statement.

About what? I think. *I didn't even do anything wrong.*

"Mars?" West touches my shoulder.

I startle. "What?"

"I asked if you're okay. I don't think you've taken a breath in the last two minutes."

"Yeah." I shake my head, trying to clear it. "I'm fine," I say more to myself than him. *It's fine. I'm fine. Not everyone has to like me.*

"Do you want to go inside?" he asks, and I realize we're back at his house. From the look on his face, we've been sitting in the car for a while.

That night, he holds me in bed and whispers apologies into the dark.

"It's not your fault," I say.

His arms tighten, crushing me to his chest. "It's explicitly my fault, and true to form, the internet is blaming the woman. You should say something."

"Like *what*?"

"Who cares? Say that you were forced to work with me this weekend. That you hate me. That I deserve every name they've called me."

"No."

"Please, Darling, throw me under the bus," he begs. He's tried to take the blame already, but his statement and apology went unnoticed. With his book recently released, the timing of it is too convenient. No one trusts him.

"It'll blow over," I insist, but my body doesn't believe the lie. I feel like I slipped backward in time. My limbs are heavy, my thoughts scattered, my appetite nonexistent. A wave of nausea rises in my stomach when my phone vibrates with a notification. Hours blur together. Days turn into nights when I don't sleep, and nights turn into days when I bite my fingernails until they bleed. I draft statements in my Notes app that I don't post, scared to anger even more people. I brainstorm ways to give my readers exactly what they want. I vow to get it right this time.

It doesn't take long for *Shattered*'s online rating to tank. It's not even published yet, and everyone already hates it. I'm accused of disrespecting and profiting off readers. I screwed them over once, and now, by associating with West, I've done it again.

West doesn't escape unscathed. For every comment calling for the boycott of my book, there are two for *Drought*. He doesn't blink when I tell him. He gives a very good impression of a man who *does not give a shit about the opinion of strangers*, but when I look closer, I'm not so sure. He has stress lines around his eyes, his fingers massaging the bridge of his nose every other minute. His face crumples into a grimace when he looks at me.

As if all of this weren't bad enough, the looming premiere of the third *Torched* movie turns a minor internet scandal into a national frenzy. (It's a bad time to remind everyone how much they fucking hated my last novel.) West and I read the *Entertainment Weekly* timeline of our relationship on my laptop, marveling over which details they get right and which ones they get wrong. After, I scroll to the comments.

West snaps my laptop shut. "Don't read the comments."

Danielle calls to check in on me. "I'm fine! I'm fine! I'm not worried! I'm fine!" I say, increasingly shrill with each declaration. By the time we hang up, I fear she's more concerned than she was before the call.

On Friday, West finds me sitting on the floor of his office. My knees gave out after a call with Whitney, and I collapsed against the wall before sinking down. He sits next to me and laces his fingers with mine.

"What happened?" he asks.

"They want to postpone the release of *Shattered* and cancel my events," I say, slightly dazed. He looks stricken. "My editor says it's to protect my mental health. They don't want a repeat of what happened last time. There's also talk of canceling the sequel." I know she doesn't trust me to write one if I'm in a bad headspace.

I can't even say that I'm surprised. I knew that at some point my publisher would decide I'm not worth the drama. It's the loudest thought in my head and the monster in my closet. It's the nightmare that wakes me up in a cold sweat. *I chased my dream, and I got it—and now there's nowhere to go but down.* In the decade since I got my book deal, nearly every thought and action has been driven by the fear of what will happen when it's gone.

"Well, fuck." West lets his head fall against the wall. "My agent dropped me." I open my mouth to let out a string of incoherent rage, but he squeezes my hand and shakes his head. "It's my own fault. My agent represents a lot of YA authors."

"Schedule another interview with that journalist. She won't ignore you this time; you're in the zeitgeist now. Make your apology tour, and your career will be fine. The Torchers will leave you alone." The second half of that sentence hangs unspoken in the air. *As long as you're not with me.*

West scoffs. "You're worried about *my* career?"

"Obviously."

He shakes his head. "I'll be fine. All I care about is what happens to you."

I swipe tears off my cheeks. "They can't postpone my book forever," I insist, though I wonder how long they'll wait. *Until the scandal blows over? Until I speak out against West?*

"I'm relieved to hear that, but I'm worried about you. Here"—

he lifts his free hand and taps me lightly on the temple—"and here"—over my heart. "I don't want you to suffer the same way you did last time."

We sit so long that we watch the light bleed from the sky, quiet surrender settling around us. With my head on West's shoulder, I track the sun as it sets, shadows lengthening until they swallow the room whole. "You're going to leave again, aren't you?" he whispers into the dark.

I suddenly wish I hadn't avoided this conversation until now. If we'd already made the important decisions without the weight of all this surrounding noise, maybe this week would have a different ending. But I'm leaving, and once again, he won't ask me to stay, because he doesn't want to be a person who holds me back. And I won't ask him to follow me, because he deserves every bit of success coming to him, and I refuse to get in the way of that.

"What other choice do I have?" I ask eventually, so long after West's question I wonder if he forgot it. "I don't want you punished for your association with me."

He drops my hands and presses his palms into his tired eyes. "Don't do that."

"Do what?"

"Use me as a convenient excuse. I'm telling you that I do not give a single fuck what the internet thinks about me. When you leave, you don't get to pretend like you're saving me from anything. You're scared," he says bluntly.

"I have every right to be scared. You have *no idea* what it was like for me last time, because you weren't there," I snap with more force than intended.

Hurt flashes across his features, an edge of resignation bleeding through. I realize with an unpleasant lurch that he told me this would happen when he asked me to read his apology letter. He knew there would come a day, sooner rather than later, when I would throw our past in his face.

He rolls his shoulders and looks me square in the eye. "You're right. I don't know, and I feel awful about what you went through. But that's not the whole story. You're leaving because you're scared of not measuring up to your warped definition of success. You don't believe you can be happy without it."

I push to my feet. "Don't act like you're the expert on me. We barely even know each other." The lie burns all the way up my throat, leaving a bitter taste on my tongue.

West's eyes flash as he stands, bringing us chest to chest. "And that. Right there. I think you're scared that I'm all in. That I'm ready to start a life with you right now."

"We live on opposite sides of the country!"

"Details."

"Big ones."

"No. I love you—*that's* a big detail. I don't want to live another day of my life without you. You think I'm going to throw my hands up based on something as trivial as location or comments on the internet? Give me more credit than that. Give *us* more credit than that."

My breath sticks in my chest until I'm choking from lack of oxygen. He *loves* me. My insides shift to make room for this new truth. It changes my brain chemistry and my cellular structure. It changes absolutely everything—except the reality of our lives and circumstances.

"You don't want to come to New York," I say.

His jaw clenches around the truth. *No, he doesn't.* "I want to be anywhere you are."

"What about your job?"

"I'll find a new one."

"What about your sister? And your home?"

He pushes his hands through his hair in frustration. "I lost you once because of distance and fear. What kind of coward would I be to not hold on to you this time?"

My body twitches with the urge to launch myself into his arms and tell him that I've loved him for so long I can hardly remember a time when I didn't. After a stilted moment in which I stand motionless, I realize that West is right about all of it. My fear is overwhelming, smothering every other instinct and thought.

Tears build behind my eyes, and a fluttery panic takes root in my stomach. It branches out and digs in until I feel woozy. You'd think experience would have prepared me to say goodbye to West, but the time and the fight and the effort it took to bring us to this moment make this goodbye excruciating.

"Maybe we can try again when things settle down," I say, a last-ditch effort to calm the beast clawing at my ribs.

He leans against the desk and stretches his legs out as he studies me. "I'm done with first kisses, Darling. I can't keep losing you. I won't survive it again."

"What does that mean?"

His hands grip the edge of the desk as he studies me. The unwavering intensity in his eyes makes my skin hot and my chest cold. He looks at me as if he'll never get another chance. "It means this is our last goodbye. I hope you eventually find what makes you happy. You deserve it." With one final, searing look, West pushes off the desk and drops a kiss to my head before leaving me alone in the office he wanted to be mine.

37

Present Day

New York is freezing when I land at JFK. It's cloudy and gray in that way that screams *seasonal depression*. The subway line to my apartment is down, because that only ever happens on what is already the worst day of your life, and it takes more than two miserable hours to get home. Inside, my fridge is empty, the air smells stale, and there's a pile of mouse poop in the corner by my bed. I have the jarring realization that I wouldn't care about any of that if West were with me, followed by the even harsher understanding that he *would* be with me if only I'd asked him to come.

New York hasn't felt less like home since my first summer here.

I never blamed Daphne for leaving the city, but I feel the sharp ache of her absence now more than ever. I'm so tired of being alone. I've learned to live with it, but at the moment it feels less like living and more like existing.

As I sit in the middle of my empty apartment, I scroll through the Notes app statements on my phone, unable to believe I've become such a cliché. Another author mired in internet scandal. I numbly delete the statements defending West. What I end up posting doesn't mention his name at all.

> Hi, Torchers! Festival schedules are often changed last minute and without any input from the participants, which is what happened to me at the Tucson Festival of Books. I will never tolerate or excuse any hate toward my readers, and I don't associate with people who do. I'm thankful for all of you, and I can't wait to see you on tour for my new book, *Shattered*, which hits shelves SOON!

I wonder if it's vaguely tacky to promote myself in a Notes-app non-apology but decide that I don't care. I type Love, Mars but delete it right before I hit post. For some reason, the move gives me a tiny buzz of vindication. The ones who will care about this note are the same ones who spent the last few days dragging West and me through the mud. I don't have to love them right now. I just have to give them what they want.

Next, I email Whitney and tell her not to postpone the release or cancel my events. I swear that I'm mentally capable of handling the job and that my name won't be associated with another scandal. I promise to keep my head down.

I'm too hollow to cry. My head and my chest and my limbs ache in a way that is unfamiliar and terrifying. Losing West has never felt quite like *this*. The days that follow are an endless stretch of gray wanting. At first, they move too slow. Every hour feels like ten. As my book tour gets closer, however, time plays tricks on me. I blink, and the sun has moved halfway across the sky.

The first morning of the tour comes too quickly, and I'm scrambling to get out the door. Just as I turn off the lights, I realize I have nothing to read on the plane, not even my Kindle, which I forgot at West's. I scan my bookshelf for whatever will distract me from my life, but I'm not in the mood for any of it. I don't want to read about people falling in love or casting spells or solving mysteries. I drag my finger across spines, stalling on a little black book I've never even opened. I put it in my bag with a heavy sigh. *What could it hurt?* I can't possibly be sadder than I already am.

I sleep on the flight to LA, where a car picks me up and drives me straight to the first bookstore, giving me plenty of time stuck in traffic to stew in my own nerves. I write a dozen disaster scenarios in my head, each one ending in my utter humiliation because no one shows up, or they do and it's a joke, or they film me saying the wrong thing, *or, or, or.*

The event is standing room only, with a line out the door. The store sells out of stock. People cry. (Not me.) I see fae ears and Fox T-shirts and a teenage girl with a tail. It gives me some reassurance to know that the fandom is alive and well and that these books exist in a universe that in some ways has nothing to do with me. A woman close to my mom's age shows up with seventeen books for me to sign: foreign editions, movie tie-in covers, original hardcovers, and more.

This is exactly the moment I've been dreaming of since I wrote the first chapter of *Shattered*, my book about a magical world that's lost its magic and the girl on a quest to restore it. I was broken when I started, but writing this book brought me back to life. It gave me a reason to get out of bed again. I carved out writing spots all over the city. I cried and complained with

Daphne. I fell back in love with stories and characters and the feeling of writing something with zero expectations.

All that work and dreaming led to this moment. For years, this was my North Star; this success would make me happy again.

"You ready to go?" a voice asks.

"What?"

"We're closing up the store."

I blink back to reality. The bookstore is empty except for a handful of employees watching me warily.

A car drives me to the hotel. I'm too tired to keep my eyes open—until the second my head hits the pillow. I stare at the ceiling and wait for sunrise.

The next day, I do it again.

The day before the premiere, Daphne flies into LA and takes me dress shopping at the Grove.

"How do you want to look?" she asks as we sort through evening gowns in the dressing room at Nordstrom. "Dramatic? Whimsical?"

I push aside dresses with sequins and bows and pretty, iridescent fabric. "Invisible." The last thing I want is to be perceived. My plan is to show up, watch the movie, check this off the to-do list, and move on to my next event. Two signings in, and I'm already counting down the days until this tour is over.

Daphne turns to the sales associate. "We'll try a little bit of everything. Color, silhouette, and style. She's dressing for revenge."

"Not true," I say.

"Anything for you?" the sales associate asks Daphne.

"I'm all set. I made my dress." She shows off pictures of the dress she designed, and the employee squeals in delight and asks if my dress should match. "I'm her plus-one, but she's walking the red carpet alone. No need to match," Daphne says brightly.

With instructions and my measurements in hand, the associate sets off, and Daphne slips her sandals off and tucks her feet up under her legs on one of the dressing room's soft lounge chairs. "Have you heard from West yet?"

"He won't call," I say as I try on a black V-neck ball gown with spaghetti straps and a fitted bodice. It fits like it was made for me; it doesn't even need to be altered. "And I don't want him to," I add as an afterthought. Daphne audibly scoffs. "You don't like it?" I turn to see the low back in the mirror.

"The dress is stunning. Your statement was ridiculous."

I make eye contact with her reflection in the mirror. "It's over, Daph."

"Except it's never really over between you two."

"You only think that because your view has been poisoned by mine." I wasted hours of her life ranting about how much I hated him, and she saw right through it.

"Or maybe it's because when we were all trapped in that Martha's Vineyard house together, I saw the way you two looked at each other. Or because I've read *Torched* and *Drought*. Or because I heard the giddiness in your voice after you ran into him in Tucson. Believe whatever you have to tell yourself, but you two still have unfinished business."

I sigh. "West and I both held on to the hope of 'maybe, someday,' but when someday finally arrived, it wasn't the right time."

"Why not?"

"We weren't ready."

"Except he *was* ready," she says.

I don't have an argument for that.

It's almost midnight when I take *Oasis* out of my travel bag. I'm alone in a hotel room, and I can't stop replaying my last conversation with West.

I'm done with first kisses. I can't keep losing you.

The thought that West and I will never have another first kiss makes it impossible to sleep. Daphne was right about West and me; even when there was nothing going on between us, there was *always* something going on between us. That sliver of hope is what allowed me to spend nearly a decade building a life without him. I chased every dream and chance of happiness, knowing that at the end of a horrible or wonderful day, I could fantasize about a future with West.

Faced with a world where I might never speak to him again, I'm scrambling to hold on to any piece of him that I can, which is why I'm finally brave enough to read his first novel.

I open the front cover, and a folded piece of paper falls onto my lap. I pick it up, assuming it's a receipt from the bookstore, but it has torn edges and printed lines like it was ripped from a notebook. I unfold the pages and smooth it out on top of the hotel bed.

My jaw drops when I see West's familiar handwriting. The words are smudged from his left hand dragging across wet ink. It's dated eight years ago in December. Before Martha's Vineyard, before the article.

Dear Mars,

I've found myself writing this letter more times than I'm willing to admit, and each time, I've thrown it away—crumpled it in the trash, buried it beneath drafts of stories that never turn out and endings I'm trying to rewrite. As embarrassing as this is to admit, even more humiliating is the circumstance that has led me to write it. There's an indie bookstore on Fulton that agreed to carry a single copy of my book, and I return every couple of weeks to see if it's been purchased. Last time I stopped in, an employee who I suspect feels sorry for me told me that she was holding it for a customer—"a famous writer!" she said with a wink and a smile. The store had a stack of freshly signed copies of Torched on the front table, and, well, here I am—with regrets piled up and a pen in my hand.

There are a hundred million things I want to say to you—a lifetime's worth of words built up over a handful of years. I kept track of them in a notebook for months: books I read and loved, books I read and hated, stupid jokes that I thought would make you laugh, things I should have said before you left. Even now, I have so much to say, but I'm scared it will come out wrong. We both know how words are, how easily they slip into a shape that's not quite the one you meant.

I live in the city now, and I think of it as your city; I can't help but imagine that you moved here and immediately stepped onto the path of world domination. I still find myself envious of the strength of your convictions. You knew that you belonged here from day one. You never questioned if you could keep up with the pace of New

York. Meanwhile, I spent years in limbo, unsure which path to take, searching Tucson for something that was no longer there, trying to make sense of something that has no shape or resolution.

I should be writing about other things—new ideas, new worlds, new characters. But no matter how hard I try, you slip through the cracks of every story I write. I should be reading new books, but instead I reread yours and find you tucked between the pages. I hear the words in your voice. My mind is a maze of haunted hallways. I drive myself crazy, remembering.

It was easier to be happy then, don't you think?

Do you remember the morning we hiked Sabino Canyon and watched the sun rise over the horizon? You had a way of infusing magic into my ordinary world—like how the sound of your voice transformed the dry, brutal heat into something soft, almost sacred. Or how your smile turned the desert into an ocean—I was always a little lost in it. The mole above your lip was my religion. Losing you, my crisis of faith. I think, deep down, I never expected that the horizon would change, but it has, and I'm still trying to find the edge of it.

I have this dream that feels like a memory, of running into you in our old spot on campus. Some coincidence or twist of fate has brought us both back to Tucson, and I find you in the place where we met and had our second first kiss. Sometimes I let myself believe it's possible.

If we ever find ourselves there again, I'll look for you under the palm trees.

The critique I always get is that not enough happens in my stories. They need more plot. With that in mind,

Mars, I'm getting to the plot: I think about you all the time, and I miss you more than is reasonable. I assume that as the years have stretched on without anything to hold us together, you don't feel the same. That's okay, but I'll close with this.

If you ever find yourself thinking of me, I'm asking you to call.

Love, West

Tears roll off my chin onto the letter, blurring the already-smudged ink. I move it to a safer position and wipe my eyes with the back of my hand. I read it again and again until the words are hazy to my exhausted eyes. Each time I finish, I'm drawn back to the same sentence.

If we ever find ourselves there again, I'll look for you under the palm trees.

He held on to that sentiment for years, and on my first return to Tucson in nearly a decade, he went straight to our spot. He was waiting for me, even after all that time.

It was easier to be happy then, don't you think?

Yes, it was.

I've been hunting "happiness" for so long that I forgot what it feels like. I expected that when I hit whatever goal I was chasing, my life would magically transform into a "happy" one.

But happiness has always been in the fleeting moments that occur between all the other necessary shit that causes the world to turn. It's stargazing with West and making him laugh. It's falling asleep on his chest. Writing something I'm proud of.

It's not the immediate, suffocating pressure of getting a book deal or the relief of hitting the bestseller list or even the overwhelming moment of seeing my characters on-screen. It's a feeling that comes with no strings or angst attached, and that, for better or worse, has never, ever been related to my success.

I can't believe it took me more than thirty years to understand something so painfully obvious.

I gather the letter, my signed copy of *Drought*, and the unsent apology that I never bothered to unpack. I trace my fingers over each one, marveling at the fact that West has been writing me love letters and sending them out into the universe for the better part of a decade. What a tragedy that it took me so long to receive them.

It was easier to be happy then, don't you think?

No wonder it's easier to write when West is in my life. *Everything* is easier with him. My natural state is one that is tightly wound with equal parts ambition and anxiety, but his presence unspools me like a typewriter ribbon.

If you ever find yourself thinking of me, I'm asking you to call.

It's the middle of the night, and I have a red carpet in twelve hours, but I pick up my phone and I call.

38

11 Years Ago
Junior Year, Second Semester

"Remind me what this movie is about?" West whispers as the lights go down in the theater.

"How should I know?" I whisper back. He's holding the bucket of popcorn between his knees, and I wonder if it would be weird for me to take some. *No, thinking it's weird is what's weird.* I grab a small handful of popcorn and resolutely ignore the squirm in my gut. West has a girlfriend. No squirming allowed.

"It's a musical?" he asks, tilting his head at the screen.

"It's Bollywood. And no one forced you to be here," I say defensively. My English professor is offering extra credit to any student who goes to a screening of an old Bollywood film at the Cinemark this semester. West's not in my class, but he offered to tag along.

He nudges my knee with his. "That wasn't a *complaint*, Jupiter. I'm ecstatic to be spending my Sunday evening watching a three-and-a-half-hour Bollywood film with you. Over the moon. There's nothing I'd rather be doing and no one I'd rather be with. When I die—"

"Oh my god." I roll my eyes and knock my knee against his with a bit more force than is strictly necessary. "That's enough. I get it."

He holds his knee against mine, refusing to be moved. I breathe slowly through my nose and imagine poisoning every last butterfly in my stomach.

The opening credits start. West leans his head closer and lowers his voice. I have to tilt so my ear is nearly at his lips. "How often do you think about what it'll be like to see one of your books on-screen?"

"The chances of that are low," I say. The look he gives me is flat and disbelieving. I bite my cheek to keep from smiling too big. "But I think about it all the time."

"I knew it." He sits up with a smug smile and tosses some popcorn into his mouth. "I call dibs," he says suddenly, his mouth again close enough to draw goose bumps to the surface of my skin.

"On what?" I remove the bucket from between his legs and settle it in my lap in case he's talking about the popcorn.

"Your movie premiere. I want to go."

"You're calling dibs on a ticket to a movie that doesn't exist based on a book that I haven't written yet?"

"Yes."

"Fine. You can come." I turn sideways and am startled by how close he is, grinning at me like he stole something. "You have to bring the Red Vines," I say, snapping a piece of licorice between my teeth.

West watches the movement closely. "It's a deal."

39

Present Day

I wear the floor-length black gown, and Daphne wears her white crocheted baby doll dress with long sleeves. "We look like we're getting married," I deadpan when she meets me outside the Peacock Theater. My hair is twisted up, and I have enough makeup under my eyes to hide the lack of sleep. I always call in the professionals for red carpets, because it would be a shame to waste all that good lighting on bad glam.

"You should be so lucky." Daphne loops her arm through mine. "Now, point me in the direction of the silver fox who plays Juniper's dad."

"Really?"

"Oh yeah. I'm a sucker for a salt-and-pepper mustache."

My hands tremble as I lift my dress and walk toward the red carpet, which is flanked by interviewers and cameras. On the opposite side of the carpet is a holding area filled with hundreds of fans carrying homemade signs. I can't wait for this to be over.

"No comment about the mustache? And did someone famous get out of that limo?" She cranes her neck to see past a cluster of security guards. The crowd erupts in loud screams. "I guess that's a yes."

"I called West last night."

Daphne gives me a sharp look. "Oh?"

"He didn't answer. It was late. I left him a voicemail."

She smooths a nonexistent wrinkle from my dress. "I'm sure he'll call soon. Let's just enjoy this. Are you excited?"

"Not really."

"That makes one of us. This is objectively the coolest thing I've ever done. Isn't this the theater where they film a bunch of awards shows?"

"I think so. My hair feels weird. Does it look weird?"

"It's perfect."

"Should I take it out? The pin is stabbing my head." I reach back for the French pin, but Daphne cups her hands around my wrists.

"Don't you dare."

"Can we leave after the red carpet?" I ask desperately.

"You don't want to watch the movie?" Her face falls.

"I don't know if I can."

She shakes her head firmly. "You forget—I was a *Torched* fan before I was your friend. I didn't make my own dress not to see how the story ends."

I sigh heavily. I have no interest in seeing Fox and Juniper get the happy ending I stubbornly refused to give them. Someone grabs my hand and pulls me toward a camera.

"I'll meet you inside!" Daphne calls.

I nod, stumbling over the hem of my dress. I feel like I'm moving underwater. Everything is slow and surreal, right up until the moment a microphone is put in my face, and I snap into focus.

"We're here with Margot Darling, the author of the *Torched* series. How excited are you to be here tonight?"

"Very," I say in a voice that is unfamiliar to my own ears. Another loud scream erupts from the crowd. I don't look, but I think the actor who plays Fox has arrived. "Everyone has put so much love and hard work into these movies. You can really feel that energy here tonight."

"Will fans of the book be happy with the movie?"

What fans of the book? "I hope so!"

"Do you think the movie closely follows the book?"

I smile until it hurts. "I guess we'll see!"

I'm ushered along the carpet for a handful of identical interviews. Once the cameras are off, I pull the pin out of my hair and shake it loose around my shoulders.

"I told you to leave it up!" Daphne scolds me as I take a seat next to her in the front row of the packed theater. In addition to the cast, crew, and family members, the studio held a contest that selected one hundred fans to come to the premiere. The room is buzzing with energy as Daphne tries to fix my updo, but the pin is difficult to maneuver, and as the lights dim, she settles for my flat, mediocre hair.

The movie is good, but the waiting is agony. I find myself bracing for impact the entire last hour of the film. The final battle arrives as the mortal and faerie realms are both unraveling, and I feel the entire theater collectively hold their breath in the moment when Fox and his wolf are supposed to die in an unremarkable, unsymbolic, unnecessary way. When they don't, the held breath becomes a gasp, followed by cheering. I watch as Fox and Juniper fight side by side, defeat the evil, and—my stomach drops.

Juniper in a wedding dress.

"She's like twenty years old," I hiss into Daphne's ear.

She squeezes my hand. "I have to pee."

"*Now?*"

"Too much soda."

"I'm coming, too."

"No." She presses her hand to my shoulder to keep me in my seat. "People are watching." She jogs out of the theater as the wolf walks Juniper down the aisle.

"Traitor!" I whisper after her. *So much for being a* Torched *fan.*

It's misery to watch Fox and Juniper get the happily ever after that West and I never will. As the audience swoons and cheers, I can't help but wonder if any of these people were the ones ripping me to shreds four years ago *or* last week. I've tried so hard to give them what they wanted, and where did that get me? Alone, unhappy, and desperately wishing for the end of what should be one of the highlights of my career.

Someone slips into the seat next to me as the credits roll and the lights on the stage come up. "You missed the worst part—" I say, but the rest of that sentence dies on my tongue as I turn and see West sitting next to me.

Around us, the crowd breaks into a massive round of applause. The director walks onto the stage alongside the actors who play Fox and Juniper as they prepare for a Q&A.

"You didn't like the end of the movie?" he whispers.

I'm dumbstruck, both by seeing him in a black suit for only the second time in my life and by the fact that he's here at all. "What are you doing here?"

"I had a promise to keep." He offers me a box of Red Vines with steady hands that match the stability in his voice and the set of his shoulders. It's a complete contradiction to the chaos in my body. I'm little more than a racing heart, twisting nerves, and a kaleidoscope of butterflies. "Sorry I'm late. LA traffic," he says. The soft regret in his expression tells me that he's talking about more than just today.

I knock my knee against his. He holds steady, trapping me in a gaze that lasts an eternity. "You called."

"I love your letter. Sorry it took me so long to read it."

"Your timing is perfect." His mouth tips toward mine.

"Can you two shut up?" a voice down the row hisses. West freezes.

"That's Margot Darling!" someone else responds.

A dozen people turn to look at once.

"Is that—?"

"Is he—?"

"What's he doing here?"

West looks sideways at me, his expression indecipherable as the whispers around us catch and spread, until suddenly the lights in the auditorium are up and people are craning their necks to get a better look. "Do you want me to leave?"

"No." I grab his hand. He squeezes tightly, then drops my hands as he stands. My heart sinks, assuming he's on his way out, when he straightens the sleeves of his jacket.

Everyone is staring now, including the director. West motions to the microphone hanging limply at his side. "Mind if I borrow that for a minute?"

My entire body flushes hot. I've never seen West purposely ask for attention, least of all in a room full of strangers. "What are you doing?" I whisper.

He glances down at me with a small shrug and a crooked smile. "Why depend on some journalist I hate to issue my public apology when I could just do it here?"

The director offers the microphone and motions to half a dozen cameras waiting in the wings. They all train on West as he accepts the proffered microphone and turns to face not only me but also the audience.

"Hi, uh—" He pulls it away as feedback screeches through the auditorium. "Sorry, is this better?"

"Who are you?" The shout comes from the audience.

West laughs nervously as he scans the crowded room. "I'm, um, I'm the guy that—I did that interview—" He cuts himself off and looks down at me with wide eyes as the reality of the moment catches up with him. I shrug helplessly. I'm dying to know where he's going with this. West takes a deep breath and pushes his hands through his curls. "Raise a hand if you're chronically online."

I cover a laugh with the back of my hand.

The actress who plays Juniper speaks into her own microphone. "This is West Emerson; he's the asshole who inspired Fox and insulted a bunch of fans. Said they needed to get a life and that no one cares about teenage love stories." She raises an eyebrow at West. "Boom. Easy."

"Yes. Succinct. Thank you." He clears his throat and straightens his jacket again. I'm overwhelmed by the urge to take his hand and drag him away from the eyes that are judging, scrutinizing, and categorizing. My biggest fans will decide right now if he's *Good* or if he's *Bad*. Nuance and context need not apply. For many, that label will stick forever, and if that label is bad, he'll be a common enemy to rally against. His career will truly be over.

"I don't need you to do this," I tell West quickly. "Let's just get out of here."

"Not yet." He addresses the confused crowd again. "I said some things that I regret deeply. I'm sorry. To everyone my words hurt, and especially to Mars."

Someone to my left whispers, "Who's Mars?"

"Margot!"

They're immediately shushed.

"We're not pathetic; you're fucking pathetic," a voice shouts.

A muscle in West's jaw works. He sticks a finger between his collar and his neck. "No, I—I didn't mean—"

I wrap my fingers around the microphone, overlapping with West's. "We're done here," I say quietly.

He grimaces and lets his arm fall. "I can explain, I can say it better, apologize better. I'll tell them you had nothing to do with it."

I place my hand on his cheek. "I don't need you to grovel to anyone but me, and you already did that in the form of a big-ass book."

His lip twitches. "What if I want to?"

"You've apologized multiple times. It's their choice what they do with your apologies, but I don't need their approval. We're done here."

He hands the microphone to an extremely confused audience member and tips my chin up with his finger. Stunned silence fills the room as he brings his lips to mine. We miss the uproar that follows our kiss as we run out the back of the theater.

"Did Daphne know that you were coming?" I ask as he pulls me down a side hall and presses me up against a wall.

He brushes his nose along my cheek. "Yes. Apparently, she approves."

"Hmm." His kiss is soft but insistent, and it's not long before I'm dizzy and overwhelmed, my hands, lungs, and heart full of him. I break away with a gasp. "There's one more thing we need to talk about before we go any further."

He draws back, curious.

"I love you. I've loved you since forever, it feels like. Since our twelve-hour first date, at least. Or maybe it started when you put your arms around me in the snow, or before that, when we laughed about the word 'heartsick' in Dr. B's class, thinking we were too clever to ever need it."

West kisses me softly and then wipes a tear from my cheek. "For a girl who hates crying in public, you do it a lot."

"And for a guy who hates PDA, you keep kissing me where people can see."

He laughs and traces my lips with his thumb. "You made that up. I've always told you that I'll kiss you anywhere you let me, as long as you'll let me."

So *this* is what it feels like to get everything you want. Happiness with no strings.

I relax into him as that lovely unspooling happens inside me. "That's pretty romantic, West Emerson. Should I put it in a book?"

Epilogue

One Year Later

"What if they rob the bank?"

West barks a loud laugh of surprise from across the small office. He turns to look at me, his fingers poised over the keyboard, his glasses resting on his nose. "Why would they rob the bank?"

"Because it's fun!" I tilt my head to the side from where I'm stretched out on the couch, legs slung over the armrest. I squint at the paint samples taped to the wall over West's head, trying to distinguish between the many shades of green. I thought it would be fun to repaint the office now that we spend so much time here. When I picked up a pretty blue paint sample, he suggested something more neutral.

Like pink? I asked, which earned me a wry smile.

Subtle as a brick, this man.

West laughs now and turns back around, fingers flying over the keys, filling the room with the gentle clacking that has become the soundtrack to my life. "'Because it's fun' can't always be character motivation," he says.

"Agree to disagree." Fun is the entire reason that West and I are cowriting this outrageous genre mishmash of a book. It is ridiculous and silly and the most fun I've had in years. West is *still* typing. "What are you writing now?"

"Don't worry about it."

"Not another metaphor."

"No. Still the same metaphor."

"West!"

"Shh. It's not your turn."

I grin at the ceiling as Hemingway puts his head under my hand and waits for head scratches. (Gabbi cast the tiebreaking vote for his name. I lost.) Some days I can barely wrap my mind around how much my life has changed in the last year. I handled what I needed to in New York while West finished up the school year, and I moved in with him over Memorial Day weekend. By that point, it didn't feel even remotely fast. I was ready to be wherever he was, and Tucson makes the most sense, at least for now. I kept my apartment, though I doubt we'll live in New York anytime soon.

"Ooh! I have an idea!" I jump up from the couch and gently swat West's hands away from the keyboard.

"Hey! I wasn't done!"

"No metaphor needs to be that long," I say as I start typing. I attempt to push him sideways off the chair with my hip, but he wraps his arms around my waist and pulls me onto his lap. He cinches them tighter as I type, resting his chin on my shoulder and reading the words as they appear on the screen.

He throws his head back and laughs. "Fine. I'll give you your spontaneous bank robbery. But I want them to kiss at the end of it."

I turn my head slightly until our eyes meet. It brings my lips very near his. "So soon?"

"He can't possibly wait another second." West traces the words against my lips.

"I thought we both agreed that these characters are *not* us."

He looks affronted. "I'm not the morally dubious crime boss?"

"Correct. Just like I'm not the time-traveling space pirate from the future."

He scoffs. "We'll see about that."

West allows me about twenty uninterrupted minutes of typing before he presses openmouthed kisses down my neck. It might be a new record for the most patient he's ever been. I shiver as his teeth softly graze my skin. I type two and a half more sentences, but when I drop my head to the side, exposing more of my neck, he knows he's got me. He twists me around in his lap, crushing his lips to mine and reaching his hands under my shirt as he pulls my hips closer.

Our goldendoodle tries to nudge his head between us. "Shoo, Hemingway," I say. "Go. Get out."

He flops down on his stomach and rests his head on his paws, unfazed.

West laughs and stands, holding me tight against his chest. I wrap my legs around his waist and kiss his jaw as he carries me to our bed. "This is why Hemingway is a bad dog name! It sounds ridiculous when we try to tell him what to do or discipline him or call him at the park—" West drops me on the bed, effectively silencing my thoughts. He has my shirt off and my hands pinned above my head in less than thirty seconds.

"I'll let you name the next one," he says as he grins down at me.

I lift my head in surprise. "The next *dog*?"

"Dog, baby, whatever comes first."

I huff a laugh. "Big talk considering we're not even engaged yet."

"Details." He drops a kiss to my lips.

"Big ones."

He laughs against my skin.

Neither of us is presenting at the Tucson Festival of Books this year, which means West and I get to wander through the tents at our own pace without worrying about signing lines or author panels. *Shattered* did well enough that my publisher agreed to the sequel, which will be published later this year, but I haven't decided if I want to tour with it yet.

The internet backlash against West and me burned hot for about a month before receding to embers that occasionally flicker to life and catch us by surprise in the form of a scathing email or angry review that focuses on our personal lives more than our work. I'm learning to create separation between my books and my life. It starts with reminding myself that my work is not *me*, and other people's opinions on it have very little to do with my life.

West found a new agent and is working on what he hopes will be his third novel. I'm also working on a new project, slowly and without putting too much pressure on myself. And we're both having the time of our lives cowriting our time-travel-space-pirate-crime-boss novel, which will likely never see the inside of a bookstore.

"You've been staring at that book for five minutes," West comments as he takes it from my hands and pays for it.

I blink back to the present. "Just thinking."

He tucks my new book under his arm and laces our hands together. "About what?"

I glance up at him and part of my brain sighs. *There you are.* I still can't believe he's mine. Finally. "Last year."

"Ah. When you were in such denial about being in love with me that you resorted to the world's worst revenge plan." He looks down at me with an arched brow.

I roll my eyes. "You loved the attention."

"And you'll never hear me say otherwise, Darling."

He's leading us away from the festival, down to our spot outside Modern Languages. "I was feeling claustrophobic back there. Mind if we hide out here for a while?"

"Of course not." I pluck my book from under his arm and walk to the bench under the palm trees.

"Hey, Mars?"

I turn, and the book slides from my hand when I see West down on one knee. "Margot Darling," he starts, and abruptly my eyes well with tears.

"Hey, no, no, no. If you start crying now, I'll never make it through this." His voice is hoarse.

I press my tongue to the roof of my mouth and blink rapidly. "I don't know if you've heard, but I have medically diagnosed overactive tear ducts."

"That sounds familiar, yes." His lilt is teasing, but his eyes are full of affection that makes my body flush. I sink to my knees and take his hands. As my eyes draw level with his, we both fight tears.

He takes a breath and starts again. "I met you in this exact spot nearly fifteen years ago, and I've been in free fall ever since. It took me too long to realize that the feeling of the ground slipping from under my feet and the desire to land by your side was love, and even longer to figure out what to do with it. I shouldn't have waited so long to tell you. I should have said it every day, in all the clumsy and ineloquent ways I know how. If you let me, I'll spend the rest of my life making sure you know that I love you." He pulls a ring box out of his pocket and opens it. "Mars, *darling*, will you marry me?"

I know I should look at the diamond ring he's holding, but I can't pull my attention from his blue-and-amber eyes. In moments like this, I swear I can see my whole world in those irises. "Yes. Of course. I'll marry you whenever and wherever you want, West Emerson."

Salt water mingles on our lips as we kiss, and when West slides the ring onto my finger, I can't help but think that I could write for the rest of my life and never capture this happiness on paper.

Acknowledgments

Thank you to my agent, Katelyn Detweiler. You worked your magic with this one. I say it every time because it's always true—I am more and more grateful for you with each passing book.

To my editor, Angela Kim. Thank you for laughing at my jokes, swooning in all the right places, and seeing the potential behind West's skinny jeans and eyeliner. (You're like Mars in that way.) I've never been more scared to submit a draft than I was to send this one to you, but your insight was invaluable in shaping this story. Thank you for taking a chance on me.

To the entire team at Berkley, including Colleen Reinhart, Megha Jain, Tara O'Connor, and Anika Bates. Thank you for everything you've done to get this book into the hands of readers. I'm so grateful to have found a home at Berkley. And all my thanks to Decue Wu for bringing Mars and West to life in my delightful cover illustration.

To Sandy, thank you for all of your help with the details of being an undergrad in Tucson. And to Dr. Blasingame, your class changed the course of my life. It's about time I keep that promise to come back and speak.

To my Friday writing crew, including Joanna Ruth Meyer, Madeleine Elizabeth, Nicole Adair, Karen Chow, and Amy Trueblood. Thanks for keeping me distracted and perpetually entertained. I'm sorry for all the writing hours you lost because I wouldn't shut up.

And finally, thank you to Scott for holding down the fort at home while I'm on deadline and dropping balls left and right. And to Owen, Graham, and Emmett—I'm sorry there aren't any dragons in this one, either. (Maybe next time, but probably not.) I love you all.

Keep reading for an excerpt of Kara McDowell's next novel.

I was raised to believe in almost everything: astrology, curses, magic, you name it. Superstitions, soulmates, and seers. Kismet. Transmutation. *You can turn anything into gold*, Mimi used to say. Aliens, obviously, but doesn't everyone believe in aliens these days? Not religion—not in such defined terms—but in the mystical and divine, certainly.

Most of it seems about as real as Sasquatch, if you ask me. Still, I find myself flinching if I exit a building through a different door than the one I entered, and I don't argue with Mimi when her eyes slide out of focus and her voice falls to a hush, even if I (mostly) think it's a bunch of theatrics. There's something sticky and fundamental about the stories you're told as a child, about the beliefs that wind through the family tree. Left to my own devices, I fostered a trust in science, facts, and evidence. And yet, on occasion, I can admit when the undeniable evidence supports the implausible myth.

As much as I once hoped to divorce myself from the Rhodes family magic, I can't deny the truth. By some stroke of good luck or misfortune, every woman in my prolific family, spanning back as far as anyone cares to look, has met the love of her life at age twenty-one.

It's not the most interesting magic—I'll take instant hair-drying powers if the universe is accepting requests—but it does guarantee a soulmate for everyone, just like the stories.

Everyone except me.

The Rhodes women refuse to accept this. If Mimi and my mom and my sisters are to be believed, it's not that I *didn't* meet the love of my life at twenty-one; it's just that I couldn't hold on to him. I had him, I lost him, and it's the saddest story in a long line of enviable romances, with the possible exception of my great-great-aunt Willa, whose husband died in World War II when she was pregnant with their first child. When reminded of Willa, they begrudgingly admit that things could be worse for me—but if, and only if, I were a knocked-up war widow who was forced to ration sugar.

They pity my personal tragedy, but there's really no need. It's liberating to know that true love is never going to happen for me. It leaves me free to live my life, to date or not, without the unbearable burden of expectation.

Take the man across the desk from me, for example. From the moment he first kissed me, in the break room after everyone else had gone home, I knew it wouldn't last. My sisters tell me this makes the decision to date my boss even *more* baffling, especially when half a dozen men like him can be found in every fair-trade corner coffee shop, with their beards and their bicycles and vast collections of flannels. And yet, in the infinite wisdom of a twenty-seven-year-old with zero hope of forever, I chose *him*. And now I'm suffering for it, because there's nothing quite as humbling as asking your ex-boyfriend for a raise.

If only someone would have warned me that dating my boss was a bad idea—someone other than my family and my common sense. If anyone *else* had warned me that one day my rent would increase 50 percent and I'd be forced to sit in Alex's office and explain to him why my time is worth more than my current salary, perhaps I would have been struck by the divine foresight not to get into a relationship with the man who signs my paychecks.

Alex would object to the label of *ex-boyfriend*. We were, after all, never official. Not in the eyes of our one-person human resources department, anyway.

As he sits across from me now, his lips turn down. "I don't know what to tell you, Piper. A raise is not in the budget right now."

I'm prepared for this response. "Kaylee left four months ago, and because her position *still* hasn't been filled, I've been doing school visits and nature workshops on my own. It's a job for two people, *at least*." Frustration and bitterness bleed through my words, because Alex knows this better than anyone. When we were together, he used to badger me to take lunch breaks and chastise me for never using my sick days or vacation time. He watched me stay up all hours of the night preparing wildlife lessons and demonstrations, often leaving for school visits on only a few hours of sleep, pushing myself closer and closer to burnout with each passing month.

Alex takes his glasses off in a show of disappointment and puts his fingers to his temples to pretend he feels a headache coming on. Sometimes he forgets that I know all his tells. "If you're in nonprofit work for the money, you're never going to be happy."

I tighten my fingers around the edge of the chair I'm sitting in. "This doesn't have anything to do with my happiness. It's about paying my bills."

Alex threads his fingers together on top of his desk and leans toward me, like we're sharing a secret. "You can't ask me for preferential treatment, Piper. It's not appropriate."

I feel my face twist in a slow-motion wince. "I haven't asked for a raise once in five years," I remind him. One look at our building—with its stuck windows, peeling paint, and leaky roof—makes the state of things very clear. We're barely staying afloat, on the verge of shutting down year after year. I knew what I was walking into when I joined the nonprofit sector; I'm here because I love teaching kids about wildlife conservation.

When our program director decided that we should expand our education to high schools, I helped her plan the new demonstrations. When she made an offhand comment about bringing live owls into the schools, I made it happen. And when I didn't feel like we were doing enough, I pitched the idea of holding weekend nature workshops outside schools and then built the program from the ground up. The more I did, the more responsibility I was given. My job title is wildlife educator, but I also keep the office break room stocked with snacks, I place buckets under leaks when it rains, and I sweep spiderwebs out of our doorways from September to November. By the time I'd been here long enough to realize that I deserved a raise, Alex and I were together, and it was too late to ask.

"All I'm asking for is a raise that is in line with the work I do and the rise in the cost of living," I tell him now, nearly choking on the words.

He tilts his head and studies me for far too long. "New skirt?" he asks, setting my teeth on edge. He knows it's not. "There's really nothing to be done about your hair today, is there?" He smiles in a way that I once would have considered affectionate but now sends shivers down my spine.

My fingers twitch. I sit on them to stop myself from smoothing wayward curls away from my face. It's late afternoon, and the bun I wrestled my hair into this morning has surrendered, allowing seditious ringlets to spring out in every direction.

Alex is not a fan.

He slaps his hands once on his desktop, making me jump. "I'll tell you what. You're right. You're invaluable, and we can't afford to lose you."

I exhale heavily. "Thank you, Alex. It means more than you know."

"Of course. Don't give it another thought." He sits back in his chair and smiles softly. "I'll have to get it approved by the board, but I think they won't object to giving you five extra vacation days a year."

A bubble of surprised laughter escapes my throat. "Vacation days won't pay my rent."

"It's a good offer."

"For *you*. I don't even use my vacation days!"

"You're free to use them anytime, as long as your request is approved," he says, a gleeful schadenfreude dancing in his eyes.

A flush of painful embarrassment sweeps across my skin.

"Or, if you prefer, we can forget about all this, and I'll help you save your butterfly."

My eyes snap to his. "What?" I ask sharply.

"Your butterfly. I assume you still want to save it?"

"Obviously." I practically spit the word at him.

"Drop your request, and I'll speak to the board about funding. I'll find out what's possible," Alex says casually.

It feels like he's sucked all the oxygen from the room. My heart beats in my throat as I struggle to maintain my composure. How naive of me to think this conversation could have gone any other way. I stand slowly, my chair scraping loudly across the floor. I smooth my shaking hands down the pencil skirt that Alex didn't like me to wear because he thought it was too tight, and take a fortifying breath. "I'll see you Monday."

He frowns. "It's not five o'clock yet."

"My work is finished, and I have plans for this evening." I flinch even as the words roll off my tongue. Answering his unspoken questions is an ingrained habit.

He kicks his feet up on his desk and surveys me again as my stomach roils in protest. "Tell your family I say hello."

"How do you know—"

He scoffs. "Who else would it be?"

I turn away and bite the inside of my cheek. I hate him for trying to make me feel small and predictable for going to Mimi's eightieth birthday party.

"Have a nice weekend," I say blandly, hoping he understands the words mean *I hope you freeze to death in Puget Sound.*

As I quickly pack up my desk, my eyes fall to the twenty-year-old photo that I have taped to the wall behind my computer. My sisters and I are gathered around Mimi. Her hand rests lightly on my head of messy curls, the ever-present twinkle in her eye piercing the camera lens. I trace my fingers over my wide smile and think about family magic and curses and how the stories we're told as children can lead us down paths we were never meant to take. If I'd met Alex at twenty-one, I'd have taken one look at his broad shoulders and his scruff and his passion for nonprofit work and tricked myself into believing that he was my soulmate. Left to my own devices, I could

easily have wedged myself into a situation even worse than the one I'm in now.

It took me too long to realize I needed to leave Alex, but when I did, it was as easy as waking up from a bad dream. One night, he was holding my keys hostage so I wouldn't meet my sisters for dinner, and the next morning, I was boxing up his beard oil and his record collection and pushing him out the front door. I couldn't fall victim to the sunk cost fallacy because I never entertained the delusion of spending forever with him. After our breakup, there was no lost future to mourn, no expectations to realign with reality.

When it comes to romantic relationships, I don't get too invested, and I move on quickly. It's not as good as having a soulmate, but at least I won't spend a day of my life waiting for a train that I've already missed.

Traffic is slow on the way home, and I have just enough time to change before I pick up Mimi. We'll be late to her own birthday dinner because we'll watch *Wheel of Fortune* (her favorite) followed by *Jeopardy!* (my favorite). I grab my mail and let myself in, kicking off my shoes and freeing my curls from their bun. The tension on my scalp dissipates, and I sigh as my hair falls to the small of my back. The air outside is thick with promised rain, and my hair has reached dangerous proportions, but I can't bring myself to tie it back again. I comb my fingers through the strands as I fan myself with the large stack of junk mail and walk into my bedroom.

My skirt hits the floor, followed by my blouse, and I drop the mail on my bed before I step into my small closet. I quickly change into jeans and a casual top, grabbing a cardigan because spring in Seattle is as moody and temperamental as a preteen, and step back into my room. I slip my feet into sandals,

grab my purse off the bed, and head toward the door. Two steps later, my mind catches up with my body.

I pause. Turn slowly. Retrace my steps. I sweep my hand over the pile of mail, uncovering a thick white envelope at the bottom of the stack. My eyes drift to the names above the return address, and for the second time today, it feels like someone has siphoned the oxygen out of the room.

First Alex and now this. Maybe I do believe in curses, because why am I holding an invitation to my ex-boyfriend's wedding?

We don't keep in touch, not even to say happy birthday. I haven't spoken to him in years, and I've never met his fiancée. The only time I even think of Lachlan is when my family decides to remind me exactly why I'm alone.

Every Rhodes woman has a soulmate, and Lachlan Blair was supposed to be mine.

Photo by Kendyl Hawkins

Kara McDowell is the author of romantic comedies for adults and teens. She lives with her husband and three sons in Mesa, Arizona. When she's not at a baseball game, she divides her time between writing, baking, and wishing for rain.

Visit Kara McDowell Online

KaraJMcDowell.com

KaraJMcDowellBooks